JENNIFER NIVEN

~~~

Becoming Clementine

A PLUME BOOK

PLUME
Published by the Penguin Group
Penguin Group (USA) Inc., 375 Hudson Street, New York, New York 10014, U.S.A. • Penguin Group (Canada), 90 Eglinton Avenue East, Suite 700, Toronto, Ontario, Canada M4P 2Y3 (a division of Pearson Penguin Canada Inc.) • Penguin Books Ltd., 80 Strand, London WC2R 0RL, England • Penguin Ireland, 25 St. Stephen's Green, Dublin 2, Ireland (a division of Penguin Books Ltd.) • Penguin Group (Australia), 250 Camberwell Road, Camberwell, Victoria 3124, Australia (a division of Pearson Australia Group Pty. Ltd.) • Penguin Books India Pvt. Ltd., 11 Community Centre, Panchsheel Park, New Delhi – 110 017, India • Penguin Group (NZ), 67 Apollo Drive, Rosedale, Auckland 0632, New Zealand (a division of Pearson New Zealand Ltd.) • Penguin Books (South Africa) (Pty.) Ltd., 24 Sturdee Avenue, Rosebank, Johannesburg 2196, South Africa

Penguin Books Ltd., Registered Offices: 80 Strand, London WC2R 0RL, England

First published by Plume, a member of Penguin Group (USA) Inc.

First Printing, October 2012
10   9   8   7   6   5   4   3   2

Photo of Jack F. McJunkin Sr. on p. 343 courtesy of Jennifer Niven.

Ⓟ REGISTERED TRADEMARK—MARCA REGISTRADA

LIBRARY OF CONGRESS CATALOGING-IN-PUBLICATION DATA

Niven, Jennifer.
    Becoming Clementine / Jennifer Niven.
        p. cm.
    ISBN 978-0-452-29810-1
    1. World War, 1939–1945—France—Fiction. 2. Intelligence service—Fiction.
3. War stories. gsafd I. Title.
    PS3614.I94B43 2012
    813'.6—dc23   2012010157

Printed in the United States of America
Set in Granjon LT Std and Park Avenue Std • Designed by Eve L. Kirch

BOOKS ARE AVAILABLE AT QUANTITY DISCOUNTS WHEN USED TO PROMOTE PRODUCTS OR SERVICES. FOR INFORMATION PLEASE WRITE TO PREMIUM MARKETING DIVISION, PENGUIN GROUP (USA) INC., 375 HUDSON STREET, NEW YORK, NEW YORK 10014.

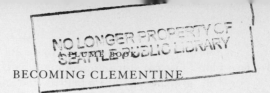
BECOMING CLEMENTINE

JENNIFER NIVEN's two previous novels are *Velva Jean Learns to Fly* and *Velva Jean Learns to Drive*, which was chosen as an Indie Reader's Group "Top Ten" Pick. Niven has also written three nonfiction books. *The Ice Master* was named one of the top ten nonfiction books of the year by *Entertainment Weekly*, has been translated into eight languages, has been the subject of several documentaries, and received Italy's Gambrinus "Giuseppe Mazzotti" Literary Prize. *Ada Blackjack* was a Book Sense "Top Ten" Pick and has been optioned for the movies and translated into Chinese, French, and Estonian. *The Aqua-Net Diaries*, a memoir about her high school experiences, was optioned by Warner Bros. as a television series. She lives in Los Angeles. For more information, visit jenniferniven.com or follow her on Facebook.

Praise for *Becoming Clementine*

"*Becoming Clementine* is a spirited tale of courage, honor, and loyalty. Jennifer Niven succeeds in not only illuminating an important and little-known role played by women during the war, but creating an unforgettable and heartfelt story that will resonate with readers far and wide."
— Pam Jenoff, author of *The Diplomat's Wife*

"Jennifer Niven has thrust Velva Jean into the realm of unconventional warfare. This is the gripping tale of a young woman surviving a plane crash in Nazi-occupied France, only to find herself in the perilous world of the French underground. It's all here—intrigue, romance, heroism. A terrifically absorbing read."
— Will Irwin, author of *The Jedburghs* and *Abundance of Valor*

"Reading this splendid novel allowed me to vicariously share wartime adventures with a sister spy. Velva Jean had everything that was required of us operatives in OSS (Office of Strategic Services), a forerunner of the CIA. She had the courage to survive undercover behind enemy lines in constant danger. She carried out life-threatening orders without question and bravely faced capture. *Becoming Clementine* is a spellbinding spy saga."
— Elizabeth P. McIntosh, OSS/CIA, and author of *Sisterhood of Spies*

"Richly textured, historically evocative, emotionally mesmerizing, *Becoming Clementine* takes you on a journey through World War II France so gripping you can smell the gun smoke. Niven's deft prose transports readers on a finely blended internal and external voyage, where Velva Jean's physical adventures are as engrossing as her emotional exploration."
— Kerry Reichs, author of *What You Wish For* and *Leaving Unknown*

"Niven has done something I didn't think was possible. She has topped Velva Jean Hart's first two stirring adventures with a third that is an epic—powerful, gripping, tragic, romantic, and inspiring. *Becoming Clementine* is a page-turner of a story, with its riveting, insightful, on-the-ground perspectives of World War II. The time, the place, and the events are as authentic as Velva Jean herself. Spellbinding."

—James Earl Jones, Tony Award–winning, Emmy Award–winning actor

"Jennifer Niven has done it again! In Niven's third adventure featuring this courageous female pilot, Velva Jean persuades the RAF to use her in flying intelligence agents to France, where she crash lands and is rescued by the Resistance. Her arrest by the Gestapo and her heroic triumph over the horrors of war (as well as her moving romance with a French agent) makes *Becoming Clementine* a riveting, 'can't put it down,' *must* read."

—Dr. Margaret S. Emanuelson, veteran of OSS and author of *Company of Spies*

"In Velva Jean's latest adventure, cloak-and-dagger buffs will recognize and appreciate Niven's artful and knowing introduction of tradecraft—techniques used to carry out covert operations. Hiding local currency in shoulder pads. Miniature compasses designed to look like dress buttons. Lethal knives built into shoe and boot heels. All are actual examples of tradecraft utilized by covert agents staging missions behind the lines during World War II. As a collector of 'spy gadgets,' and as a fan and student of real-life female agents, I found Niven's authentic application of tradecraft a hidden gift in the espionage thriller that is *Becoming Clementine*. Read it for the intriguing tale *and* the intriguing tradecraft."

—Linda McCarthy, founding curator of the CIA Museum

Praise for *Velva Jean Learns to Fly*

"An endearing portrait of a young woman with a big heart—*Velva Jean Learns to Fly* illuminates the power of going after a dream and the courage it takes to never let go."

—Beth Hoffman, bestselling author of *Saving CeeCee Honeycutt*

"Velva Jean's story delves into the contributions made by amazing women during World War II and tells a compassionate story about adventure, love, and war. This is a wonderful book—very hard to put down."

—Ann Howard Creel, author of *The Magic of Ordinary Days*

"I devoured *Velva Jean Learns to Fly* and immediately began spreading the word: This one is not to be missed!"

—Cassandra King, author of *The Same Sweet Girls*

"Velva Jean Hart is a heroine with grit, grace, determination, and enough humanity to hook readers with ferocious tenderness, making them want to find and befriend her. Niven's writing shines."

—*Booklist* (starred review)

"A sweeping adventure that takes the reader from the streets of Nashville to the belly of a WWII bomber."

—Benjamin Percy, award-winning author of *The Wilding* and *Refresh, Refresh*

"In this fun, fast-paced, heartwarming sequel to *Velva Jean Learns to Drive*, we follow the beloved young heroine from her mountain home to Nashville. But soon after Pearl Harbor is attacked, Velva Jean begins singing a new song—one full of patriotism, courage, and feisty independence. The perfect read for any girl of any age who yearns to soar beyond her dreams."

—Susan Gregg Gilmore, author of *The Improper Life of Bezellia Grove* and *Looking for Salvation at the Dairy Queen*

Praise for *Velva Jean Learns to Drive*

"A touching read, funny and wise, like a crazy blend of Loretta Lynn, Dolly Parton, a less morose Flannery O'Connor, and maybe a shot of Hank Williams . . . Niven makes some memorable moon-spun magic in her rich fiction debut." —*Publishers Weekly* (starred review)

"In this story Jennifer Niven creates a world long gone, a mountain past where people suffer failure, loss, and betrayal, as well as the strength and joy of connection and deep love. *Velva Jean Learns to Drive* takes us far into this soaring, emotional country, the place where our best music comes from." —Robert Morgan, author of *Gap Creek*

"A fluid storyteller." —*Wall Street Journal*

"Velva Jean learns to . . . not only drive, but to soar. This beautifully written coming-of-age story captivated me, and I recommend it to anyone who has ever longed to 'live out there.'"

—Ann B. Ross, author of the bestselling *Miss Julia* novels

"Spirited." —*Parade*

For Louis,
my Colonel Brandon

He is the kindest and best of men.

—Jane Austen

Where there is doubt, faith.
Where there is despair, hope.
Where there is darkness, light.
Where there is sadness, joy.

—The Prayer of St. Francis

Acknowledgments

$\mathcal{F}$lannery O'Connor said, "Writing a novel is a terrible experience, during which the hair often falls out and the teeth decay."

Because writing really can be a terrible—and lonely—experience, it helps to have support. Or, more accurately, life support.

I couldn't have written this book without:

My mother, Penelope Niven—fellow writer, mentor, cheerleader, commiserator, cohort in over-jubilation, *Bachelor*-watcher, and best friend.

My home team—Louis Kapeleris, love of my life, and our three literary kitties: Satchmo, Rumi, and last, but never *ever* least, Lulu, all of whom spent hours by my side while I was writing. Special thanks to Louis for spending long weekends helping me sort out the plot, index card by index card, and for continually reminding me I could do this.

My unparalleled literary agent, John Ware, who is not only a terrific agent and one of the very best people I know, but one of my dearest and most cherished friends.

My superb and savvy editor, Carolyn Carlson, who knows and cares for Velva Jean almost as much as I do, and who once again worked editorial magic. And the wonderful folks at Penguin/Plume who have given Velva Jean such a good home: Amanda Brower, Milena Brown, Elizabeth Keenan, Ashley Pattison, Clare Ferraro, Kathryn Court, Phil Budnick, John Fagan, Kym Surridge, Lavina Lee, and Howard Wall, not to mention the marvelous sales team. Heartfelt thanks also to art director Jaya Miceli and Elena Giavaldi, designer of the gorgeous cover.

The OSS Society and its president Charles Pinck, Roy Tebbutt and the Carpetbagger Aviation Museum, Linda McCarthy, founding curator of the CIA Museum, Dr. Margaret Emanuelson (former spy!), and others who are mentioned in greater detail at the end of this book for their invaluable contributions to the story.

Joe Kraemer, for much-needed fun and best friendship, Angelo Surmelis, Ed Baran, Lisa Brucker and Peter Mervis, Dan and Magda Dillon, Gay Diller McGee, Gloria McGee Hope, Lynn Duval Clark, the entire von Sprecken clan, Terri Day McJunkin, Florence Moore (who sent me a package of family history and letters, including one written by my grandmother that appears in the afterword of this book), Gayle McJunkin, and the rest of my family and friends, too numerous to name. I love them, each and every one. (Pay close attention, Learyn and Annalise—I have written you into these pages. . . .)

My early readers—Mom, Louis, and friend and fellow writer Valerie Frey Stone. Also Will Irwin, for his counsel and expertise regarding Special Forces, Special Operations, and the military; John Thomas, my consultant on all things World War II; Dan Dillon, my expert on all things flying; Michael Hoppé; Darren Thorpe; Marie Toma of Playclothes Vintage Fashions; and musician and kindred spirit Briana Harley, who has so beautifully brought Velva Jean's songs to life, and whose song "Live Out There" (lyrics cowritten with my mother) appears at the end of the book.

Rachel Sheeley Muzzillo, Frances Owens Draughn, James Fleming, and Briana Harley for coming up with ideas for supercool spy weapons, code names, and, most important, lipsticks.

Mary Duff, surrogate cat mom.

Physique 57 and Bootcamp LA (led by Jay and Marcella Kerwin), which got me away from my desk so I could not only exercise but clear my head.

And, last, my literary inspirations: Flannery O'Connor, Shirley Jackson, Harper Lee, Ernest Hemingway, the Brontë sisters, and my mother, who taught me to "live out there."

Contents

~ *1944* ~

PART ONE

Fare you well (fare you well)
So I left my dear old home. . . .

—"A Distant Land to Roam"

ONE

Somewhere over the Atlantic Ocean, we flew into a cloud bank. The weather had been nice as could be from Greenland to Iceland, and from Iceland it was nothing but blue skies and calm winds. The closer we got to Great Britain, the more the sky changed, going suddenly gray, then dark gray, then a darker gray, then black.

They said the B-17 had mythical powers, that it was magic because it could defend itself, even with the pilot knocked cold and no one at the wheel, and that it could return home even if it was blown apart. It was the fiercest fighter of the war, the Flying Fortress, a daylight precision bomber that flew smooth for being so big and heavy as smooth as Three Gum River, back home in North Carolina, on a sunny, cloudless day. But now I had to hold on tight to the wheel and the throttle to keep the plane from dropping or turning or rattling away from me.

I was going to be the second woman in history to pilot a bomber across the Atlantic Ocean. I was dressed in my Santiago Blues, the official uniform of the WASP, or Women Airforce Service Pilots, with a smart little hat and a fitted navy skirt designed by Bergdorf Goodman in New York, and I had a .45 pistol strapped to my hip. I was flying a crew of eleven, and three of those were girls—Helen Stillbert, who was also a WASP, and my friend Beryl Goss, or Gossie, who was serving in the Women's Army Corps, and me. Helen sat in the copilot's seat. She was going to fly the B-17 back across the ocean on our return.

Suddenly, the bomber shuddered and for one second I wondered if we'd been hit. It rocked and rolled side to side, and just then, I didn't care about being the second woman in history. The only thing I cared about was getting to Scotland in one piece because I was on a secret mission: I was on my way to Europe to find my brother Johnny Clay.

I climbed up and up, pushing the B-17 heavenward through the winds and the fog because the thermals were usually calmer the higher you flew. Thermals were giant trees of air that rose above the earth, caused by the change in temperature. I climbed higher, right up into the thunderclouds. I was flying almost blind, so I dropped a bit, trying to get below the winds. In my headset, I could hear Helen saying, "Can't we get above these clouds, Hartsie?" She sounded cross—and scared.

Johnny Clay had gone missing, and the only person who knew I was planning to find him was me. I didn't have a clue in the world where he was, but the last letter I had from him was dated October 18, 1943, from a base in England. Johnny Clay was a paratrooper with the 101st Airborne. His unit had made the jump on the Normandy coast on June 6, a little over a week ago, but Johnny Clay hadn't jumped with them, and no one could tell me why or where he was. Over three hundred thousand troops had landed or gone ashore along a fifty-mile stretch of beach to fight the Germans. I knew Johnny Clay better than anyone, and if there was one thing I knew for certain, nothing on earth—not a gold mine stuffed fat with gold or our own dear mama herself, come down from heaven—would have kept him from jumping out of that plane on D-day.

Suddenly, the B-17 dropped twenty-five hundred feet, knocking the breath right out of me. It was the heart-in-the-throat, stomach-in-the-knees feeling of free falling, the same feeling I'd had practicing parachute landings from a platform at Avenger Field in Sweetwater, Texas, where I learned to be a WASP. I could see the dark blue-black of the ocean below me, and clouds overhead and on all sides closing in tighter and tighter on the B-17, as if they were trying to smother the life right out of us.

The last place I wanted to die was in a bomber flying over a freezing cold ocean, my family far away and missing me, my brother captured or dead without me even knowing what had happened to him. And what if he needed me? What if just that minute he was calling my name, hoping I'd come rescue him?

The plane dropped again—twelve hundred feet this time. In my headset, I could hear the flight engineer and tail gunners swearing. I could hear the bombardier being sick on his stomach over and over again and the navigator yelling something at me, but it sounded like he was underwater. Then, from the back of the plane, I could hear Gossie, her voice as dramatic and loud as Katharine Hepburn's: "It's cold as a witch's left teat, Mary Lou. Don't you dare crash this plane." Mary Lou was what she called me, since the moment I'd met her on a Nashville street, back when she thought I was a down-and-out and took me in to live with her above the Lovelorn Café, before I ever knew how to fly or went to Texas to become a WASP.

I yanked off my headset and threw it on the floor of the cockpit. I could feel Helen looking at it, looking at me. I thought, To hell with this. And then I pulled back the throttle and pushed the nose of the plane up and up, just like I was headed straight for heaven and my mama and a boy named Ned Tyler who I'd loved and lost.

I climbed till I couldn't see the ocean, till we were above the clouds, above the overcast. Ceiling and visibility unlimited, Ty used to say. And only then did the air even out and the plane stop shaking, gliding once more like the waters of Three Gum River, high up in Sleepy Gap, North Carolina, on a mountain named for my mama's people.

One hour later, the B-17 broke through the clouds and the wind and the rain and soared toward the runway at Prestwick, Scotland. We'd left the ocean to cross over land miles before, but the earth was darker than the water because of the blackout regulations in Great Britain. I'd been told there was a short runway and a new runway, which was wider and longer and crossed the other one to make an *X*. The runways were grass, not the paved ones of Avenger Field or Camp

Davis, North Carolina, where I was stationed after graduating from WASP training, but the long one was under construction to be paved. Because of this we weren't supposed to use it.

The rain was heavy and driving in our downwind leg, but we were back to dry weather again on the base leg. As I made the final approach, I put my headset back on, and we went right back into the storm. The water was beating down so hard I couldn't see an inch in front of the windshield, which was completely misted up. When I was two hundred feet over the runway, the visibility cleared enough so I could just make out the ground lamps that were there to guide us, the only light for miles. They didn't look any brighter than candle flames.

Then I heard the control tower. A male voice came blurring through, growing louder and louder. He was shouting at me to pull back up. He said, "There's a C-54 with broken landing gear in the middle of the old runway. You'll have to use the new one. Use the new one!"

A flash of red exploded right in front of us. Another flash exploded to my left, and then another to my right. Helen said, "They're shooting at us!"

"Flare pistols!" I couldn't see a thing. I thought to myself: Breathe. Breathe. Breathe. Then I pushed the throttles forward, faster than you were supposed to, and I got almost to flying speed. Just as we were coming up on the C-54, I hauled back on the stick and jumped over the wreck, like I was fence-hopping again with Ty around the farms that surrounded Avenger Field.

Two work trucks sat on the new, longer runway. The grass had turned to mud, and Helen said, "We don't have enough room to land, Hartsie."

I could see two, maybe three hundred feet at the end of the runway, just beyond the trucks. Then the new pavement gave way to gravel, and then nothing but grass and, beyond that, water. I hollered, "Hold on!"

I thought of everything I'd been taught as a WASP—to trust my judgment, to know my compass, to fly blind if I had to, to picture an imaginary airport in the sky where I could land my plane safely, easily. I pictured it now as I came in over the ground—as black as a cave—so low that I thought we were going to hit those trucks and knock them into the sea. I flew as low as I dared, and then, after I cleared the second truck, I took the B-17 down, easing up on the throttle, my engines at fifty percent, then lower and lower again. I put my flaps to full landing and released the landing gear. We hit the earth, bumping once and then twice, and then one more time. I slammed the brakes as hard as I could, but we were sliding too fast across the runway toward the gravel and the water.

I'd taught myself to drive when I was seventeen years old. I'd learned to fly when I was twenty. I'd been singing since I was a girl, dreaming of the day that I'd stand on the stage at the Grand Ole Opry. Ever since I was little, before Mama died and my daddy went away, I'd saved my money to go to Nashville, Tennessee, so that I could be a singer. But then came the war and then I learned to fly, and now here I was, all the way across the ocean.

The B-17 came to a stop, front wheels on the gravel, back wheels on the grass. It was an almost perfect landing.

I climbed down from the plane, knees shaking, trying to get my land legs again, trying to get used to the feel of ground beneath my feet. Helen climbed down after me, pulling off her helmet and goggles and smoothing her dark hair with a slim and elegant hand, and then she sat right on the wet ground and held on to the grass and the gravel as if she were afraid she might go spinning off into the air. The navigator, the flight engineer, the gunners, and the bombardier came down after us, and then Gossie came lumbering out, stocky legs wobbling, landing ginger as a cat, a smile on her brightly painted mouth. One of the men said, "Swell landing, Waspie." He slapped me on the back and I tried to remember his name. People ran to meet us, coming out of the moonless dark like fast-moving haints.

There I was, Velva Jean Hart—twenty-one years old; from Fair Mountain, North Carolina; daughter of Lincoln Hart, blacksmith, wanderer, no-account, and Corrine Justice, who died too soon; Harley Bright's ex-wife; singer and mandolin player and owner of a Mexican guitar; writer of songs, some good and some not-so-good; driver of an old yellow truck; WASP; the second woman to ever fly a bomber across the Atlantic—thousands of miles from anything I'd ever known or seen in a whole other country on a whole other continent. It was June 16, 1944, and I was in Scotland.

TWO

$\mathcal{P}$restwick Airfield sat on the west coast of Scotland, some thirty miles southwest of Glasgow between the villages of Ayr and Troon. The Scottish names, like the Scottish accents, sounded like music to me. The way people spoke reminded me of being back home, only I thought we were a lot easier to understand. A couple dozen American pilots, just arrived from the States, rambled over the base, getting ready to fly out to join their bombardment groups. But mostly the base was filled with British officers and pilots, young and sturdy, flying in and flying out, onto other airfields around Great Britain.

It was Saturday, June 17. Helen and I had gotten a telegram that morning from Jacqueline Cochran, head of the WASP, saying, "Congratulations WASP Hart and Stillbert on remarkable achievement." But other than that, no one was paying much attention to us and the fact that we'd just flown across the ocean.

At seven o'clock on Monday morning, Gossie would sail for France, where she would meet up with other WACs and work with the 3341st Signal Battalion in Paris, and Helen and I would leave for home, unless I could figure out a way to stay here. I hadn't said anything to either of them about Johnny Clay, but I was working on a plan.

We ate breakfast at the mess hall, and while Gossie and Helen talked about how to spend the day, I stirred my food around and tried to think. I was here. I'd done it. I'd come this far. But what was next?

While I was busy thinking, five young men came wandering over, swaggering as if they were in a movie, and sat down at our table. I knew by their uniforms that they were Americans. They'd arrived in Scotland the night before, not long after us. One of them was burly shouldered and good-looking, though not as good-looking as he seemed to think he was. He said, "Y'all are WAAF, right?" He sounded like he could be from Mississippi or maybe Louisiana.

I said, "WASP, and Gossie here is a WAC."

He said, "Girl pilots. What d'ya know?" He looked at the other men and waggled his eyebrows, and I couldn't tell if this meant he thought it was a good or a bad thing. "Lieutenant Alden." He held out his hand and I shook it.

They asked us our names and where we came from and how did we ever get into this war and all the way to Scotland. They said they were with the 801st Bombardment Group, and they were on their way to an airfield in England to join the rest of their squadron. When Gossie asked what kinds of missions they'd be flying, they clammed up, except for Lieutenant Alden, who seemed to love hearing himself talk.

He said, "Dangerous ones. Our group has flown three hundred missions since just before and after D-day, and only one hundred seventy-three of those came back."

Then, without telling us where they had flown or what the missions had been, Lieutenant Alden and the others started talking about a pilot buddy of theirs who'd been shot in the neck, right through the larynx, but still made it back to base. They told us about another friend, someone they had gone to training camp with, who'd flown one mission—his first and only—and had been shot down and killed over Saint-Lô, which was somewhere in France. They told us about another who'd been captured by the Germans, and another who'd been shot in the head as he was flying over the drop zone. They told us about other pilots who'd just disappeared and never come back and no one had ever heard from them again.

The girls and I sat in silence, not eating or drinking, and the men looked smug, like that was exactly what they wanted, like maybe they were trying to teach us a lesson for being there. Helen took a drink of tea, which was all you could have now that coffee was so hard to find, and I saw that her hand was shaking.

Suddenly, the beginnings of an idea popped into my mind. I said, "It sounds like you've got a shortage of pilots."

Lieutenant Alden said, "That's why we're headed that way, honey."

Gossie squinted at me across the table just the way my older sister, Sweet Fern, did when she knew I was up to something. I didn't catch her eye, even though I knew she wanted me to, and I didn't say a thing, just nodded and took a sip of my tea, like a proper lady.

Base Commander Colonel McNaught, wide and unsmiling as a brick wall, sat behind his desk. The light poured in through the window behind him, making what was left of his pale red hair glow like the sun. He'd offered me a seat when his secretary first showed me in, but now he looked as if he wanted to take it back.

He said, "It's unheard of."

I said, "You need pilots. The 801st Bombardment Group has suffered losses. Great losses." I couldn't believe it, but my voice sounded as calm as if I were discussing the weather or the list for the market.

He shook his head. "It's not done, Miss Hart. Women in combat, flying bombers."

I said, "I've survived a crash in a B-29, the biggest bomber on earth, when someone cut my rudder cables. I've flown a B-17 Flying Fortress across the ocean because General Henry Arnold and Jacqueline Cochran believed I could. I'm a good pilot. I'm a great pilot, and I'm volunteering. I can be useful in this war besides just ferrying planes from base to base." I thought: What are you doing, Velva Jean? What are you getting yourself into?

He leaned over his desk and folded his hands and stared at me good and hard. I stared right back at him, not blinking, something I'd learned to do from Johnny Clay. For one minute, I thought he was going to yell at me and tell me to get the hell out of his office and off his airfield, and maybe even out of Scotland.

Then he sighed. "It's dangerous work. It can be deadly work." But he said it in a bored way, as if he were tired of saying it, tired of things that were deadly and dangerous, as if they'd lost all meaning and were just a normal way of life now. In those two lines, I could hear how worn out he was from years of war, how ready he was to have it be over so he could go home. My eyes glanced along his desk to a picture of a woman and two little girls. Home to his family. I wondered when he'd seen them last. His eyes followed mine to the photograph and lingered.

I glanced up at the wall, at the pictures of Winston Churchill and President Roosevelt. Just above his desk was another picture—it was a photograph of Colonel McNaught and Eleanor Roosevelt, the first lady. Beside her he was warm and smiling, the tired lines around his mouth and eyes cleared away.

I looked back at him—the real, live him—and his eyes were still on the picture of his family. After a moment they wandered back to me. Before he could say anything, I said, "Eleanor Roosevelt says, 'We are in a war and we need to fight it with all our ability and every weapon possible. Women pilots are a weapon waiting to be used.'" It took all the strength and willpower I had to sit with my hands folded in my lap, my back straight as a board, and not glance up at the picture of him and Mrs. Roosevelt. I thought about how I must look to him, dressed in my Santiago Blues, my silver wings pinned on my shoulder. I didn't smile because I didn't want him to think I was some silly female, wasting his time with chitchat. Instead, I stared at him straight, like we were regular men having a discussion.

Finally, he said, "I would have to get approval from General Arnold and Miss Cochran, of course."

"Of course." I told myself: Stay calm. Don't smile. Breathe.

"Among others."

"Yes." Don't look too happy. Don't make him take back what he's saying. Don't make him change his mind.

"I doubt they'll agree to it. It's just not done. Just not done." He muttered something to himself, but I couldn't make out the words. "I leave the decision to them. I assume that's fine with you." This sounded a little jeering, but I didn't change my expression. I sat as cool and calm as the Virgin Mary, and nodded. I thought of asking him if he knew anything about where or how to find my brother, but decided not to push my luck.

"Do you think your base can spare you?"

I thought of Camp Davis, North Carolina—the swamps and the mud and the ugly wood barracks, the five hundred Army Air Force pilots who didn't want women there, the jabs and looks and mean comments, the sabotage that had killed my friend Sally Hallatassee, one of the best flyers I'd ever known, that had nearly killed me. I thought of Butch Dawkins, part Creole, part Choctaw, blues-playing and blues-singing guitar man, my friend and maybe more, who used to be there too but now was somewhere in Georgia or England or maybe even France. And then I thought of Johnny Clay, who wasn't in the United States but was somewhere over here, and how I'd made up my mind to find him, no matter what.

I wasn't sure if the colonel was mocking me again, but I said, "Yes, sir. I think they'll be just fine."

I walked outside and stood in the hard, summer light—a mix of sun and clouds—surrounded by the green of Scotland, a green brighter than emeralds or Fair Mountain on a full spring morning. Under blue sky and sunlight, it was hard to imagine bombs and machine guns and tanks and people bleeding into the earth.

Gossie and Helen stood by the door, arms folded, waiting. Helen said, "What did you do, Hartsie?" I looked at Gossie, and by the look in her eyes I knew she'd figured it out.

I said, "I'm not ready to go home." Not without my brother, I added in my head. "One hundred twenty-seven men killed while they were flying missions over France, and that's just one division. Think of them all. This is what we trained for. How can I go back home to ferry planes when they can use me here?" As I said it, I knew suddenly that every single word of this was true, and that this was bigger than Johnny Clay.

Gossie said, "Did he go for it?"

"I think so."

She said, "Well done, Mary Lou." Something cracked in her voice, just enough to let me know how proud she was of me. She coughed once and started clearing her throat, patting her chest, pretending she'd swallowed a bug.

Helen had a strange look fixed on her face. I knew she was anxious to leave, to be the third woman in history to pilot a bomber over the water. I looked at her and she looked at me, and finally she said, "Oh hell." Then she sighed and tossed her head back in a way that I was always desperate to copy. It made her seem as confident as Bette Davis. She marched off into headquarters, the door banging shut behind her.

The next morning, Colonel McNaught called Helen and me to his office and read us Jackie Cochran's message: "Glad you can use WASP Hart and Stillbert. Let them know our pride in them. The world will soon see what women pilots can do."

As I listened to the words, I thought of all the centuries of stories in Prestwick and Troon and Ayr. I came from a place in North Carolina where the mountains were the oldest mountains on earth, but everything else felt new. I guessed I was a part of the history of this place now too.

When he was finished giving us Miss Cochran's message and finished giving us our orders, Colonel McNaught said, "Just for the record, I want you to know I believe this is a bad idea and I'm against it."

Helen and I stood like soldiers. I listened to everything he had to say about why we shouldn't be flying and why we should be going home, leaving the war to the men, and the whole time he talked I stared at the picture of him and the first lady. I thought, You can talk all day if you want to, Colonel, but it doesn't change the fact that Helen and I are going to England to help our boys in the invasion of France.

Attention: Commanding Officer
Upottery Airfield
Devon, England

June 18, 1944

Dear Commanding Officer,

I'm sorry I don't know your name or who to direct this to, but my brother Technical Sergeant Johnny Clay Hart is a member of Easy Company of the 506th Parachute Infantry Regiment, U.S. 101st Airborne Division. According to Colonel Bradley Burns of the Bluie base in Greenland, Johnny Clay did not jump with his unit on D-day, and hasn't been heard from since winter of last year, when I believe he was sent to Upottery.

I hope you will write to me if you can at Harrington Airfield, Station 179, attention Velva Jean Hart, WASP, to let me know where he is. If you can't tell me, I hope you'll at least write me and let me know he's okay.

Thank you very much.

Yours truly,

Velva Jean Hart

THREE

*A*s we touched down at Station 179, a black-bellied B-24 took off, its nose pointed south. Helen and I sat strapped into the fuselage of our B-24, which was a retired D model, hollow and rattling like a bag of old bones. We sat with Lieutenant Alden and the four other pilots from Prestwick, who hadn't said a word to us since we boarded the plane.

After the engine growled to a stop, the men didn't even wait, but shoved on out ahead. Helen looked at me and said, "Welcome to England."

There was a hum about Station 179 that made me think of the way Fair Mountain hummed after a rainstorm. This was the home of the U.S. 801st Bombardment Group, which was also called the Carpetbaggers. Men in uniform covered the ground like ants. I didn't see a single girl anywhere.

As we lined up on the runway, collecting our things, sorting our gear, Lieutenant Alden and the others walked past as if they didn't want to be seen with us. Most of the other men, the ones already on base, stopped and stared, and an officer came bounding toward us. The air was dank and misty, and I could feel my hair begin to curl. Except for the control tower, the buildings were low and long, looking like grain silos lying on their sides, half-buried in the ground. The officer was ruddy faced, with a chin that faded into his neck. He said, "This way to the operations block."

He pointed out buildings as we went—the sick quarters; the mess hall; the PX, or postal exchange; the Service Club; Tent City, an enormous area just off of Harrington-Kelmarsh Road covered with row after row of tents, some five hundred in all; and headquarters, or HQ, which was as ugly a place as the others. A railway line ran along the western edge of the airfield, but the officer said you couldn't see Station 179 from the trains because Harrington was a secret, self-contained town, which was why it was camouflaged.

It was what they called a Class A airfield, which meant it was a base for heavy bombers. Instead of grass runways, concrete runways joined and crossed, and the main one was almost a mile long. Planes waited on the edges—an A-26, a C-47, a smaller plane I didn't recognize, and twenty or so B-24 Liberators, a few painted camouflage green, the others painted black.

Helen and I were taken straight to the base commander, Lieutenant Colonel Heflin, a serious-looking man with brown hair swept up in the pointy tuft of a Kewpie doll. His second-in-command, Major Fish, had thick black hair and thick black eyebrows and a downturned mouth that made him look like a brook trout.

Lieutenant Colonel Heflin welcomed us and told us he was glad to have us, and the whole time he seemed to be off somewhere in his head. I thought a man like this must have more to do in one day than the President. He said, "We're glad you're here. As you know, we have a shortage of pilots. As soon as we run FBI checks, we'll clear you for takeoff."

I looked at Helen and she looked at me. I thought: What in the world is an FBI check? And why would they do one on me? I knew the FBI was the Federal Bureau of Investigation because before he wanted to be a movie cowboy or a gold panner or Red Terror, Russian spy, Johnny Clay had decided he would go to Washington, D.C., and become a lawman. I wondered if this FBI check was something the lieutenant colonel was making up just to keep us from flying or if it was a real thing that every pilot had to go through.

Lieutenant Colonel Heflin said, "We'll notify you as soon as you're cleared." And he stood, which meant he was done. Major Fish opened the door for us, and Helen went on out. I stood, still facing the lieutenant colonel, who said, "You're dismissed, pilot."

I said, "Thank you, sir. But I have a question." Helen hovered in the doorway, trying to decide whether to come back in.

Major Fish sat down in one of the hard-backed chairs and folded his hands across his stomach. He looked back and forth between the lieutenant colonel and me.

"Yes?"

"My brother Technical Sergeant Johnny Clay Hart, of the 101st Airborne, is missing. No one's heard from him since winter of last year, and the last letter he wrote me was dated October 18, 1943. He was supposed to jump on Normandy, but he didn't. He hasn't been with his unit for a long time. I was hoping you might help me find out where he is."

Major Fish stared right at Lieutenant Colonel Heflin, his mouth twitching.

The lieutenant colonel said, "I'm sorry, but I can't help you." He sat down and began rummaging through the papers on his desk.

I said, "The commanding officer at Bluie, the base in Greenland—a man named Colonel Burns—he looked at the telegraph reports and did some checking, but he couldn't turn up anything. I was hoping maybe you could—"

Lieutenant Colonel Heflin barked, "I'm sorry, Miss Hart." My eyes started stinging, and for one horrible moment I thought I might cry.

Instead I pulled myself up to my full height, which was almost five feet seven inches tall, and I said, "Thank you, sir." And then I walked out of the office, trying not to see the smile on Major Fish's face or the way Lieutenant Colonel Heflin shook his head and rolled his eyes. I heard their voices as I shut the door—rumble, rumble, rumble, then laughing.

Outside, the sky was dull and thick with clouds. Helen said, "That went well."

I said, "I had to ask."

A Jeep rolled past carrying two women and two men. The women were attractive and young. They were laughing and smoking cigarettes and looked as if they were out for a Sunday drive. One of them caught my eye and I felt a chill. I'd never seen anyone look so cool and confident. I stood still as a statue, like I was carved out of stone or rooted into the earth like a tree—Helen's voice in the distance, her hand tugging at my sleeve—watching them until they drove out of sight.

At four thirty in the afternoon, a large American car with curtained windows arrived at Station 179. Helen and I stood outside our Nissen hut—one of the sideways silos—where we were bunking with some Red Cross girls who were stationed there. We watched as three men in paratrooper uniforms got out of the back of the car.

The men were met by officers who led them to one of the other huts. The three men were young, so young, and they carried duffel bags with their names on them. As they walked past, one of them looked our way and I caught his eye, just for a second.

Helen said, "Look at them." And I knew what she meant—these were just boys from farms and mountains and little cities and big cities, which they might never see again. I thought, Any one of them could be Johnny Clay, and thinking it made my heart drop low in my chest.

We didn't see the men the rest of the day. We looked for them at mess, but there wasn't a single sign of them. After we finished eating, Helen and I started back toward our barracks, and suddenly we spotted the men coming out of the same hut they'd gone into earlier. This time they were dressed in helmets and large padded gray-green jumpsuits that made them look like giants. The same officers were walking with them, and they put the men into the same car with the curtained windows and drove them off toward the airfield.

I said, "Let's go!" And I grabbed Helen's hand and we started running. The airfield was probably half a mile from the mess hall. We ran as fast as we could, getting there in time to see the three men climb into one of the black B-24 Liberators, its engines already churning. Behind it, lined up on the runway and the airfield, were three more B-24s, ready to go. We stood, trying to catch our breath, wind whipping our hair around—I could feel a storm brewing in the distance—and watched as the doors closed behind them and the officers, still on the ground, stepped away. The Liberator rolled down the runway and took off, followed by another and another and another, into the night sky, the moon shining bright as fox fire.

Sometime before dawn it started raining and it didn't stop for three days. Early in the morning, a car with curtained windows drove onto the base carrying three men, followed an hour later by three cars carrying ten men, only all the planes were grounded, so no flights went out that night or the night after. The newspapers said it was the worst storm in forty years. The reports from Normandy were gloomy— eight-foot waves slamming the beaches, grounding eight hundred Allied vessels and stopping five hundred others from getting where they needed to go. The Army Air Forces couldn't fly in to drop reinforcements, and the navy couldn't get through to make deliveries, which meant the six hundred thousand troops that were waiting were short of supplies and help and ammunition.

On the fourth day, the rain started to let up, and by the afternoon of the fifth day, June 24, the sky was gloomy but dry. We were called into the sick bay and given physicals by one of the Red Cross nurses. And then she gave us shots: tetanus, typhoid fever, malaria, and dengue fever. We would get the rest—smallpox, cholera, typhus, yellow fever—in a couple of days. She said, "These may make you feel a little bad later."

We were too sick to do anything the rest of the day but lie in our beds and sleep. I was dizzy and hot and mad at myself for coming here and dragging Helen with me when I didn't know what they were planning to do with us. I'd never even heard of dengue fever, but it sounded horrible. Like something one of the Lowes would have up on Fair Mountain. Like something you would get from a possum.

From her cot, Helen said, "Well, I'm bored to death. I might just die of boredom. Let's study our French before I lose my mind."

Helen had learned to speak French during her year of college and, before that, at Miss Porter's School for Girls, which was a fancy boarding school where her mother had gone, and her mother before that. She took me through different words and phrases, just as she'd been doing since Camp Davis, all things she said I should know when and if we ever got to France. Afterward, we went over our maps of France, trying to learn the names and coordinates of every town.

I said, "That team of four people in the Jeep. The two men and two women. They weren't dressed like soldiers, but they were important. I think they were spies."

Helen said, "Oh, Hartsie."

I said, "What?"

She said, "All this spy talk."

I said, "What else could it be?"

She was quiet. One of the good things about Helen was that she didn't always insist on being right. If you talked to her long enough about something, sometimes she came around. She said, "Well, my mother did know a girl at Miss Porter's who said her mother was a spy in the First World War. Mother said she was never sure whether or not this girl was telling the truth, but she figured she didn't have any reason to lie."

I thought about how Johnny Clay and I used to play Spies on a Mission, which was our favorite game when we were growing up. I was Constance Kurridge and he was Red Terror, and we would creep through the woods as silent as haints. We were the best spies for fifty miles.

Hours later, I woke up to the dark, my cot shaking underneath me. I said in Helen's direction, "What is it?"

She said, "The drop. There's a drop tonight." All flights over enemy territory were made during the moon periods when the weather was good. This was so pilots in the middle of the blackout could find their way by using rivers, lakes, railroad tracks, and towns as checkpoints. Helen's voice was blurry. She said something else, but I couldn't understand it because she was fading away into the darkness.

I said, "I wonder where they're going?" I closed my eyes again. My head was spinning right into the pillow, right into the floor. I said, "I wonder if they'll come back?" And then I fell asleep.

The next morning, one of the Red Cross girls was on her way out the door of the Nissen hut when she turned around and poked her head back in. She said, "There's something out here for you all."

Helen propped herself up on one elbow and said, "Gosh, I hope it's roses." And we both laughed because that would be the last thing ever left on our doorstep at Harrington.

I followed the nurse outside, my legs wobbly as an old man's, and saw a stack of newspapers sitting in the dirt. It was starting to rain again. I said, "How do you know they're for Helen and me?"

She said, "Because some of the articles are circled." She bent over to study the papers and then she picked them up. She straightened and frowned at me, and it was a sorry kind of frown. She was a nice girl. Mary Phillips, from Pittsburgh, Pennsylvania. Before the war, she'd been a telephone operator. She said, "I just want you to know that the girls and I think what you and Helen are doing—what all of you girls are doing—is pretty damn swell." I looked down at the newspapers, my eyes going right to the circled story. I flipped through each article in the stack and saw story after story marked with a black pen.

"What is it, Hartsie? Why are you sitting here in the rain?" Helen leaned against the doorframe, rubbing her eyes. "God, what an awful day."

I kept flipping through the papers, and she sat down beside me, brushing the dirt off the step, pulling her knees in tight, and started reading over my shoulder.

All the articles were about the WASP, some from recent newspapers, some from months ago. The latest one, dated June 23, had a headline that read: "WASP Bill Defeated." It said that on June 21, the United States Congress met to discuss the WASP militarization bill. Male civilian pilots had been campaigning for months to fight the bill, and they were helped by reporters like Drew Pearson, who wrote regular columns for the *Washington Post* demanding that the WASP deactivate, and *Time* magazine, which had published an article called "Unnecessary and Undesirable" that said the program was too expensive and that men could have been trained more quickly. These articles were also in the stack.

The hearing in Washington had lasted less than one hour, and when it was over, 188 to 169 voted against the militarization bill. The House recommended "immediate discontinuance of the WASP training program." Jacqueline Cochran was told that all current students—the ones already at Avenger Field—could finish their training. But five days later, a brand-new class of WASP recruits had to turn around and leave Texas as soon as they arrived, paying their own way home.

═══════

Velva Jean Hart, WASP
Harrington Airfield
Station 179
Northamptonshire, England

June 23, 1944

Dear Velva Jean Hart,

I am sorry, but we have no record that Technical Sergeant Johnny Clay Hart was ever at Upottery.

I wish you all the best in locating your brother.

Sincerely,

Ann-Marie Paget
Secretary to General Maxwell Davenport Taylor,
Commander 101st Airborne Division

FOUR

On Monday, July 3, in the early hours of the morning and on into the day, the B-24 Liberators returned to base, one by one. Around noon, a bomber limped into Harrington with over a thousand bullet holes shot through it. Officers, pilots, crew, and nurses came hurrying out of the control tower, the tents, the lodges, the Nissen huts, HQ, and the sick bay, rushing over the concrete of the airfield to look at the B-24. A gaping hole had been torn into one side of the bomber, and the glass of the windshield was splintered into a million little lines and rivers running this way and that, up and down and across. The engine was smoking, and one of the wings was cut in half like someone had chopped it with an axe. Before they could talk to anyone, the crew was driven away by a group of officers.

Lieutenant Alden and another pilot stood on the flight line, dressed in their flight suits. Helen and I walked up, standing just behind them.

Without looking at us, Lieutenant Alden said, "You need to remember something and really think it over. Back home, you may have been a WASP, ferrying planes and what have you, flying them from base to base." The way he said it made it sound like all we'd done was sit around and go to tea parties. "But this is a war zone. No one was shooting at you." I thought of the gunners firing at our airplanes during target towing practice. "No one was trying to kill you." I thought about the sabotage on our planes—sugar in the fuel tank, sand in the carburetor, rudder cables cut in two, my friend Sally, trapped in her

A-24, burning to death because someone had tampered with the canopy safety latch. "But here, you're a weapon of war."

That afternoon, we were called into Lieutenant Colonel Heflin's office, where we sat in the straight-backed chairs across from him, learning that our FBI checks had come back fine and we were now cleared for duty.

The lieutenant colonel said, "You will be flying to France, dropping off supplies or teams of men, and then returning back to base. I know you both check out on the B-24, but I'm having Lieutenant Colonel Dickerson go over the bombers you'll be flying since they've been modified for our purposes. When flying, you'll wear your WASP uniforms. If your plane is shot down, you're to keep your uniforms on because they entitle you to POW protection under the Geneva convention, even if you aren't technically military."

He leaned forward over his desk, clasping his hands together and resting on his elbows like he was about to pray. He said, "It's not too late. We're asking a lot of you. We ask a lot of any man who goes up right now." He didn't say it, but we knew what it was he wasn't saying: We're asking even more of you because you're women.

I waited for Helen to tell him we were sorry, that we just couldn't do it, that we were taking our B-17 and flying back to Camp Davis, North Carolina. I waited for me to say something, to turn this around so that it had never happened, so that it never would. Helen uncrossed her legs and recrossed them and stared unblinking at Lieutenant Colonel Heflin. Neither of us said a word.

He sat back, his shoulders sinking a little. He said, "All right then. You report to Dickerson this afternoon. Dismissed."

We stood and saluted him and we walked toward the door, first Helen and then me. Behind us he said, "One more thing, ladies." Helen's hand was on the doorknob. We turned to look at him. "If you tell anyone about the work you are doing, you will be executed."

At noon on July 13, I reported to the Group Operations Building. The officers looked up when I walked in.

"Velva Jean Hart?" The voice came from a tall and lanky man. I guessed he was in his thirties.

"Yes, sir."

"Captain Putnam. Your squadron commander. I want you to meet your pilot, Captain Baskin, and your navigator, Second Lieutenant Glenn. Officers, your copilot, Velva Jean Hart."

Captain Baskin was close to forty and made me think of Daryl and Lester Gordon, boys I'd grown up with back home—short and beefy, with a head as square as a cinder block. He slapped me on the back and told me it was good to have me aboard, and then he said, "You and me, we're going to get along fine, just so long as you remember who the pilot is." He sounded as though he were shouting every word.

Second Lieutenant Glenn was as small as Captain Baskin was large, slight and neat, not a hair out of place, with the look of someone who liked to stay inside reading books or studying mathematics. He held out his hand to shake mine and I was surprised at how firm it was.

He said, "Nice to meet you, ma'am," and his voice sounded just like home.

Before I could ask if he was from North Carolina, Lieutenant Colonel Heflin cleared his throat and began our briefing. The wall behind him was covered with a giant map of Europe, and it was stuck with pushpins, each one holding up a small piece of colored paper. The map showed mountains and rivers and forests. Looking at it, I could almost see the villages and the people and their houses.

At the back of the room, Lieutenant Colonel Dickerson, squint-eyed and sour, stood watching. With Dickerson, Helen and I had gone over the B-24 Liberator and the general rules of flying drop missions into a combat zone: First and foremost, don't get shot down, and if you do, don't tell anyone anything about your mission. He'd spent two days with us, and that was it.

It was up to Captain Baskin and Second Lieutenant Glenn and me—under the direction of Captain Putnam—to choose the route and draw up our own flight plan. After the general briefing ended, we went over our map, a smaller version of the one on the wall. We looked for the presence of flak, or antiaircraft fire, on the S2 flak maps, and selected our route and the checkpoints we would make on the way to our target: Rouen, the capital city of Normandy, France. The only thing I knew about Rouen was that it was where Joan of Arc had been burned at the stake.

Captain Putnam said to me, "The best thing you can do is memorize the route to the drop zone so that you never have to use the map. The top pilots can read their way by moonlight, memorizing landmarks and finding their way on their own."

Second Lieutenant Glenn said, "The trick is to fly in a dogleg pattern, which means you never fly a direct course for longer than thirty miles. This is so we can avoid antiaircraft guns and night fighters. Obviously we want to make sure we get in and out and don't get involved in an air fight."

I felt a terrible chill run through me, just like I had dengue fever.

He said, "Sometimes you have to fly miles farther into enemy territory after you complete a drop so that you can disguise the actual drop zone. You never know if an enemy's tracking the plane or if maybe they got tipped off that you're coming."

Captain Putnam and Captain Baskin started arguing about the route, and I looked down at our target, at the word *Rouen*, which was just a dot on a map of France.

Second Lieutenant Glenn leaned toward me and said, "Why are you here, Velva Jean?" He said it low, as if he didn't want the two captains to hear him. "Why did you agree to this? What kind of mission are you on?"

I looked him square in the eyes and thought of all the things I could say, starting with my brother and how he was missing and how I needed to find him, to make sure he was okay and alive, and then going on to the WASP and Jacqueline Cochran and all those men at Camp Davis who said we shouldn't be here, that we shouldn't be flying at all.

I said, "I want to be a weapon of war."

At 1800 hours, two hours before takeoff, our crew met up in Squadron Operations at the crew room they had assigned to us. I was dressed in my Santiago Blues, my beret pinned to my head because if I crashed in France, I didn't want to risk losing any part of my uniform.

The weather operator gave the latest weather report to Second Lieutenant Glenn, and he handed in our flight plan to Captain Putnam. Lieutenant Sullivan gave me crew kits to hand out to everyone, and these contained candy and chewing gum, cigarettes, flares, first aid kits, and emergency packets.

At 1900 hours, Helen and I sat in the mess hall pushing our food around on our plates while the men ate and ate and ate. I said, "I'm not hungry."

She said, "Me neither."

I said, "Do you know what kind of drop this is?" The one thing they hadn't covered in all our hours of briefings was what our mission was—who were the men we were dropping (they called them "agents") and who was waiting on the ground in France to receive the supplies we were carrying.

She shook her head and pushed her tray away. "Listen, I think we need to have a way to send each other a message, you know, if we get shot down. Some sort of code something or other. A poem."

"Or a song," I said. This was regular spy stuff, and I was surprised at Helen for thinking of it.

We eventually decided on "In the land of crimson sunsets, skies are wide and blue," which was from a hymn to Avenger Field, the song we'd sung at our graduation. If we crashed and were somehow stuck or even captured, we could say those lines to folks on the ground, hoping they might repeat them somewhere else and then the message would get carried along. This way we'd each know that the other one was okay.

At 1930 hours, Captain Baskin and the crew and I were driven to our B-24 Liberator, which was already loaded with the containers and packages to be dropped. Some of the men on my crew weren't happy having a female copilot. In the hours before takeoff, a few of them had gone to Lieutenant Sullivan and asked to be reassigned.

Except for Second Lieutenant Glenn, none of the men would look me in the eye or say anything to me, not even "thank you" when I handed them their crew kits. While we rode, I glanced from face to face, wondering if they knew about the newspaper articles, if maybe they'd sat up late the night before with scissors, cutting out one story after another.

As we climbed out of the car, my heart started going faster and faster, like it was racing down a hill. I was wearing a fleece-lined flight suit over my Santiago Blues and boots, carrying a pair of GI shoes, the smallest pair of men's shoes they had, which we all carried in case of a crash.

The rain and clouds were gone, and it was the clearest night I'd ever seen, with a moon so big and bright it looked like you could touch it. The B-24 stood waiting like a gigantic metal monster, black as the night. I told myself that flying a B-24 Liberator across the English Channel to France wasn't any scarier than flying an AT-6 over the San Francisco Peaks or a B-29 across the North Carolina mountains or a B-17 across the ocean, all of which I'd done.

I sat in the cockpit next to Captain Baskin, one hand on the wheel, one hand on the throttle, engine rumbling. The B-24 wasn't as sleek as the B-17. It was a heavy plane, as wide and ugly as a freight train. It wasn't made to be pretty—it was made to haul bombs high and far.

Helen and I knew the B-24 like our own faces, thanks to our WASP training, but these B-24s were different. The ball turret had been taken out and only the tail and top turrets were left in. The hole where the ball turret used to be was lined with metal and covered by a plywood door that hinged in the middle. This was called the Joe hole because when it was time for the drop, the door would come off the hole and agents—called Joes—and supply containers would be dropped through it with parachutes. Flash suppressors had been installed on the guns, flame dampeners had been installed on the turbo-superchargers, and blackout curtains hung over the waist-gun windows. This was so that we were as invisible as possible. All the lightbulbs were painted red and the bottom of the bomber was painted black so that enemy searchlights couldn't spot us.

The entire plane was blacked out except for one dim light in the navigator's compartment. I flicked on the fuel booster pumps and then reached for the accelerator switch. Captain Baskin advanced the number three engine throttle to one-third open, and then I pushed the accelerator switch, holding it while I jabbed at the priming switch. I pushed the crank switch, and the engine coughed and wheezed before catching. The captain took us through our checks—oil pressure, vacuum pumps, anti-icers, deicers—and then he taxied out to the runway, where we went through the last checks before takeoff. I called out the airspeeds as he held the throttles against the stops, and then the B-24 broke ground at 110 mph. Captain Baskin and I went through one more series of checks and then we took off.

As we climbed higher into the night, the B-24 gaining speed, I breathed in and out, in and out. It was good to be flying again, even if I wasn't lead pilot and even if I couldn't make out anything below me—because of the blackout, the ground was dark as tar. Second Lieutenant Glenn's voice was in my ear, giving us checkpoints, telling us coordinates, but I had the same itchy, mean feeling I always got when I knew I should be able to do something that I wasn't being allowed to do—like flying the plane or finding the way.

I thought about Upottery to the southwest of me and Omaha Beach to the southeast and I wondered what would happen if I took over the Liberator and pointed it toward either place. And then, instead, we headed for France.

FIVE

We crossed the English Channel above six thousand feet because it was easier to avoid antiaircraft fire up high. The old hollowed-out bomber rattled and coughed. As we reached the shores of France, Second Lieutenant Glenn and the bombardier started working together on the navigation, and Captain Baskin took the plane to two thousand feet because the lower you flew, the less chance you had of getting hit by a night fighter and the less chance you had of being spotted by the enemy by either sight or sound or radar detection equipment.

The bomber bucked this way and jigged that way, and I wondered what Captain Baskin saw that I couldn't. I kept my eyes trained out the window, watching for lights. Around 2100 hours, I heard Second Lieutenant Glenn in my headset: "We're closing in on the drop zone," and then the dispatcher shouted, "Running in!"

We were making the drop near Rouen, which wasn't all that far from Paris. I looked through the glass at the ground below and thought about Gossie.

Suddenly, the plane shuddered and the B-24 lurched, nearly rolling over on its side. Captain Baskin swore into his headset and righted her again. He said to the rear gunners, "Where in the bloody goddamn hell is that coming from?"

Looking back through the window, I could see the tip of the right wing glowing red, smoke spinning out and away from us into the sky.

One of the rear gunners said, "I think it's ground fire."

The other gunner said, "Schräge Musik."

Whatever that was sounded terrible. I said, "What is it?"

Captain Baskin shouted, "German night fighter. Upward firing. Damn things get you from below where you can't spot them."

The bombardier sat on a swivel seat in the glazed nose reading off landmarks to Second Lieutenant Glenn, who was shooting his fixes and giving the captain directions. The turret gunner, who was also the plane's engineer, reported on the engines, saying we'd lost the number two engine but the other three were in working order. I knew we'd be okay with only three engines as long as our fuel held out, and as long as we didn't lose another one. Captain Baskin turned the vacuum valve to the good engines. The radio operator sat in the upper fuselage just aft of the cockpit, and I could hear him telling headquarters about the attack.

Then I heard the *rattle-rattle-rattle* of machine guns from the rear of the plane. The rear gunners swore and then one of them said, "Nine o'clock," which meant it was to the left of us. There was another *rattle-rattle-rattle* and then the other rear gunner shouted, "I'm hit!" The radio operator swung around and grabbed the second waist gun and started firing, the used-up shells hitting the floor like hard, metal raindrops.

From the middle of the plane, the waist gunner, who was in charge of dropping the agents and supply containers through the Joe hole, climbed into the top turret. A minute later, he shouted, "Bastards nearly shot my head off!"

I strained to look, my hand on the wheel, on the throttle, hovering over the controls, the trim tabs. Captain Baskin said, "Take your hands away, Hart! You think I need a girl to help me fly this plane?"

I was so surprised I yanked my hands away and sat with them on my lap. Captain Baskin was gripping the throttle so hard his knuckles had gone white, and his jaw was so clenched up it looked as if it would never come unhinged again. That great, heavy B-24 was quaking and bobbing and pitching, and all around me the men on the crew were shooting or barking orders or shouting to one another, working together, everyone but me.

The captain said, "I want you all to fasten and adjust your chutes," and then he asked Second Lieutenant Glenn to plot their position again. The plane filled with the smell of gasoline, so strong it burned my nose, and Captain Baskin ordered the bomb bay doors retracted in case we had to bail out. He lowered the nose and pushed the power levers to their stops, and then leveled off with plenty of airspeed, and then he cranked the aileron trim wheel to bring the wings level again so that the bomber would stop rolling toward the dead engine.

I sat there in a fury, not allowed to do anything, the restraint straps digging into my waist and chest and shoulders. Somewhere over the coast of France, one of the rear gunners hit the night fighter, which exploded like a firework. I watched as it dove downward and disappeared into the black of the water. I heard the splash in my mind even though the only thing in my headset was the sound of men whooping and hollering and congratulating one another, and the sound of my own pulse pounding like a man's fist.

Captain Baskin said, "Let's make the goddamn drop," and there were cheers in my headset as he pointed the nose of the B-24 south, back toward Rouen.

When we were just a few miles from the target area, we all looked out the window, searching for the flashlights of the reception party. There would be three high-powered torches placed in a row, with a fourth at a ninety-degree angle so that we would know the direction of the drop. Captain Baskin selected half flaps and made the run in at 135 mph, which wasn't much above stalling speed. He circled the drop zone once and then the bombardier guided him in and the B-24 went in low, till we were about six hundred feet off the ground. Behind me, I could hear the agents lining up at the rim of the Joe hole.

And then I saw them—three faint flickerings of light. From where I sat, they were beautiful. Bright spots in the middle of nothing. A series of stars blinking in a row.

Captain Baskin began lining up with the lights. He dropped to three hundred feet, which meant I could just make out figures on the ground, and I guessed that these were the members of the reception party. I wondered who they were and where they came from. And that's when

I saw that the people on the ground were holding the flashlights, but there were people behind them—just shadows on the tree line—with helmets and uniforms and guns. Something flashed again and again, and one of the rear gunners said, "Ground fire . . ."

I said, "Pull us up." Granny always said I had eyes like a cat's, able to see far and wide, deep into the dark, deep into the blinding sunlight, farther than anyone.

Captain Baskin shouted, "What?"

I said, "Pull us up. The Germans have got them." I could hear the dispatcher giving orders to the first of the agents. I turned in my seat, even though I couldn't see him, and hollered into my headset, "The Germans have got them. Stop the drop!"

In the headset, the dispatcher asked the captain if this was true, and then the bombardier started shouting, "Pull her up! Pull her up! Get us the hell out of here!"

The captain tugged on the yoke, which controlled the elevator, to pull the nose up, and at the same time he advanced the throttles for more power. From inside the plane I heard a roar, like a thunderclap, and the B-24 shook so hard that I waited for it to explode. The waist gunner swore and then he said, "We've been flak-blasted. Shell exploded . . . inside waist . . . torn in two . . ." The radio buzzed and clicked, and I could barely hear him. Another jolt, another blast, and the plane jerked hard to the right and then dropped down even lower. This time we were shot in the nose.

I looked over at the captain, and he didn't say a word. The plane flew along at 130 mph, 120 mph, dipping back down to five hundred feet, four hundred feet. I said, "Captain, get us out of here!" And that's when I saw the blood dripping onto his flight suit.

I grabbed the wheel and slammed back the throttle and pointed what was left of the nose of that great, hulking bomber into the sky. I shredded the rudder and elevator controls to try to maintain directional and altitude control. I said into my headset, "Throw all the extra weight overboard, and get yourselves above the weak point."

I heard the men scrambling, and one by one they showed up behind me. I didn't turn to look because I needed to bring her out straight and level. I poured on more power to overcome the drag. The B-24 felt like it weighed twice as much as the B-29. I shouted, "Get your chutes ready!" before I remembered that Captain Baskin had already ordered them to do this. And then I began to sing.

> *In a cavern, in a canyon,*
> *Excavating for a mine*
> *Dwelt a miner forty-niner,*
> *And his daughter Clementine.*

"Oh My Darling, Clementine" was one of the songs Johnny Clay and I used to sing when we were little because it gave us the spooks and made Sweet Fern have fifteen fits. For some reason it came into my mind before any of my own songs that I'd written myself.

I looked down at the captain and suddenly I felt woozy from all the blood. So much blood.

A voice said, "Keep singing." It was one of the agents from the belly of the plane—I could tell from the gray-green parachute smock he wore—and he was standing over the captain, wrapping him in bandages from his kit, his hands covered in blood. So much blood.

I said, "What?"

He said, "Sing, goddammit." His voice was cool and even and sounded French. In the dark of the cockpit, I could only see the red of the blood, the white-red flash of antiaircraft fire.

> *Ruby lips above the water,*
> *Blowing bubbles, soft and fine,*
> *But, alas, I was no swimmer,*
> *So I lost my Clementine.*

I pushed the bomber up and onward. I thought, Please, Jesus, if you can hear me. Help me get us out of here.

I looked at the Frenchman. His hands were working, working. I said, "Is he okay?"

There was blood everywhere. The Frenchman had his hands

pressed against Captain Baskin's neck. Second Lieutenant Glenn was behind him now, and then so was one of the other agents, handing him bandages from their kits. The Frenchman said, "Sing." His voice was a command, as if he were used to giving orders and having them followed.

> *Oh my darling, oh my darling,*
> *Oh my darling, Clementine,*
> *You are lost and gone forever,*
> *Dreadful sorry, Clementine.*

To my right I heard a pop—like a distant star exploding. I thought: I wonder what that was? I wonder if a star makes a sound when it dies? I wonder if we're hit? I wonder if I'm hit? I wonder if I'm dying right now, just like a star? I could smell the blood. I could feel the wet of it all the way over in my seat, in my lap, flowing down my arm. I could almost taste it.

And then there was nothing but blackness.

SIX

Suddenly I felt a sharp sting on my cheek. I tried to hide my face by turning in to my shoulder, but there was a sting on my other cheek, as if someone had taken a hot poker to it. I was weak and I was weary, and I didn't have much breath left in me, but I threw back my head and screamed.

A voice said, "Be quiet, idiot girl. *Chut! Chut!*"

I started coughing from the smoke, from the fire, but when I tried to keep screaming, I couldn't. The smoke was filling my lungs like air in a balloon so that all the breath was squeezed out of me and I felt as if I were drowning, or being smothered by a pillow. I shouted, "Please don't let them burn me alive!"

"No one is burning you alive, you fool."

And then there was another sting against my cheek, and my eyes opened and all I saw were flecks of light, just like lightning bugs, coming at me out of the dark. I was hot, so hot. I felt like I was on fire. I could hear a crackling and hissing, and then I turned and saw where it was coming from. It was a giant bonfire—flames bursting up from the ground, climbing into the sky.

I sat straight up, trying to get to my feet, my body throbbing and aching and stinging, and saw a face, strange and exotic. It was a serious face, an angry face, with something simmering in it that made me think of an animal. The eyes were dark and burning, the lips full, the cheekbones high, the eyebrows arched. At first I thought it was the devil himself, and before I could scream, a hand went over my mouth.

I was sitting on the ground and he was kneeling over me, and I thought, Dear Jesus, he's going to kill me. I wanted to bite him, to kick him, but I couldn't move my body. It was as if I were underwater or in quicksand or stuck in the muddy bottoms of Three Gum River. And then I knew I wasn't in hell. I was in France, and that bonfire was my B-24.

Little by little, I could feel my body waking up. First I felt pinpricks of pain in my right ankle, then a sharp pang in my knee. A soreness in my hip, an aching in my wrist, a throbbing in my shoulder. A sting on my right cheek and my left cheek. A dull pounding in my head.

I said to the Frenchman, "Did you slap me?"

He said, "Yes. Shall I do it again?" I wasn't sure he was French at all. Maybe Spanish. Or from a place where gypsies lived.

I said, "Why would you do that?" I wished I could slap him back, right across the face, but I couldn't move. My whole life, no one had ever slapped me.

He said, "We must go. Can you walk?" He stood, blocking out the sun. But no, it wasn't the sun; it was another great burning ball of fire. The other half of the B-24, I thought. I started coughing again. He swore, but the words sounded like nonsense words. The only way I could tell he was swearing was because of the tone and because of the look he wore on his face. He walked around behind me and pulled me up. I went dizzy, holding on to his arm, and then I looked down and saw the blood.

I said, "I'm dying."

He said, "*C'est seulement une égratignure.* It is just a scratch." He put my left arm around his shoulders and started half-walking me, half-dragging me, fast as he could, away from the fire. Smoke was everywhere, billowing and pillowing around, filling the air like fog.

He kept dragging me along, bumping me over stones and twigs. He had the stealthy, swaggering walk of a panther. We were in the woods somewhere, surrounded by tall, slim trees, thick as soldiers on a battlefield. Beech trees, I thought. We had ones just like them in North Carolina. And other ones. Tall trees. So tall. Where was the sky? Where was the moon?

I said, "What day is this?"

"July fourteenth."

I said, "Where are we going?" The night air closed in around me.

"Away from here. The Germans will see the fire. It is only a matter of time."

"Where are the others?"

"Dead. All but you, me, and my team. The ones who made it."

Captain Baskin. Second Lieutenant Glenn. The gunners, the bombardier, the dispatcher. My crew. Everyone dead. Everyone gone.

Fifty miles later—or maybe it was fifty yards—he dropped me onto the ground as if I were no more than a sack of potatoes. A shadow came out of the trees, and before I could scream again I saw that it was one of the other agents, dressed in the same gray-green parachute smock, and that he'd been shot in the eye. He'd made himself a patch from a bandage and spots of red were seeping through.

He said, "The goddamn radio's blown to hell. How am I supposed to let London know what happened or tell them where to drop supplies? All I've got left is this." He held up a square of silk that looked like a very small handkerchief, but it was covered in writing. "How am I supposed to help us without a fucking radio? We don't know where the Krauts are or where headquarters is and we don't even know where the fuck we are." He was American. He had a face like a boxer's, nose and chin jutted out to spite the world. He was lean and wiry and looked as if he were ready for a fight. He took off his helmet and threw it on the ground and I saw that he had a wild shock of dark hair.

The Frenchman said, "We will borrow a radio where we can. My aid kit was lost in the crash. Do you have an extra bandage?" The boxer threw him the whole kit, and the Frenchman stood, sorting through it.

I said to the boxer, "Your eye is bleeding." I reached out like I could touch it all the way from the ground, and like I might somehow be able to fix it.

He said, "Who the hell are you?"

The Frenchman said, "Our copilot." He tore the bandage in two and wrapped one of his hands, which was red from the blood.

"Great job on the landing, sister."

The Frenchman said, "Enough." He wrapped the other hand.

Before I could say anything, two more shadows came out of the trees. The taller one said, "Crown, Gelman, Miles, Sterling, Chapman—all dead." These men wore the same gray-green smocks. The taller one was dark and built like a truck. His face was scarred and craggy, as if he'd been left out in the sun too long, and there was a bandage just above one knee, where he was bleeding. The shorter one was short, with thinning hair and the nervous look of a mole. One of his arms was wrapped in a makeshift sling.

The short one said, "Who is she?" He was British.

The Frenchman said, "Our copilot."

"We can't take her."

"We cannot leave her either. Not for the Germans to find."

They started pulling off their parachute smocks. The craggy one rewrapped his leg and then he dug a hole, and the men threw the smocks into this. The flight suit was warm and waterproof and I was chilled from the night, from the damp of the air, from crashing, from almost burning to death. I didn't want to take it off, but I knew we had to bury the smocks so no one would see them. I pulled off my suit and handed it to the craggy one. He dropped it into the hole and covered it up with dirt.

The other men bent over the ground and started sorting through the gear, tossing the things they didn't need or couldn't carry into a pile while the craggy one dug another hole. When it was ready, they threw everything in.

Suddenly a fifth man appeared from out of the trees. He was as handsome as Tom Buccaneer, a hero in dime-store romance novels who always saved girls by throwing them onto the back of his horse. This man had white-blond hair and a strong, square jaw. He looked as if he should be wearing shining armor instead of an army uniform.

He said, "As far as I can tell, we're at least fifty miles west of the drop. We'll put as much distance between ourselves and the plane as possible. The Germans know we're out here, and even though we managed to get far afield from the zone, they'll have seen the flames, and, if they haven't yet, they'll find the crash site." He was American too, and other than a scrape on his neck, he didn't seem to have a scratch on him. He looked at me then, as if he was only just noticing me, and said, "You took over the plane when the captain was killed."

I said, "Yes, sir."

He shook my hand. "Good work, soldier." And then he smiled and it was the glittering smile of a movie star.

I thought, Thank God you're here. The others were glaring at me as if I'd shot them down myself. It suddenly dawned on me that I was alone in enemy-occupied France with five strange men. I didn't know the area, barely knew the language, didn't have a weapon, didn't have any clothes other than my Santiago Blues.

The Frenchman, who seemed to be in charge, said, "We need to keep moving." He looked at me. "Can you run?"

I felt myself bristle. I said, "Of course." I tried not to think about the fact that I was hurt and bleeding.

He looked at Tom Buccaneer then, waiting.

Tom Buccaneer said, "Let's go."

We'd lost our food and water in the crash, not to mention all sense of direction. No one seemed to know where we were, not even the Frenchman, who was at least in his own country. When it was clear he didn't know where we were going, except away from the crash—that none of them did—I said, "Wait." I didn't look to see if they'd stopped, if they were listening. I reached into my pocket and felt for my compass, the one Ty had given me, and held it as steady as I could in my palm. As far as I could judge, the plane had crashed to the west or southwest of the drop; it was hard to know how many miles. My hand was shaking and I held it steady with my other one. I squinted at the sky, at the stars, at the moon. I'd grown up in the woods. I'd learned to find my way home by the streams and the sky.

When the compass pointed northeast I said, "This way." And this time I took the lead. The boxer grumbled, but Tom Buccaneer told him to shut up before he shut him up, and from then there was only the sound of our footfalls and our breathing. Each of the men wore a pistol on his belt and extra magazines, and each one carried a large rucksack. I wished I had my pistol, the one they'd issued me for the B-17, but they'd taken it away once we landed at Prestwick.

For a while we followed a creek bed, ducking through brush and bramble, and when this ended we kept pushing forward through the trees. I thought: I am in a forest in France. I am running from the Germans. I'm with strange men I barely know. I am a weapon of this war.

We ran for hours, until the woods thinned out and suddenly, spreading out in front of us, was the flat land of a farm, a little thatched cottage in the distance, outlined against the sky, a rickety half-timbered barn behind it. My nose wrinkled at the smell of cows and chickens and fertilizer and something else—something sweet and bright, like sunshine on Fair Mountain: apples. Tom Buccaneer stopped and held up his hand. We all froze in our shoes and listened.

He said, "We should tuck in here for a couple of hours, get some rest," and I was glad he'd said it because I was so weary, counting every step, and I didn't think I could walk much longer.

The Frenchman said, "We should keep going. We do not know how near the Germans may be." His voice was edgy. I thought, So Tom Buccaneer is the one in charge, and the Frenchman hates this.

Tom Buccaneer said, "We'll go back in the forest and take shifts."

We ducked into the trees, where the air was fresh and cool, and where the only smell was of leaves and dirt and us. The men, all of them, were filthy and bloody, scratches on their faces, uniforms raggedy and torn. I thought for the first time about how I must look— hair wild and windblown, lipstick faded off, dirt on my clothes, on my skin, dried blood on my uniform, on my hand. We opened our survival kits. All I had was a stale chocolate bar, and I chewed on this, making sure to take my time with it, to chew each bite fifty times, because I didn't know when we'd find more food or water. I didn't say one word because I was scared to ask another question, to have them see how green I was.

While we ate, the Frenchman, in a voice as low as the breeze through the leaves, told us stories about France. As he talked, he pulled off his helmet and set it on the ground. His hair was as black as the devil's cave, up on Devil's Courthouse back home. He told us about the Hundred Years' War, William the Bastard, who later became known as William the Conqueror, Joan of Arc, Napoleon Bonaparte. For as cool and swaggering as he seemed, there was a weary air to the Frenchman, as if he'd been fighting in this war for fifty years, even though he couldn't have been much more than thirty-five.

After we were done eating, Tom Buccaneer said, "We'll take shifts. At first light, we go in search of the Resistance."

The short man, the British one, said, "She's injured. We don't want her bleeding on the run. She'll only slow us down."

Tom Buccaneer said to me, "You're going to need to take off that jacket." He pulled a bandage from his pack and wrapped my arm, up around the shoulder, just under my sleeve.

The boxer said, "We can't take her with us." Then to me: "Look, sister, we can't guard you and hold your hand. We ain't goddamn babysitters. We don't take prisoners because we got enough to do out here without looking after someone. We're fighting for our own lives."

No one said anything. The Frenchman sat watching me, his mouth still, his eyes dancing, almost like he was amused, almost like I was some sort of prey.

The boxer said, "When paratroopers jump behind the lines, you kill everything between you and your objective, and that includes pilots."

Tom Buccaneer said over his shoulder, "That's enough." He looked at me and, even though there was only moonlight and starlight, I could suddenly see how clear and blue his eyes were—so clear and blue that they were almost eerie. "You have my permission to ignore him." I thought, That's exactly what I plan to do. "Now," he said, "where are you from?" He tied the bandage good and tight.

My arm shot through with pain and I sucked in my breath. "North Carolina."

"Southern belle." He said it like this explained everything, then added, "I didn't even ask your name." He smiled, broad and blinding, brighter than the moon. I thought he was the best-looking man I'd ever seen. He held out his hand to me. "Captain Perry O'Connell."

I said, "Velva Jean Hart."

"It's a pleasure, Velva Jean Hart." He nodded at the others—the boxer, the craggy one, the Brit, and the Frenchman. "Barzetti, Ray, Coleman, and Gravois." Then he said, "I'll take first shift." He took off his jacket and held it out to me. "You can use this as a pillow."

As I lay down, the men gathered in a huddle, the captain shining a flashlight over the compass Barzetti was holding—Ty's compass. My compass, which I'd let them borrow even though they'd done nothing but complain about me. Someone said something about needing to reach Rouen by the nineteenth, before it was too late, so they could get there before the Allies and be ready. I closed my eyes and thought, Be ready for what?

They took stock of the things that we'd carried away from the crash and those we hadn't, the things they'd buried and the things they'd kept. Coleman said he was short on detonators and would have to make some of his own. Ray said his rifle had made it, but he only had half the ammo. Barzetti complained about the radio again.

Then Coleman said, "What are we going to do with her?"

Barzetti said, "We leave her here. Let her find her own way."

The Frenchman said, "We are not leaving her in the woods."

The captain said, "She's the reason any of us survived."

I opened my eyes, careful not to stir, careful not to give myself away. Gravois said, "We will drop her with the first Resistance group we find. They can get her back to England."

They were finished then, and everyone but the captain stretched out on the ground to sleep. Gravois was a few feet away and Barzetti, Ray, and Coleman just beyond him. In a moment, I heard a snore, but the Frenchman lay flat, arms folded underneath his head, glaring up toward the stars. He was staring up at the sky just like he could see over it and past it and right into the heart of Hitler himself.

The last thing that went through my mind before I drifted off, just before the sun came up, was, You're not leaving me anywhere.

SEVEN

When I woke, I thought: I am not alone. Someone is watching me. Suddenly, I knew where that feeling of being watched was coming from. I opened my eyes and looked down as if I were looking at my feet, only I wasn't looking at my feet—I was looking past them at a grove of trees. The trunks were all lined up, and with them, just like trunks, were two dark trousered legs. I inched my gaze up the legs till I saw that they belonged to a man.

This man was not Perry O'Connell or any of the others. This was a man who was standing as still as I was lying, and he was looking right at me.

Before I could scream or pull myself up to run away, he took five long strides in my direction, till he was standing over me, blocking out the sun. He said, *"Vous êtes allemand?" You are German?* I blinked up at him. With the light behind him, he was just a giant shadow, tall and dark as a monster. He was carrying something, an axe. *"Vous êtes boche?"* He shouted it.

I told myself to be calm, to not give myself away, because people, like animals, could smell fear. I stammered, *"Je ne parle pas français."*

He leaned over me then and I thought, To hell with being calm. I raised up my foot and kicked him as hard as I could, aiming for the spleen. I'd learned self-defense in my WASP training, even though I'd never had to use it. He staggered backward, and I started to run. Suddenly I heard a stream of French, and Gravois pushed me behind him so I went flying into the captain, who caught me and then stepped in front of me like a shield. Gravois and the stranger went at it, back and forth in rapid French, until I was waiting for the stranger to chop him down with his axe just to get him to be quiet. Then Gravois turned to us and said, "He will take me to a house near here."

Captain O'Connell said, "I'm leader of this team." The other men stood around in a half circle. A knife glinted on Ray's belt, and his hand rested near the handle, as if he were ready to grab it at any minute, even though he looked like he could kill a man bare-handed. In the daylight, these men looked fierce—like warriors—and I wondered what kind of mission they were on.

Gravois said, "My French is better." He looked at the captain without blinking, and I wondered who was really in charge here.

Captain O'Connell said, "We'll both go."

Coleman said, "They might be Milice."

I said, "What's Milice?"

Barzetti said, "Goddamn cowards."

Coleman polished his glasses with a small green cloth. He said, his voice quiet, "Soldiers and farmers and shopkeepers and convicted criminals, all working for the Germans against their own people. They are the worst kind of traitor."

Gravois said, "We are going to have to take a chance. We need a radio and supplies. We don't know where we are, but we need to find out. If anything happens, take the girl and get out of here." And then he and the captain followed the stranger out of the woods without waiting for anyone to say another word.

The men gathered up the few things we had and then we sat or stood, waiting. I looked at the faces of the men I was left with and thought, Not a one of them wants me here.

Coleman sat off by himself, resting against a tree trunk, eyes closed. His spectacles were pushed up onto his head. He had the narrow, shrewish look of a bookkeeper, but I knew sometimes this was the most dangerous type of man. Ray sat still as could be, and I thought if he were a dog his ears would be tilting in the direction of every noise. Except for the scars and the weather-beaten skin, worn as an old glove, he would have been almost handsome. Five minutes later, he got up and walked off without saying a word. I watched as he went creeping into the trees, and I thought that as good as Johnny Clay and I were at sneaking about, I'd never seen someone walk so soundlessly.

I turned to Barzetti then, who scared me most of all because I'd known men like him back home. They were the men you never could predict, except that they were always the first to start a fight and the first to end it. He was studying me, just like I'd seen a cat study a fox or a squirrel, something it was hunting. He said, "You kicked that guy right in the spleen."

I said, "Yes, sir."

"You were aiming for it."

"That's right."

He didn't say anything, just kept studying me.

I said, "How did he get the scars on his face?"

"Ray?"

I nodded. I thought: If you try to kill me, I'll fight you back.

He said, "Prisoner of war. Depending on who you ask, he was captured two, maybe four times. Maybe more. Prison camps, a German death camp. He escaped each time. When they were forming these teams, they went after him. I mean, the guy's a fucking bulldozer. Strong as a tiger, able to outmaneuver whole German platoons."

"Did you train at Camp Toccoa?"

He narrowed his eyes at me. "How do you know about Toccoa?"

"My brother's a paratrooper. He was at Toccoa and then at Camp Mackall in North Carolina."

Coleman opened his eyes, small and squinty and deep set, and looked at me. After a moment, he closed them again.

Barzetti said, "I was at Camp Tombs and Camp Mackall too."

My skin went prickly. "Then you must know him. Technical Sergeant Johnny Clay Hart."

Barzetti took his time answering, making me wait. He said, "There were a lot of fellas at Camp Tombs. You really only knew the ones in your platoon."

Something rustled in the brush and I almost grabbed his arm, but stopped myself before I touched him. Barzetti's hand flew to his gun. He hissed, "Stay here."

He slid into the trees, pistol out and ready, and I watched him as long as I could before the woods swallowed him whole.

Barzetti's rucksack was a few feet away. I glanced at Coleman, who sat, eyes closed, not doing a thing to protect either of us. I reached a hand for the bag, trying not to make a noise. I inched over to it, thinking I might find a gun or something to defend myself with. Inside there were eight books, all the same—*Cipher Codes*, they said on the cover. There was a box as big as a book that held batteries. There was some clothing, a few rations, and a canvas belt that had some U.S. dollars and something that must have been French money. ID papers with Barzetti's picture, only the papers said his name was Claude Lessard. A .32-caliber pocket pistol, which I picked up and held by my side, just in case. The gun was cold in my hand. I didn't know if it was loaded or not, but I was hoping that wouldn't matter, that I could just point it at anyone who might come at me and scare them away.

Each moment passed like a funeral, each minute taking longer than the next. Even though the pistol was light, my hand started to cramp and even shake a little. I counted each second as it went by, starting over with each new minute. I was up to six minutes when something cracked in the brush to my right. I decided to keep the gun at my side, to wait and see if I would need it at all. Two more minutes went by, and then I heard another cracking, followed by a rustling, and suddenly Barzetti came out of the trees, and, just after him, Ray, looking big as a giant, a rabbit dangling in one hand, his rifle in the other. There wasn't a single drop of blood on the rabbit, but it was as dead as a Christmas goose.

Barzetti said, "It's just us, sister." He saw the pistol at my side and said, "Did you go in my rucksack?"

Coleman said, "Yes." I looked at him and saw that he had drawn his gun too.

Ray didn't say a word through any of this. Instead he threw the rabbit onto the ground in front of me and took out a knife. Before I could look away, he began to skin it in long, sweeping strokes. The body was probably still warm. After a moment he looked up, his eyes cool—the darkest eyes I'd ever seen. He said, "Lunch."

*   *   *

An hour later, we heard a whistle, a bright little song. Barzetti whistled back and the captain and Gravois ducked toward us through the trees. They weren't alone. A figure came along behind them, slight and quick. It was a girl, not much older than me, and she was carrying a basket.

The girl said, "Call me Delphine."

Delphine wore her hair short, just above her shoulders. She wasn't beautiful, but she had the darkest lashes I'd ever seen, and a sprinkling of freckles—like stars—on her nose. She said, "*Bonjour,*" and then she started pulling things out of her basket: apple cider, bitter and strong, and chunks of bread covered with butter and cheese. We couldn't risk making a fire, but Ray peeled long pieces of meat off the rabbit and offered them to us on the point of his knife. Everyone but Barzetti said no, and then he and Ray ate piece after piece until they'd finished the whole thing.

I ate my bread and cheese, trying not to watch them. When Barzetti was done, he said, "You never know when you'll eat again." For some reason, he said this right at me.

While we sat underneath the trees, Delphine told us she was a schoolteacher. She said, "The schools are closed right now, but because I am a teacher I can travel on my bicycle around Normandy. It seems, how do you say, natural."

At the word *Normandy*, my heart beat a little faster. Normandy was where Johnny Clay was supposed to have been dropped with the 101st Airborne. Just because he hadn't dropped with his unit didn't mean he wasn't here and that he couldn't have gotten here some other way.

She said, "I carry messages from one Resistance group to the next, sometimes for a hundred miles or more. We are like a chain, linked from one city to another, one village to another, one forest to another. It is like a telephone line, passing information and sharing supplies and weapons, the things we need to fight." She smiled, and I saw that she had a gap between her two front teeth. She said, "I hide the messages in my seat stem or in the handlebars of my bicycle."

I suddenly wished for a gap between my own front teeth. I thought: Who would I be if my old ancestor Nicholas Justice and his family hadn't left France for Ireland way back when to escape the Huguenots? I might be sitting here in these very woods with these very people, only I would be the one serving up cider and bread, with a charming accent and freckles like stars.

While Delphine talked, Gravois sat on his haunches, watching the woods. Perry handed him something—a patterned scarf, a brilliant blue—and Gravois smoothed it on the ground. It took me a minute to see that there was more to the pattern, that behind the little leaves and flowers was a map of France. He said, "We are here." He pointed to a dot on the map, about twenty or so miles northwest of Lisieux: Beuvron-en-Auge. "Delphine tells us this area is crawling with enemy patrols."

Delphine said, "You must wait here until after dark. I will come back then and take you to the leaders of the Resistance." As she said it, I glanced at Captain O'Connell and the other men, one by one, trying to see how they felt about this. What if she was planning to take us to the Germans instead?

After Delphine had disappeared through the trees, I said to the men, "How do we know we can trust her?"

Perry O'Connell said, "We don't." He folded up the scarf and stuffed it in his pocket. "But we need to trust someone, and we're going to have to choose whether to trust the people we meet here or kill them." I thought about the way Ray had killed the rabbit, the way he'd skinned it and eaten it raw. Something must have crossed over my face or behind my eyes because the captain said, "It's wartime, love." And he smiled, but it was a hollow smile, dimples and all. The way he said it carried the weight of the world, as if he'd suddenly aged fifteen years.

EIGHT

Delphine returned an hour after sunset. "*Suivez-moi,*" she said. *Follow me.* She led us out of the woods and along the dirt road, which wound through the countryside. The night was bright with stars, and the moon hung low in the sky. We went along like this for miles, until we came to a blanket of fog so thick you couldn't see two feet in front of you. In a low voice, Delphine said, "Here is where the Orbiquet, Cirieux, and Graindain rivers meet, which is why there is always this fog." The mist made her voice seem as if it were coming from as far away as England.

We formed a chain, Delphine leading the way. I could hear the sound of running water, and suddenly we were in the middle of a village. It sat in darkness, not a single light or streetlamp to show that anyone had ever lived there. All at once, the fog cleared so that I could see half-timbered houses and storefronts, one blending into another, all attached, sitting around a market square. Behind me, Coleman said, "'Germelshausen,'" and at first I thought this must be the name of the village, but then he began to sing a song, his voice as low as a brook, and it wasn't any language I recognized.

Finally, we turned off the road and cut through some trees, and there, standing on a little rise in the ground, was an ancient-looking farmhouse, two stories, partly made of stone and partly thatched, with a steep roof, like something out of *Grimm's Fairy Tales*. Flower boxes lined the windows and flowers sprang up in beds on either side of the front door. The windows were dark, but Delphine pushed the door open and by the dim light of candles we could see a group of men sitting around a table. I counted twelve of them, and they were all ages—the youngest around fifteen, the oldest around sixty. They were dirty and bearded, and as Delphine closed the door behind us, every single one of them stopped talking and stared. I recognized the stranger with the axe, the one from the woods.

Thick black curtains hung across the windows, pulled tight so that no light could get out or in. Delphine said, "I must go." Then she said something in French to the men. She looked at me with her dark-lashed eyes, and said, "I wish you luck. *Bonsoir*."

As she left, one of the younger men stood and shook our hands. He said in English, "I am Marcel. We have been waiting. Come—sit, eat, and let us plan." He had a nose like a beak and smelled like wine.

Before I could think about it, I was sitting on a hard wooden chair in between Gravois and the man with the axe, who didn't seem to have the axe right now. The man looked at me and I looked at him, but I didn't say I was sorry for kicking him because I wasn't. I thought Gravois seemed out of place among these men, the only Frenchman with eyes like a gypsy's and a cultured, scornful voice. He didn't look or sound anything like them. He was like something out of *The Arabian Nights*.

Marcel said, "The Allies are advancing, yes? Carentan, Saint-Lô, Caen. You are part of the advance party that we have been waiting for."

Another man said, "There are four hundred enemy troops in the area. They are fanning out and moving into the forest. They have been here once, but they are coming again."

Another said, "We have more than thirty organized Maquis groups, and other people from Lisieux, from here, who want to help. Gregoire Auvain, the butcher. François Ledeux, that runs the music hall. André Mael, who has a restaurant. We are ready for the fight. But they tell us wait, wait."

And another, "We are cutting the lines for telecommunications. We are blowing up railroads and ambushing the Germans on the roads. But we can do more."

And then all the men started talking at once, voices rising, asking Captain O'Connell what the plan of action was, where were their supplies and guns, and when did they need to round everyone up, when could they start the fight and kill the *boche*, the nasty Germans.

Suddenly Gravois slammed the table with both fists so that the plates jumped ten feet in the air. The men fell silent, staring at him. Gravois stood and said, in a voice so cool and calm it sounded as if he were measuring each word, "We were supposed to drop in Rouen, but the Germans intercepted us. We have men there we need to meet. We cannot wait here with you, do you understand?"

He plucked a lit cigarette from the mouth of the man next to him. He took a long drag and then he blew three perfect smoke rings into the air. He handed the cigarette back to the man, who sat staring dumbly, and then he walked outside. The door swung closed but didn't catch, and I could see him standing on the step, arms crossed, glaring off toward the woods.

The men stared after him and you could have heard a pin drop. There was a bristling in the room, at the table, which set me to thinking of the way the air felt—charged and electric—before a tornado.

Captain O'Connell said to the table, "As soon as we have a radio, we'll ask them to send another team."

Marcel said, "I know a man in Cambremer that might have a radio. But we have this one here, not one you can transmit from, but one you can listen to." He checked his watch and flicked it on so that we heard a fuzzy sound of static. He said, "There are Germans, but not so many as in the other towns. Henri will take you if you wish." He waved at the youngest of the men, a boy of fourteen or fifteen.

The captain said something about how we didn't have time to go for the radio, how we must be moving on because we had a date to keep, and then Barzetti started arguing with him about how the radio would help them. What if the date had been changed? What if there was something they needed to know before they got to Rouen?

Marcel said over them, "Let me know what you decide," and then he rolled the dial on the radio back and forth, and suddenly an English-sounding voice announced that we were listening to the BBC. Everyone leaned in as the news was read. It was all war related, of course, listing which Allied troops had entered Rome or France or North Africa. Afterward, the French-language BBC service came on and the men seemed to pay particular attention to this. They leaned in closer, as if they were waiting for something, but it didn't sound like anything more than silly personal messages—"Marie-Claire Sezanne wishes to be remembered to Monsieur Jordain." "Bernice Troyes and Maurice Theureux report that the roses are in bloom in Arles." And so on. They are coded messages, I thought.

Marcel clicked the radio off, and they all began to talk at once again, in French and in English, and as they did I watched the flame of the candle flickering and waving. Coleman said something about needing supplies, the light glinting off his glasses. Did they have acid, vinegar, black ash, sulfide, sugar? He said baking soda and bicarbonate would work too.

My eyes began fuzzing up a bit, and then they grew heavy and heavier, till I was suddenly hit with a weariness I'd never felt before. How long had it been since I'd slept?

Then I heard the captain's words: "We need to trust someone, and we're going to have to choose whether to trust the people we meet here or kill them." Where was my brother? Where was Helen? I wondered if they were in France too, having to take a chance on trusting total strangers.

The next morning, Barzetti was taking his shift at the barn door, a cigarette in one hand, a gun in the other. I sat up and saw the lines of sunlight on the dirt of the floor, falling across the hay. I said, "Good morning." Barzetti didn't even turn around.

I said, "Where did you sleep?" The barn was empty except for the two of us.

He took a drag on his cigarette, still facing away from me. He said,

"We slept in the woods and took turns keeping watch. Captain thought you could stand a night off from the forest floor." He said this as if I'd asked for a bed of feathers and a blanket spun out of silk.

I said, "Why did you sleep outside?"

"Safer that way. Never good to be boxed in. Never give yourself just one exit." I looked around. I only saw one way in and out. "Better to be in the open, where you have a choice which way to run."

I stood up, brushing the hay from my uniform. I said, "Those men last night, who were they? Are they soldiers?" I thought, He may not like me, but he loves to talk. I decided to be nice to him, to try to win him over, and also get some information out of him while I was at it.

"Combat virgins. They want to be soldiers, and maybe they will be if they take the time to learn how to shoot a gun and not jump at the first fucking Nazi they see. Goddamn Frogs. They'll lose the war for us, shooting off their mouths and their guns without waiting for the plan, for someone to show them how to hold a fucking gun. That's not why we're here though—not our team, at least."

I said, "And those men, they're part of the Resistance?" When he didn't say anything, I said, "You're the radio operator, right?" He didn't answer. "I learned Morse code in WASP training."

"That so?" He still wasn't looking at me. "That where you learned self-defense too?"

"Yes." I inched toward the door.

He wasn't wearing his patch anymore, and I could see a long red line, mean as a rattlesnake, at the corner of his eye. He looked at me then and said, "I'm not going to let you fuck up this mission." He smiled and it was the smile of a jackal.

I stared right back at him and said, "Why does your ID say 'Claude Lessard'?"

"Christ, sister. Anything else you want to know? My shoe size? My briefs size?"

I said, "I just wanted to know what to call you."

He took a long drag on his cigarette, his eyes on me the whole time, and then blew the smoke out of the corner of his mouth, so it rose up sideways like a mist. Never taking his eyes off me, he rummaged for something in his pocket and handed me my compass, the one they'd borrowed from me our first night.

"Barzo," he said. And then he lifted his arm and let me pass.

NINE

The French clothing was tailored and cut in a different way than American clothing. Even the seams were different and the buttons were different. When Delphine handed me a dress, I told her I would rather have trousers. I said, "I can move faster in pants."

She said all she had brought with her was a dress, but she searched through the chest of drawers until she found something. Afterward, I looked at myself in the old mirror that hung in the narrow farmhouse bedroom, the one where Marcel must have slept. The pants and shirt were simple but well made. The trousers were a deep, dull green-brown, the color of balsam fir, with a dark brown belt, and the shirt was green. I cinched the belt tight and rolled up the sleeves and rolled up the pant legs so I wouldn't trip over them. Instead of my flight boots, I was wearing low-heeled shoes that felt tight on my feet, and Delphine had given me a bag like hers and a sweater in case I got cold.

"The men do not like you because they are worried for you," she said. "They do not want the responsibility."

"I know, but I want to help." And find my brother. And not get left behind.

"You must blend in. You must disappear. You must not call attention to yourself because if you do, you not only risk your own life but the lives of those around you. There are things you need to know if you want to pass as French." I hadn't wanted to take off my uniform—Lieutenant Colonel Heflin had said to keep it on in case we were shot down, that it would entitle us to POW protection. But the uniform was muddy and torn and needed cleaning and mending, and the men said I must be inconspicuous.

She handed me an ugly brown scarf. "Wear this on your head."

I tied the scarf over my hair.

"When you eat, you must eat with your left hand. Everyone but Americans holds their fork with the left hand. This is one of the surest ways to give yourself away. You must learn more French phrases. You should learn three phrases perfectly, with an accent so French no one will ever know you are American." And then she went over some with me. She said each word again and again and I repeated them, and all the while I thought how funny it was that Delphine could say a word like *noir*, which meant "black," and it would mean the same to both of us, but sound so different.

Finally she said, "You learn the words quickly but your accent, how do you say, interferes. You must speak with your smile, Velva Jean, and if anyone asks, you say you are an American actress who lost her French husband to the war."

She crossed the room and picked up a basket and started handing me things out of it. "You should carry these with you." French money, a comb, a compact, a small knife with a pearl handle, and a lipstick— Rouge Captif, which Delphine said meant Captive Red. When I pulled it out to paint my mouth, she said, "Not too bright."

I said, "I know. Blend in."

She said, "*Oui*. Yes."

I said, "Why are you helping me?"

She shrugged. She pulled a package of cigarettes out of the basket and a box of matches. She set the basket on the floor and lit the cigarette. As she inhaled, the red end of it glowed like an eye. She said, "We are both women, and this is not just a man's war."

When I came downstairs, the men were gone. An old woman was wiping the table with a rag, and Henri, the boy, was sweeping the floor. Marcel stood in the doorway smoking a cigarette. He was talking to someone outside and at first I thought it might be the captain or Gravois or Barzo, but when I went to the door I could see it was an old man, maybe his father. He muttered something in French to Marcel and then squinted toward the woods.

I said, "Where did they go?"

Marcel looked at my trousers, which must have been his. "Rouen." I heard Delphine come down the steps after me. He turned to her. "We are to get her to the Freedom Line." He turned back to me. "Where is your uniform?"

Delphine said, "Here." She held it out to him.

"Bury it in the woods so it will not be tracked to us." Before I could say anything, he handed me a piece of blue cloth, pressing it into my hand. He said, "A souvenir from your captain. Tonight I will take you to the Freedom Line and they will get you out of France, but you will have this in case something happens to me."

I opened my hand and the piece of cloth was the blue map scarf. I tied it around my neck, and then I turned to look at Delphine and Marcel and Henri and the old man and woman, who were just strangers, daring them to say something and trying not to let them see the tears I was blinking back.

An hour later we ate dinner in silence. Every now and then Marcel, Delphine, Henri, and the old couple would discuss something in French, and then they would talk to me in English, asking the simplest questions—where was I from and did I have any sisters or any brothers fighting in this war and how had I learned to fly.

After supper, Delphine helped the old woman clear the plates, stacking them beside the small sink in the kitchen, which was nothing more than a carved-out counter along one wall. She said, "I must get back."

I said, "You're not staying?"

"No, I need to get home. But all will be well." She gave me a sad little smile that was meant to cheer me on and make me feel better about being left alone with people I barely knew. She pulled her bag over her shoulder and chest so that it rested on the opposite hip, and then she kissed Marcel on both cheeks and then his daddy and his mama, Henri, and then me.

As I watched her shut the door behind her, the old man murmured something in French to his son. Marcel said to me, "He says perhaps you would like to read a book."

The old man held something out to me, a small book, no bigger than a fried pie. *As You Were*, by Alexander Woollcott. *A Portable Library of American Prose and Poetry Assembled for the Members of the Armed Forces and the Merchant Marine.*

"Where did you get this?" I wondered if they had shot it out of the hands of an American soldier or stolen it from his pack after they had slit his throat.

Henri said, "One of the Allies sold it to me for fifty cents." He sounded proud.

I thanked them for the meal and pushed my chair away from the table. "I think I'm going to get some fresh air." I picked up a hunk of my unfinished bread and *As You Were* and the bag Delphine had given me, thinking how light it was. Everything else I owned—Mama's Bible, the record I'd made for Darlon C. Reynolds, my Mexican guitar and mandolin—was back at Harrington in the barracks I'd shared with Helen and the Red Cross nurses.

Marcel said, "We leave in an hour. Don't go far. Sit out back, out of sight."

"Je le ferais." I will.

I slipped outside and walked around the house to the back, which faced the barn. There was a stoop with two stone steps, and I sat on one and started flipping through the book. After a while my eyes adjusted to the moonlight, and I tried to concentrate on the words, tried not to be mad over being left behind by men I barely knew, like I didn't matter, like I was something to be gotten rid of.

I read Abraham Lincoln's second inaugural address, which talked all about the Civil War and the slavery that had to end and how there was still important work to be done. He wrote: "Let us strive on to finish the work we are in; to bind up the nation's wounds; to care for him who shall have borne the battle, and for his widow and his orphan . . ."

This made me think of my brothers, but especially Johnny Clay. I'd come all this way, but I wasn't any closer to finding him. If I let Marcel put me on this Freedom Line, which would get me out of France, what would happen to Johnny Clay then?

I turned back through the book and found a poem by Emily Dickinson. The first line read, "To fight aloud is very brave."

To fight aloud is very brave. . . .

I thought of Ray escaping from two or more prison camps and at least one German death camp. Then I heard Butch Dawkins's voice in my head: *I figured if my destiny wasn't coming to me, I would go to it.*

I laid the little book aside and fished in my bag for my compass. It was just one of my talismans, my good luck charms that I always carried, like the rip cord from my parachute, the one that saved my life when I jumped from the B-29, and the little flying girl carved from a dogwood tree by my friend the Wood Carver, back home on Fair Mountain.

I untied the map scarf Captain O'Connell had left for me and studied it till I could see France and not the pattern. Rouen was a dot to the northeast, sixty, seventy, maybe eighty miles away. I followed the line of the road from there to where I thought we were, based on our walk the night before, and then I held my compass steady in the palm of my hand. I waited till it gave me the direction and then I looked up toward where it was pointing. One of the things they'd taught me in the WASP was to trust my judgment and know my compass, and my judgment and my compass were both telling me what I needed to do.

I retied the scarf and stood up. I left *As You Were* on the steps, where I knew Marcel and the others would find it. I pulled the bag across my shoulder and chest so that it fell against my other hip. Then I started across the farmland toward the woods, just like the men must have done.

I kept to the woods at the side of the road. I stayed close to the tree line, inside the first row of trees, because I didn't want to be spotted by anyone who might drive by, but I was careful not to go too deep into the holler. I knew from my mountains and my own woods that dark and horrible things lived in the forest.

The light from the clouds and the moon and the stars filtered through the treetops, making them glow like haints. The moon was set high in the sky, but I could see clouds in the distance. It took my eyes a while to adjust and be able to make out a path. I walked faster, tripping over a rise in the ground—maybe a root or a limb that had fallen or been cut. Or maybe a dead body. I walked even faster, tripping over this and that, my bag bumping across my chest, against my hip. I could feel the hunk of bread inside it and wondered when I would get my next meal. Would I have to kill and skin a rabbit and eat it raw?

The air was cool and the damp was rolling in from somewhere—England, I guessed, where it always seemed to be wet and misty. Along the way, I saw certain things I recognized from when Delphine was leading us to the farmhouse—a road sign, a cottage, a fence, a grove of trees. I'd learned in the WASP not to rely only on maps. I knew how to fly blind and find my way by the land and the stars. I cocked my head back now and peered up at the sky, which was half-covered in clouds. I searched until I found the North Star, the only one that never moved.

I heard a rustling to the left of me and then to the right of me. Then I heard something cranking down the road—a car, a truck, a tank? I left the tree line and slipped deeper into the woods.

The car or truck or tank—I was too far away now, too deep in the trees to see which it was—crawled past, slow as a turtle, heading in the opposite direction. I stopped moving, waiting for it to go, and finally, after what seemed like days, I heard it wind away into nothing. I crept along again, moving as fast as I could in the dark over sticks and rocks, limbs snapping me in the face.

An owl hooted. An animal rustled in the brush. Something scuffled across the forest floor.

I paused in the shade of a tree and got out my compass again. I held it flat as I could, but my hand was shaking. I made a fist and shook it, and then I opened my hand again and this time it was still. The compass ticked this way and that, finally settling on a direction.

I slipped the compass back into my pocket and strained my eyes for landmarks. Things were beginning to look the same. This house, this barn, this road sign. Was I going in circles? I'd been so sure I could find my way, but now everything was blending together. I remembered a sign on the side of the road that said "Cambremer" when Delphine had led us through. Where was it now?

The mist and the smoke were spreading across the floor of the forest and starting to reach up toward the trees, like flames. I stood still, feeling like the only person on earth, and then I got down on my knees and put my ear to the ground. I listened for the water of the rivers, which was something Granny once taught me. This came from the Cherokee in her, the part that was connected to nature in a deeper way than everyone else was. My mama's only living brother, Uncle Turk, had the most Cherokee blood of any of Granny's children, and he lived down by the creek bed with his Indian wife and sometimes creek-walked from one stream to another, all over the mountains, keeping one foot in the water at all times. That way, he said, he could never lose his way. He called the creeks his roads.

For a moment I couldn't hear anything because my stomach was growling as loud as a bomber engine, like I hadn't eaten in weeks. I closed my eyes and tried to hear past my stomach and the cry of a bird, high and shrill, and the breeze that was picking up in the trees, making them seem alive, as if they were waking up from a long nap, stretching their arms and legs and shaking the sleep off them. I half-expected to open my eyes and see them moving toward me, limbs held out like mummy arms, knots in the wood opening and shutting like eyes and mouths. I tried to hear past my own doubts and worries and all thoughts of Perry O'Connell, Gravois, Barzo, Ray, Coleman—Johnny Clay most of all—and I just listened to the earth. Granny and Daddy Hoyt, who had been trained by the Cherokee as a medicine man, both believed the earth could talk to you and tell you its secrets, as long as you were able to listen.

I listened a minute. Two minutes. Three minutes. I was about to give up when I heard it—a faint trickling, like a mountain stream after days without rain. Then it was a swooshing, picking up speed and power, then a rushing, a gushing, and it was more than a single stream or river I was hearing—it was three coming together to make one.

About a half mile later the air grew heavy as a blanket, the fog rolling around me till I couldn't see ten feet in front of my nose. It was rolling toward something, as if it were being called, and there, across the road, I could see a fog bank, wide as a train crossing the tracks. I listened, but all I could hear was the rushing of water. I climbed up onto the road and started across, and I saw the sign that said "Cambremer," which I knew was on the way to Rouen.

Suddenly, I heard the sharp burst of a rifle. Then a second shot and then another. The darkness tossed the sound around like a boomerang so that I couldn't tell where it was coming from. I threw myself into the ditch, landing on my sore shoulder and clamping a hand over my mouth to keep from yelling out.

From somewhere, the churning *chug-chug* of a motor and then a single headlight, dimmed but blinding because it was the only light for miles. Then another headlight. And another. The last motor paused just above me and slightly ahead, sputtering and rattling in place, and I heard talking. It was a language I didn't know, strange and harsh, spoken by men. Germans.

I lifted my head enough to see that it was a line of six, maybe seven German motorcycles, all with machine-gun-mounted sidecars. The last driver had his feet on the ground and was standing over the bike, scanning to the left and right and talking to the man in the sidecar. The machine gunner said something and then they started backing up the bike, the engine still idling. The driver walked it backward till they were just behind me.

I heard more talking and then, all at once, machine gun fire directly over my head, as if they were shooting at the woods to the left of me. I turned and started scrambling forward like a crab, arms and legs grabbing at the ground, kicking up dirt and rocks. My knees were scraped raw against the ground, and I could smell the vinegary scent of blood where I'd cut my hand. There was a blast and then another, louder than a machine gun.

Another blast followed and then, from the ground, a wailing that made my hair stand on end. It was the wailing of a person or people being murdered. The air was filled with a great humming roar, and suddenly a plane soared past, low to the ground. Even in the dark and even with its blacked-out belly, I could tell it was a Royal Air Force Beaufighter, which was a double-engine long-range bomber.

The Beaufighter circled once more before it disappeared over the fog bank, climbing higher and higher, pointed toward home. I waited another minute and then I raised myself up on my elbows and then on my hands, and I peered over the edge of the ditch. The motorcycles sat in the road, single eyes gleaming, but I couldn't see the men. I sucked at the place on my thumb where it bled.

I stood up slowly, as if I had all the time in the world, ready to throw myself back into the ditch or hurl myself over the hedgerow or across the road toward the village of Cambremer. My eyes went to the first bike and then to the ground where, flat on his back, the driver lay in a heap, covered in blood from his head to his waist, the red seeping across the dirt of the road, shining black in the dying beam of the headlight. His machine gunner was half in the ditch and half on the road. His head had been blown right off. On down the road, it was more of the same—a body here, a head there, an arm, a leg.

The only dead body I'd ever seen was my own mama's. I remembered standing by her coffin, up on a step stool, while everyone else was asleep. I'd reached inside and touched her skin and it had been hard and rubbery.

I looked at those men and I thought, I'm glad they're dead. And this made me feel like the worst kind of person, like a criminal. I wondered if they had families back home in Germany who were saying prayers for them right now, hoping they would return safe.

Then I said out loud, "Mama, if you're watching, I'm sorry for what I'm about to do."

I walked across the road to the dead German soldiers and I bent down over the first driver. He wore a gun on a holster strapped to his hip, and I pulled the gun out and then I took the holster too. Because I didn't have anything else, I wrapped the gun in Delphine's sweater and I put it and the holster into my bag, even though I wanted to wear it right then. Someone might see me, though, and I knew the last thing I was supposed to do was call attention to myself.

The driver's eyes were open the whole time, like he was watching me—staring up at me, at the sky, at God. I thought of a thousand things I wished I could have said to him in life, and then I fixed the bag across my shoulder and laid my hand on top of it, just where the gun was, bumping against the hunk of bread, and walked into the fog.

TEN

Cambremer sat on the top of a steep hill, and its streets were silent. The half-timbered houses and storefronts were closed tight like fists, and the town had the look of a place that had been interrupted in the middle of something. Some shop windows were boarded up and others were half-boarded or open but bare, nothing inside them, and others were picked through as if someone had come by in a hurry and taken what they wanted.

I took off my shoes, even though the ground was wet in places from the rain that had been falling off and on since we'd crashed. The street felt cool and damp on the bottoms of my feet. The central square went sloping down the hill. I paused against the face of a hat shop, the hats in the window as grand and beautiful as wedding cakes and covered in a layer of gray-brown dust.

Where were the Germans? Signs were posted around the village, stuck to shop windows and lampposts, that showed they'd at least been here or maybe were still here. Some of the signs were in French and two or three were in English: "All persons of the male sex who should aid directly or indirectly the crews or personnel of enemy airplanes dropped by parachute will be shot on the spot. Women who are guilty of a similar offense will be sent to concentration camps in Germany."

The hairs on the back of my neck bristled, like someone was blowing on them, and I realized it wasn't just the signs that were spooking me. It was that suddenly I knew I wasn't alone.

I slid around the side of the hat shop, into an alleyway of shadows. I pressed myself into the cold stone of the building, willing myself invisible. From here, I could see almost everything—my eyes went up the street to the left and then down the street to the right and then straight ahead, from ground level to the windows above. One window was cracked open, just a couple of inches. The breeze blew the curtain. Or had someone moved it?

There you are, I thought. I slid against the building, deeper into the alley. In the distance, I could hear the cracking of gunshots. I froze until it stopped, counting the seconds till it started again, as if I were counting the seconds between thunder and lightning. Twenty-six seconds later, it started again, and I wondered how many miles away it was, how far sound could carry in the night. I couldn't see the Germans, but I thought not seeing them was worse than if they had been marching up and down the village streets.

I thought I would slink down the alley and come back behind the buildings so that I could approach the house with the open window from the other side of the street. I slid back, back, back into the shadows until I was out of sight of the open window. When I was deep enough in shadow, I turned around, quiet as a little brown mouse, and found myself nose to nose with Gravois.

"*Bonsoir,*" he said.

Before I could scream, he clamped a hand over my mouth. "Idiot girl," he whispered. "Do you want to get us killed?" I thought about biting him, but I was too frozen. I glared at him over his hand and he glared back at me.

Finally he said, "Okay?" I nodded. He took his hand away. "You should not have come." He took my arm and dragged me deeper into the alley.

I said, "Where are the Germans?"

"They do not go out alone because they are afraid of being killed in the streets. Or perhaps they have already come and gone. Moved on to the bigger villages." He stopped and motioned for me to stop too. He peered around the edge of a building and then he started pulling me along again.

"But why are the people still hiding?"

"Curfew."

"How did you find me? I was coming to find you."

"When O'Connell left the map for you, I knew you would come after us."

"You're not sending me back, are you?"

"Yes." He led me down another alley and although I didn't want to, I admired the way he moved, so soundless—even loaded down with his gear—like it was second nature. We went back the way I'd come, through alleyways and over the humpback bridge where the rivers met. We walked through the fog bank that surrounded the town and then through the woods just on the outskirts, only a mile or so from where I'd run into the Germans. There was a ruin of a farmhouse, as if the place had burned long ago and all that was left was the shell.

I said, "Please don't send me back. Please keep me with you. I'll stay out of the way. I'll do what you need me to do. Just please don't send me back there to strangers."

He said, "*Je suis désolé.*" *I'm sorry.* But I could tell he wasn't, not one bit.

Gravois and I crept back over the hedgerows that lined the road and through the woods, back past the murdered German motorcycle patrol, stopping only so Gravois could loot the bodies for ammunition and supplies. He was leading the way and he wasn't saying two words. We walked in silence, and every now and then he held up his hand and we stopped. We would hear the *rat-a-tat-tat* of gunfire in the distance, and then we would press on. He walked so fast sometimes I had to hurry to keep up with him. He didn't need a map, and seemed to know the way by heart.

The whole time we walked, I was trying to think of a way to get him to let me stay with them so that he wouldn't leave me at Marcel's farmhouse.

Finally I stopped walking. I thought, Let's see how far he gets if I just stand here. He kept on, broad through the shoulders, black hair gleaming under the moon. I thought he had the look of a wolf about him.

He turned, his eyes flashing at me. "Are you hurt?"

"No." We talked in whispers. "I'm just not going any farther."

He shook his head at this and said, "Come," like he was talking to a dog. And he kept walking.

I didn't move.

He turned back and said, "We must go." His voice was cold. "It is not safe for us to keep you. We are on a mission, and we cannot pull you into it; we cannot let you ruin it. If we're captured, we will be executed, and because you are with us, you will be executed too."

I said, "Please don't leave me there." We stood looking at each other—the guns rat-a-tat-tatting in the distance, the breeze gusting through the trees, making the limbs and leaves dance, blowing my hair across my face. He sighed and I thought: He's going to back down. He's changed his mind. And then he picked me up and threw me over his shoulder and kept right on walking.

Ten minutes later, he set me down and grabbed my hand and dragged me along behind him. Half an hour later, I could tell that we were getting closer. I recognized a rambling barn, a cluster of trees, a sign on the road, which I could see just beyond. We crept closer to the tree line, and I could smell something burning. He said, "*Merde,*" very low, and he stopped walking.

Before I could ask what we were doing, what he had seen, I saw explosions of red in the distance and I heard the sharp rattling of a jackhammer, which sounded as if it were coming from just a few hundred yards away. Gravois pulled me down so that we were crouching. He said, "No, no, no," and it was a whisper. We walked like this a few more feet and then we stopped again. "Damn."

He was looking through the trees and across the road at a great, raging fire. Germans were everywhere, crawling in and out of tanks and Jeeps and shouting at one another. Hundreds of them. It took me a minute to realize where we were and what we were looking at—that the bonfire was coming from Marcel's farmhouse and barn.

Gravois said, "They will be searching these woods."

We started creeping in the other direction, back the way we'd come, still hunched down, still low to the ground, as silent as could be.

The jackhammering machine guns got farther and farther away, but I could still feel the heat of the fire, still smell the smoke, which was in my nose and in my skin and in my throat. There was a snapping of twigs to the right of us, and we froze.

Gravois said, "Get behind me. Behind that tree," and he reached back and pushed me away.

I ducked into the shadow of a wide tree trunk, and Gravois stepped forward, silent as a cat. Suddenly, I could see the outline of someone against the dark, and he was wearing a helmet and a uniform. Even in the night, I could see he was German, and I thought, I don't want to die.

The German had his weapon drawn. He called out something to someone I couldn't see, and then he turned around, right in place, slow, steady, as if he knew we were somewhere nearby. I reached into my bag and pulled out the Luger. He said, "Come out, come out, wherever you are," and he was saying it to us. I held my breath.

I didn't even see the knife until it was over and the German was lying on the ground, blood spurting from his neck, hands at his throat, trying to stop the bleeding. Blood was everywhere, flowing across the ground toward my feet. I backed away so I wouldn't have to step in it, and this made me feel horrible and cruel.

I stared at the man on the ground and then at the Frenchman. He said, "Where did you get that?" He was pointing at the Luger.

"Off one of the dead German soldiers, back when I was following you. There was another man—just now." I looked down at the man on the ground. "He was calling to someone." We listened to the voices in the distance.

Gravois said, "We must go." And he grabbed my hand and we ran through the woods, away from the fire and the Germans and the man that he'd killed.

Suddenly Gravois pulled up short. From nearby, a snapping of twigs, a rustling. I grabbed his arm, and he pulled out his knife again. Then someone stepped out of the trees and said, *"Ne me tuez pas!"* *Do not kill me.* It was a man, or a boy, and he was holding up his hands.

Gravois said, *"Êtes-vous seul?"* *Are you alone?*

"Oui," and then the boy came forward and it was Henri, and he was crying.

According to Henri, three German soldiers had stopped at the farmhouse to ask for directions and one of the Resistance fighters opened fire. He killed two of the men but only wounded the third, who was able to leave the house and report what had happened. Hours later, the Germans came back to the farm—some three hundred of them—shooting and killing everyone and burning the buildings to the ground. Henri said they were paratroopers, which were the best combat troops Germany had in France.

We pressed on, past Cambremer, past another little village and then farm after farm. We walked on the outskirts so as not to cut through the towns in case the Germans were patrolling after curfew. Gravois said we needed to keep our distance from villages and farmhouses because the Germans would be conducting searches. Every now and then we could see, in the distance, a few of the French people who lived on the farms or in the villages, but they didn't see us, or if they did they pretended not to, and I remembered the signs in Cambremer.

We left Henri at the farm of his sister and her family. I decided I wanted to go with Henri because he was young and innocent and had probably never killed anyone, but Gravois took my hand and dragged me off and then we went deeper into the *bocage*, which was what he called the hedgerows of shrubs and trees, some as high as twelve feet, that bordered the fields and the roads.

To fight aloud is very brave. . . .

I yanked my hand away. Gravois said, "Take my hand. It will go faster and I need to keep track of you."

I said, "No."

"You are still upset then."

He stopped and turned and I could see right into his eyes, right into the dark brown-green that circled the black dot of the iris. He said, "For your own sake, you need to understand this. You must do things in war that you would not do otherwise. It is a different world with different rules, and you must adapt or you won't live to tell the story," and then he turned around and kept walking, not even bothering to see if I was there.

I thought about going in the other direction, about trying to find my way back to Henri, and then I started after the Frenchman before he disappeared into the trees.

We walked for hours. We headed north, following an old forest road. German rifle and machine gun fire from the west forced us to turn eastward. At one point, I stumbled and lost my footing and grabbed onto his jacket so that I wouldn't fall on my face. He glanced back at me and instead of looking annoyed or angry, he gave me a look of concern. He took my hand and led me onward, his palm rough and warm and strong.

As we went, I said, "What's your first name?"

"Émile," he said.

Émile Gravois.

He said, "You have a nice voice. Have you always sung?" He was making polite conversation, probably to help me stay awake and keep me going. "My mother had a lovely voice too. She would sing us asleep and sing us awake. There was one song in particular. *'Qui a mordu dans la lune, Il n'en reste qu'un croissant, Où donc est la pleine lune, Toute en or et en argent. . . .'*"

His voice was rough but good, like the swinging of a sturdy wooden gate.

I said, "What do the words mean?"

"I am not sure of the English. Something like 'Who took a bite of the moon? There's just a crescent moon left. Where oh where can the full moon be, All dressed in gold and silver, So much of it disappeared, That soon there'll be nothing left.'"

I said, "We have a song we sing to that same tune."

Twinkle, twinkle, little star,
How I wonder what you are. . . .

My voice sounded thin and small when you compared it to the tall, tall trees and the night sky, but even though it was my own voice, hearing it made me feel less alone and less far away from home.

Then the traveler in the dark
Thanks you for your tiny spark;
He could not see which way to go,
If you did not twinkle so.

I sang all four verses, and then Émile Gravois said, "I like your words better. There is more hope in them."

Early the next morning, before the sun came up, we reached the outskirts of Lisieux, which Émile said was the largest town in the Pays d'Auge. He said we would meet the rest of the men outside the city—from there we would all go to Rouen—and so we only circled the town, picking our way through the farms and woods that surrounded it. The faded smell of smoke and death lingered in the air. Whole patches of trees were missing, burned to the earth, and farmhouses were crumbled, just three walls or a chimney or a pile of wood on the ground to let you know they had ever been there at all.

Tanks ground up and down the narrow roads, and groups of German soldiers walked together and drove together. This time local people were mixed in with them, going about their business as best they could.

If it wasn't for the tanks and the burned-up woods and the bombed-out houses, I could see it was probably a charming place, a beautiful place. I wondered what it would have been like to be here before the war, holding the hand of a strong and sexy Frenchman because we were in love and happy and not running for our lives.

ELEVEN

*A*t dusk we found the men on the outskirts of Lisieux. By then it was drizzling, and my hair hung around my face, soaked through. Inside an old church, we huddled under a corner of the choir loft, the only place where there was roof left. I tried not to stare at the bombed-out walls, the piles of stone. I missed my flight boots and my flight jacket. My feet were blistered and sore and Delphine's shoes soaked up the water like a sponge.

Captain O'Connell stood by himself under the roofless sky, water beating down on him, catching on his eyelashes so that his eyes looked even more like pools. He said, "Why is she here?"

Émile gave the captain a cold little smile, like a cat swallowing a canary. "She had a map." Then he told him about the farmhouse and about the Germans.

Coleman waved his hand, as if he were swatting away a fly. "We will drop her with the first Americans we see."

I said, "You're not leaving me with strangers."

Coleman looked at the captain. "It's a mistake to take her."

They were talking about me like I wasn't even there. I said, "Half your team is dead and I'm guessing that's put you all in a bind, but I'm here and I'm strong and I may not be a paratrooper or an agent, but I was trained by the military just like you were, and I went through a lot to do that training from men who didn't want me to fly and men who thought they would teach me a lesson and make me go home where I belonged. But I didn't go home. I came here, and I can help."

I stared at them and they stared at me until Barzo said, "There's no time to leave her anywhere unless it's right here."

Émile said, "She won't be left." He walked over to me and said, "Give me your bag."

"I'm not giving you my bag."

Émile opened the bag himself, right there on my hip, and pulled out the Luger. I said, "Hey!"

He held up the gun. "It is best not to be caught with a German weapon." Then he found a corner of the floor that had been blown away, where the earth rose up through the stone. He sat on his heels and dug a hole with the end of his rifle and dropped the Luger into it.

Barzo said, "Maybe we can use her." I wasn't sure I liked the way he said it.

Ray said, "Can you shoot a gun?" His voice was low and soft, but the sound of it threw me because he hardly ever spoke.

I said, "Yes, sir. My daddy taught me to shoot when I was eight years old. And then I learned all over again in the WASP. I've got three older brothers, so I know all about shooting and protecting myself and fighting back. I grew up in the mountains, so I know how to live off the land and walk through the woods by moonlight as quiet as you can, so quiet not even a panther can hear you. And if one does, I know what to do about that too. I also know how to find my way by the stars and by a compass. If you remember."

No one said a word, and the men took their time looking back and forth at one another. The captain folded his arms across his chest and said, "There are other things you need to know. Better French, for one." He looked at Émile. "Can you help her?"

Émile stood up. He was lighting a cigarette. He stopped, the match still lit, the cigarette in his mouth. He said around it, "I will try."

We walked through the night and most of the next day, stopping when the Germans came too close, hiding in the shade of a tree or the ruins of a building, waiting them out, sometimes an hour or two at a time. The rain fell as if it had always fallen and always would. The roads and fields were mud, and the earth was churned up and piled with stone and rubble, some of the piles as high as hills. Finally, we came upon a drainage ditch, which looked empty and wild, covered up by a thicket of spiny, prickly shrubs. One by one, we crawled inside. I tried not to think about what kinds of animals might live in there. Instead I pulled out the chunk of bread I'd taken from Marcel's house and I offered it to the men. They shook their heads and said no thank you because they had their own supplies—rations from their kits, water collected at Marcel's—and so we sat, eating and not talking. Every so often Captain O'Connell passed me his canteen because I didn't have one of my own. As soon as he finished his meal, Émile disappeared.

Ray handed me a submachine gun, a plain, compact, old-looking thing that looked as if he might have made it himself. It had a wooden butt, a pistol grip, and a bayonet lug. He said, "Sten gun. Already loaded. It can take German nine-millimeter magazines. So easy, even the dumbest man in France can shoot it. Remember—never hesitate. Never freeze. If you're going to shoot, shoot. A man's second best friend over here is his gun." And then he lay down on the cold, wet concrete of the ditch, as if he were tired from talking so much, and closed his eyes.

I said, "What's his first best friend?"

"Luck."

One by one, the rest of the men lay down, so I lay down too. As I closed my eyes I wondered what would happen if the Germans decided to look in here themselves, taking shelter from the rain and the wind. Then I decided that I would keep watch if no one else would, and so I crept across the ditch to the opening, Sten gun across my shoulder, and sat down.

The night was still except for the tanks. One would pass by and then there would be nothing for a good while, only silence. No crickets. No birds. No breeze. Only rain falling, soft and steady. When a shadow came walking up sometime later, I trained my gun on it, and before I could cock the hammer the shadow whistled, a bright little song, like the one I'd heard in the woods when I'd waited with Barzo and the others for the captain to come back. A voice—French with something else mixed in—said, "Are you on watch?"

I said, "Yes. Someone had to be."

Émile squatted down next to me. I wanted to ask where he'd been, but I didn't. I hadn't heard any tanks for a while now. The night was quiet. In the shadows, I could only see half his face. He said, "Did you know Joan of Arc died in Rouen?" His voice was low. "Rouen was under English rule then. Victor Hugo called it the city of a hundred bell towers."

In the wet and the dark, his voice gave me the spooks. I thought, Telling stories for him is like singing for me—it helps us to think; it makes us feel better.

Émile was saying something about the river Seine and Joan of Arc's ashes being scattered to the winds.

I said, "Tell me your favorite poem or song, but tell it to me in French."

He said, "You won't understand."

"I don't care. Just tell it to me. Maybe I'll understand some of it."

Inside the drainage tunnel, someone began to snore. The sound of it mixed in with the rain and the splashing of the pools, and it was almost like music.

Émile narrowed his eyes at me like he was thinking. At last he said:

> *Un petit cochon*
> *Pendu au plafond*
> *Tirez-lui le nez*
> *il donn'ra du lait . . .*

He kind of half-talked, half-sang the words. His voice was warm and soft, as if he had just painted a memory and he wanted to be as delicate, as gentle as possible so as to get it right and not disturb it.

He said, "It is the song my mother sang to me each day when I awoke. It is just a silly little song, a simple children's nursery rhyme, but when I sing it I can hear her voice."

I said, "It's beautiful." The rain fell harder. I watched it splashing against the earth and the pools that were collecting there. I thought of Émile's mama, who must be waiting for him to come home, and of my own mama.

He said, "It is a song about a pig."

"A pig?"

Émile started to laugh, hardly making a sound, his shoulders shaking. When he laughed his entire face changed. He ran his large hands, strong and wide and skinned at the knuckles, through his hair, and then he looked up at me, gypsy eyes tearing. When he smiled his face didn't seem so proud or so full of itself. He looked almost handsome. He said, "It is a song about a pig that lays eggs if you hang it from the ceiling. If you pull hard enough on its tail, it lays some gold."

It took me a moment to let this sink in, but then I started laughing too.

He said, "French makes everything beautiful, no?"

At the same time we said, "Even pigs." I thought, Even you.

Above us, on the bridge, I heard the sound of walking. It took me a minute to realize where it was coming from. I couldn't tell if it was one set of footsteps or several. I laid my hand on Émile's arm. He went still and quiet.

I whispered, "Is it the Germans?"

"Yes. I want you to wake the men and tell them to move, and then I want you to stay close to me."

I ducked back into the tunnel and shook the men awake, putting a finger to their lips so that they would know to be quiet. We gathered our things and crawled to the door. From above, there was the sound of heavy boots.

Émile signaled to us, and I knew enough to know it was code to tell us how many men were out there and where they were.

From the bridge, a blast of gunfire exploded, so loud it hurt my ears. Coleman crept out of the tunnel, away from the bridge, from the sound, from the footfalls, his gear over his shoulder. He gave a hand signal of his own and then a salute. He said, "Whatever happens, lads, we do not get caught."

The men looked at each other, from one to the other. Barzo said, "No prisoners."

"No prisoners," Émile said, followed by Perry, by Ray. I didn't like the way this sounded, and suddenly Coleman was gone.

"Where is he going?" I could barely hear my own voice.

Émile held up his hand, which I knew meant to be quiet. The gun-fire blasted again, this time to the left of us. He said, "We need him alive. In many ways, he is the most important of us all. He is taking his equipment and going as far as he can."

Perry pulled out his carbine.

Émile said to me, "If I say shoot, you shoot."

I said, "No prisoners."

Ten seconds later, the five of us left the tunnel and half-ran, half-crawled to the woods. Up on the bridge, I could see dark, outlined figures moving across and down along the river and then off into the forest till it was hard to tell which of the tall, straight shadows was a soldier and which was a tree. We ran right for a briar patch, dropping to our hands and knees and crawling into the center until we were sliding across the dirt on our stomachs. I could feel the thorns tugging and tearing at my face and hair, at my clothes. I kept crawling. I heard gunfire and then a cry, the sound of someone being shot.

I said, "Coleman!"

Émile said, "No, the Maquis, the Resistance."

We flattened ourselves against the earth, which smelled like fresh-cut grass and dirt and mud and cows. My head went dizzy from the smell and the sound of gunfire getting closer, but I couldn't tell what direction it was coming from—the left, the right, front, back. We were surrounded.

More shots, more cries. Through the thick, wiry branches of the bramble I could see bodies hitting the ground. Then I could see heavy hobnail boots, the boots of German soldiers, and they were coming toward us. There was talk, very low, and they called out, "We know you are there."

They came closer, closer, till they were in front of the bramble bushes. They were talking to one another, to us. They fired off shots into the bushes, trying to flush us out. On either side of me, Ray and Émile raised their weapons, holding them steady, pointed at the hob-nail boots. I raised my Sten gun, my hand shaking. Never freeze.

A shot went off and I heard something buzz past me. Then another buzzing to my right, just in front of Émile. Another over my head, so close I could feel the wind from the bullet.

Suddenly I heard a voice, cool and British. It said, "Why don't you speak English, you bloody Krauts?"

Coleman.

He said, "Or are you as daft as you appear?"

"*Was ist los?*" Silence. Then another German shouted, "*Was ist los?*"

The hobnail boots were turning. They were walking away. One man stood alone now, and he fired his gun once more into the bramble before going after the others.

"What's he doing?" I whispered it to either Ray or Émile, whichever one. It didn't matter. We were all the same. They were all the same.

Barzo said, "Bastard's letting us go." I could see the hobnail boots gathering together. Forty pairs of them. Maybe fifty. Maybe more. I could see the bodies of the Resistance scattered on the ground.

Émile said, "Does he have the detonators?"

Barzo said, "He must have hidden them."

I said, "We have to save him."

Ray said, "I can pick them off." He was squinting through something that looked like a telescope attached to the top of his rifle. He moved the gun from one German to another. "One by one by one."

Perry said, "You shoot that gun and every last one of them will be on us."

I looked to my right, to where Émile was studying the Germans over the muzzle of his carbine. He had his finger on the trigger. After a minute he let it go. "*Merde, alors.*" His eyes darted this way and that, taking it in, trying to figure out what to do, how to take on fifty Germans by himself.

Finally he said, "He is saving us." And he yanked me with him— harder than he needed to—as he backed away, silent as a snake on the earth. Ray was the last to follow. I waited for a gunshot, for the sound of a body hitting the ground, but the Germans were going away now, away from the bridge and away from us. And they were taking Coleman with them.

*   *   *

We ran through a field, down a winding road, and into a valley filled with wildflowers. We didn't stop running till long past the sun came up, sometime the next afternoon. We came to a hill surrounded by trees, and in the distance I could see the tall spires and bell towers of what must have been Rouen.

At the very top, with views across the valley, was a tiny building with walls of rough stone laid out unevenly, as if the person who'd built it had done so quickly and used what he could find. Two narrow towers rose up on either side, and a chimney in the middle was made of the same crumbling stone. The roof was thatched, and a few yards away was a waterwheel and a spring. A bicycle lay on its side in the grass.

The captain walked to the door and knocked once, then again, two sharp raps. The men cocked their guns. We waited. The captain knocked again—once, twice—and this time the door swung open. A woman stood, framed by the candlelight that spilled out from inside. When she saw us, she smiled, a perfect gap between her two front teeth.

TWELVE

Delphine lived in the house with her mama and daddy and little sister, Mathilde, who was ten. Her father, Monsieur Babin, was a neat, trim man with a gray mustache and a small cap of gray hair in the center of his head. He invited us to stay with them for as long as we needed to.

After a supper of bread and butter, Perry checked his watch. He nodded at the others and they stood, gathering knives, guns, ammo. I stood too, wondering why we weren't staying.

Monsieur Babin took out a pipe and a bag of tobacco, which had been folded and refolded, and said, "Other than a radio, do you have everything you need?"

Perry pulled a slip of paper from his pocket. "We need to get this message to the Allies. Without a radio, it's our only way to let them know our status and to let them know Coleman's been taken."

Monsieur Babin said, "As far as I know, the nearest Allies are east of Caen, one hundred kilometers from here."

Delphine took the paper from Perry. "I will deliver it for you. There is a professor in Rouen. He works with the Resistance. He is British by birth and is said to be in close touch with the British army."

The men seemed to be hurrying, collecting the last of their gear, throwing their rucksacks over their shoulders. Barzo bent over the fireplace and stirred his hand around in the coal and ash. He smeared streaks of black on his face like war paint. When I reached for my own bag, he said, "Not this time, kid."

"But—"

Émile looked at Monsieur Babin. "Make sure she does not leave."

Perry said, "Someone will be back for you, Velva Jean. You have my word." Then he picked up his bag and paused at the door, blinking back into the room, as if he were trying to remember something—as if he were trying to remember himself from a long time ago. He smiled at Delphine's mother and touched his forehead in a kind of salute. "A lovely meal, madame. *Merci*." I thought that even with shadows under his eyes, Captain Perry O'Connell looked like a knight or a king who had temporarily lost his way. I wondered if I could fall in love with him, if we were in a different place and there wasn't a war going on.

Perry opened the front door and, one by one, the men filed out. I stood watching from the doorway as they crossed the grass before disappearing down the hill. Émile was the last, walking backward so that he was facing me, and then turned around without a word.

The Babins and I spent the evening reading and talking. While I played a game called Bilboquet with Mathilde, Delphine and her father spoke in low voices about the professor in Rouen. His name was Alain Fontenay, and he was retired from teaching history at the city's university. He lived at the very end of Rue de la Seille, in the shadow of a great cathedral, with his wife. Delphine would go in the morning to deliver the message.

Monsieur Babin had heard through the Resistance network that the Germans were moving southeast, toward Paris, west toward the Normandy beach towns, and east toward Germany, but a few of them still lingered around the area of Rouen, so Delphine promised to be on her guard.

I wanted to help, to prove that I could be part of things, and not just some girl in everyone's way. That was when the idea came to me: If I couldn't go with Perry and Émile, there was no reason why I couldn't take that message to Rouen in Delphine's place.

After everyone went to bed, I untied the map scarf and spread it underneath the candlelight. Here was Rouen, eleven kilometers away, and there was Rue de la Seille. I wouldn't take my Sten gun because it was too bulky and big, but I would take the knife with the pearl handle that Delphine had given me. I pulled the paper out of Delphine's bag and tucked it into my pocket. It was nothing but numbers and symbols, a kind of code. I would leave at dawn.

I was up before anyone else. I washed the dirt and mud off my skin and out of my hair, and tried to make myself look as clean and tidy as possible, and then I wrote a note to Delphine to tell her my plan. I slipped outside, silent as the dead, shutting the door behind me, careful to not make a noise. I picked up the bicycle and unscrewed one of the handlebars. I rolled the paper tight, thin as a pencil, and slid it inside. I screwed the handlebar back in and set my bag in the basket that was attached to the front. As I was wheeling the bicycle away from the house, I saw Mathilde standing underneath a tree. She held a piece of bread in one hand and was tearing off bits of it with the same hand, throwing the crumbs up into the air and onto the ground for the birds. When she saw me, she stopped, head cocked to one side.

I said in French, "I was hoping I could borrow your sister's bicycle."

"That one is mine."

"Do you mind if I use it? I promise to bring it back."

"No. Do they know you are awake?"

"No."

She seemed to consider this. Finally, she said, "Do you like seashells?" I nodded. She reached into the pocket of her skirt and held out her hand. There were three little pink shells, the kind you pick up on the beach by the ocean or the sea. They winked in the early light. She held her hand to her face so that the shells were eye level, studying them. Finally she chose one and handed it to me.

I wasn't sure whether she wanted me to keep it or look at it, so I leaned in and said, "It's very pretty."

She said, "For you. It will bring you luck."

At the base of the hill, I climbed onto the bicycle. I wobbled off, across the field and down the dirt road. I'd only been on a bicycle twice in my life, back in Texas, and I'd discovered then that riding one was ten times harder than driving a truck. I bobbed and swayed, and even as I bobbed and swayed, I tried my best to look French, dressed in a pair of navy pants and a gray blouse of Delphine's, brown scarf over my head, wearing old brown boots that belonged to Monsieur Babin.

It was Thursday, July 20, a warm, cloudy day, and as I steered the bicycle along the dirt road, swerving to miss a stray cow or pothole, I hit a bump and the front tire wobbled and suddenly I found myself on the ground.

I brushed myself off and climbed back onto the bicycle and pedaled slowly, trying to get my rhythm, as if I were in the middle of a song. I practiced using the brakes, and when I was able to drive straight for a mile or two without wobbling or falling off, I started going faster, happy to be doing something, scared about what might happen, anxious about whether the men were ever coming back, worried about what they would do to me if they did come back and found out I'd gone to Rouen, but feeling useful for the first time since I'd left Scotland.

A mile or so later I came to the city. As I saw it rising up in front of me, I set one foot on the ground and took it in. Even in the clouds, I thought the church spires looked like jewels, and that even if I tried, I would never be able to write a song with words as lovely as the spires themselves. I stood another minute, and then I set my foot back on the pedal and went on. I passed a man on the road, walking with a loaf of bread under one arm. He didn't even look at me from under his cap. I passed a woman and a man and their little boy, who was crying. The man stopped to pick the boy up and the woman wiped his wet face with her shawl. I rode by them, concentrating on blending in.

I wove through the streets of Rouen, picturing the map, getting my bearings. Rouen was set in the middle of low hills with the Seine—where Joan of Arc's ashes had been scattered—on one side. I couldn't even count the church spires. As I came up on the Left Bank of the city, I slowed down because suddenly so many of the buildings were gone and there was nothing but rubble and ruin. You couldn't tell where the buildings had stood.

Before I knew it, I had stopped in the middle of the street, the blue-gray sky hanging over me and this city—what was left of it—like a great, gloomy tent, the buildings crumpled and scattered across the ground, just hollow shells or piles of wood and stone, some higher than an actual building. Walls, chimneys, stairs, all unattached and sitting by themselves. A tire here, the engine of a truck there, a church pew, a painting, a table, a chair. Up in a tree was a bright bit of red—a scarf or a shirt, some sort of clothing. Suddenly the whole city seemed gray, and not because of the weather. It looked like the earth had exploded underneath Rouen.

I heard the rumble of an engine, and a car full of German soldiers came flying past. My heart sped up and my throat closed in, and I told myself to keep pedaling, to go on until I reached the professor. Somehow I got my feet working and rode down the cobbled streets until I was beyond the Germans and beyond the part of the city that had been bombed. The professor's house was just up on my right, I knew, and as I headed toward it, I suddenly came upon the largest building I'd ever seen. It wasn't just a building—it was a church with at least twenty spires and archways and windows and staircases and doorways and angels, all made out of stone the color of wheat, and black marble.

At that moment, the car full of Germans turned around and started rolling back down the road toward me, slowly this time. I hopped off my bike and wheeled it up to the front door and placed my hand on the giant gold handle and ducked inside. The ceilings were as high as the sky, curved and vaulted. It had the feel of a giant air hangar or a barn, but fancy—so fancy I wondered if God lived there. I held my breath and listened, and there was nothing but quiet. A long hall led up to the altar, with arches and doorways on either side and a ceiling that looked as if it were made of gold. I wondered who came here on Sunday to pray and talk to Jesus and if Jesus would listen to them more because they were praying from this beautiful place, or if he could hear you just as clearly from the one-room church that we'd built ourselves up on Fair Mountain.

I heard the clackety-clacking of footsteps then, and they echoed on the stone floor so that it sounded like a thousand men marching. I pushed my bicycle fast toward a hallway, tucked to the side, and down this to another hallway, this one with windows. I opened door after door, looking for a way out, the footsteps growing closer. And then I opened another door that led me outside into the day, this time at the back of the church. I seemed to hear German voices everywhere, from all directions, and instead of climbing onto the bike, I walked alongside it, keeping my head down.

The professor had a brown beard and wore a brown sweater over a brown button-down shirt, which gave him the look of a rumpled bear. His wife was small and gray and waved her hands when she was speaking. Their house sat at the very end of the street, just as Delphine had said, and was narrow and cramped and filled with books, stacked from floor to ceiling. The smell of something sour and warm came from the kitchen—cabbage soup or potatoes in vinegar.

When I told them I knew Monsieur Babin, they asked me in, inviting me to sit in the parlor. Every now and then the professor glanced at the window just past my head. He said, *"Êtes-vous américain?"* Are *you American?*

"Oui."

"Let us speak English then."

"I have a message that needs delivering." I pulled it out of my sleeve and gave it to him. I watched as he unfurled the paper and read. His wife stood, crossing to the windows on the other side of the room.

When the professor was done reading, he looked up, his face troubled. "He was taken day before yesterday?"

"Yes."

He said, "I will see that your message is delivered." His wife gestured to him and he stood. "You must forgive our manners. Normally we would serve you tea and biscuits, but it will be best for you if you are on your way. It is a dangerous time for you to come. The Germans are on alert because of an air raid last night on prison Bonne-Nouvelle here in Rouen. I understand that many German guards were killed and that many prisoners escaped. These prisoners are French Resistance, but they are also political prisoners and spies. They say the prison was attacked from both the air and from the ground."

"Of course." I stood, and at that moment there was a knock at the door, and a man's hard voice, speaking French with a German accent.

The professor's wife whispered, "Go."

The professor took my arm and led me down a narrow hall to a bedroom. He opened a closet door and stooped to move shoes and more books. He pushed aside the clothes and felt along the wall and suddenly it seemed to spring open—just a small square door, large enough to crawl through. Inside I could see guns, boxes of ammunition, medical kits, and other gear. I bent over and crept in, knees tucked under my chin. He said, "I will let you out as soon as they are gone." He closed the door and I was swallowed by the dark. I could hear him moving the shoes and books back into place, and then his footsteps fading away down the hall.

There was the sound of a door opening and voices. I tried to make out what they were saying. The voices moved away until I could barely hear them. I held on to my knees, reminding myself to breathe. Minutes later, the voices grew louder and then louder as they headed toward me. I could hear two sets of footsteps, one heavier than the other. They seemed to be coming through the hallway and then into the bedroom. I was drawn in so tight that I suddenly felt as if I were going to fall over. I reached my hand out and grabbed on to the first solid thing—a box of some sort. I steadied myself and waited.

The heavier footsteps came closer, and then I could hear the creaking of the closet door as it opened. I held my breath and held on to the case and prayed I wouldn't fall over. Hangers skimmed back and forth on the clothing rod. I could hear the professor now, and then the German, only a foot or two away on the other side of the wall. In English he said, "You have heard about the raid."

"Yes."

The closet door slammed. The voices and footsteps moved away. The box was cutting into my hand, or maybe my hand was cutting into the box, but I didn't move, didn't breathe. A door opened and closed somewhere. Silence.

Then footsteps again, lighter and faster than before. The closet door opened. The shoes and books went sliding. The hangers skimmed across the clothing rod. A square of light came pouring in and I could suddenly see the professor's face. He said, "All clear."

He reached for my hand and pulled me out, and the box came dragging along behind me. He had to peel my fingers off it because I couldn't seem to let go. His wife appeared and he told her, "She is all right. Just frightened." He rubbed my hands until I could move them again. "You must go now, while you can."

He helped me to my feet and I looked down at the box, which wasn't a box at all. It was a suitcase, small and black and ordinary. I asked him a question then, even though I already knew the answer: "Is that a radio?"

out the bullet. Ray didn't flinch. When the older man was finished, he straightened and held up the bullet, pinched between the tweezers, and carried both to the sink. Ray opened his eyes and watched him as Delphine's mother mopped up the blood and cleaned the wound, and then Delphine handed her a sewing kit.

Ray and I both stared at the needles and he held his glass out to me. I said, "Another?" He nodded, and then he drank the second glass down like the first.

Five minutes later, he was all stitched up, and making his way through the bottle of whiskey. Émile sat across the room, off to himself. I poured a glass and took it to him. He looked up at me and said, "*Merci.*" I could see that he was tired. He pulled out his cigarettes, laying the package on his knee, and then he pulled out the matches. I watched as he lit a cigarette and took a long drag, eyes closed, head tilted back, breathing it in. His fingernails were still stained with blood.

When I asked how it had gone—even though I didn't know what "it" was—he said it hadn't gone as planned, and left it at that. He said, "Where were you?"

"I delivered your message."

The room went still. I picked up the bundle of bread. I set aside the loaves and unwrapped the plain black case they'd been hiding. I walked over to Barzo and held it out. "I brought you a radio."

I waited for the men to say something. I waited so long I thought: You'll never be one of them. No matter what you do, you won't ever make them think of you as anything but a burden.

Finally, Delphine got up and poured two glasses of whiskey and handed one to me. She clinked her glass against mine and said, "*Santé,*" and drank. Then her daddy began to clap, and he jumped up to pour whiskey all around, even a drop or two for Mathilde. He and his wife handed out the glasses.

Barzo held his up. "Anyone want to join me for a little crow?" He tipped the glass in my direction, and drank it down.

Émile sat with his arms crossed. I said, "You're angry with me." I took little sips of the whiskey and my head began to feel light, as if it could float away on its own.

THIRTEEN

By the time I reached the Babins', the men had been back for thirty minutes, faces and hair wet, uniforms spattered with dirt and mud and water. I looked, and they were all there. Ray lay on the sofa, head back, face white, eyes closed. His pants were split from thigh to shin, and Delphine's mama and daddy were kneeling beside him. I stood over them and could see the blood—on his leg, on the couch, on the floor. His leg was slashed open and bleeding from the middle of his thigh to his knee. Mathilde and Delphine rushed to fetch towels and bandages, and bottles of something—iodine, alcohol.

I set down the bundle of bread I was carrying, wrapped in white cloth, the one the professor and his wife had packed for me. "What happened?"

Émile said, "Ambush." But that was all. He had blood on his hands, and I wondered if it was Ray's or his own or someone else's.

Ray said, "Whiskey?"

Delphine's daddy didn't look up. "In the right-hand cupboard."

I went to the cupboard, which held three bottles, all half-full. Two were wine and the other was a rich dark brown. While Émile stood at the sink, washing the blood off his hands, I poured some of the dark brown one into a short, fat glass, and carried it to Ray, trying not to stare at his leg.

He drank it down straight. Monsieur Babin looked at Ray and Ray nodded, closing his eyes and moving his lips in a silent prayer. Monsieur Babin bent over the leg with what looked like tweezers and dug

He said, "You should not have gone. It was a stupid thing to do."

"But I delivered the message and got you a radio. Everything worked out fine."

"Yes, this time. War is not a place to be impetuous, to be reckless. You come here and you say, 'I will do this. I will do that. You cannot leave me. You must take me along.' Why do you think we left you behind? Because you would have gotten in the way. You give us no choice. And then you do what you damn well please."

"Are you mad because I could have been killed? Or because I went without you knowing?"

Barzo poured more whiskey and started singing "Run Rabbit Run," only he changed the words to "Run Adolph Run"—and one by one the others joined in. I sat watching them, my face hot, my eyes burning.

Perry raised his glass to me and said, over the singing, "Velva Jean Hart, when this is all over I'm going to buy you a new uniform. One without a rip in the shoulder. I'll buy you the fanciest gown in Paris, and we'll celebrate the Liberation with champagne. No more hiding, no more running. We'll climb the Eiffel Tower and take in the view." He drank down the whiskey, and as the other song ended he began to sing "Roll Out the Barrel."

I could feel Émile staring at me. I turned back to him, meeting his gaze. They were watchful eyes, ones that held secrets, that collected information and stored it away and made judgments without telling you what they were. They were eyes as old as centuries. He said, "Are you this much trouble in America?"

I said, "Yes."

At nine o'clock, Barzo picked up the black case and left the house. He would carry the radio into the woods because this way he could avoid the German vehicles that patrolled the roads, picking up radio signals and tracking them to the agents transmitting messages. Barzo was going to send a message to London and see if he couldn't get one in return.

By ten o'clock, the Babins had gone to bed. Perry, Ray, Émile, and

I sat up, waiting. We read and the men smoked and drank, and no one talked.

At eleven, Barzo walked back in. He set the radio on the table and said, "Swan's been moved."

Émile said, "Where to?"

"Fresnes."

"Still alive?"

"As far as they know."

I said, "Who's Swan?"

Barzo poured himself some whiskey. "A little package we've got to pick up and take home with us."

I said, "Swan was at the prison in Rouen, the one that was raided. You were trying to break him out." When they didn't say anything, I knew this was true. "What about Coleman? You can't leave him."

Barzo said, "We tried, kid. We did all we could."

I looked from one to the other of them, and finally Perry said, "He's gone."

The weight of his words filled the room, making the air heavy. I didn't ask how they knew.

I said, "And me? Are you going to leave me too?"

After a moment, Émile said, "No."

I said, "Where are we going?" I thought: Thank you. Thank you. Thank you.

"Paris."

"When do we leave?" I am safe, I thought. For now, I'm safe and not alone. They're taking me with them.

"The day after tomorrow."

The following night, three B-24s dropped three hundred containers filled with fifty tons of arms and supplies in fields or clearings around Rouen. We divided into welcome parties—Perry leading one, Émile another, Barzo another. I went with Émile.

I stood in the woods, holding my breath as Émile and the other men waved the plane in with their flashlights. I kept my eyes open for Germans. The supplies fell from the sky—canisters that gleamed silver in the moonlight, attached to parachutes that looked like giant mushrooms. The chutes billowed out and then collapsed when the canisters hit the ground. The men rushed forward and emptied them, burying the containers and then dividing up supplies and hauling them away in wheelbarrows or baskets.

I knew this was the most dangerous time of a drop—the time that came after. If the Germans had heard or seen the plane they would be on their way—by air or by land.

I carried a bag full of food and two Sten guns, slung over my shoulder by their straps. Émile walked ahead, listening, watching, clearing the way. He wore a black cap that nearly matched the one I was wearing.

Two or so miles from the farmhouse, we climbed up over a hedgerow and there was the road. We dropped down into the ditch, which was too shallow to hide us, and waited, listening. A glow of lights came toward us. We had nowhere to go except across the road, nowhere to hide on the side we were on, and we couldn't cross because we'd be spotted.

Émile said, "Drop your weapons. Drop your bag." He was watching the lights coming closer, moving toward us swift and sudden. He dropped his and I did the same without asking him why. He said, "Do as I say." He pulled my hat off so my hair came spilling out and said, "Trust me, Velva Jean." The way he said my name was a way I'd never heard it before, French and flowing, like a lovely old-fashioned dance.

Then he shouted at me in French and shook me hard. He took my hand and pulled me in, and, just as the lights were coming up on us, he turned me around so my back was to the road and placed his arm around my waist. I was so close to him, I could feel his heart beating against mine. I heard the car slow and stop, engines chugging, and Émile drew me even closer. "We appear like two lovers quarreling in a field." He smiled. "It is the best I could do with such short notice." Then he kissed me.

It was soft at first, his lips barely touching mine. I wanted to shove him away, to knock him down on his back and give him a good kick in the ribs. Then I felt myself go floating out of my body until I was hovering with the clouds in the air above us, watching.

I stared up at Émile for a good long while, and then I closed my eyes and let him kiss me. The whole time, I was thinking: Not since Ty, not since Harley, better than Ty, better than Harley. Different. Is this how Butch Dawkins would kiss me? Is this what it's like to be kissed by a man? Not a boy, but a man? Does Émile want to kiss me or is he only doing it to save us from the Germans?

Then I wrapped my arms around him and forgot to breathe and felt the hard muscles under his shirt, the way his arms felt as if they could crush me just by holding me, his hands in my hair, the roughness of his beard, and I kissed him and he kissed me, there under a watery French sky, with the Germans looking on, yelling catcalls and clapping their hands.

Suddenly Émile broke away, looking off toward the Germans while I looked up at him. One of the Germans shouted something, and I couldn't tell if it was French or German or maybe even English, but Émile nodded and called back, "*Oui. Son père est très strict.*" Yes. *Her father is very strict.*

There was laughter from the Germans and one of them said something. I whispered into his chest, "What did they say?"

He said into my hair, "They are repeating what I told them. That your father is strict, which is why we are out here."

The Germans laughed again and then they shouted something else and Émile answered, and they went back and forth, back and forth. The whole time, he held me close, and I rested my head on his chest, solid as a tree, because it seemed natural and like something a farm girl with a very strict daddy might do. His heart was beating fast and hard.

The Germans called out something else, and then there was a grinding as the car moved forward over the dirt of the road, and I could hear them driving off. Émile drew me to him again as they passed. I thanked God it was dark and that he couldn't see how red my cheeks must be.

As soon as their taillights faded into the black of the horizon, just dots like stars, Émile said, "They knew about the drop."

"What does that mean?"

"I don't know. We are lucky they were drunk and happy and decided not to stop us longer."

I waited for him to say something about the kiss or maybe even kiss me again, but instead he headed across the road, not touching me, a great distance growing up between us like a creek, then a river. I followed him, fast and silent, and slipped through the field on the other side. I knew where we were now—we had to cross two small fields and two small farms, and then another field, which was almost the size of Alluvial, and which was where one of the other drops had taken place, and then the woods that lay beyond. Soon after, we would reach the hill, and then, at the top, the farmhouse. There we would share our food and organize the weapons and the money.

By the time we reached the third field, I was still thinking about the way Émile had kissed me. My lips throbbed and burned. As we walked through the grass, I could see the fresh-turned earth where the canisters were buried. In my haze, from a far-off place, I thought: I shouldn't be able to see where they buried these. The ground should be put back just the way it was so that the Germans don't notice.

I brushed my lips with my fingers, as if I could conjure up the kiss again by touching them. They burned so much I wondered if my lips were bleeding. Up ahead, something gleamed on the ground. It was a container, and then there was another.

Émile said, "Something is wrong." The kiss was fading fast, disappearing into the night. He bent over one of the containers and there was nothing inside. He bent over another and it had been picked through—the only things left were wool sweaters, gloves, and a medical kit, which lay open and empty. All the weapons that would have dropped with them—grenades, rifles, revolvers, carbines, submachine guns—had been taken.

We walked faster, through upturned earth and more canisters, flung here or there. We stepped over more sweaters, bandages, a broken radio, which looked as if someone had smashed it with a hatchet or the butt of a gun. "They were interrupted," Émile said, but it was like an afterthought because we knew this already. "We need to bury the canisters and any of the supplies that we cannot use or carry away."

But he wanted to push on first, to see how much more there was, if anything was left that would be useful to us. On the edge of the field was one last canister, larger than the others. Something about it made my heart stop.

Suddenly we were at the container, lying on the ground—only it wasn't a container. I saw everything in pieces—a leg, a shoe, an arm. The body was lying on its side, arms reaching out toward something, although there was nothing there. The ground underneath it was dark and wet, and the hair glinted white-gold in the moonlight. And then I saw the eyes. They were open and staring up at the sky—like clear blue pools.

Together, Émile and I buried Perry in the field, along with three of the Maquis who lay nearby and all of the containers and the supplies we didn't need. We dug the graves with our daggers and our hands, working as fast as we could in the dark. My hands went numb and blistered. My fingers bled. The graves weren't deep, but I prayed they were deep enough to hold the men and keep them there without anyone coming along—a German, an animal—and digging them up again.

We worked fast, knowing the Germans could come back at any minute, and we didn't speak a word. As I dug, the motion of the dagger Delphine had given me—in and out, upturning the earth—and the feel of the dirt in my hands made me feel as if I were doing something. Something necessary. Something important. It made me feel helpful instead of helpless, strong instead of weak. I'd never dug a grave or buried someone before, even though I'd lost plenty of folks I loved. I thought if a person ever wanted to know about death, they just had to dig a grave and feel the dirt, cold and moist, under the fingernails, and smell the mustiness of the earth all around. I tried to imagine what it would be like to be inside one of these holes, smelling the musty earth and the damp forever.

FOURTEEN

*L*ong before dawn on Saturday, July 22, Émile, Barzo, Ray, and I climbed in the back of a pickup truck with two British pilots and three large pigs. The truck was owned by a local man named Armand Leveque, who was a farmer and a friend to the Babins. His son worked in a local factory as a mechanic and, since the war began, had been smuggling a cup of gasoline at a time from the factory and storing it away in an old shed behind his daddy's house, where he kept the truck up on blocks, the tires hidden in the barn.

I wanted to be behind the wheel of that truck. Anywhere but lying in the back under a pile of straw, knocking against the men, tarp drawn tight over us so no one could see in, pigs grunting and squealing over each bump in the road. I didn't know who smelled worse, the men or the pigs.

The motor was loud but smooth, and we rode with the headlights off, which meant Monsieur Leveque had to find his way in the dark along winding country roads. Each time we passed through a blacked-out village, he would cough loudly and hit the gas, and the men lifted the tarp just enough and pointed their guns out.

I knew we were following an old forest road southeastward, and that the Germans were moving in and through the area, raiding farms and setting fire to the woods and the houses. They were destroying the villages and shooting innocent people just because they were French and the enemy. Sometime the day before, according to the BBC, Hitler's own men had tried to kill Hitler at his Wolf's Lair field headquarters, where he'd sat in a conference room with twenty-four other people. Someone had put a bomb in a briefcase and slid it under the conference table. When the bomb went off, the room was destroyed and four people were killed, but Hitler survived. I couldn't let myself think about what his death might have meant to me, to us, to everyone. If Hitler had been killed the war might be over, just like that. Johnny Clay, if he were still alive, would be safe. We—those of us still here—could go home.

Every now and then we heard the buzz of a plane overhead and then blasts of fire. The male pilots and I tried to guess the planes by the sound—an RAF Beaufighter or Spitfire, an American Liberator or Flying Fortress, a German Messerschmitt—but they all sounded terrifying to me.

We knew there would be roadblocks along the way, but when we were stopped the first time my heart began pounding so fast and loud I could hear it in my ears. I was sure the Germans could hear it too.

The truck shook as it sat there, engine still humming along. I heard voices—German—and then Monsieur Leveque. They were speaking French. One of the Germans asked to see Monsieur Leveque's papers. Then it was quiet except for two or three of the Germans talking to one another in low voices, the sound rising and falling like the buzzing of crickets on a summer night.

I could hear Monsieur Leveque, and then the German who'd asked to see his papers. I didn't know what they were saying, but suddenly the truck began to move, and soon we were jolting over the winding, bumpy road again. Émile said, *"Nous sommes bien." We are fine.*

The second time we were stopped, the Germans asked for Monsieur Leveque's papers and there was quiet followed by the sound of a door slamming. One of the Germans said in French, "Stand where I can see you." He said something else that I couldn't understand.

Émile whispered, "They want to search the back to see what he is hauling."

We all froze—Émile, Ray, Barzo, the British pilots, and me. We were pushed as far away from the tail of the truck as we could get, smashed together against the back of the cab.

Suddenly there was the blinding beam of a flashlight. The pigs squirmed and squealed, and from where I lay I could see the face of one of the Germans, wrinkling his nose. Monsieur Leveque had lifted the tarp only enough to show the pigs, but I could feel the men go rigid around me, and I knew they were afraid like I was. I waited for the whole tarp to be yanked back, all the way. I waited for the Germans to see us and raise their guns and shoot us on the spot.

Another soldier walked over and took a look and shook his head. He said something in German and then the tarp dropped back into place, and I could hear Monsieur Leveque tying it down again. The voices and footsteps faded away from us. The truck settled a little as Monsieur Leveque climbed back in. The door slammed. I heard him say, "*Bonsoir. Merci.*" And then the truck rattled off, bumping and thumping down the road.

We weren't stopped again, and somewhere along the way I fell asleep, my head bobbing against Émile's back. The last thought I had before I nodded off was, I can't believe I'm going to arrive in Paris in the back of a pig truck.

~ ~ ~

Paris was bridges and trees and grand gray-white buildings that looked as if they'd been built hundreds of years ago by kings and for kings. Every single one of them was as fancy and regal as a museum or a palace, even the normal ones, the ones Émile said were nothing but shops or apartments. Cars and trucks full of German soldiers hammered through the streets under a wet morning sky, horns honking. The sun was barely up, but already soldiers and regular, everyday people jostled and pushed or sat outside in cafés. Trees and streetlamps lined the streets, making it look like a kind of city forest. The smell of bread was in the air, and I could hear music even though there was none playing. Even in the rain, Paris looked like a picture book, a fairy tale. Émile said, "The best view is from the rooftops," and I could hear the warmth in his voice, as if he were talking about a girl he loved.

Monsieur Leveque dropped us on a quiet street just off the Champs-Elysées, which looked as if it must be the longest street in the world. Émile said it was two kilometers, which was a little over a mile, but it seemed to stretch forever, like if you walked along it long enough you might cross the ocean and find yourself right back on Fair Mountain.

Monsieur Leveque held the tarp back while the engine of the truck kept running, and we climbed over the pigs and out of the truck onto the sidewalk under a row of handsome trees, clipped and pruned like schoolboys fresh from the barber. He saluted us all and then rattled off, the truck sputtering and coughing like an old man. I wondered if he would make it all the way home.

We stood on the sidewalk, dirty and tired. Émile and Barzo exchanged names with the pilots so that if any of us made it out of France we could report on what happened to the others. The pilots said they were going to join the Freedom Line, that there was a woman in Paris who was smuggling out Jewish children and downed airmen, that she was famous for all the people she'd saved.

I watched the men, waiting for them to tell me good-bye and send me away with the other pilots so they could get rid of me, like they'd been wanting to do from the beginning, but they just stood there, shifting their packs over their shoulders. Ray pulled on a cap that looked like something a fisherman might wear. Barzo and Émile both put on hats as well.

As the pilots waved and turned away, I said, "Wait," then went running after them. I said, "My friend Helen Stillbert is a pilot too, a WASP. There's a song we agreed on before we left base, one that we could use to find each other if we got lost." And then I told them the lines and asked if they would keep an eye out for her, just in case she was in France too, when they reached the Freedom Line. One of the pilots said the lyrics back to me and I thanked him, and then I ran to join the men, who were waiting in the shadows of the trees.

Émile said to Barzo and Ray, "We split up. Take the Metro car to the Arc de Triomphe, and meet at the square du Roule." Then he took my hand and the two of us set off down the street and up another, passing people and buildings and cafés. Barzo and Ray fell behind,

Ray barely limping, even though I knew his leg was causing him pain. When I turned to look for them, Émile said, "Don't call attention."

I said, "We already smell like pigs. If that's not going to call attention, I don't know what will."

We passed people—men in hats and slacks and crisp white shirts, women in summer dresses, their hair cut short and smart, their heads wrapped in bright scarves or flowered hats, flowers tucked behind their ears, boys selling newspapers, old men selling vegetables, and German soldiers, riding or marching through the streets. There were so many of them, walking in great lines, and I sucked in my breath. They drove past in cars without tops, six to a car, as if they were going to a party. They saluted each other and called out to each other in German, and the French people on their bicycles or horses steered to get away from them.

Émile's hand tightened around mine. He said, "You are with me. Better for Barzo and Ray to go alone so you aren't three Americans together. If we get stopped, I am here."

We passed streetlamps, pretty as a picture even unlit, and cobbled streets and alleyways that tucked behind the rows of buildings just like secrets. Some of the houses were narrow and tall, pressed close to each other or into each other, and others were palaces, angels and kings etched into the sides, looking as if they were trimmed with brocade and lace. Flowers bloomed in gardens and neat window boxes, and the sky was a pink-gray-white, which made the city look pink-gray-white.

Émile pulled me toward a stairway that disappeared into a cave in the earth, and my other hand brushed against the black iron railing as we went down so far I thought we'd end up in China. While I waited beside him, he bought two tickets and we went through the turnstile and down more stairs to a platform packed with people. We stood close together, Émile facing me and rubbing my arms up and down with his hands, just like I was cold. And maybe I was cold. I shivered a little and had chill bumps on my skin. I looked up at him and he smiled at me, the lines around his eyes and mouth crinkling as if someone had etched them there. He said, "If a pig can make gold." And this made me laugh.

A wide, black arrow was painted on the wall of the Metro, winding away from us. I said, "What does it mean?"

"It directs you to the air-raid shelter. If you ever hear the sirens, this means the Allies have been spotted in the skies, and you need to run before the bombs start dropping."

A train rumbled toward us, fast as a B-17. It stopped with a squeal of brakes, and Émile said, "We are lucky. The Metro is closed most of the day and all night because of the electricity shortage." The doors to the cars cranked open and the crowd pushed forward. Émile tugged at my hand so we wouldn't lose each other, and suddenly we were boxed inside, smashed against everyone else. I looked up at the strap overhead, but I couldn't raise my arm to grab it because I was wedged between Émile and a man to the left of me, a large woman to the right, and a family of three to my back.

The doors ground closed and then we were moving, all of us together, swaying this way and that as the train traveled through the dark. I swayed right into Émile. He took one hand away from the strap above his head, pressing the other into the curve of my back to steady me. Without thinking, I leaned up and kissed him. For just a few seconds, I closed my eyes and felt the warmth of him. No matter what happens to me, I thought, I am kissing this man right now in Paris. We are spies posing as lovers, and now everyone will believe it. When I pulled away, his face was hard to read, but his arm tightened around me.

The train rattled fast through the underground, traveling through dark and light, dark and light, till I thought I would get dizzy. I heard shouting, and to the left of us I could see a fistfight between two men or three men, I couldn't tell. The air was close and tight and I breathed through my mouth because the smell was worse than in the pig truck.

The train stopped once, then twice, and on the third time, Émile pulled me toward the door and we stepped out onto another platform and climbed another set of stairs, my hand brushing the black iron railing, until we were up on the streets of Paris again, blinking into the pink-gray-white sky, the color of pearls.

The Arc de Triomphe was just like its name—it sat at the end of the Champs-Elysées, a giant archway made of sand-white stone. Angels and naked soldiers and wise men in robes were carved into its face, on either side of the upside-down U-shaped opening, and just looking at it made me want to be good forever and write a song that would be worthy of it. People passed back and forth under the archway and as we stood staring up at it, Émile said in French, "Napoleon had it built to remember the generals and soldiers who fought in the Revolution, fighting for French freedom. The Arc represents victory for the troops." At the top, planted like a candle on a birthday cake, was a black, white, and red flag—the swastika of Germany.

As he talked, we walked toward the Arc. In the distance, across the Seine River, I could see the Eiffel Tower, rising up like an exclamation mark, pointing straight at heaven and God himself. It was graceful, with the fine, delicate features of a beautiful lady, but it was much larger than I'd ever imagined, standing like the fiercest soldier, one who was guarding his country and all he loved and good luck getting past him. The sight of it made me think of Perry, who would never get to climb to the top and take in the view.

We walked under the Arc, and I could see that it wasn't just the Champs-Elysées that stopped here. There were streets on all sides— twelve in all—that ended at the Arc's front door. Émile said, "They call it Place de l'Étoile, or Square of the Star." He was still speaking French so as not to draw attention.

We strolled by the men and women, old and young, and the soldiers, and I wondered what they thought when they looked at us. Did they think we were two young lovers on our way to a café? Or brother and sister out to do an errand for our mother? Or could they look at us and see what we were—a secret agent and a pilot who'd just arrived in Paris in the back of a pig truck?

We strolled until we stopped at a rectangle of concrete with a bronze circle, like an upside-down pot lid, at the head of it. It was laid out like a grave, and there was writing on it that made me think of a tombstone, and the dates 1914–1918.

I said, "What is it?"

Émile said, "The Tomb of the Unknown Soldier. It is meant to honor all the heroes of the last war, the ones who never found their way home or got a proper burial. All the missing. Usually there is a flame that burns there." He pointed to the copper circle. "The eternal flame. It was extinguished in 1940 when Hitler came through the city."

"What does it say?"

" 'Here is a French soldier who died for his country.' "

I let the words sink in. How many more graves would there be like this before it was all over? My fingernails were still black with dirt from burying Perry. Somewhere, a long way off, I heard a melody starting in my head. I tried to follow it, but it ran away from me until there was nothing left except the thought that was playing in my mind like a record: I had come to Scotland and then to England and then to France to find Johnny Clay, but he was still lost, like an unknown soldier.

"Goddamn France." We turned and there was Barzo, standing behind us, breathing hard, wiping the sweat off his forehead with the back of a hand, and just behind him, Ray.

Barzo said, "Whose grave?" Before we could say anything, he leaned past me and read what was written there. He whistled, then swiped the hat off his head. He closed his eyes, just for a minute, and it looked as if he were offering up a prayer. When he opened them again his eyes were watery. He cleared his throat and said, "Where to?"

Émile said, "This way," and I followed him away from the Arc de Triomphe. We passed trees lined up like soldiers at attention, green and full, but neatly clipped and trimmed. We walked across the Avenue des Ternes and followed the street to the Boulevard de Courcelles, and then we turned from there onto Rue de la Néva, which was a handsome street filled with enormous overstuffed buildings, all linked together, that looked as haughty as old maiden aunts. We crossed the street and a little square of green park, and that was where Émile and the others stopped and he said, "We leave you here."

I said, "What do you mean, you leave me here?"

He said, "We cannot stay together in this city. The Germans are everywhere and more are coming, along with the Allies. It is only a matter of time till the battle for Paris, and we will be watched."

I said, "I'm going with you." The words sounded silly and weak as soon as I said them. I was sorry I'd kissed him.

"Not this time. We have work to do. I want you to walk down this street and go to the fifth building—the fifth door. A man will answer, my height, age fifty or so. It is him and his wife and their two children. They are friends of the Resistance, of Monsieur Babin and his family. You will tell them, 'Such bad weather we're having,' and he will say, 'Yes, for the past week, but I think it will be clearing soon,' and you will know it is him and that it's safe to go in. He will rent you a room in his house and you will wait for me there." He talked to me like I was a child.

"You're going to find Swan." I looked from one man to another.

Émile said, "Yes."

"I could help you."

Barzo said, "It's too dangerous, kid."

I was good and mad now. "How do I know you'll come back for me?"

Émile said, "You don't." He pressed something into my hand—a wallet. He said, "Keep these with you." Inside the wallet were French money and a French identity card and a driver's license. There was my picture, the one from my WASP ID, that he'd somehow taken from me without my knowing it. Beside the picture was the name Clementine Roux.

I said, "Clementine? Like the song?"

"Like the song. You are an American who moved to Paris just before the war to marry a Frenchman—Pierre Roux. You stayed on even after he was killed because you are part German on your father's side. You are staying with friends in Rouen. It is hard for you to leave here because it reminds you of your husband, and because of the war, of course. Your cover is shaky, but it is the best we could do on short notice. You must memorize this information and become her."

> *Thou art lost and gone forever*
> *Dreadful sorry, Clementine. . . .*

Émile said, "I want you to remember this. If you are going to lie you need to make it as close to the truth as possible. You must bury your beliefs. Lies must become real to you. You have to become somebody else—this Clementine Roux—and believe that."

"What does that mean?"

"You must lose your identity. An agent has to give up everything—friends, family, and himself."

The last thing I wanted to do was give myself up. I'd worked so hard to find myself—after Mama dying and Daddy leaving and me marrying Harley and divorcing Harley and going to Nashville and then to Texas to fly planes. I said, "I don't know if I can do that."

"What you want doesn't matter. Who you are doesn't matter. You must make a new story, become a new person. You have new papers, a new name." From his pocket, he handed me a slim gold band. "Wear this on your left hand."

"Where did you get this?"

"Never mind. Put it on."

I thought of everything I would have to let go to be Clementine Roux, like learning to drive and learning to fly and writing my songs. I slipped the ring onto my left hand and it felt cold against my finger. My own ring, the one I'd worn when I was actually married and not just pretending, was somewhere in North Carolina, up in Devil's Kitchen, on the hand of a new woman. The new Mrs. Harley Bright. I rubbed the ring with my thumb and shivered. The ring was too small. It pinched the skin in a way that made me feel as if I couldn't breathe.

He took my hand and held it, just for a moment. *"Au revoir,* Clementine." Then he turned around and Ray and Barzo turned around, and the three of them left me there. I watched them go, watched them split apart and walk in three separate directions. I followed them with my eyes till they disappeared.

I thought: I'm not Velva Jean. I'm Clementine Roux, wife and widow of another man. None of those men are my husband. They're not even my friends. They're not my comrades. I'm not part of their team. They're just soldiers doing their duty, just like me. Émile didn't

kiss me because he wanted to. He kissed me to throw off the Germans. And then I threw myself at him on the train.

The thought of all of it made me feel stupid and tired, and suddenly I wasn't sure I could walk the rest of the block, not even the length of five doors.

I looked up at the sky and down at the green of the grass. It was such a little bit of garden surrounded by so much concrete. I pulled my bag tight on my shoulder and walked down the street counting houses—one, two, three, four . . . When I came to the fifth one, I climbed the stairs to the door, my steps heavy, and rang the bell. I waited. After a minute, I rang the bell again. I looked around and there was no sign of Émile or Barzo or Ray. I thought, They could have at least waited to make sure the man was at home.

I pressed my finger to the bell again, but before I could push it, the door swung open and a man stood there, bearded and graying, thinning brown hair and glasses tucked in his shirt pocket. There was a book in his hand, his finger marking the page.

He said, *"Bonjour, mademoiselle."*

I said, *"Bonjour.* Such bad weather we're having."

He squinted at me and I held my breath. What if he said, "I don't know what you're talking about"? At least the sky was dreary and gray, so even if he was a stranger I wouldn't seem as if I were talking nonsense, although I wasn't sure how I would explain walking up to his door out of the blue. I thought of all that was hinging on just a few words. These were people I'd never met, and the only thing I had to let me know I could trust them was a password.

After about a hundred years, he said, "Yes, for the past week, but I think it will be clearing soon." And then he smiled, and it was a shy smile but a kind one.

From behind him, from another room, a woman's voice called out, *"Qui c'est, cher?"* Who is it, dear?

He said, "It is our guest."

FIFTEEN

I waited in the house for two days. Monsieur Brunet went in and out, sometimes gone for long periods of time, while his wife, Bernadette, worked in the kitchen. She was always cooking, and every time I offered to help her, she waved me away with a smile, saying, "You are our guest."

For half an hour after dinner, the electricity flickered on, and Monsieur Brunet would turn on the radio. He said the Germans were trying to block out the broadcasts from the BBC, but you could just hear the news through the static. After that half hour, the house would grow dark again and we would sit and talk or read by candlelight.

On my second night there, I asked Monsieur Brunet if he had a map of Paris I could borrow. I didn't plan to leave the house, but I thought I could be studying the map just as I'd studied the maps of France before flying out of Harrington. That way I would be prepared when Émile and the others came for me.

He said, *"Oui, mademoiselle."* And I followed him to the living room, where there were bookcases along one entire wall. While he searched for the map, I wandered around the room, which was cluttered but clean. Everything was a deep, warm red, even the curtains on the windows. A fireplace sat opposite the bookcases, with a basket of wood beside it and a sofa and three chairs facing it. On a side table next to one of the chairs was a record player the size of a bread box.

As he searched for the map, he said, "I hope you slept well."

I said, "Yes, sir." I didn't tell him that I'd tossed and turned for an hour before I curled up on the floor with my pillow and blanket, where I stayed the rest of the night. I wasn't used to beds anymore.

He said, "Bernadette has pulled aside some clothes for you and left them in your room. She thought you might be able to use them."

I said, "Yes, thank you. That's awfully kind."

He said, "I understand you have some experience working with the Resistance." His voice was vague and turned away, as if he were talking to the bookshelf.

I said, "Yes." I didn't tell him what my experience was.

On a table just inside the door was a glass jar with matchboxes. I picked these up to look at the names of the places they were from, but they were all the same—square, plain black boxes. I moved from there to a book, a glass vase, a pipe, cigarettes, a bottle of wine. I leaned in to read the label, and when I straightened up Monsieur Brunet was next to me, holding out a map.

"Here you are," he said. His voice was short and clipped, as if he suddenly wanted me to go. I thought the Brunets were pleasant but I could tell they weren't excited to have me in their house. I walked up the stairs, back to my room, the map in my hand, and thought: Émile, where are you? Please come.

On the morning of the third day, when the men still hadn't come for me, I put on a skirt and blouse that Bernadette had given me, and picked up my bag and walked outside. I stood blinking in the sunlight, trying to adjust my eyes. The first morning I'd woken up to the crowing of roosters, and I thought for a minute I was on Fair Mountain, back at Mama's house. After I woke up to roosters on the second day, I asked Monsieur Brunet where they were coming from. He said the French people had to do what they could for food, that each house was given a certain number of ration tickets, that you could bicycle thirty or forty miles into the countryside to buy meat and vegetables from peasants if you dared, or spend 1.84 francs— forty cents—for one egg, and forty-six francs—about ten dollars—for a pound of butter on the black market. If you were caught you'd pay a fine, so some people, the lucky ones, kept goats or rabbits or chickens in their house to feed themselves and their families.

Monsieur Brunet lived next door to Gestapo headquarters. He said this wasn't the only one, that there were others across the city, and that up until last year it had been just a regular house. The couple it belonged to was Jewish and wealthy, and they had been taken away by the Nazis, who then took over their home and turned it into offices. Every evening at six o'clock, a man with black-rimmed glasses and a square face like bread dough marched up the steps and into the building, and any officers standing outside saluted him and moved out of his way, which made me know he was important.

As I walked out the front door and down the steps to the sidewalk and past the Gestapo, I held my breath and counted to twenty-five, which was how long it took me to get to the end of the street and make the turn away from there, away from the Germans. Nazi flags were draped across roofs and shop windows, and signs were posted everywhere here, just like in Cambremer, Lisieux, and Rouen. They were mostly in French, but a few were in English. They said:

"It has come to our attention that our troops do not act with sufficient harshness. Do not hesitate to shoot, hang, and set fire. There is to be no exception. For instance, when crossing territory infested by the French underground, place French women in front of German convoys for protection."

While I walked, I looked for Émile in the faces of the men in the street. It had been three days since he and the others left me, and so far they hadn't sent one word as to what I should expect and when. Monsieur Brunet said, "He will come," as if he knew I was waiting for only one of them.

I memorized the way by landmarks, unfolding in my mind the map I'd borrowed from Monsieur Brunet. I kept one eye on the Eiffel Tower and one on the church of Sacré Coeur, which sat above the city, high up on Montmartre. This way, I thought I could figure out where I was. As I walked, I studied the people who were obviously French and I did what they did so I would blend in. I crossed and recrossed streets, stopping to glance in shop windows, just as I would have done down in Hamlet's Mill or Nashville. There were no buses running, and no taxicabs. The French seemed to get around on foot or on bicycle or on horseback. The streets and sidewalks were filled with bicycles.

I knew that Gossie was in Paris with the WAC, working with the 3341st Signal Battalion. So far, the only thing I could find out was that the 3341st Signal Battalion was still in the city, but no one—not Monsieur Brunet or his friends in the Resistance—could tell me where.

I walked like this for two hours and then I turned back. Most of the local people wore shoes with thick wooden soles that made them sound like horses as they clopped along the sidewalks and streets. These were the only shoes you could get right now, and I moved with them, clopping just like they did. I passed by Gestapo headquarters and climbed the steps to Monsieur Brunet's, and I called "Hello" after I shut the front door with a snap.

Monsieur Brunet came shuffling out of the kitchen, eyes blinking as if he'd been asleep. I could hear the clattering of pots and pans coming from the kitchen and the sound of Bernadette talking to her daughters. He said, "*Bonjour*, Clementine."

"*Bonjour.* Any messages?"

"I'm sorry." This time he didn't say, "He will come." He said, "Perhaps he has been delayed." The way he said it made me wonder if he knew something, and then it hit me that he thought Émile was someone I loved and fancied, that this was why I was so anxious. Monsieur Brunet said, "Did you have any trouble?"

I wasn't sure what he meant exactly, but I said, "No. I didn't even take the map with me, and I didn't get lost once. One of the first things they teach you in the WASP is how to learn your way without one."

He said, "Good. But you must be careful out there. The Germans are worried about the Allied approach and because of this they are beginning to lose confidence."

"That sounds like a good thing."

"They are scared, and when a person is scared he lashes out, like a caged animal. He will fight to the death." He leaned in the doorframe and I could see he had something in his hand—it looked like a lump of coal. He said, "There are rumors. Hitler hates the Jews and he hates France. He was a corporal in the First World War and here during the surrender. When Hitler came into France in 1940, he made us surrender at the very same place where the Germans surrendered twenty years ago. Some say he wants the city burned to the ground before the Allies arrive and that he has set explosives at all of the major sites—the Eiffel Tower, Notre Dame, the Sacré Coeur. He wants Berlin, and not Paris, to be the most beautiful city in Europe."

His words climbed into me like germs, till I was so tired I couldn't hold my head up. I was suddenly mad at everyone—Hitler, Émile, Barzo, Ray, Perry, Coleman, Jacqueline Cochran, President Roosevelt, Johnny Clay. Especially Johnny Clay, who was nowhere to be found. I was sick and tired of this war.

I laid my hand on the railing of the stairs, on the shiny wooden globe that sat on the first post. I felt the smooth coolness of it against my palm. This wasn't my city, even if I could find my way in it. These weren't my people. It didn't matter to me what happened to them. I thought: Save yourselves. Just leave me alone. I wanted to go upstairs and lie down on my floor and sleep for fifty years. I said, "I'm sorry."

Monsieur Brunet nodded and said, "Dinner will be at six o'clock."

That night I lay on the floor of my room, curled up on my side, the pillow folded beneath my head, one eye on the door because I didn't like to sleep with my back to it. I thought about Johnny Clay and Émile and Perry and Barzo and the others till they became jumbled in my mind and eventually I worried myself to sleep. It was a heavy, dreamless sleep, but I was pulled out of it sometime later by the sound of screaming.

I sat right up and grabbed for my bag, where the knife was that Delphine had given me, and then I waited, watching the door, half-expecting someone to break it down and come inside to grab me. The night was silent and still. I didn't remember dreaming, but the night was so quiet, I told myself I'd dreamed the noise. I lay back down, my bag to my chest, eyes open and staring toward the ceiling.

Out of the darkness, another scream and then another. At first I thought it was coming from the street or maybe downstairs, that something had happened to Bernadette or one of the girls, but then the night was broken by another scream, louder than the others.

All of a sudden, it stopped short.

The sound of silence after that was worse than the screaming, and I knew then where it was coming from—the Gestapo headquarters just next door.

SIXTEEN

On Thursday, July 27, my fifth day in Paris, I bought a ticket to the theater and went to see a play called *Antigone*. Inside, the theater had the musty smell of a closed-up church. I walked down the aisle as the lights were dimming, and the only other people were a few young couples, and a mother and her children, and a German in uniform who sat by himself. I wondered if I should leave, if it was safe to be there, but then he looked up at me and I thought it might be worse to turn around and walk out. I smiled at him, just slightly—not too big, the way Americans smiled—and then I took my seat, two rows ahead of him and far over to the side. In a minute, more people started coming in, walking down the aisles, arms linked, until almost all the rows were filled. Who were these people who could stop to see a show in the middle of the day?

The play was in French, and even though I couldn't understand all they were saying, I figured out that it was about a girl whose brothers were killed in battle. One was buried, but the other was left where he fell, out where the animals could get him. When Antigone tried to give him a proper burial, she was taken prisoner and was told she had to choose life or death. When she chose death, I felt the tears sliding down my cheeks, right off my chin and onto my hands, which were folded on my lap. I didn't even bother wiping them away. I sat there thinking about Johnny Clay and where he might be and what would happen if I found him and had to bury him, just as we'd buried Perry. It was starting to occur to me lately that I might never find him.

Then I started thinking about Émile and how he might not come back for me. And how there could be dynamite under this theater. It could be set to go off any minute. Hitler could blow up this theater, and I would be gone and no one would know, and Johnny Clay would never get his proper burial. This made me cry harder, and so I cried through the rest of the play, only wiping my face dry when the lights came up again.

I was at the end of the row, close to the wall, which meant I had to wait for the people around me to get up and leave. Everyone stood up, talking, brushing themselves off, and headed out into the day. I fell in behind them and with them, one of the crowd, while the German still sat, staring at the stage. The mother and the children were walking past him now, holding each other's hands like a daisy chain. The littlest child was kicking each seat as he walked, and when they passed the German, his mother yanked him close to her so he wouldn't be able to kick his too.

I came out onto the sidewalk and the people started fanning away so that I was by myself again. I blinked in the sunshine. The air smelled fresh and green like rain, but the clouds were disappearing and the sky was a bright blue. I turned to my right, back toward Monsieur Brunet's. People bustled by in the street, and I was happy to see them, happy to disappear in the crowd.

A minute later, a voice said, in French, "Did the play make you sad?" It was the German, and he had fallen in step beside me.

I thought of shaking my head to let him know I couldn't speak at all. I wanted to say: Go away. Leave me alone. My heart is broken. But instead I said, in French, "It was a sad story."

In English he said, "As soon as I saw you, I knew you were American. I would have known it anywhere."

Damn, I thought. I wasn't sure what to say to this, so I didn't say anything. I figured the less I said the better.

He said, "Are you an actress?"

"No." I was counting the streets we crossed, trying to remember where to turn. With each building we passed, I wondered if there were explosives planted underneath.

"You are beautiful like one."

In French I said, "I'm a singer."

"An American singer in occupied France."

He was still speaking English. In French I said, "My husband was French." The skin under my collar was growing damp.

"He is dead?"

"Yes."

"The war?"

"An accident." Ty's face flashed before me, like a snapshot. "He was a pilot."

"I am sorry for your great loss. Why are you still here?" His tone was friendly, but I thought he was asking too many questions. Because I refused to speak English, he had switched back to French.

I said, "The war began and I couldn't leave, so I am here with my friends."

He said, "Do I know these friends?"

I didn't like the way he said it. My back was dripping wet. I could feel little drops of water on my upper lip and forehead. I hoped he couldn't see them. Then I thought of what Delphine had said, about letting my smile speak for me. I looked up at him and smiled my brightest smile, the one I'd used when I was little on Sweet Fern when I needed her permission to do something. "I don't think so. They are simple people, like me."

He said, "I don't think somehow there is anything simple about you." I wondered if he was flirting with me. Except for his accent, he would have been the all-American boy—young and sturdy, with a friendly face as open as a field.

Up ahead, I could see Rue de Courcelles, which would take me back to Rue de la Néva. I held out my hand and he looked down at it in surprise. He put his hand in mine and I shook it. "It was a pleasure to meet you, but I am almost home."

"But I didn't get your name." I wondered if he was going to ask for my papers. I reminded myself to breathe.

"Clementine. Clementine Roux." I waited for him to say: That's not your name. Your name is Velva Jean Hart. What are you playing at? Who are you trying to fool? You're just a mountain girl from

North Carolina, and you are trying to fool me, a German officer working for Hitler, the cruelest man in all the world.

He said, "It's a pleasure, Clementine Roux. I am Fritz."

I said, "So nice to meet you. Good-bye." And then I waved to him and walked off, making my turn. I wanted to look back to see if he was following me, but instead I went on, casual as could be, every now and then stopping at a shop window or to pet a dog that was sitting outside on a stoop. At one point, I ducked into a drugstore and bought myself a lipstick—Rouge Ardent, which meant Fiery Red.

I turned onto the next street and the next, and when I was finally on Rue de la Néva, I counted the doors, walking past the Gestapo headquarters, and walked up the steps to Monsieur Brunet's. Inside, there were happy sounds coming from the kitchen, which was at the back of the house. I followed the sounds and there was Bernadette, in a blue apron with red trim, her sleeves rolled up above her elbows, cutting vegetables, the ones she grew on the roof now that food was so scarce—potatoes and radishes and strange vegetables I'd never heard of, like the Swedish turnip and the Jerusalem artichoke. Because there wasn't electricity or cooking fuel, she was boiling water in the fireplace, using scraps of newspaper as kindling. The children, Learyn and Annalise, were cutting shapes into the potato skins that fell on the counter and on the floor—stars and rabbits and trees.

Bernadette saw me and smiled. She blew a piece of hair out of her eyes and said, "*Bonsoir, Clementine.*"

"*Bonsoir.*" The counters were stacked with loaves of bread and muffins—fatter and prettier than any in a bakery—set out to cool. I wanted to help, so I picked up a knife and a rutabaga, thinking I would slice it for her, but it was heavy and hard, like plaster.

I stared down at the rutabaga and then Bernadette stared down at the rutabaga, and then I looked up at her and she looked up at me. She wiped her hands on her apron and whisked the rutabaga away from me, setting it back into the bowl, careful as could be. She smiled and said, "*Non, non.* I will call you for supper."

I said, "*Merci,*" and turned to go, the laughter and sounds of home fading behind me. My foot was on the first step, going up to my room, when I stopped and turned around. I walked back to the kitchen and said, "Madame Brunet?"

The girls were laughing now, sticking the potato skins on their faces, trying to make them stay there. Annalise said, "Come join us, Clementine!"

Learyn said, "*Oui!* You must try!" She made a mustache out of the skin and marched around the kitchen like a soldier.

Bernadette watched them, laughing. Her hands were kneading and kneading. She didn't look up. "*Oui?*"

"Do you have a pair of cutting shears I can borrow?"

My room was neat and clean but small, just a bed with a flowered blanket, a chair in one corner, large enough to sit in with your knees up, and a chest of drawers. The walls were papered in roses, heavy and fat and red. There was one large window, and through this I could see the Eiffel Tower.

I picked up the cutting shears that Bernadette had given me, and I walked into the bathroom, which was down the hall. I wrapped a towel around my shoulders and then I looked at myself in the mirror. I was freckled and sunburnt from the day's walk. I looked thin. My hair was wild and too long. I'd taken to wearing it tied back by a scarf.

I took a hunk of my hair and smoothed it against me. It fell to the middle of my chest. I smoothed it as if I were petting a dog or a cat, and then I raised the cutting shears and cut clean through the hair till it fell just over my shoulders. French women—especially the ones who lived in Paris—had short hair and were smart and suntanned and elegant, even those struggling to survive.

I reached for another section of hair, and sliced it away so that it fell into the sink. It was easy to cut it—my heart panged, but only a little—and this surprised me. When I was done cutting, I got out the box of hair dye I had bought on the way home. I covered my head in Brun Foncé, the deepest, darkest brown, nearly black, and I didn't even stop to think about what I would look like or what I had done. It was time I learned to blend in.

After I was finished, I stood in front of the mirror brushing my hair, trying to get used to the new shape of it. I set down my brush and I looked at the girl looking back at me and decided I didn't recognize her.

When I went down to supper that night, Monsieur Brunet and Bernadette acted as if they had expected it. Bernadette said, "You are looking lovely, Clementine," and Monsieur Brunet said, "The dark hair makes your eyes more green."

All through the meal, I caught Learyn and Annalise staring at me until finally Anna said, "You look like everyone else now." She sounded disappointed.

Monsieur Brunet said, "Annalise."

I said, "No, *c'est bien.*" *It is fine. It is good. It is okay.* It was what I wanted, to blend in, to become invisible, to disappear. I was trying not to miss my hair, which sat upstairs in the trash can, as dead as Velva Jean Hart.

After dinner, when the dishes were done, Bernadette took the girls to their room, down the hall from the kitchen, to read them a story and tuck them into bed. The bread was stacked on the counter, and, careful not to make a sound, I picked up a loaf. It was heavier than a regular loaf, but only by a little. It smelled like bread but something else too that I couldn't put my finger on. I set it down, careful as I could, just in case, and then I picked up a muffin. It was also heavier by a little, and also smelled slightly off.

Monsieur Brunet called out, "Bernadette?" The sound was muffled, as if it were coming from inside the wall.

I set the muffin on the cooling rack, just as it was before. There was a blank wall between where the counter ended and the doorway to the toilet began. A calendar of food advertisements hung on this, but that was all.

I stood in front of the wall and studied it, remembering the secret door in the professor's closet in Rouen. I tapped on the wall, and Monsieur Brunet's voice said, *"Oui? Qu'est-ce que c'est, mon cher?" What is it, my dear?*

I pushed on the wall, right at my waist level, just inside the line in the wood, and a door swung open. It was a small square of a room stacked with books and maps and papers. Monsieur Brunet stood, bent over the desk, gathering up his keys and his billfold. He looked up at me, and I couldn't tell who was more surprised, him or me.

"Clementine." His eyes darted past me into the kitchen and beyond.

"What is this place?"

He reached past and shut the door behind me with a click. The office smelled of potatoes and onions. As if he could read my mind, he said, "This was once the pantry."

I said, "And now it's your office."

"Yes."

We stood staring at each other.

He said, "I hear you crash-landed a team of agents into Normandy."

"Yes," I said. "What is it you do for the Resistance?"

He took his time answering, and I knew he was trying to decide what to tell me and how much. Finally, he said, "I am an inventor."

"What kinds of things do you invent?"

"I make equipment for the Resistance fighters."

"Spy weapons?"

He raised his eyebrows and then he nodded. "Yes."

I felt my stomach twitch like it was the first day of school. It was both a good and a bad feeling, but mostly a good one. "Can you show me?"

He sighed. I said, "I'm sure you don't want me here, especially because of the work you're doing, but you can trust me. I give you my word, and where I come from, sir, that's as good as a blood pact or spitting in the dirt."

Monsieur Brunet smiled at this, just barely, and then he said, "Come."

He pressed a button on the door and it swung open again, and I followed him through the kitchen and down the hall and into the living room. He walked over to the bookshelves, where there was an entire shelf of record albums. He pulled one out and I could see by the cover that it was *Mlle Lucienne Boyer—Dans la fumée*. He slipped the record out of its package and held it up, twisting it back and forth so I could see the grooves on its face.

He said, "See there?" He pointed to one of them. "It looks almost the same as the others. But when you place the needle on it, it triggers an explosion."

He slid the record back into its sleeve and returned it to its shelf. He reached for a pair of white candles in matching gold candleholders, which sat on the fireplace mantel. "These explode when the wick reaches a certain level." He set them down and waved to the basket of wood. "Fake wood with explosives inside."

From the bowl of matchboxes, he showed me a matchbox that was really a camera. He picked up the cigarettes and showed me how one of them was a pistol, and then the pipe, which was really a gun. The wine bottle was actually an explosive pump, and he showed me how it was painted with transparent green paint, which made it look like glass.

I followed him into the hallway then, where there sat, on the hall table, a pad of notepaper and an ink pen, and a red bowl filled with keys. He picked up the pen and unscrewed it and showed me how it shot darts, and then he picked up a door key, which hid microprints.

On the top shelf of the hall closet, he reached for a pair of handsome black pumps with high heels. He turned them over and snapped off the heel, which was sharp as a dagger. He reached for another pair of shoes, this one for men, and twisted off the heel, which had a hidden opening packed with bullets.

Back in the kitchen, he brought out a knife that strapped to your forearm so it could be hidden under a sleeve and a knife the size of a safety pin that could be sewn into the collar of a jacket. In the bathroom, there was face cream that could frost glass or write in invisible letters.

We stood in the doorway to the bathroom. I said, "It's everywhere. Nothing's what it seems to be."

"Hidden in plain sight."

"What about the girls? What if they get hurt?"

"They know what to touch and what not to touch." He pulled a pack of chewing gum out of his pocket. "This is the only temptation. Each stick is an explosive. I'm afraid it looks so real, they forget, and I have to carry it with me."

I said, "You should make hairpins that act as knives or poison darts. Or a perfume bottle that squirts poisoned gas with one of those sprayers." I made a squeezing motion with my hand so he would know what I was talking about.

"An atomizer."

"Or it could be sleep gas. Phosgene or chloropicrin or lewisite. Not lethal, but damaging. Maybe mustard gas, which gives you blisters and sometimes pneumonia, or nerve gas, which attacks the central nervous system." I thought about this. Back in WASP training, we'd had to crawl through every kind of gas until we could identify each one. "Or soman, which only takes two minutes to kill a person. The only thing is, you need a liquid if you're going to put it in a perfume bottle. In that case, you'd want something like CS gas, which is a type of tear gas."

He was staring at me. "We can use you in our work."

I said, "I would like to help."

"But you are waiting for your friend."

"He knows where to find me." If he comes. If they come. "I want to stop Hitler from killing people. I want to stop him from blowing up this city. And there is one more thing. I'm looking for my brother. But I need help."

"I will do what I can to ask, to see if anyone knows anything." I thought of what Delphine had said about the Resistance messengers being like a chain that linked all of France together, from forest to farm to village to city.

He reached into the pocket of Bernadette's apron, hung on a hook by the oven. He pulled out a lipstick, sleek and shiny. He twisted off its cap and showed me where the single bullet shot out, right where the colored part was. Then he capped the lipstick and handed it to me. "You are sure?"

"Yes."

"You know the dangers. . . ."

"I do." I'd actually known them for a very long time.

"We must work on your French, day and night. Bernadette, the girls—we will all help you."

I said, "I want to learn as much as I can."

He said, "In the morning then. I have somewhere to be first thing, before you are awake, but when I am home I will send you on an errand. I must go now." He brushed past me and then he turned and in the light coming through the kitchen window, I could only see half his face. "Thank you, Clementine. *Merci*."

~ 1944 ~

PART TWO

When our hearts are bound in sorrow
And it seems all help is gone. . . .

—"Sunshine in the Shadows"

SEVENTEEN

At noon on Friday, July 28, I left Monsieur Brunet's house for the Grand Hotel, which sat at 2 Rue Scribe. I walked right past Gestapo headquarters and right past the Germans who were standing outside. One of the buttons on my dress had been switched out with a tiny compass that looked just like a button, and my Rouge Ardent lipstick had been switched with the one that looked like a lipstick but was actually a gun. I was wearing the black pumps with the knife in the heel, and a black skirt and white blouse belonging to Bernadette. I wore the blue map scarf tied at my neck. I had left everything else behind except my papers, Ty's compass, the seashell, the rip cord from my parachute, and the wooden flying girl. Monsieur Brunet said I must travel light and take my things with me in case something happened to him or to me and I couldn't go back.

As I turned off our street, away from headquarters, I heard the sound of music coming from the Champs-Elysées, and there was a long line of German troops headed by a brass band, Nazi flag flying, everyone marching in rhythm. Monsieur Brunet said the Germans had been doing this every day at noon since the Occupation began. They always marched the same path—down the Champs-Elysées to the Place de la Concorde—and played the same song, "Preussens Gloria," which meant "Prussia's Glory." Monsieur Brunet said this was done to destroy the spirit and pride of the French people.

I waited for the parade to pass, and when I was able I crossed the street with the others who were waiting, some of them muttering curses at the Germans, others calling out after them and shaking their fists. The sound of the music—too loud, too bright—still rang in my ears as I let myself be carried along from street to street and sight to sight without anyone even noticing me. I felt nameless and faceless in the wave of soldiers and Frenchmen and travelers, and for once I was happy to be invisible.

While I walked, I went over all the things I had learned as a WASP that would help me be a spy: navigation, meteorology, physics, airplane mechanics and maintenance, Morse code, parachute landings. I'd also had lessons in knowing my compass, flying blind, flying the beam, dead reckoning, packing a parachute, and trusting in the instruments and in myself. I knew about fuel systems and carburetion, radio compasses, survival training, how to identify nerve gas, and how to handle emergency situations.

The walk to the hotel took thirty minutes. Monsieur Brunet had given me a French magazine to carry, and inside the magazine were two sealed envelopes. I didn't know what was inside them, but I knew they were important. I was to go into the lobby of the hotel and give the magazine with the envelopes to a man wearing a hat and carrying a cane, who would ask me how I was enjoying the weather. In exchange, the man would give me two names of key Resistance leaders— men who had infiltrated the German guard—to give Monsieur Brunet. Monsieur Brunet said it shouldn't take long, and that I would be home well before midnight, which was the city's curfew.

The Grand Hotel was exactly like its name. It sat on an entire block near the Paris Opera and the Galeries Lafayette, which was a ten-story department store. Throughout the city, trenches had been dug into the grass and flower beds of public parks, and the glass storefronts and showcase windows were covered in paper and sticky tape. Bernadette said the trenches were in case of air raids, and the paper was to keep the glass from splintering when bombs dropped. I stood outside staring at the Galeries Lafayette, forgetting who I was and what I was supposed to be doing. The hotel was just as large. Napoleon himself was responsible for having it built.

But the most beautiful building of all was the Paris Opera. There

was nothing homey or small-time about the opera, like there was about the Grand Ole Opry. The building itself was the finest-looking I'd ever seen—the same sand-white stone of the Arc de Triomphe, with seven arched doorways and a balcony of windows on the level above. On the very top was a copper dome aged green and two gold angels, like turrets, on the corners of the roof. It looked like the kind of place where magic would happen.

I stood staring at it until, somewhere, church bells chimed one. I walked inside the hotel. The lobbies were crowded with soldiers and officers. I pretended I didn't notice them, and walked past, looking for an open seat. I tried to think of myself as a swan, gliding through the rooms, not nervous, not scared, not wanting to spin my head around this way and that, looking for an empty chair or sofa.

I saw one finally that was free and that you could see from the front doors. I sat down and crossed my legs, and the high-heeled pumps shone blue-black. I opened the magazine, careful that the envelopes didn't fall out. The magazine was in French, and I ran my eyes up and down the page. I tried to time each line as if I were actually reading it, in case anyone was watching.

I sat there for five minutes. German soldiers came and went. A group of three of them stopped in front of me, lighting cigarettes and talking. I glanced up and one of them was looking at me. I caught his eye, just for a second, and smiled kind of far off and distant, as if I couldn't be bothered.

In a few moments, they walked away.

Ten minutes.

To pass the time, I made myself think of other ideas for Monsieur Brunet's inventions. A woman across from me pulled out a compact, and I imagined one that was packed with dynamite powder and another that was packed with sleeping powder.

Fifteen minutes.

An older lady strolled by, dripping with jewels, and I imagined a brooch that was actually a hand grenade or a ring that could shoot a single bullet.

Twenty minutes.

A couple entered through the lobby doors and paused as he lit a cigarette. I thought, What if the lighter wasn't a lighter at all but a blowtorch? He adjusted his tie, his jacket, and the buckle on his belt flashed. What if the belt was lined with piano wire that could be used as a garrote?

Twenty-five minutes.

I uncrossed my legs and was just getting up to go when a man walked past. He was blond and slim and wore a hat. A magazine was folded under his arm, but I couldn't see the title. He stopped in front of me to light a cigarette. I thought that instead of a blowtorch, the lighter could be a camera or a recording device. When the man saw me watching him he nodded. In French he said, "A lovely day. Are you enjoying the weather?"

He wasn't carrying a cane, but I sat back down on the edge of the chair. In French I said, "It's nice to see the sun after so much rain."

He settled himself in the chair beside mine, crossing his legs and blowing a plume of smoke at the ceiling, never looking away from my face except to glance once—for several seconds—at my legs. He said, "My flat is not far from here. It has the loveliest view of the city."

This wasn't what he was supposed to say. My hand tightened around the magazine. I said, "Pardon?"

He glanced at my legs again. "Just up the street. Only a five-minute walk. You do like exercise?" He smiled a leering sort of smile and blew another plume of smoke.

I said the only French phrase I could think of that was fit to say in public: "You must be thinking of another girl." And then I stood and headed for the door. I didn't turn to see if he was following me.

I walked so fast out onto the street that I crashed into a man. He wore a hat and leaned on a cane, and he carried a magazine—the same one I carried. He said, "*Ah, bonsoir.*"

He kissed me on each cheek, like we were old friends. He smelled of cigarettes and soap. He said in French, "How are you enjoying the weather?"

My heart was racing, but I said in French, "It is nice to see the sun after so much rain."

He said, "Isn't it? I was beginning to despair."

He took my arm and we began to stroll. He was saying the right lines, but I still thought: What if he's a double agent or an informer? What if it's a trap? What if the man with the cigarette was a spy or a rat?

There was an ice cream dealer across the street. We darted through the traffic, and the man led me over to the cart. In French he said, "Which flavor?"

I said, "Chocolate please."

He said to the man selling the ice cream, "One chocolate, one vanilla."

He bought our ice-cream cones and we stood there a moment eating them. As I put my mouth around the ice cream, feeling the coldness on my lips and on my tongue, I closed my eyes, just for a moment, and suddenly it was summer and I was on Granny's front porch, my family all around me.

I opened my eyes and looked at the Galeries Lafayette, at the Grand Hotel, at the opera. I wondered if the Germans had put explosives underneath them. I thought these were exactly the kinds of buildings that Hitler must have hated most.

Before I was finished with my ice cream, the man in the hat said, "It has been a pleasure."

I handed him the magazine and he said, "Christophe Franck and René Pascal." And then he was off, and I was still standing with my half-eaten cone.

A group of Germans came driving down the avenue, shouting at people on the street. I crossed to the opera, telling myself I would stay only till I finished eating. While I stood there, I stared up at the building.

Christophe Franck.

René Pascal.

I felt a little thrill creeping up my spine. In the end, it had gone smoothly, and it had been easy to pretend, to be someone else. All around me, the Germans and the French people walked by and no one looked at me twice. I thought: I should go to Hollywood. I could be an actress.

*   *   *

The first thing I saw when I turned on Rue de la Néva was a line of cars outside Gestapo headquarters, and officers marching from the cars into the building, dragging along three men who I could tell were American, even if they weren't in uniform. I knew it by the way they walked, the way they carried themselves, the way they stuck out their jaws as if they were daring the world. I stopped in the patch of garden and bent down, pretending to fix something on my shoe. The Germans were leading the Americans into the building, and as I glanced up I caught sight of a man with black-rimmed glasses and a square face like bread dough—the same man who arrived at headquarters every evening at six o'clock—and beside him was the German from the movie theater, the one called Fritz.

Seconds later, they were all inside, and I walked fast up the street until I was at the Brunets' front door. One of the first things Monsieur Brunet had done when I moved in was to give me a key and tell me to always lock the door, no matter what, that the only reason it would ever be left open was if something had happened to him or to them. The door was locked, and I let myself in.

Bernadette was working in the kitchen, kneading bread dough. She said, "Clementine. You're back. I've left dinner on the stove for you."

I said, "*Merci.*" I leaned against the counter and watched her. "Madame Brunet? Why do you still live here when the Gestapo is right next door? Don't you worry? Isn't it dangerous?" I thought of the weapons her husband made, of the plaster vegetables in the bowl on the table that I was pretty sure were explosives.

She said, "It is, but anywhere we would live there would be a danger. The thing about living here is that we hope it might be the last place they would suspect—after all, who would stay next door to the Germans if they had something to hide?"

The loaves of bread and the muffins were gone. I said, "Is the bread you're making now for us to eat?"

She stopped kneading, her hands resting in the dough. "My husband says you can be trusted and that you are now working for him. He told me you have worked for the Resistance." She seemed warmer than her husband but also more cautious. "The bread is made with Aunt Jemima. It is a plastic explosive that looks just like baking powder. We got it from the Americans. It is easier to transport this way behind the lines. But if anyone tastes it, it's poison."

"If my aunt Bird saw the muffins, she'd want the recipe, and she never asks for recipes."

Bernadette laughed. "They are the best-looking muffins I have ever baked. When I am trying to make them with regular baking powder, you should see how sad they are." She smiled, but her eyes were tired. "Now eat the food I set out for you. And afterward I will show you how I bake the bread."

I thought of something Barzo once told me. "You can turn anything into a deadly weapon."

"Yes. I almost forgot." She set down the dough and wiped her hands on a rag. "I have this for you." She pulled something from her pocket and handed it to me. It was a number and the name of a street.

"What is it?"

"The address of your friend at the 3341st Signal Battalion. The one you call Gossie."

EIGHTEEN

*R*ue Royale was an important-looking street, as handsome as a man in a tweed coat and hat. In the middle of it sat a restaurant called Maxim's, with elegant people tripping in and out, even in the middle of the day. When I stepped inside, I felt as if I'd fallen down the rabbit hole, just like Alice, or walked right through the looking glass. It was a world of gold and heavy red velvet, of red leather and deep brown wood rubbed to a shine, of naked women painted on the walls, and mirrors as large as barn doors. The carpet was the color of blood, the lamps on each table glowed a warm, dim gold, and the stained glass windows were etched with flowers. I caught a glimpse of myself in one of the mirrors and adjusted my hat, which was wide and black and hid my face.

When the man at the door said, "Can I help you?" in French, I said in French, "No. Thank you. I am meeting someone." There were different rooms—he called them salons—and I went from one to another and stood inside the door of each one, scanning the tables and trying not to feel out of place.

Suddenly, I saw Gossie, dressed in her WAC uniform. She hadn't spotted me yet, and as I crossed the room to her, I thought she looked exactly the same, which made me feel both angry and grateful. I wanted to run right to her and have her wrap her big arms around me and remind me who I was and why I was here. But I was busy blending into the carpet and the velvet and the stained glass, taking my time, pretending I belonged.

I stopped at her table, resting one hand on the back of the chair across from her. Gossie stared at me as if she didn't know me. After a good minute, she said, "Sweet mother of pearl, Mary Lou. What have you done to yourself?" Then she hugged me so tight I couldn't breathe or move. She pulled away and sat down, the chair creaking under her weight. She said, "What the hell happened to your hair? And your clothes? Where's your WASP uniform? You look so goddamn French."

I felt my ears go pink with pleasure, and I couldn't help it—I smiled. I said, "*Merci.*"

A waiter swept in then, black hair dripping with pomade, a mustache so neat and trim it looked painted on. In French, he asked what we wanted, and in French I told him that I would like to see a menu and have a glass of water. He said, "No need for the menu. Mademoiselle has already ordered." When he walked away, I looked across the table at Gossie. She said, "Start talking."

And so I told her all I could, sitting at a table surrounded by people who might overhear me and learn too much. I was careful to leave out the part about the team of agents and the Resistance and Delphine and Coleman's capture. I didn't mention kissing Émile, or Perry lying dead in a field or anything about a man named Swan who had to be rescued. Which meant the only thing I'd really told her was that I'd crash-landed and had somehow found my way to Paris in the back of a pig truck. I could tell her the rest later when we were alone, or not.

Even though I'd left almost everything out, she sat back, smoking a cigarette, eyes wide. When the food came—pâté de foie gras, boeuf à la mode, salad, wild strawberries, and a bottle of Nuits-Saint-Georges 1934, according to the waiter—I folded my hands in my lap and thought, I don't know how I'm going to eat that. I'd been eating nothing but boiled rutabagas and bread and cider and watered-down tea for weeks. The sight of all that fancy food, all those fancy people, turned my stomach inside out.

Gossie said, "Aren't you hungry?" She was eating with her right hand, just like an American, her fork spearing strawberries and salad and beef all at once. She took a large sip of wine and, when I asked her about her work, she started talking instead about a play she'd seen and a concert she'd been to and a dress she was able to buy on the black market in spite of the shortage of good cloth.

While we sat there, people kept stopping by the table to say hello to her—a fat man with a cane made of ivory and a stomach that spilled over his pants like a sack of potatoes; a tall gray man with a scarf tucked into his collar and a dry, polite cough; a man and woman, bright-eyed as cockatoos, their arms linked together, drinking champagne and swaying in place, just like they were dancing. Gossie seemed to know everyone. She chatted with them about the weather, the theater, the pâte de foie gras, their voices rising and falling like chickens in a yard. After the last one was gone, she said, "They're going to wonder who my French friend is."

I picked up my fork then, careful to hold it with my left hand, and I reached for a strawberry. It was ripe and red and plump. I popped it into my mouth without saying a word and held it there, letting the sweetness of it sink in.

Two young men stopped at the table and chatted with Gossie about the war in North Africa, how they were able to get out of serving and had spent most of the war at a friend's house in Barcelona where they had nothing but laughs all day long. A group of Germans walked into the salon then, eight of them, and the young men stopped talking. They watched as the Germans took two tables nearby, making the French men and women that sat at them move somewhere else, pushing the tables together, pulling off their gloves and examining the room and the people.

I finished my strawberry and took another. The young men went off on their own, prattling and laughing and slapping the backs of people they met on their way across the room. Gossie frowned at the Germans, then she looked at me, her face settling back in from somewhere away. She said, "You're awfully quiet, Mary Lou."

"Am I?"

"What's wrong with you?"

"Nothing." Everything. I knew I sounded short and cross, but how could I say to her: Everyone is letting me down and now you're doing it too. How can you sit here eating this fine food and talking to these fine, terrible people while our men are being captured or shot dead in fields?

I said, "How is Clinton Farnham?" Clinton Farnham was Gossie's fiancé, who was serving in the navy.

"That rat. He's fine, as far as I know. I send him letters but I don't know that he gets them. It's been a long time since I've heard anything." She lit a cigarette.

"How long?"

"Four weeks and two days and, oh"—she checked her wristwatch, a slim gold band—"four hours and twenty-three minutes."

I said, "You'll hear from him. He's probably fighting or out of reach." Or off doing a mission without you, when all you wanted was to come along and help, and now he's just gone and left you on your own in a strange city where you don't even speak the language.

"Or dead." She stubbed out her cigarette and lit another. "What about you, Mary Lou? Have you heard from your Indian? Do you know where they shipped him off to?"

"No."

She leaned forward. "Listen. When real love comes, you'll know it and it'll happen when you least expect it. It may be Butch Dawkins or it may be someone else. But it will happen. There's no way it won't happen for you."

"Why do you say that?" My mind went to Émile and this made me mad. It was a week now since I'd seen him and the others.

"Because you're the sort that was born for true love and storybooks." She sat back. "In the meantime, here we are. Not exactly a time for storybooks. Maybe I'll see Clint again, maybe I won't. But for now I'm alive and I'm here and I intend to make the most of it, every goddamn moment."

Before I could ask her what she meant by this she said, "Christ. I can't get over how bloody French you look." She tapped her lips with her little finger, the one on the hand holding the cigarette. She said, "Have you taken up smoking?"

"Of course not." I'd only smoked once in my life, back when Johnny Clay and I were little, just after Mama died, and had gotten hold of some rabbit tobacco. It made me sicker than a dog.

She blew a perfect ring of smoke. "It's awfully French." She smiled at me, stubbed the cigarette out, and said, "Do you want any more to eat? You barely had a thing."

I said, "I'm good."

"Dessert?"

"No thanks."

"Suit yourself." Gossie craned her head around, looking for the waiter. One of the Germans nodded at her and she nodded back as if she knew him. When the waiter walked over, she asked for the check. Then we sat and smiled at each other, but it was the kind of smile you give a stranger or someone you're only being nice to until you can make your excuses and get away.

The waiter with the mustache brought the check, and from a red change purse, Gossie counted out coins and two paper bills and handed these to him. "I'd like to take the rest of this home with me." She nodded at the table, at all the food that still sat there. As the waiter took the plates away, I held out money to her and she waved it aside. She said, "Your money's no good here, Mary Lou."

In the street outside, Gossie said, "Come back to my aunt's flat with me and have some tea or worse. We can really talk there." She laughed. "Tell me you're still not drinking."

I said, "Not really." All I wanted was to go back to Monsieur Brunet's and wait for Émile and the others. What if they came while I was away? Would they leave a message? Would they come to find me? Would they wait for me there?

Three young women tripped out onto the sidewalk in front of us, laughing. One of them said, "Beryl Goss. Look at you in that sweet little uniform. Aren't you the cutest thing?" They were American. They air-kissed her on each cheek, first one girl then the next and then the next. They chattered on about Gossie's daddy and brothers, their daddies, Paris, Maxim's, and then they glided down the sidewalk like a parade of geese.

Gossie said to me, "Reporters. Coming over here to find an adventure, to see Paris, and to hell with the battlefield or anyone who might actually be doing something to win this war." She glared after them and suddenly she looked and sounded like her old self.

She turned back to me. "Are you coming?"

"Yes," I said.

NINETEEN

Gossie's aunt lived across the River Seine in Montparnasse, which Gossie said was also known as the Latin Quarter, or just the Quarter. She said this was where the writers Ernest Hemingway and Gertrude Stein and F. Scott Fitzgerald had spent their time in the 1920s, back when they were living and writing in Paris. I thought this made sense because the air was different in the Quarter, rich and colorful like it had spices in it, and it was the first time since leaving the States that I'd felt the old itch to write a song. Except for the Palais du Luxembourg, which rose up in the midst of it, a kind of elegant mountain, the buildings were smaller and not as grand, and the streets were narrow and twisting instead of broad. The people seemed less grand too.

Gossie's aunt owned a shop that was part bookstore, part bakery, part tavern. The building came racing to a point, just four feet wide, at the corner of two streets, so that it looked like a giant wedge of cheese, and the door to Breedlove's was cut into that same point. Up above it were three stories of windows and black iron balconies. Two little tables and two sets of chairs sat out front, and these were filled with German officers, eating and drinking. They raised their cups to us as we walked past.

Inside, the shop was open and bright, with two more tables and four more chairs, a counter with stools, and, in back of the counter, another counter lined with bottles. Bookcases pressed up against the walls, floor to ceiling, and stacks of books sat on the floor. A young boy sat on one of them, reading a book in French.

A woman worked behind the counter, cutting a loaf of bread for a customer, another boy, who looked French and not German. The woman had dark hair and fat red cheeks like apples. She said, *"Bonjour."*

Gossie said, *"Bonjour*, Sylvie, is my aunt home?" Her eyes flickered to the window, where we could see the Germans drinking their wine. They flickered over to the boy, who didn't look up. *"Bonjour*, Philippe," she said to him. He nodded his head.

Sylvie said, "She's upstairs."

Beyond the glass case was a door, and Gossie opened this and I followed her inside. Bookcases stood on three walls. She shut the door tight behind us and plucked a book out of the middle shelf. I watched as she pressed a button in the wood. Another door swung open, which led into a small room. Rising up out of the middle of it, like a ship's hatch, was a narrow set of stairs with no railing. We climbed up these until we were standing in a bright and airy room, which led to another room, and another. Tall windows, shaped like rectangles, let the light in. The air smelled like bread baking, wafting up from down below.

Gossie called out, "Cleo!" She said to me, "She usually spends the summer in the country or by the sea, but with the trains and roads out of the city cut or blocked, she's staying here." She stood in the middle of the room a kind of entryway with a window seat stuffed with pillows and more bookcases and a giant painting of a naked man with legs like a goat.

"How was lunch?" A woman's voice came singing through the rooms, even before she got to us.

"Awful. Maxim's is overpriced and overstuffed, and so are the folks who eat there." Gossie unpinned her hat and slid off her shoes, kicking them into a corner by the window seat. She waved at me to do the same. "Cleo's nutty when it comes to her floors."

I looked at the floors, which were a beautiful, shiny wood, the color of cherries. And then I looked at Gossie and raised one eyebrow, which was a look I always gave Johnny Clay. She let out a bark of a laugh and said, "You should see your face. Oh, Mary Lou. Did you believe that act?"

She shook her cigarettes and lighter out of her purse and threw the purse onto the window seat. She inhaled, closing her eyes, and then held her hand out to me. It was shaking. "Do you see how that got to me? Sitting there like that, listening to those wags carry on as if they aren't afraid, as if they don't go home and lie awake at night, scared to death but too proud to show it?" She took another drag on the cigarette and blew out the smoke, making rings. "Why do you think they go to Maxim's during the day and get so stinking drunk? Because they can't bear to live with themselves."

I said, "But why . . . ?"

"Because if I don't go and carouse and make a show of it, they'll say something's wrong, that fun-loving old Beryl Goss, rich girl, isn't herself these days, that, mark my words, she's up to something."

A woman marched into the room with all the sureness of a bull. She was tall and redheaded and had broad shoulders and a narrow waist and bosoms as big as Sweet Fern's. She was the kind of woman Johnny Clay and the Gordon boys back home would have whistled at, even if she was old enough to be their mother, maybe even older than that. She wore a long sweater that looked more like a robe, with all the colors of a peacock, and gold slippers that showed her toenails, which were painted red. The sweater swirled around her ankles as she walked past us to the window seat and glanced outside, her entire face—eyebrows, mouth, eyes—seeming to gather together like a bouquet as she drew it all in and sighed. "They've been sitting out there for two hours." Then she looked me up and down, from top to bottom, and held out her hand. She said, "Cleopatra Mayhew Breedlove. For God's sake call me Cleo."

I shook her hand, which was firm and strong as a man's even if it wasn't any bigger than mine. I almost said: My name is Clementine Roux. I was married to a Frenchman who was killed in the war, and now I live here.

But before I could speak a word, Gossie said, "This is Mary Lou from Nashville, the pilot I told you about, the one I found on the street way back when, looking like an urchin. My very best friend."

In that moment, with those words, everything I'd lived through since I last saw her in Prestwick, Scotland, came rushing up at me. I said, "I think I need to sit down."

Gossie said to her aunt, "I told her to eat, but she didn't touch her lunch." She handed Cleo the food box.

Cleo said, "Come with me."

I sat on a pillow as big as a chair, my hat on my lap, and ate an entire plate of strawberries and a slice of thick bread covered in butter. While I ate, I didn't say one word because I was too busy staring at the framed pictures on the walls—twenty or so on the wall across from me, thirty on the wall behind. They were mostly paintings of landscapes and people. A piano, its top covered in a bright orange-and-green cloth, sat in one corner. A potted palm in another. On the narrowest wall, the one above the street corner, there was a single window and the head of a stuffed buffalo.

While I ate and looked around, Gossie and her aunt made small talk about the menu at Maxim's and who we'd seen, and Gossie told me about her work. She said the office was inside a former German blockhouse, with concrete walls ten feet thick. There were eighty-two teletype machines and thirteen radio circuits, and she sat at the cable desk and also answered the telephones, and between them all, the WAC traded about a thousand messages a day with the War Department. She said some fifty thousand messages were handled each week, and that around ten to fifteen photographs were radioed to the War Department every twenty-four hours.

Fifteen minutes later, the Germans left, sauntering off down the street, still wiping their mouths from their meal. We watched them from the window, and then Gossie said to her aunt, "All clear." When Cleo frowned at me, Gossie said, "You can trust Mary Lou."

Cleo stood up from her seat across from me and said, "Fine. Leave the curtains, though. We don't want anyone to look up and wonder why we've shut them before dark." She walked off, shoulders and back straight as a general's, hips swaying like a metronome, peacock robe swirling around her ankles.

I set my plate down and said, "Your aunt is wonderful."

"She's the only one of my family I can stand. My mother's aunt, so more of a great-aunt, actually. She's the black sheep, like me."

I heard footsteps, more than one set, and Cleo returned with three young men. They stood like deer, shy and awkward, until Gossie said, "For heaven's sake, sit down right now. Wait till you see what I brought you."

They moved together in a bunch to the settee and sat, all at the same time. I would have thought they were triplets except that they didn't look one bit alike. One had curly black hair and a big, looping smile, another was fair and balding and serious, and the other was tall and brown-headed and wore glasses.

Gossie waded off toward the kitchen, bare feet slapping on the wood floors. Cleo said, "Mary Lou, meet George, Nathan, and Daniel." I didn't bother telling her or them that my name wasn't Mary Lou.

"Bone joor," George said. He grinned his looping grin.

I sat up. "You're American."

Cleo said, "They all are."

"What are they doing here?" I asked this as if they weren't even sitting there, as if they couldn't answer for themselves.

Cleo said, "We're getting them home." And then she told me about her work with the Freedom Line, which was the escape line that started in Brussels and ran all the way through Paris to San Sebastián in Spain to Gibraltar. She said the trick was to reach the downed fliers before the Germans did, that the Germans sent out patrols of men and dogs to search for any Allied airman who was shot down. Food was already hard to find, and they had to rely on the black market and forged ration tickets to feed the men. The airmen stayed with them for two or three days, which was how much time was needed to arrange for train tickets and guides to take them to the Spanish border, where native mountain guides would lead them over the Pyrenees and into Spain.

There was one train that traveled out of the city, and it only went as far as thirty of the 120 kilometers to the region where the Maquis waited to meet the airmen and guide them on their way. The airmen were given civilian clothes and new shoes because so many of the men had worn theirs out, and they were given false papers and were moved from house to house along the line. They had to make their way from one safe house, one village or city to another until they reached the Spanish border, where the Germans patrolled the mountain passes with hunting dogs. A French man or woman was sent with them as a guide.

Cleo said sometimes the line got broken by Germans posing as Allied pilots. These men had gone to British or American schools before the war so they could speak perfect English. When a spy was discovered in the Freedom Line, they were turned over to the other Resistance fighters and tortured or shot.

Gossie came back with three plates, balanced in her arms. She set them down in front of the men, and then she went off again and came back in a moment with a bottle of half-finished wine and four glasses. She sat on the edge of her chair, smoking cigarette after cigarette and drinking. She chimed in now and then as her aunt was talking, saying the work she was doing for the WAC was just a cover. The real work was helping her aunt on the Freedom Line.

I said, "Are there a lot of you?"

Cleo said, "On the line?" She turned her gaze on the three men. The men wiped their mouths and shoved their plates away, sitting back, wrists dangling over knees, listening. I'd never seen anyone eat that fast unless they were in a pie-eating contest. She said, "Hundreds. Maybe more. We smuggle Jews too, when we can. But there are thousands of others working for the Resistance. Railroad workers make up the Iron Network. They send shipments to the wrong place and cause derailments. They destroy sections of track and blow up bridges. There's a line of postal workers that intercepts important German military communications, and telephone workers who sabotage phone lines."

Gossie said, "We have signals for the others we work with and for the couriers who take messages between us. If the curtains are open on all sides, that means the coast is clear, come on in. If the curtain above the store is closed—just that one—it means keep away."

I said, "Johnny Clay. Have you—has anyone on the line—have you heard anything?"

"No, honey. I've been keeping my eyes and ears out for him." She said to the pilots, "Her brother's gone missing. Paratrooper with the 101st. They lost track of him long before D-day." She took my hand. "Still nothing?"

"No. I feel like I don't know what else to do, but I also feel like I'm not doing anything."

Gossie said to her aunt, "The best thing to do is put the word out as far and wide as we can." Cleo nodded. "We make sure everyone in the Resistance knows, from here to Versailles."

The talk wandered off then, to Paris and the movies and America. The pilot named Daniel had a wife and two babies back home and every now and then he would tell us a story and sigh as if there were more he wasn't telling and this was the only way he could say it. It felt so good to be sitting there with Gossie and her aunt and these three young Americans, pilots like me, that I lost track of time. Somewhere a clock struck six, and I said, "I should be going."

Gossie said, "You should move in here with us, Mary Lou. We've got plenty of room, don't we, Cleo? Even with all these extra men around." She winked at the pilots.

Cleo said, "You absolutely should."

I said, "I can't." I didn't tell them I was waiting. Every day, waiting. If I moved in with them, Émile and the others might never find me once they came back. If they came back.

The pilot called George stood up and put on a record and suddenly there was music, bright and fast. "Not too loud," Cleo said.

Gossie walked to the window. She said, "All clear."

George said, "Do you know the Big Apple?" For some reason, a homesick feeling had ahold of my throat and my chest. "It's the latest thing. Just follow me." He and the other boys pushed aside the furniture. He rolled up his sleeves and held out his hands, and I placed mine in his. He said, "Ready?"

Before I knew it, he was twirling me and spinning me all over the apartment. The other boys joined in, and then Gossie and Cleo started dancing too. We jumped and dipped and clapped and swayed, and someone said the dance came from Harlem, New York, and that the Negroes had started it. For that one song, I forgot about everything and danced.

Gossie's bedroom had a table with a chair in front of it, but it wasn't a desk. She called it a vanity table, and spread on top of it, like a picnic, were lipsticks and powders and perfumes. I sat on the chair and stared into the mirror that hung above the vanity, so you could see yourself if you were sitting down. Gossie said, "I've been wanting to do this since I saw you walk into Maxim's." And she pulled out a brush and took it to my head, curling this piece of hair, smoothing that one, until I didn't look so dull and dreary, but actually kind of smart, like someone who could eat at Maxim's even if she didn't want to.

Gossie said, "Christ, that's better. The day you start looking like a plain Jane is the day I marry Hitler." Then she picked through the lipsticks, tossing them aside till they lay in a pile. Finally she plucked one out and held it up like she was the Statue of Liberty and this was her torch. She said, "It'll be easier if you do it," and she handed the lipstick to me.

I turned to the mirror and painted the color on my lips. It made me think of the heavy roses on the wallpaper at Monsieur Brunet's house and blood seeping across a field. There was nothing about it that blended in or made me invisible, and because of this I did two coats.

Gossie said, "Yes. Take it, it's yours. It looks a hell of a lot better on you."

I turned it over to read the bottom. Révolution Rouge. Behind me Gossie sank down onto her bed, crossing one leg over the other and swinging it back and forth. She propped herself up on her hands, arms back behind her, and said, "Now start talking." She fixed her eye on me in the mirror.

I said, "What do you mean?" I pretended to fuss with my hair, my scarf—Perry's map scarf—the lipsticks, picking them up and reading the bottoms, then standing them back up again.

She said, "I'm not stupid and I'm certainly not blind. You're up to something, Mary Lou. Something secret, and you're not leaving here till I know what it is." When I didn't say anything she said, "It takes one to know one. I'm playing a role right now, a kind of cover, so that no one will know what kind of work I'm really doing. I think you're doing the same."

I turned around in my chair and looked at her. There were about ten thousand things I wanted to say, but I didn't know if I should say any of them. I opened my mouth and closed it, and then I opened it again and closed it again.

She said, "Mary Lou, you can trust me." She leaned forward, tucking her feet up under her bottom. Her bobbed hair waved toward her face and she shook it aside. She said, "Go."

I thought: I can be Velva Jean here. I can be Mary Lou. This is the only place I can be myself, but out there I'm someone else. I heard Émile's voice and Delphine's—where was she now?—telling me it was all or nothing, there was no such thing as halves, that I needed to become another person and stick with that, memorize it, live it.

I said, "Actually it's not Mary Lou. It's Clementine. Clementine Roux. My husband was French but was killed at the start of the war. I couldn't go home, so I stayed. I eat only with my left hand. I know not to wait more than twenty minutes for my contact. I never sleep anywhere that doesn't have at least two exits. I know the difference between a Sten gun and a forty-five, and I can shoot both. The top button of my dress is really a compass. The heel of my shoe is really a knife. My lipstick can fire one shot at close range." I recited every single thing I'd been told about my cover, as if I were reciting a lesson out of a schoolbook. "I'll go back after the war is over because there's nothing here for me now. My husband—he was a pilot—he took that with him when he died." Before I knew it, I was crying, the silent kind, tears running one by one down my cheeks. "I am a singer and a spy. I am a weapon of war." I'm afraid I am in love with a Frenchman who left me here.

And then I said the entire thing over, as best I could, in French.

I'd never known Gossie to go speechless, but for one whole minute she sat staring at me, her mouth open so wide I could see her fillings. After that minute was up, she snapped it closed and said, "I'll be damned."

TWENTY

$\mathcal{E}$ach night, I practiced my French with Monsieur Brunet, and each morning I practiced with Bernadette and the girls. I could still understand more than I could speak, but I was getting better and my accent was improving. When I wasn't practicing, I delivered messages for Monsieur Brunet and helped Gossie and her aunt take care of the airmen before they were smuggled out of Paris. The three pilots I'd met were gone now, on their way to Spain with a French-speaking guide, and five new airmen had moved into Cleo's apartment above the bookstore.

It was August already—August 2, Granny's birthday. I tried not to think about my family celebrating back home on Fair Mountain as I went to the market for Cleo. She bought most of their food on the black market, but once a week she shopped at an open market on the Left Bank, which the Germans let the public use on Wednesdays. There you could trade in your stamps to buy two eggs, two ounces of margarine, three ounces of cooking oil, and a share of meat that was smaller than a subway ticket. Cleo had a friend at one of the stands who put aside all the food that the Germans didn't want—bread and vegetables that were too old and stale, and maybe a rabbit or a chicken that was too scrawny. The Allies were cutting off northern routes in France, which meant food was even harder to come by. The Germans were using up as much of what they could find in the markets and the restaurants, and the people of Paris were hungry.

The Luxembourg Gardens had been taken over by the Luftwaffe, which was the German air force, with cannons and machine guns and tanks sitting smack in the middle of the flower beds and the pathways and the little pond that was there. The gardens weren't far from Cleo's apartment, and around eleven o'clock each morning, the German tanks rolled out of the gates and on down Boulevard Saint-Michel, shooting at random at the people walking by.

I did my best to stay in the middle of the crowd, to walk a zigzag so that I would make a harder target, to keep my eyes and ears open for the patrols. Men and women fighting for the Resistance were setting up roadblocks throughout the city, which made it difficult for the Germans to drive in their cars and trucks and tanks. The barricades were made of piled-up stoves, wardrobes, dustbins, and other furniture, and members of the Resistance sat behind them wearing armbands and pointing their weapons at the Germans. Cleo said that of the twenty thousand Resistance fighters in Paris, not even half were armed. The ones who weren't cut communication lines, pierced the tires of German vehicles, destroyed road signs, and bombed gasoline depots and railroads.

The day was fair and warm, and on the way back to Cleo's I walked through the street as gingerly as a cat so as not to trip because my arms were full of groceries, as many as I could buy with the ration stamps real and counterfeit—in addition to the vegetables her friend had given me.

I was three blocks away from her apartment when a man ran into me, running down the street after someone. I lost hold of the bag, and it dropped onto the sidewalk, margarine and cooking oil and bread rolling in all directions. I bent down and, fast as I could, tried to fetch everything. I didn't look up because I was afraid of the police stopping me and seeing what I'd bought and how much of it there was.

A boy walked by and handed me the margarine. A group of women stepped around me, crushing one of the eggs and kicking two of the potatoes into the street. I couldn't hear the traffic rushing by or the people talking around me because my heart was beating so loud in my ears.

A hand reached down and held out the loaf of bread. It was a large hand, with long fingers and round, clean nails. For one minute, I let myself think that it belonged to Émile or Barzo or Ray. I was always looking for them in the faces of men on the street. Every day, I read the newspaper and sat by the radio, waiting for reports of a raid on Fresnes prison, where I knew they must be headed.

I looked up and it was the German from the movie theater. He kneeled beside me and gathered the last of the groceries, handing them to me one by one.

He said, "Clementine." I didn't say a word, just put the vegetables, the oil, the bread into the bag. He said, "I am Fritz. Remember? We saw the play."

He was talking in English, but I replied in French, "Of course, thank you for your help."

He smiled. His eyes moved to the bag. He said in English, "You are cooking a big meal. An American Thanksgiving?"

I said in French, "Oh no. It's for my friends. One of them is sick and she can't shop for herself, so I'm helping her."

He said, "You are a good friend."

"I try to be." I thought, Go away, go away, go away.

He said, "I would like to take you for coffee sometime."

I wondered if I could be shot right here on the street for saying no. I said, "I'm sorry." I hoped it was enough. I hoped he thought I was missing my dead husband, that this was why I couldn't make a date with him. I thought, Please don't ask me again.

He said, "It is a no then?"

"No." I held my hand out. I said, "Thank you again."

"Fritz," he said.

"Fritz."

He took my hand. I hoped he couldn't feel it shaking. I wondered why he didn't ask to come with me to meet these friends of mine, why he didn't take me into headquarters right now for questioning. He held on to my hand and looked down at me without blinking, the smile fixed on his face, and I could tell he was reading me, trying to see what was there behind my own smile. I concentrated on thinking of the most innocent things—Ruby Poole's baby, Russell, or the stained glass window of the Virgin Mary in the Little White Church back home. I thought if I could think of something like this he would see it in my face and let me go.

I said, *"Bonsoir,* Fritz. *Merci."*

"Bonsoir, Clementine."

TWENTY-ONE

On August 5, I sat in the lobby of the Grand Hotel, across from the opera, a handkerchief in my hand. It was thin as a razor and made of fabric you could eat if you had to. Monsieur Brunet said it would dissolve on the tongue in seconds. I knew that the handkerchief contained a grid for decoding messages, and that whatever I did, I had to make sure it didn't fall into the wrong hands. If anything about the exchange seemed off, I was supposed to get out of there and swallow the handkerchief and make sure I wasn't followed.

My contact was an older man with a newspaper under his right arm and a blue beret. The man seemed nervous, watching left and right over his shoulder. He sneezed and I offered him the handkerchief, and he walked off without saying good-bye.

I waited three minutes before leaving, and out on the street I saw two Germans in uniform step from behind a streetlight and stop the man in the beret on the sidewalk. I started walking at once in the other direction, fast as I could. I didn't look back, but I kept imagining the Germans chasing me down and dragging me off, the way they'd done with Coleman.

Just in case they were following me, I took a zigzag route back to Monsieur Brunet's house. When I reached Rue de la Néva, I walked past the house, down to the corner, and stepped into a dress shop. Then I went next door to the little store where they sold makeup and jewelry, and then the one next door to that, which was a bakery.

After an hour or so, I stepped out of the shops and back onto the street, which was empty except for a man and two children, walking away from me. The little girl had a yellow balloon, and I watched as it bobbed in the air above their heads, swaying when a breeze blew past, tugging at its string.

I walked back to Monsieur Brunet's house, and there was Bernadette standing in the doorway to the living room, as if she'd been watching the door. She said, "Clementine, are you all right?"

I said, "Yes. Is Monsieur Brunet at home?"

"Not yet," she said. "He went out." She was worrying her hands, fingers clasped, turning them inside out and outside in. She had been worrying since last night, when we heard the news that Warsaw was burning after the people there rose up against the Germans. She said, "So much noise next door. They have been shooting their guns in the back garden and walking up and down the street knocking at the doors."

I said, "Do you think they suspect?" I thought of the man with the newspaper and the beret, led away by the Germans—did he have time to swallow the handkerchief? I thought of George with the looping grin, and Daniel with the wife and two babies, and the other pilots arriving in Nesles, trying to get to Spain.

"Je ne sais pas." I don't know.

That evening, Cleo hosted a party downstairs in the bookstore. The latest group of pilots had left that morning, and so the place was free of airmen, at least for now. The guests would be people Cleo had known for years. She said they were freethinkers and artists, but some had become Nazi sympathizers to make it easier on themselves. She had invited some of the German officers too, because she needed to do whatever she could to keep them from suspecting her and her work on the Freedom Line.

I stayed to help get ready for the party. As we swept and dusted and rearranged the stacks of books I said to Gossie, "How can the Germans go to parties with these people, eating their food, drinking their wine, when they must know we hate them?" The day before, the Germans had bombed and destroyed five of the six bridges in Florence,

Italy—including one designed by Michelangelo—before they ran away from the Allies.

She said, "These parties are a kind of truce, don't you know."

We set up the food on a table in front of the glass counter—beef and potatoes and salad and wine, which I knew must have cost Cleo a pretty penny on the black market. People would eat standing up and there would be a man strolling through the shop playing violin.

When it was time for the party, I went upstairs and shut the door tight and sat on the settee and ate alone. I couldn't risk being noticed by the Germans. When I was done eating, I leaned my head against the pillows and listened to the voices below, rising and falling. I had told Bernadette that there was a party at a friend's, that I might stay the night. I didn't want to be out after dark and risk being caught past curfew, and I didn't want the Brunets to worry.

I tried to read, but I kept hearing the voices and the music. Finally, I put the book aside and closed my eyes. An hour or so later, I heard the sound of footsteps in the hall. Before I could hide myself, a woman, plain and small, appeared in the doorway. She was dressed all in black. She said, "*Bonsoir.*"

"*Bonsoir.*"

The woman was small but sturdy, with short, dark hair brushed back from her face and pinned into a bun, and round spectacles like half dollars. I guessed she was near fifty years old.

In French she said, "I hope I didn't startle you. I am a friend of Cleo's. I do not like parties and I do not care for Germans. May I?" She waved at a chair.

"Of course."

I sat up straight and she perched on the edge of the chair, lighting a cigarette. She looked around the room, her eyes lingering on the different paintings hung on the walls.

In English she said, "You know Hitler fancies himself an artist." Her accent was thick but her English was perfect. "He applied to the Academy of Fine Arts in Vienna, but was rejected. The Jews were the ones who turned him down. He hates modern art because he thinks it's impure and degenerate. After he took power, he passed a law which said degenerate artists were not allowed to paint." I thought about Harley telling me I couldn't sing anymore, when singing was all I wanted to do.

She said, "Now he destroys the art he hates and steals the art he loves." Then she told me about how they had moved the *Mona Lisa* from the Louvre before Hitler made his trip to Paris in 1940, how the painting rode in an ambulance with the curator. She said, "There is a song that says a long, long time after the poets have disappeared, their music will live in the streets. At times such as this, it becomes more important for art to survive. If it can outlast a war, it means that beauty can triumph over horror, that the stories in these paintings and sculptures live on, and that life can be created from them again."

I tried to memorize the words as she was saying them because they were important and beautiful and true. She leaned forward toward the coffee table and stubbed her cigarette out in the ashtray. She stood and smoothed her skirt and then shook my hand. In French she said, "I must get back before I am missed. Thank you for letting me interrupt your evening."

Two hours later, the voices began to quiet, and twenty minutes after that, Gossie and Cleo came upstairs and sat down. They looked tired and spent. Cleo was holding a wineglass. She drank it down and said, "Entertaining like this is damn hard work."

I asked Cleo about her friend, the woman with the spectacles. I couldn't get her words out of my head: *At times such as this, it becomes more important for art to survive.*

Cleo said, "Her name is Rose Valland. She works at the Jeu de Paume museum. She is also a captain in the French military. The Nazis are looting all the museums and private art collections in France and the Jeu de Paume is where they are sending it all. More than twenty thousand pieces of art stacked in corners and up against walls so that the Germans can have their choice of what they want. Rose is keeping track of it all—where the pieces are being sent, who they are going to. They don't know she speaks German, and so she goes home at night and writes down everything she remembers. She has a mind like an elephant." But she looks like a mouse, I thought. She blends in. "If pieces of art go out in a shipment by train, she lets the Resistance know so that they won't accidentally blow up the line."

"What will happen to her if she's caught?" I thought about how, after the war was over, millions of lives would be lost but these paintings would still be here.

"She will be shot."

I said, "She's very brave. Just like you."

Cleo said, "There are other women like her, equally as brave. There is a woman who works at night all alone, poisoning the German food supplies that pass by in freight cars on the railroads in France, and another who gathers information about the movements of Nazi troops and submarines and transmits them to Britain."

Rose Valland was just one person, just as Cleo Breedlove was one person, and so was the woman who poisoned the food supplies, and the one who reported information about the German troops, and so was Delphine Babin and so was Gossie and so was I. But when it came down to it, I thought we were all fighting together.

Cleo said, "In war, you do what needs to be done."

TWENTY-TWO

By Sunday, August 6, the day after the party, the BBC reported that the Allies had captured the Belgian towns of Namur and Charleroi, as well as Mortain, France. Turkey had cut off commercial and diplomatic relations with Germany. South African troops had reached the outskirts of Florence, Italy. United States naval carriers had bombed the Japanese in Iwo Jima and Chichi Jima. And the Allied forces had cut off the Breton peninsula. Every day, there were more rumors that the Liberation was almost here, and this seemed to make the Germans even more determined to round up all of the Jews and members of the Resistance they could capture and send them to prison or to the camps.

It was just after six thirty in the evening when I started back to Monsieur Brunet's from Cleo's. I left later than I meant to, and this made me walk faster and look over my shoulder again and again.

It must have been eight o'clock by the time I turned onto Rue de la Néva and counted the steps—twenty-five—past Gestapo headquarters and up the stairs and into the house, which sat like something forgotten. The door creaked open as if it had been waiting for a very long time, as if we hadn't all been going in and out, in and out, this week. It was unlocked, and this was how I knew that Monsieur Brunet and his family were gone.

I stood on the step, trying to decide whether to go inside. I'd just decided to turn and walk away, fast as I could, when a group of Nazi officers came ambling up the street. I pushed the door open and then shut it again behind me. The house was quiet, but not just quiet—there was nothing alive in it. I knew what this felt like because of the still, sad way Mama's house had felt after she died. It was as if the air was let out of it. But it was also the feeling of the air being heavy, as if it had nothing to do but settle in on itself and grow even heavier because no one was there to breathe it. My eyes went to the table in the entryway, just by the parlor, where there would have been a message if someone had left one. The table was as blank as the house.

Everything I owned was in my bag, the one Delphine had given me, the one that was slung over my shoulder right now. I knew from Émile and his team and from Monsieur Brunet that you always left a room as if you might never go back to it, just in case something happened. My mind spun, trying to remember if I'd left anything behind in my room upstairs, anything at all, even a hairpin or a lipstick. I stood in the hallway and went over the entire room in my mind.

Instead of going back out the front door, where the Gestapo might see me, I walked through the hallway on tiptoe, trying not to make a sound, and through the kitchen to Monsieur Brunet's office. The door hung open, and papers, maps, books were scattered across the desk and the floor, as if someone had come in and turned it upside down. I sorted through his things to see if there was anything I should take, anything that needed hiding from the Germans.

Then I started moving through the downstairs, putting things into my bag because you never knew—I might need them. Candles, a lump of coal, buttons with hidden compartments, a matchbox camera, cigarette pistols, and, from the bathroom, a box of bobby pins that were actually knives, just like I'd suggested. Things had been tossed here and there—I found the pack of chewing gum under the hall table—searched and gone through, but all his inventions were thrown aside because the Germans hadn't figured them out.

As I closed up my bag, I saw something shiny on the floor beneath the sink. I dropped to my knees and wrapped my hand around it, whatever it was. I pulled it out and there in my palm was the sweetest perfume bottle, made of violet-colored glass, with an atomizer attached to the top of it. I held the bottle to my nose. CS gas.

Then I backed out of the room, leaving the office door open just as I'd found it, and walked through the kitchen to the back door. There were vegetables on the counter, beside the pot Bernadette used on the fire. Radishes and carrots were stacked in a messy pile, the dirt still covering them. I paused, hand on the knob, and without moving the curtain, peered through a corner of the window, toward the Gestapo headquarters. I looked and I listened, and I couldn't see or hear anything.

Suddenly I stiffened. Something had moved behind me. I looked at my hand on the doorknob, and I thought: Turn it. Just go. The sound had come from the front hall.

A voice said, *"Ich weiß, Sie sind es."*

I turned the doorknob, but it wouldn't budge. I turned it again. Nothing. Then I saw the keyhole and remembered that you had to unlock it from the inside. The key. Where was the key?

There were footsteps in the hallway. The voice said, *"Bonsoir?* Hello? You cannot run."

I searched the ledge above the doorframe, the mat on the floor, the counter nearby, the windowsill. A potted plant sat on the counter, beside the sink. I'd seen Bernadette reach inside this before. I felt in the dirt, in the space between the plant and the pot. I lifted the plant so that it came out, dirt and all, and at the bottom I saw the thin gold key. I was just sliding it into the keyhole when a voice behind me said, "You cannot run."

He lunged for me with his bare hands, and I tried to push him away. He wrapped his hands around my throat and began to squeeze. I tried to kick him, but he moved his lower body away and then he slammed me up against the door. The breath went out of me so that it felt like I was cut off from my lungs and could only breathe from the throat upward. I gasped, and this only made him squeeze harder. I thought: Breathe. Don't panic. Don't black out. I closed my eyes, so he would think I was about to swoon, and at the same time I reached into my bag and felt around, pulling out the first thing I could grab.

I lifted the perfume bottle and sprayed it into his face. He staggered back, coughing violently, eyes closed, and I covered my mouth and nose with a dish rag so that I wouldn't breathe the mist in myself. The thing about most tear gas was that the immediate effects of it wore off in minutes, but CS gas was more toxic. The man fell to the floor, the skin of his face and hands as red as if he'd burned them. He wheezed like a bellows and tried to grab at me, even though he couldn't see where I was.

From a hook on the wall, I grabbed Bernadette's apron and ripped it in two. I tied his feet and his hands in a constrictor knot, which I'd learned from Johnny Clay. It was the tightest knot you could tie. If you did it right, the only way to break it was to cut it with a knife.

Then I turned the key in the lock and threw the door open. I stepped onto the landing, which was covered on all sides, with a door that led to the left, away from the Gestapo and down an alley that ran behind. I slipped through the yard and into the alley and, without even looking to see if anyone was watching me, I started running away from the Brunets', away from the Germans. I ran until I got to the Arc de Triomphe, and then I went down into the ground to see if the Metro was working, but the station was as shut up and quiet as the house had been.

I came back up, this time glancing about me to see if anyone might be following me. When I didn't see anybody who looked strange or German or official, I began walking right down the Champs-Elysées. The streets were quiet. Everyone seemed to be inside, off the sidewalks, out of the cafés. What time was it?

I walked fast as I could, as if I were late for a dinner date, all the way past the end of the Champs-Elysées, right past the Jeu de Paume and the Louvre. I kept one eye on the Eiffel Tower. When the Champs-Elysées ran out, I walked along the Seine. The sky was dark now and the streets were thinning faster as people disappeared into doorways and behind gates, doors slamming shut behind them. I slipped off my shoes because they were too heavy. They would make noise on the pavement.

My heart sped up and so did my feet. I didn't want to be caught in the streets after dark or after curfew. But which way was Cleo Breedlove's apartment? Was I still too west of it? Was I east enough yet? I couldn't get my bearings or seem to remember the way. As soon as I could, I crossed the Seine on one of the bridges that linked the Right Bank of Paris with the Left Bank. The part of my brain that was still ten years old said, "Haints can't cross over running water," which was something I'd learned from Granny. This made me feel better, as if the Germans were ghosts and not real.

I saw a restaurant I'd passed once with Gossie. I saw a market I recognized. Then, rising up like a mountain, I could see the Palais du Luxembourg. I started for it, veering off just before I got there, onto a neat little square where narrow streets collided.

The sky was dark. The buildings were dark. The streets were black. I started off down one of the narrow streets, and when I realized it was the wrong one, I headed back to the square. I tried not to think about the Luftwaffe, so close by at the palace. I turned down another street, and just as I was thinking it was the wrong one, just as I felt the panic rise in my chest, I saw a little corner with a doorway cut into a building that was shaped like a wedge of cheese.

It was black all around me now as I ran for the shop, which was as closed and dark as the other buildings. The curtains were still open, though, which meant it was okay, that I could go up there if someone would just let me in. A face appeared in the window, a hand reaching to pull the curtain. I thought, Look down, look down. I could hear something coming—a car rattling over cobblestones. The only people who drove at night in Paris were the Germans. If they turned on the street, they would see me standing there and I knew they would stop and question me and then who knew what they would do.

Look down, look down.

Rattle, rattle, thump. The blast of a horn.

The curtain was drawing closed, but then the face in the window looked down at me. The curtain hung there, in the middle of the glass, half-open, half-shut, and the face blew a ring of smoke and started to smile but stopped at the rattling, thumping sound of the tires and the engine as the car or truck or tank, whatever it was, turned down the street toward us. I pressed myself into the doorway, trying to disappear into the frame, into the dark wood. I could see the dim blue of the headlights coming for me. I tried to will myself invisible, to become a part of the door, of the darkness. I felt my body go light. I felt my head start to spin like a propeller. Suddenly, the door flew open and I was yanked inside, and then the door slammed closed on the darkness, on the street, on the Germans.

A voice said in French, "Do you want to get yourself killed?" Outside the truck roared past, the sound of Germans shouting at one another and firing their rifles into the night. I sat where I'd fallen, on the cold stone floor, limp as a rag doll, and Émile crouched down beside me. He reached out and tugged at one of the waves in my hair till it was smooth and flat in his fingers. In the dark I saw the corners of his mouth turn up. "Clementine Roux," he said in English. "What have you done?"

TWENTY-THREE

*I*t was three hours before I learned where Émile had been. First we sat with Gossie and Cleo and the airmen—two Jewish boys, one from New York and one from California. I watched Émile while he talked to the others, easy, smiling, his very best self. His face was smooth, as if he'd just had a shave, and he was dressed in different clothes than the last time I'd seen him. He smiled and laughed and was almost charming, and I sat not smiling because I'd been waiting for two weeks for him to come back for me, not knowing if I'd ever see him again. There was no sign of Ray or Barzo.

When the clock struck one, the pilots turned in first, and then Cleo got up, gathering her peacock shawl around her. In the doorway, she turned back to the room. She said, "Gossie? They may want to catch up."

Gossie leaned forward, stubbing out her cigarette. She said, "Mary Lou, you can bunk in with me. Let Émile have the sofa." She stood, unfolding herself like a broad paper fan, scratching her calf with the toe of her other foot. Émile stood too, like a gentleman. For some reason this made me even madder.

I said, "Thanks, Gossie." But I sat right where I was, legs tucked under me. I sat and Émile stood and neither one of us moved.

Gossie smirked at me and said, "Night, kids."

She lumbered off and Émile sat down again, next to me this time, on the other end of the sofa. He said, "I cannot get used to your hair."

I looked at him without saying anything and concentrated on

drawing myself up and in, trying to sit as far away from him on that sofa as I could get. I was so far away I was practically sitting on the arm.

He said, "It suits you."

"Does it?"

He said, "Not a bit." Without thinking, I kicked him, just as I would have Johnny Clay. I wanted to kick him good and hard, but he grabbed my foot and held it and my skin went hot all over. He said, "But it's still very becoming."

I couldn't tell if he was fooling or not. He rubbed the top of my foot, and I snapped it away, tucking it in with the other one. I said, "I didn't think you were coming back."

"I said I was going to."

"Where were you?"

"I went to see my wives and children."

He was joking and this only made me madder. "And how many do you have?"

"Ten of each." He threw one arm back on top of the cushions and held up the palm of his hand. "I am much older than I look."

"And now you've come for me."

He reached for a strand of my hair. "If only I had done it sooner."

"How did you find me? How do you know Cleo?"

"Remember that the Resistance links us all."

"I've been waiting two weeks for you to come back. I think the least you can do is tell me where you really were." He rested his head on his hand and looked at me, and I could see the lines around his eyes, the shadows underneath them. I said, "You left me, and now they're gone, Monsieur Brunet and his whole family. Just like they were never there. I don't know where they are or what's happened. They may be dead, and the only thing I can think is that I could have been taken too."

His face changed then, and even though he didn't move a hair, everything about him turned serious. "My mother lives in Paris."

I heard her songs in my head, the one about the moon and the one about the pig. Just like that, the anger was gone. "She must have been glad to see you, to know you're okay."

He said, "She is Jewish, Clementine." And I felt my heart sink like a stone because I knew that being Jewish in this war was about the worst thing you could be.

"Is she all right?"

"She is." He stared off toward the pictures on the wall, even though I knew he wasn't seeing them. He told me then how he had grown up in Paris, the oldest of five—three girls and two boys—the son of a baker (his daddy) and a scientist (his mama). Everyone but his mother was captured in July 1942, when the French police rounded up some thirteen thousand Jews and told them they could take only a blanket, a pair of shoes, a sweater, and two shirts, but that they had to leave everything else in their homes. Émile, his brother, and their daddy—who was part Russian, part French, but not Jewish—were sent to the Vélodrome d'Hiver cycling stadium, which had only one water tap and no bathrooms. They lived at the Vel d'Hiv for four days, and Quakers and Red Cross workers brought them food and water. Émile's sisters were sent someplace else, but he didn't know where.

On the fifth day, Émile, his brother, and his daddy were transferred to a prison camp at Drancy in sealed wagons, and his brother died on the way there. When they learned the prisoners were being sent to the German death camp Auschwitz, Émile and his father planned their escape. They broke out in early August, managing to return to Paris, where they lived in a friend's attic for ten days until the friend turned them in and they were captured by the Gestapo. Émile's father was shot on the spot, and Émile was sent to Paris Austerlitz, a train station in the center of the city where Jewish prisoners were forced to clean and repair and pack up furniture and toys and clothing and other things to send to families in Germany.

He said, "We unloaded the trucks that brought these things to the station. We sorted the paintings, and the German officers took what they wanted. I knew but I wasn't sure where these things were coming from."

"From the Jews?"

"It was everything they'd been forced to leave behind, even photographs. One day I came across a picture of my father when he was very young, and then a picture of my mother, of me as a baby, of my sisters, and then a framed photo from my parents' wedding day. I found the silver that had been handed down to my mother from her mother, and the harmonica I'd played when I was young. I found books and clothes and other things. I stole a grocery sack and I filled it with the photos, the harmonica, a brooch my mother loved, my father's pipe, the baby cup that was mine and then my brother's. I managed to escape from there too, but the Gestapo came after me and captured me, and they took the sack of memories and made me watch as they set fire to it and burned every last thing. I never did believe much in God or heaven, but for me, what little belief I had in either died right there, right then. I was taken back to Paris Austerlitz, and the next day I escaped again. This time I got away, but with nothing."

"And you became an agent."

"Because I am French, we are given different names, not just on our papers, but for everyone to use, for the other agents to call me. This way, my family is safe, and the Germans cannot use them to get to me."

I'd only ever known him as Émile Gravois. Now he was telling me he was someone else. He had another name, just as I had another name. Émile Gravois. Clementine Roux. I wondered if anyone in this war was who or what they seemed. I said, "What's your real name then?"

"It doesn't matter. I have not been that person for a long time."

"Where is your mama now?"

"She is in Salpêtrière. It is a mental asylum here in the city. In many ways, she has not survived this war either. No one knows she is Jewish, and she is safe; otherwise I would take her out of that place now and put her on this Freedom Line. So, you see, in a way the Germans took her too. They took everything."

I wanted to find the Germans who had done this to him and his family and fly over them in my B-17 and blow them straight to hell. I said, "But they didn't. I used to think I had to carry a hatbox around with me with all my memories: clover jewelry Mama and I made when I was little, back before she died; her hair combs; her wedding ring; the first wooden figure, a singing one, that the Wood Carver gave me; my secret decoder ring; my record album; the emerald my daddy brought me from the Black Mountains. But that hatbox is back in England, and I still have those memories with me. I can talk about them or think about them, and suddenly there they are, just like I can touch them, and the good thing about being able to do that is that they don't get old and chipped and yellowed like the real things do."

I reached my hand out and rested it on his, the one that lay on the back of the sofa. "You gave me a new name and new memories and told me to forget myself and everyone I know and love, to leave that all behind, but I can't because they're a part of me. And you don't need to do that either."

He was watching me behind dark eyes. He looked as if he were going to say something, and then, with the hand that was on the sofa cushion, he pulled me to him by the back of my head. He rested his forehead against mine so that I could feel his pulse and feel his breath. He smelled like wine and cigarettes and something woodsy and green. His eyes were closed and I wanted to tell him to open them, to look at me instead of looking back at all the things that had happened.

As if he'd read my mind, he lifted his head away and opened his eyes and looked at me. He traced the line of my face with a finger and drew me in close and kissed me. It wasn't a standing-in-a-field, trying-to-trick-the-Germans kiss, or a quick, riding-on-a-train-in-Paris kiss. It was soft and deep and strong, and something about it made me keep my feet on the ground this time so that I didn't go floating off above us. I was right there in it, feeling his hand on my neck, his mouth on mine, his breath and my own.

There was a thank-you in that kiss, and something else. Just when I thought and hoped it might never end, we pulled apart and sat, the only sound the ticking of the clock above the hearth. He held my hand in his. I'd never focused on what great, broad hands he had. I had big hands for a girl, but his were twice as big as mine.

The clock ticked, ticked, ticked, and suddenly I thought about all the time that had gone by, that was going by now, that would go by in the future, if there was a future. We might all be gone tomorrow.

With my other hand, I reached for Émile, touching the light V of hair that appeared just above the top button of his shirt. I circled the button with my finger while he watched my face. I circled that button round and round and then I pinched it so that it came open. I touched his chest again, his skin warm, circling the hair of it like I'd circled the button. My hand reached for the next button, and then he pulled me to him. I thought, What are you doing, Clementine Roux?

I heard Gossie's words: *I'm alive and I'm here, and I intend to make the most of it.*

And then I kissed him.

When I woke up in the morning, I felt the weight of him next to me. The clock still ticked. It was just after six. Émile slept beside me, one leg thrown over me, an arm under my head, the other across my chest, pulling me into him.

I didn't want to move because I didn't want to wake him. I wanted to lie on the sofa and feel him around me and keep him around me so that I wouldn't have to stand back and think about the night before too closely.

He said, "You are awake."

"Yes. I thought you were still sleeping."

He sat up, rubbing his jaw, his eyes sleepy and unfocused. He kissed my shoulder. "We should get up before they come in." He stood and I tried not to watch as he searched for his shirt, tried not to look at his naked chest. I could still feel the curve of it, still feel the firmness of the muscles, the warmth of his skin.

I wondered what I looked like to him, rumpled and half dressed. As he pulled on his jacket, I buttoned my blouse and smoothed my hair and clothes. I folded the blanket and settled myself on the edge of the sofa, adjusting the hem of my skirt over my knees. He laughed at this. Then he sat back down beside me and frowned. "You are too beautiful in the morning." He brushed a piece of hair off my face, tucking it behind my ear, but I could see in his eyes that he was moving past me already.

I touched my hair where he'd touched it. The shortness of it still felt strange. I said, "Where are Barzo and Ray?"

"They are staying with families, ones that work for the Resistance."

"Why did you come back?"

"Because we need your help."

"What do you need me to do?"

He pulled a cigarette from his pocket and lit it. He rubbed his forehead with his thumb and inhaled and then exhaled the smoke. He said, "This Freedom Line your friends are involved in." He looked toward the door in the direction of the bedrooms. "It is for downed pilots."

I said, "Yes."

"You are a downed pilot. I think you should free yourself. Get out of here and go back to England and be safe."

He was saying it to test me. It was just something he felt he should say. He didn't want me to go back to England any more than I wanted to go back to England. I said, "I'm not going anywhere."

"Yes you are."

"No I'm not. My brother is here. I can't go home till I find him." I stared at Émile and he stared at me and the clock went *tick-tick-tick*.

"He is in France?"

"I don't know. I think so." And as I said it, I believed it. He was in France. He had to be. "But I can't just sit here, and I'm not leaving France without him. What do you need me to do?"

"I need you to rescue someone."

He pulled something from the inside of his jacket and handed it to me. It was a photograph of a woman with curly dark hair, eyebrows that arched over merry, light-colored eyes, and a widow's peak that made her face look like a heart. She could have been eighteen or forty or anywhere in between. I studied the picture but I still couldn't tell whether she was frowning or smiling. Her expression seemed to change in front of me.

I said, "She's pretty." She looked like a nice girl, like someone I might have been friends with if I'd met her in Nashville or Texas or at Camp Davis in North Carolina. "Who is she?"

"I am not sure."

"Swan."

"Yes."

"A spy?"

"Probably."

"They don't tell you?"

"They only tell us what we need to know, nothing more."

"What's her name?"

"She has the code name of Swan, but she is also called Eleanor. Not her real name, I'm sure." He returned the picture to his pocket. For one minute, I wondered if she was someone he knew, maybe a girlfriend. I stared at his pocket, thinking of the photo next to his heart.

I said, "Why didn't they kill her when they took her?"

"We don't know. From what we can tell, she was captured by Hugo Bleicher, one of the most ruthless pursuers of enemy agents. One of the worst of the spy hunters, or the best, depending on how you look at it. He has disabled entire networks, and he has been able to turn agents so that they betray England or France or America and go to work for him and for Germany."

"So she must be an agent."

"Yes." He didn't seem to care either way, but I cared. I wanted to know everything. I thought about the female agents I'd seen at Harrington.

"So why didn't he kill her?"

"Maybe they hope to get information out of her, to turn her against the British. Or maybe they want to torture her, to make her suffer first. It doesn't matter. What matters is getting her out. That was the purpose of our mission in Rouen, but she had already been moved. We had no radio, so we couldn't know." The raid on the prison, the one the professor had talked about. "We have tried here, but there are only three of us. Coleman was the demolitionist. His equipment is gone. We can get more, but we need someone from the inside to make sure they do not move her or execute her before we can break her out."

I said, "What do you need me to do?"

"I need you to get arrested."

"Arrested?"

"She is being held at Romainville on the outskirts of Paris. It is where prisoners are sent before being sent on to other places like the concentration camps."

I said, "I thought she was in Fresnes."

"She was moved. I would go myself, but there are no male prisoners at Romainville anymore, just women, and I need you to break her out from the inside. They are most likely keeping her in an isolated cell. England is sending another team to assist us in the next few days, as soon as they can get a plane out. Once you are in, we will help free you."

My throat had gone dry as a pile of twigs. I could feel my pulse fluttering like a bird.

Émile said, "We must hurry. The Allies are coming, and before they get here the Germans will start executing prisoners. We do not have long." I knew that the Allies were moving closer to Paris, and that the Germans were prepared to defend it to the end, digging in and building bunkers and pillboxes on the streets.

He said, "But you need to know that Romainville is not just a prison. It is a hostage camp, a place of torture. If something goes wrong for the Germans, say they are attacked by the Resistance or bombed by the Allies, they might retaliate by harming the prisoners. They call it Death's Waiting Room."

His words settled around me. I said, "How important is this woman?" I wanted to know if her life was worth mine.

"Very important, or else they would not go to so much trouble."

I said, "Did you—was last night because you wanted me to help you?"

"Last night was because of you and me. No one else."

He was quiet and I was quiet. For some reason I wasn't thinking about myself. I was thinking about Johnny Clay. I was picturing him on that last day in Nashville before he'd left to get on the train, the last day I'd seen him, maybe the last time I would ever see him. He'd been so gold and proud and brave and fearless, and he wasn't looking back for a minute at the old safe life and all that he was leaving behind. *At*

least I'll know I was doing something good, he'd told me, *something bet-*
ter than sitting around and waiting. I'm going to die one way or another
one day, and I figure I might as well do some good before I do.

I said, "I'll do it." I had known from the start, from the moment
he'd mentioned it, that I would do it, so all that was left was to say it
out loud.

Émile took my hand in his. I looked down at our hands, thinking
how nice it would be if we were just a regular couple in regular times,
sitting here on a sofa side by side.

I said, "When do I go?"

"Friday."

August 7, 1944

Dear family,

I know it's been a while since I wrote, but this is the first chance I've had to mail you something. I can't say much, but I want you to know I'm fine. I can't tell you where I am or what I'm doing, but I am in this war and being as safe as I can. I hope it will be over soon, and then I'll come home and show you for myself.

Have you heard from Johnny Clay or Linc or Beachard? What about the Deal boys—Coyle? Jessup? Write me at the address I gave you before, back in June, even though I'm not there right now. And I'll write again when I'm able. Just remember that I'm missing you all and hoping everyone is as good as can be. I think of you all the time, and it's a help to know you're out there in this world when I feel so far away.

I love you.

Velva Jean

TWENTY-FOUR

*A*t two o'clock on Friday afternoon, I was to ride by the Palais du Luxembourg. I would take a spill off my bicycle, right in front of the guards, which would lead the Germans to question me. No matter what they did to me, I wasn't to give anything up—not my real name or where I came from. Émile said they had someone on the inside, a man he called Niklaus Reiner, working secretly among the ranks of the Gestapo, and he would make sure they didn't torture me and that I would be sent to Romainville and nowhere else.

I would wear a jacket with seventy thousand gold Francs sewn into the shoulder pads, which I was to use to bribe the prison guards. I would wear a lapel knife in my collar and carry the pack of chewing gum with sticks of gum that were actually explosives. Émile said some of this might be taken from me, but if all went according to plan, his contact at Romainville would see that I was released in just under twenty-four hours with the woman called Eleanor. They would make it look as if we'd escaped. If it didn't go according to plan, Émile and his team would be there to get us out.

Émile gave me a map of the prison—a military fort that was over a hundred years old—which I was to memorize and destroy, and on this map was an *X*, which marked the part of the prison where Eleanor was being held as well as the easiest escape route out of there. He also gave me L, K, and TD pills. The K pills were liquid knockout drops, the TD tablet was a truth drug, and the L pill was lethal. If something went wrong and I was tortured or fell into the wrong hands, all I had to do was swallow one and that would be it—I would be dead in a minute.

I kept the K and TD pills but I handed the L pill back to Émile. I didn't want to think about what it could do. I didn't even want to look at it or have it near me. "No prisoners," I said. "I don't plan on getting caught."

On Monday morning, the pilots left for Nesles, and in the afternoon I re-dyed my hair and studied the map of Romainville. On Monday night, Émile, Ray, Barzo, Gossie, and I went to a little place in the Quarter that served liquor and played a kind of Afro-Cuban jazz music, bright and loud. I wore a flower tucked behind my ear, and when he saw me, Barzo whistled. He said, "Nice hair, pilot."

Normally I would have bristled at him, at this, but my mind was as far off as the moon, so that the music and the dancing and the laughter and the colors of the band and of the room—blues and reds and greens and oranges and yellows—swirled all around me, but it was as if I were in a bubble, in a separate room from everyone else.

Gossie and the men talked and drank, and at some point I said to Émile, "I want to go over the plan again." It made me feel better to go over it. It made me feel more in charge, more in control, like if I went over it enough nothing could go wrong

But Émile said, "Not here. Not now." Underneath the table, he rested his hand on my knee. He looked at Gossie. We hadn't said a word to her about what we were planning to do because that way, if something happened and they somehow traced me back to her and Cleo, they could honestly say they didn't know anything. "Tomorrow," he said, and he raised his glass to me and drank. I knew it was all about appearances—going out to this restaurant, acting as if we weren't planning a raid on one of France's toughest prisons.

The rest of the night, Émile draped his arm across the back of my chair or held my hand as I smiled and talked. But I was standing a far way off from everything, watching myself smile and talk like I was an actress in a movie.

Gossie said, "You should get up there and sing, Mary Lou." She'd had a letter from Clinton Farnham, her fiancé, that morning. He was getting leave soon and coming to see her, and she was as high as the moon.

I said, "I don't feel like singing."

"We'll find him, honey, don't you worry. If Clinton Farnham can find me in this war, we can find your brother."

I smiled and tried to pretend that this was all that was on my mind, and before Gossie could say anything else, Émile leaned in to her and said something in her ear that made her throw her head back and laugh. He raised his glass to me and I looked away, pretending to watch the dancers, pretending I could think of anything but Friday. Barzo said, "I think I'll have another. *Garçon!*"

He waved to the waiter, and I watched as the man passed through the tables, through the crowd, and then I watched as he was shoved aside by a man rushing through the door of the nightclub from the street. The waiter fell on the floor, shaking his head back and forth at the surprise of it, and the man shouted something in French, too fast and muddled for me to hear. Ray got to his feet and helped the waiter up, and the man shouted again, over and over, the same thing, and suddenly everyone was out of their seats and running toward the door, and we were in the middle of them, Émile taking hold of my hand, and the others just behind me. We ran out into the night, which was warm and balmy, and we stood on the Boulevard Saint-Michel, where all the people from the restaurants and cafés and clubs and bars were singing and waving as a great line of Germans went roaring past in their cars and trucks.

"*La libération!*"

The Liberation!

"*La libération est arrivée!*"

The Liberation has arrived!

"What is it?" I had to holler over the noise. "What do they mean by that?"

Gossie said, "Paris is liberated." She took my other hand. My heart jumped. If the Allies were here and the Liberation was here, maybe Eleanor would be set free and I wouldn't have to go to Romainville at all.

Someone began singing:

Allons enfants de la Patrie,
Le jour de gloire est arrivé. . . .

This was "La Marseillaise," the national anthem of France. Everyone joined in, raising their voices and their glasses to the warm night sky.

Émile's eyes traveled up and down the street, watching the people who were dancing and kissing and waving and singing, and the Germans driving by. "It's too soon," he said.

All at once, there was the sound of a shot. I looked up, waiting. A woman standing at the edge of the street, just feet away, dropped to the ground. There was another shot and this time a man fell, the drink still in his hand. Émile said, *"Descendons!" Get down!*

He yanked me to the sidewalk, and I hit the pavement with a smack, pain shooting through my knee and up my leg to my hip. I lifted my head enough to see that the Germans were standing up in their cars and trucks, aiming their machine guns into the crowd. Ray lay to the right of me, his cheek pressed against the ground, and Gossie was just past him. Ray said, "Keep your head down, Clementine."

I closed my eyes and began to pray: *Dear Jesus, please don't let me die here on this sidewalk in France. Dear Jesus, don't let anyone die here.* I prayed for a B-29 to come out of the sky and drop a bomb on each and every German.

Men and women and children were falling to the ground all around me. Flat on our stomachs, we started edging over to the doorway of the nightclub an inch at a time. Bullets buzzed over my head. I heard the sharp *clink, clink, clink* as they hit walls and doors and then the pavement. I heard the screams of people falling where they were shot.

All the while, the cars kept rolling past, until suddenly the last car drove by and all was quiet. I lay there a minute. Two minutes. I looked up and saw others all around me looking up too. A Red Cross truck came racing toward us, stopping in the middle of the street, and medics and nurses climbed off, carrying stretchers. Émile said, "Are you all right?" He was next to me, reaching for me.

I couldn't do anything but nod. He stood and I wanted to shout to him to get down so that he wouldn't be hit. People were standing, brushing themselves off, wiping their eyes, picking broken glass out of their hands, their arms. And all around, other people lay still and cold on the sidewalk or in the street, the blood pooling around them.

Émile said, "It is okay, Clementine." He leaned down and studied me and rested a hand against my cheek. It was cool against my face, which was burning like an oven. He said, "Come." He pulled me to my feet, and Gossie was already standing, shaking her fist in the direction of the cars, cursing the Germans.

The sidewalk was red with blood. The Red Cross workers carried off the dead and wounded. Several feet away, a woman was holding a man in her arms, the blood turning the blue of her skirt a dark purple, the color of blackberries. She was singing:

> *S'ils tombent, nos jeunes héros,*
> *La terre en produit de nouveaux,*
> *Contre vous tout prêts à se batter....*

I helped lift the bodies onto the stretchers. We left the dead and went for the wounded, stepping over bodies to get to them. The faces of the dead blurred until they were the same. I looked down and saw the red of my footprints on the concrete. I stepped over a man. I thought he was dead, but then his eyes fluttered open and he opened his mouth to say something. His ear was blown away and a part of his skull. The rest of his face was craggy, as if he'd been left out in the sun too long. I bent down and untied the map scarf from around my neck and wrapped it around his head, trying not to look, trying to stop the bleeding. There was so much blood—too much blood.

I held his head in my lap, waiting for the medic to come get him. He looked up at me, at the sky, and it was hard to know if he could see me. I said, "Ray. Stay with me. I'm here."

He said, "Is it the Liberation?"

To my left, the woman was still singing.

> *If they fall, our young heroes,*
> *The earth will produce new ones,*
> *Ready to fight against you.*

His eyes were closing. I could see the light going out of them as I held his head, his blood covering my lap, my arms, my legs, my hands, so much that I wondered if they would ever wash clean.

"Yes," I said. "You are free."

TWENTY-FIVE

That night, I hardly slept. I was thinking about Ray, picturing his head in my lap, his eyes closing, his blood everywhere. I'd scrubbed my hands and arms and clothes for an hour, but I could still feel the sticky wetness of it, could still smell it on my skin. Émile and I lay on the couch at Cleo's, my head on his chest, his arms around me, and I told myself: Sleep, Velva Jean. Sleep, Clementine. But every time I closed my eyes I saw the scene on the Boulevard Saint-Michel.

Émile stroked my hair, the way Mama used to do, and told me stories of Paris before the war. Finally he said, "Is it helping?"

"No."

He tilted my chin so I could see him and then he leaned in and kissed me. "Is this helping?" It was a whisper.

"Not yet."

He pulled me closer and kissed me again, harder this time. His hands were in my hair, not gently now, and I kissed him back just as hard, just as fierce, then harder, then fiercer, as if we were trying to push everything else away but us.

We fell asleep just before dawn, and I woke two hours later, alone. I checked the time and dressed in a hurry in a black skirt and white blouse that I'd borrowed from Bernadette, a thin black blazer, a pair of dark green sandals, and a green scarf, which I wrapped around my hair like a turban. I picked up my bag and set out, following the crooked alleys and tangled streets, like a maze, that made up the Quarter. I was meeting Émile and Barzo at a café in Saint-Germaindes-Prés because Barzo was staying near there and the Quarter was too crowded with Germans. Émile had gone ahead without me because he didn't want to risk traveling through the streets together.

I left in such a hurry that I forgot the rest of my things, including a heavier jacket in case the day turned cool and an umbrella in case it turned rainy. I was halfway to the café and thought, I can turn back or I can keep going. I knew I should always travel with everything I had, just in case. But it was warm outside and the sun was shining. If I went back I would be late.

I kept going. The Eiffel Tower rose up ahead, the swastika at the top flapping in the wind. In the bright sun, the people on the streets looked shabbier and more worn out, as if they had been in this war for all their lives and they knew they would always be in it, until they died.

The sun turned the day hot, then hotter. I was glad I'd left my jacket. I took off the blazer and rolled my shirtsleeves over my elbows. I passed a little park where people were sitting on the grass sunning themselves. Skirts were pulled up over knees and shirt collars were unbuttoned, faces tipped back, eyes closed, soaking it in.

The café sat on the corner of two busy streets. The inside was red seats and dark wood walls and mirrors, but I sat outside under the white awning. I'd brought a French magazine, and I pretended to read this while the sun slanted in at an angle over my legs. I moved them a little so that they would be fully in the light. I didn't see many Germans here, only locals filling up the tables and chairs and hurrying down the street. Even though it was a hot day, I ordered coffee—just bitter chicory with saccharin to sweeten it.

For twenty minutes, I sipped the coffee and waited. When Émile and Barzo didn't come, I waited ten more minutes, my pulse starting to race. I was already on edge from the night before. The waiter asked if I wanted anything else and I said no, not today. I told him I had someplace to be, even though I didn't.

Something had happened. After thirty minutes, I got up and started the walk back to Cleo's. Maybe they were there. Maybe our signals had gotten crossed and they were waiting for me right now. I walked faster, following the river, along to my left, until I found myself back in the twisting, narrow maze of the Quarter. I turned down Cleo's street, my bag thumping against my hip, my heart thumping in my chest. But what if Émile and Barzo weren't there? What if they'd been captured?

Breedlove's was closed. Before I reached the door I looked up, out of habit, to check the windows. Only one curtain was drawn—the one on the front window. *If the curtain above the store is closed—just that one—it means keep away.*

I glanced up and down the street, making sure no one was watching me, that I wasn't being followed, and then I turned the corner and another until I was in front of a café with a raggedy red awning. Outside, a waiter was unstacking the chairs and tables, and the people who were waiting for them sat down. The cafés only served alcohol four days a week now, and one of the other waiters stood in the doorway drinking wine. Because there wasn't any more room, I sat inside, at a table by the window, and ordered a glass of wine myself, even though I didn't like wine, and watched the people walking by.

I waited five minutes, ten minutes, fifteen minutes. Something was wrong. First Émile, now Cleo. The wine tasted like vinegar, like blood. *Blood everywhere.* I pushed it away. I decided I would give it thirty minutes and then I would walk back by Cleo's to see if the curtain had moved. It had to move. She and Gossie had to be there. And Émile had to be there too.

Twenty minutes.

The wail of a siren made me jump, spilling my wine on the table and on my skirt. *Just like Ray's blood.* One of the waiters said something about the Allies—*"Ils larguent des bombes,"* which meant, "They are dropping bombs"—and everyone rushed out of the café and into the street. I looked up at the sky and it was thick with planes, like giant birds, circling and soaring toward us. I wanted to stand and watch them, to wave to them, to shout at them: "I'm one of you!" Then the first round of bombs crashed to the earth, and I was jolted against one of the waiters, who was standing beside me and looking up too.

He shouted, *"Allons-y!"* We must go!

A hand wrapped around my arm and pulled me toward the Metro station on the corner. Émile said, "Come, Clementine."

Before I could ask where he'd been and where he'd come from, we pushed our way down the stairs, bumping against all the others who were pushing and bumping. A black arrow was painted on the wall, and we all followed this to the air raid shelter, which sat right smack on the train tracks.

The tunnel was dark except for a pale blue light that glowed like fox fire in the woods. People coughed and shouted and pushed, and the children were crying. From up above, I could hear a rumble like thunder. I prayed right then for the Allies to take out every last German but leave Paris and the people of the city unhurt. Someone grabbed my waist in the dark, and then my leg, inching a hand up my skirt. A man's face leaned in to mine. His breath smelled like liquor, and I pushed away from him, deeper into the crowd. I tried to make myself as small and quiet as I could, as if making myself small and quiet would help me disappear. Émile reached forward and punched the man in the jaw, sending him reeling backward. Hands caught him and shoved him away.

The bombs boomed and thundered, and all around us the walls and ground shook. I focused on the dim blue light up ahead. I stared at it long enough to believe it really was fox fire glowing in the woods back home, and if I just went toward it I could pick some and take it back with me to Mama's. I stared at that light until I could see the woods of Fair Mountain and everything that grew there—fox fire, balsam trees, grass, moss, wildflowers—and the streams and the hollers. Three Gum River. Mama's house. Granny's house just behind it. Daddy Hoyt's fiddle workshop. The house where Linc and Ruby Poole lived, and the one where Aunt Zona lived with the twins and Aunt Bird. I could hear the rain on the tin roof at Mama's and smell the lavender and lye soap that she and Granny made in summer.

Suddenly, everything above us got quiet. We stood together, hundreds of us, not saying anything, barely breathing. I looked up at Émile and he looked back at me, calm, cool. I whispered, "I waited."

He said, "We were detained." Something about the way he said it gave me a chill. "We came just as you were leaving, but you were too far ahead."

"Something's wrong at Cleo's. The curtain—"

"I know."

The sirens sounded again, which meant it was all clear and we could come out. Everyone started moving then, and I knew we only had a short time to get off the tracks before the electricity came on.

We moved like a herd of cows, like a flock of geese pushing upward till I could see the blue of the sky and feel the sun on my face. I wanted to get right down and kiss the ground, but there were too many people—you could barely move. My hand was in Émile's, but everyone was pushing behind us and around us, and my hand broke free. For a minute, I lost sight of him. I ran my eyes over everyone as I moved forward, carried by the crowd, until I saw him, four people away. Then I heard the high, shrill screech of a whistle. Germans in uniform wound their way through the crowd on the sidewalk and in the streets.

Men, women, and children were still rushing up from underground, and the Germans rounded them up as they came out onto the street. The Germans made a wide circle around us, a kind of rope, and they waved their machine guns. I looked everywhere for Émile, but he was too far away. He was reaching for me across the people who were blocking his way, keeping us apart. He was shoving them aside, trying to get to me. Suddenly I felt something hard and cold against my back, and a voice said, in French, "Move!"

A truck waited on the street, black with a canvas roof. The something hard and cold against my back was a gun and the person holding it was a German officer. No one had ever pointed a gun into my back before, and my mouth went dry and my throat went tight and I could feel the beads of sweat collecting under my hair on the base of my neck. I looked for Émile, but couldn't find him.

There were fifteen of us in my group, and they lined us up next to the truck. The guards went up and down the row, emptying everyone's bags and looking at their papers. I pulled my bag across my chest and laid my hands across it. Out of all the things I was supposed to take with me Friday, the only thing I had with me was the chewing gum. In my hair, I was wearing some of the bobby pins Monsieur Brunet had made, but I didn't have the jacket with the gold francs in the shoulder pads. I didn't have the lapel knife or the button compass or the T and K pills. In my bag, I had my Révolution Rouge lipstick, Ty's compass, the wooden flying girl, the seashell for luck, the rip cord from my parachute, and the map of Romainville.

One of the guards said, "Give me your bag." He had wormy eyes and thin lips with a scar through the top one. I wondered if I could knock him down. I would run through the street and I wouldn't stop running till I got to Spain. He grabbed the bag from me, map and all, and I watched him go through it, my breath frozen in my chest. I thought: Stay calm. Don't tell him anything. I know nothing. I know nothing.

The guard said in French, "What are you doing in Paris when your papers say Rouen? When your husband is dead?"

I know nothing.

In French, I said, "I'm here looking for work, hoping that someone will hire me to sing at a nightclub or on the radio." Émile had taught me to say this exact phrase, and also told me to say I had friends who lived here, but I didn't want to risk them going after Gossie and her aunt.

He said in French, "You have an American accent." He looked closer at my card. He said in English, "You were born in the United States?"

I said, "Yes, but I'm French by marriage. I took my husband's nationality when I married. I have the right to circulate." Émile had told me to say this too.

The guard frowned at me. I said, "If that's all, I really need to be going." I tried to sound like I knew what I was doing, like I wasn't shaking all over, about to faint dead away. I hoped Émile was far off by now, that they hadn't rounded him up too.

The guard said, "Not so fast." He pulled out my lipstick, unwinding it to make sure it was only a lipstick and nothing else. He rustled through the compass, the wooden girl, the chewing gum like they were nothing. He held up the rip cord and squinted at it and then at me before tossing it aside. He held up the map and I sucked in my breath, hoping somehow, by some miracle, he wouldn't know what it was. I waited for him to say something, for him to show the other men, for him to raise his gun and shoot me between the eyes. But just then, beside me, an old man began to cough, and then he spat into his handkerchief and onto the ground, just missing the guard's shoe. In French, the guard shouted at the old man, "Silence!"

He shoved the map back into my bag and handed the bag to me, then he pulled a handkerchief from his pocket and wiped his shoe till it shone like a new quarter. As he did, the old man looked over at me and winked.

They loaded us into the truck and the guards climbed in after us, three in front and two in back, sitting in the open door, a leg each bent under their chins, the other swinging off the side. They held their guns with one hand, pointed straight at us.

The seat was hard and damp, and as we drove over the cobblestones I had to hold on so that I wouldn't pitch right out of it. Two cars followed along behind us filled with more soldiers and more guns. One of the women was crying. She started wailing: *"Mon Dieu! Mon Dieu!"* over and over. *"Ayez pitié."* Have pity.

Please let Émile find me, wherever they're taking me. Please don't let him be captured. I tried not to think about what would happen to me if he were picked up too.

A little girl sat in the seat next to me, and beside her was a little boy who must have been her brother. She was holding his hand in hers and singing him a song, very low, so that the Germans wouldn't hear her. The little boy glanced up at me and then he popped his thumb in his mouth. The girl kept singing:

> *Où donc est la pleine lune*
> *Toute en or et en argent. . . .*

I tried not to think about Émile and his mama and the day he sang that song to me. My bag lay at my side, and my eyes flickered over the guards in the front seat. I slid my hand into the bag, keeping it tight and close, and felt around for the map. I thought: This isn't the plan.

It's only Tuesday. I was supposed to have until Friday. Émile and Barzo aren't ready. I'm not ready. What if they send me to Germany or Belgium? How will Émile ever find me?

I touched the cool metal of Ty's compass and slipped it out, quick as I could, when the guards weren't looking. I pulled up the hem of my skirt and worked the compass into the lining, and then I plucked a bobby pin from my hair and slid it over the hem, holding it closed. One of the Germans turned around and narrowed his eyes at us over his long nose. He sat like that for a good minute before turning back around.

I slid my hand into the bag again and this time my fingers touched paper. I began tearing it into bits, right there inside the bag. I ripped it into tiny pieces, and then I felt around for each little shred and gathered them up in my hand.

The boy looked up at me again and I smiled at him. I wanted to say: It's okay. Your sister is here. I'm here. We won't let anyone hurt you. But I didn't know if this was true because I didn't know what was happening or why this was happening, and so instead I began to sing.

> *When the blazing sun is gone,*
> *When he nothing shines upon,*
> *Then you show your little light,*
> *Twinkle, twinkle, all the night. . . .*

The girl raised her eyes to my face, letting them rest there for a minute. I wondered where her mama was. She said, "*Savez-vous les mots dans le français, mademoiselle?*" Do you know the words in French?

"*Oui.* I think so."

Together we sang, our voices hiccupping and skipping with each bump of the truck.

TWENTY-SIX

After twenty minutes or so, the truck ground to a stop. I pulled my hand out of the bag, still holding the ripped-up pieces of paper. I stuck my hand in my pocket so no one would ask what I was holding in it, and I followed the woman, the old man, the little girl and her brother, and the others onto a narrow street. By now I didn't have any idea where we were or what part of the city we were in, but we were standing in front of a white stone building that seemed to take up almost an entire block. I couldn't tell if it was one huge building or a dozen smaller ones linked together. The number eleven hung beside the door.

The guards marched us out of the truck and across the three feet of sidewalk through two black iron doors. We paraded across a courtyard and through another door. We walked through the hall to a room at the end, where there were other people rounded up—French men and women and children and Allied airmen, British and American, and French soldiers. Germans in uniform moved through the crowd as if they were at a party.

I stood with the fourteen others I'd come with, and the old man coughed and wheezed and spat in his handkerchief. Some of the others glared at him, mouths twitching, eyes flinching with each cough or rattle. I knew they wished him dead right then because he was calling attention to us all. But there was so much bustle in the room, with uniformed police walking in and out and so many others rounded up and waiting, that I could see that nobody was paying much mind to us.

I bent down, pretending to fix the strap of my shoe, and popped the bits of paper into my mouth. Fast as I could, still bent over, I chewed and chewed. My throat was so dry and the paper was so dry that all I was doing was moving the pieces around and around.

One of the Germans tapped over to us and I straightened, jaw clenched, trying to look normal and natural. He barked at us to follow him, and we were made to sit on a long bench just inside the door. Another German came up then and took the old man away and out of the room. My eyes were watering and I chewed a little, barely moving my jaw so that no one would see, and then I finally thought to hell with it and swallowed all the pieces whole.

After what seemed like hours, the old man came back and then the next person was led out of the room and down the hall. When she came back, the next person went and then the next, and the next. I sat with my arm around the girl and boy, studying the other people who were waiting in groups like ours, at the pilots who looked brave but weary.

A guard walked up and stopped in front of me. It was the same man with the scar on his lip, the man who had looked through my bag. He said, "Come with me."

I had to walk ahead so he could watch me with his gun, which he pointed into my back, pushing me. With the nose of the gun, he steered me into a room at the other end of the hall that was large and airy, with two big windows that looked down on the street and a desk in front of each of them. A man with a flat gray face and sagging cheeks sat in one of the chairs, his desk covered with ink pads and rubber stamps and files and papers. He didn't even look up when we came into the room.

The man with the scar said, "Give me your bag." Without waiting, he took it from me and emptied it upside down on the other desk, the empty one. He said, "Where is the paper?"

"What paper?"

"The one you were carrying."

I know nothing.

"I don't know what you're talking about." The man behind the desk looked up, his neck sagging around his collar.

The man with the scar turned my bag inside out. I thought: Please don't notice the compass is missing too. He held something up and I felt my breath catch in my chest. It was a tiny piece of paper.

"You ate it."

I thought about saying no, I don't know what you're talking about, but instead I said, "Yes."

The man behind the desk said, "*Du bist ein Idiot.*" He started laughing.

The man with the scar snapped at him in German and then moved his eyes back to me so that I could see the fury there. But there was nothing he could do. I knew he wouldn't want to look like a fool in front of anyone else. He said, "Come with me."

In another office, two German women in uniform made me undress. They searched me and then my clothes, patting all around my body and my hair, which was still wrapped in the scarf. As one of them went over my skirt, I prayed she wouldn't find Ty's compass. She must not have been looking too hard or too carefully because soon she gave it back to me along with my other things, and I was told to get dressed.

I was taken to another office, where I was asked a round of questions—my name, age, birthplace, and the whole history of my life: schools I'd gone to, who my parents were, where I traveled, what I did for a living, who was my husband—as a secretary wrote down all my answers. The more I replied as Clementine Roux, the more I could feel Velva Jean Hart slipping away. No one mentioned the map.

I was sent to another office, where the officer there asked me about the Freedom Line. When I said I didn't know what he was talking about, he said, "You are involved in this like the other Americans and like the French. I know you are. At night you have to live with yourself knowing that you dare to save the men who cause so much death and destruction. You have been helping murderers."

I said, "I know nothing."

I was sent to one more office after that, and this last one was larger than all the others. The man it belonged to was probably forty, maybe older. He sat on his desk, his legs dangling off, and a big dog with red fur lay on the floor in front of him, staring at me. The guard with the scar stood at the door, behind me, and I stood before the desk, wishing I could sit down because my legs were as weak as matchsticks.

The man in charge said, "I advise you to talk because it will make this easier for all of us." He took his time speaking, like English wasn't easy for him. "If you lie, I'll know it. You will probably be shot tomorrow morning anyway. We haven't had time to judge people since the Invasion."

Framed pictures sat on one corner of his desk—different pictures of three children and a blond woman. They sat turned out toward the room, as if he wanted everyone to see.

He said, "Mademoiselle Roux, what is your profession?"

"I am a singer."

"And where do you sing?"

"Everywhere," I said. "I sing whenever and wherever I can."

I thought, If they shoot me, they shoot me. I figured they were going to shoot me anyhow, so I might as well not give anything or anybody away.

"You are a member of the Resistance." It wasn't a question.

"No, sir."

"Why were you arrested then?"

"I don't know. I was coming out of the shelter with everyone else."

"You say you are not in the Resistance, but you know people that are?"

"Isn't everyone in France resisting this war in some way?"

The dog had inched its way over to me on its belly. It stood now and walked to my side and I leaned down to scratch its head.

The man said something in German to the man with the scar, and then he said to me, "You will be held until your papers are verified."

I said, "Is this your family?" I nodded at the photographs on his desk.

He kept his eyes on me. "Yes."

"You must miss them." I was thinking about how much I missed my family and how I would give anything to see them right that minute.

"I do."

"Your dog is beautiful. My brother had a dog when we were growing up that used to follow him wherever he went. Still does, whenever we're home. He grew up alongside us just like he was one of my mama's children."

The man glanced down at the dog, which was sitting beside me now, tongue out, smiling. The man said, "*Tag. Komm hier.*" The dog went to him.

I said, "What does *Tag* mean?"

"It means 'Day.'" I nodded like this was fine, like I understood. I thought the dog must stand for better days past and better days to come. Even though this man was a German and on the wrong side of the war, it was still the right side to him, and he was probably as tired of it as we all were.

The man sat looking at me, and then he snapped his fingers at the guard and said something in German. The guard marched out of the room.

We were quiet for a long time. Finally, the man on the desk said, "My wife is expecting a baby."

"When is she due?"

"February."

"Congratulations, sir. A big family is a healthy family." It was something I'd heard Granny say, once upon a time. He nodded at this, just slightly.

The guard returned with a bologna sandwich and a cup of ersatz coffee, which was made out of cheap flour and potato starch and, some said, sawdust.

I said, "Thank you," and I stuffed the sandwich into my bag because I didn't know if or when I'd be given food again, and then I drank down the coffee, which tasted worse than dirt.

I sat on the floor of what must have been a cell, although I couldn't see anything in the dark. The smell of it was strong and musty and sour, as if something or someone had died there, and a single beam of light slithered in like a snake from a grille in the upper part of the door. It shone down on the floor, making a small white square. I crawled forward and sat in that light and listened to the doors opening and shutting up and down the hall—bolt, key, key and bolt. It was like the rhythm of a song.

I closed my eyes and tried to remember what it felt like to be beyond the keep, which was something we'd said to each other in Sweetwater, Texas. It was how the other girls and I felt when we were flying—free and strong and beyond the keep of anyone or anything. I pictured myself up in the air, up in the B-17, with nothing but land and ocean and sky below me. I felt the wind against my cheeks and in my hair—my long, wild hair that I missed. I could feel the throttle in my hand, feel the roar of the engine moving through me.

I still had my bag with me, but I didn't know how long they'd let me keep it. Feeling my way in the dark, I took Ty's compass out of the hem of my skirt and then I slid off my blazer and worked the compass into the shoulder pad, which was large and cushiony, and where it wouldn't be as easy to find. I slid the bobby pin over the opening I'd made and put the blazer on again. When my stomach started growling, I pulled out the bologna sandwich and ate half, and then I wrapped it back up and saved the rest.

I must have drifted off, because I woke up sometime later to the sound of sirens. I was lying on the floor, the cold stone pressed to my face. It was black in the cell—no shapes, no shadows—but I could hear planes flying overhead, and then a whine of bombs as they fell to the earth, shaking the walls. I prayed for the bombs to shake the cell wide open, but after a while the night grew quiet again and there was nothing to do but lie down on the floor and go back to sleep.

I woke again later, this time to the sound of crying. It was loud at first, then softer, then louder. It was a woman, and she started talking in French, saying the same things over and over, just like she was mad. She would talk and cry, talk and cry, and I could hear other voices trying to quiet her. I wanted to call something out to the person who was doing it, to tell her it would be okay. I wanted to tell her to stop it, to be stronger than that. I wondered what had happened to the old man and to the girl and boy.

The crying and the talking stopped then and I lay on the cold, hard ground listening to the silence. I rolled onto my back and then onto my side and then onto my other side, and I didn't sleep again.

The cell turned light with the morning. I watched it slowly unfold itself in front of me, and what I saw was a dank gray room, stone floor, stone walls, heavy wood door with bars, window with bars, and there, in the corner along one wall, was a body. Its back was to me, and at first I thought it was a dead body, but then I could see the midsection rising and falling. From what I could tell, it was a woman.

My stomach started to grumble until I was sure I could hear an echo, and I pulled out the sandwich and ate half of the half, saving the rest of it for the woman. I wanted to talk to her, to ask her why she was in there, how long she'd been in there, but instead I set the sandwich down beside her and sat looking around the cell at the window and the walls. A thick metal ring was attached to one wall, and a chain hung from this. A single lightbulb glared down from the ceiling like an eye.

That was when I saw the writing, some in French, some in English: words and sentences carved into the walls of the cell or written with a pencil, with lead, or with blood.

> *Guillaume loves Marianne.*
> *I cannot sleep for thinking about my parents and my husband.*
> *France above all.*
> *Roger: your father, your cousin, and Colette's father came through here 24-5-1944.*

I sat up and leaned in and touched the words with my fingers, tracing each letter. I thought of the people who had written them and wondered where they were now. For all I knew, these might have been their last words.

> *Never confess.*
> *Good-bye forever to France.*
> *I am afraid.*

The words made me think of my brother Beachard, who, before he ever went to war and became a hero, had wandered the woods and mountains carving messages on rocks and trees and railroad ties and barns: *Jesus weeps, Jesus waits, You are loved.*

I lay my hand flat against the wall.

> *Life is beautiful.*

I reached into my bag and pulled out my lipstick and wrote: *Beyond the keep.* Then I pulled a bobby pin from my hair and twisted off the dull rubber caps that covered the ends. Two little knife points, sharp as needles. I started scratching over each letter so that the words would still be there long after the lipstick faded.

Outside the white stone building, number eleven, long black cars without windows were backed up to the door. I was lined up with the old man, the brother and sister, and the rest of my group, as well as fifty or sixty more, including the waiter from the restaurant and others I recognized from the Paris underground.

People were put into the cars in groups of fifteen or twenty, and as soon as one car was filled, it would drive off and another would take its place. A guard shouted, "Prison du Cherche-Midi." He read off the names of the people he wanted, and they moved up and into the car, and then it roared off and up came another.

"Forte de Romainville." He read the names one by one. My heart jumped. If I was being sent there after all, it would be okay. Just two days early, and Émile would know—he would have to know by now where I was. He might already be in touch with his contact at the prison, to let him know to watch out for me. I would be out by tomorrow, Thursday at the latest. I would be back at Cleo's by Friday.

People were herded into the car and driven off. Another car pulled up, its motor rumbling. I watched after the car that drove away, thinking: It's okay. They can send more than one group to Romainville. I thought about the map I'd swallowed. I pictured every room and cell and hallway in my mind.

The guard said, "Prison de Fresnes," and called out names: "André Massaud. Jean-Louise Voison. Luc Voison. Thomas Olin. Clementine Roux . . ."

Prison de Fresnes.

There'd been a mistake. This wasn't the plan. I said to the guard, "I'm not supposed to be in this car."

His eyes were like ice and he said again, "Prison de Fresnes." Another guard came forward and slapped something cold and hard around my wrists—handcuffs. He cuffed me to another woman and to Jean-Louise, the little girl, and then he pushed us into the car. Her brother started crying, and she lurched for him, pulling me with her. The guard shoved us back, and inside there was a narrow passage down the center of the car. A handful of tiny cells, each no bigger than a broom closet, opened onto this. Each cell was only large enough for one person, but they pushed two or three inside, and the extra prisoners had to stand in the passageway that ran in between. A guard with a machine gun sat next to the driver and another guard climbed in and blocked the rear entrance. An open car followed behind and in it sat four armed police.

Next to me, the little girl was crying, and I squeezed her hand to let her know that she wasn't alone.

I couldn't go to Fresnes. This wasn't the plan. I thought maybe I'd heard wrong, that maybe it had something to do with no sleep and only a little food. I said to the guard at the back of the car, *"Pardon?* Where are we going?"

"Prison de Fresnes," he said. And then he smiled, and it was a smile that turned me cold. "For you, the war is over."

TWENTY-SEVEN

I crossed the courtyard at Fresnes prison, still handcuffed to Jean-Louise and the woman. Guards marched behind us and in front of us as we went up a short flight of steps into the entrance hall of the main prison building. The air was close and warm and shut up like a tomb. We lined up as they read our names off a list, and then the women and men were separated, some of them tugging at each other, trying to hold on. The prison matrons came forward for the women, and the matrons wore light blue uniforms with their hair pulled back from their faces in tight buns. They marched us down a wide hallway, and then through a locked door and into another long hallway, this one with ceilings as high as the church in Rouen.

The light was the first thing I noticed. After that it was the ceilings, which curved like the palm of a hand and were interrupted every few feet by skylights. Hundreds of narrow doors spread forward and above on either side of the hall on the balconies, and in each one was a window, more like a peek hole. On the second, third, and fourth floors, the two sides were linked by rickety metal bridges, and everything was cement and iron, which made the sound carry up and to the ceiling, bouncing off the skylights and back down again.

Armed guards marched across the balconies and prison matrons opened and shut doors with a hard clanging sound. I stood looking up through the skylight above my head, knowing there was blue sky beyond it, and then I tried counting the doors. One of the guards shouted names from a list, as if we were deaf or standing a long way off, and the women went forward as they were called. A prison matron would stop at a cell and unlock it, heavy keys rattling, and one by one, the women disappeared behind the doors, until there weren't many left of us.

"Clementine Roux," the guard shouted, and I stepped forward with Jean-Louise and the woman, who I was still handcuffed to. A matron with a nose like a turnip and thick blond hair rolled into braids grabbed our wrists and unlocked us. "Go," she said to me in a flat, blank voice. Another matron led me down the hall and up the stairs. Her mouth turned downward like a horseshoe and she smelled like onions.

I followed her up the stairs, her wide bottom waggling from side to side, looking like something that would win a contest at the county fair. We went up one flight, two flights, three flights, to the fourth floor, which was the highest you could get, and then I followed her down the balcony to cell number 401. Her keys rattled and she said to me, "Inside."

She pushed me in and the door slammed behind me, and the clank of it was like the echo of a church bell that had just stopped ringing. The room was about three yards long and two yards wide. It had high ceilings and whitewashed walls and a good-sized glass window on the wall across from the door. To the left was a shelf with hooks and an iron cot, which was folded up against the wall, and to the right was a toilet with a brass faucet hanging over it, and a table and chair that looked as if they were made for a child. These were also attached to the wall. Underneath the window were four straw mattresses and on top of this was a blanket and on top of this sat two women playing cards. The younger one was pretty, with a small, pointed face that reminded me of a mink. Her brown hair was short and she looked like she belonged outdoors, climbing trees and taking in the sun. The older one was tall and blond, with a hard, proud face and a judging look.

The older one said, "*Bienvenue à la maison.*" *Welcome home.*

I said, "*Merci.*"

"You're American then."

I wanted to say: No, I'm not. I'm actually French, which shows how much you know. But instead I said, "Yes."

She stood, and she was even taller than I'd expected. Her blond hair brushed her shoulders and was pinned back at the top. Her nose was long and her mouth drew in at the corners, and there was nothing pretty about her face but there was something stylish about her. "Mildred Reynolds Wallace. Watertown, Wisconsin. Call me Millie."

I almost said, "Velva Jean Hart, Fair Mountain, North Carolina," but instead I said, "Clementine Roux," and I felt like a liar all over again, like I always did when I told someone the wrong name.

"Not your real name, I'm guessing."

I said, "No, it's not."

Through it all, the younger girl was sitting on the mattresses, her eyes moving back and forth between us. I leaned down and held out my hand to her—"Hello"—and she shook it.

She said, "Annika Vadik," and her accent was thick. Then she said something in a language I'd never heard before. I thought she looked about my age, maybe a couple years older.

I said, *"D'ou viens tu?"* *Where are you from?*

She said, *"La Russie."* *Russia.*

Millie said, "She speaks very little English and very little French, so I'm glad you're here for my sake, of course, not yours." But she sounded as if she couldn't care less if I were there or not. "You don't have any cigarettes, by chance?"

"No."

"Just as well." Millie sat herself down in the chair at the desk and waved at me with one long hand to take her place on the mattresses. I sat next to Annika, the straw poking me in the legs. "What can I tell you about this place? We take turns sleeping on the bed. You'll get used to the fleas eventually. They feed us coffee in the morning, soup at noon, and bread at night. We get an extra ration of cheese or meat twice a week, and we get one Red Cross parcel a week to a cell—sugar and jam if we're lucky, crackers, cheese, some sort of fruit paté, and candy bars. It's up to us to ration it out and make it last. Of course it'll be harder now that you're here."

I said, "You're right. Maybe I should tell them I've changed my mind and I don't want to be here after all."

She stared at me and I stared at her, and Annika looked back and forth between us. Millie said, "Sorry," and I could tell that saying it was as hard for her as chewing nails. "Prison makes me irritable. Why are you in here anyway?"

I said, "I was picked up after an air raid, coming out of the underground." I didn't tell her anything else: *I'm a spy working with the Resistance and a group of secret agents, and I'm supposed to be on a mission right now.*

Millie nodded, drumming her fingers on the desk, and I could tell again that she didn't believe me. There was chipped red paint on her nails. She said she was a reporter, sent by the *Chicago Daily News* to cover the war. She said she'd had to fight like hell to get the assignment in the first place, but that so far she'd covered the war in Italy with the Free French troops, flown along on a dangerous night combat mission in the skies over Germany, and dressed up like a soldier and stowed away on one of the boats invading Omaha Beach on D-day. Even though I didn't want to be, I was impressed.

She pointed to Annika, who sat, legs out and crossed in front of her, ankle over ankle, leaning back on her arms. I thought prison must be so much worse when you couldn't understand anyone else. Millie said, "That one's the real hero, better than you or me, I'll wager, whatever you're really up to."

Annika nodded at me. She blew a stray piece of hair out of her eyes. Millie said, "My Russian is bad, at best, but from what I've been able to learn, she was a history student at Kiev University before the war, and when Russia entered the fight she joined the Soviet Army as a shooter for the 25th Infantry Division."

"A woman shooter?"

"Don't you know? The Soviets are much more evolved than the rest of us. Women are allowed into the army alongside the men. There are some two thousand female snipers fighting in Russia. Of course, at least a thousand of these are already dead or wounded."

Millie said something to Annika and Annika said something back to her, and then Millie said to me, "She's not sure how many Germans she's killed, but she thinks it's around three hundred."

I stared at Annika, who smiled at me. I said, "What is she doing here? In France?"

"She was injured last year and the army dismissed her. She came over here to fight with the Resistance."

Annika said something in Russian, and Millie said something back, and then she said to me, "She says, from what I can tell, that the key to being a sniper is patience. You have to know how to wait. You have to stay still for hours and know how to blend into your environment."

I said, "You have to lose yourself and become invisible." Just like being a spy. Just like being Velva Jean Hart. You have to forget everything you've ever known and everybody you ever knew. You have to give yourself up.

"Yes." After a pause, Millie said, "Do you have people on the outside?" I knew she meant did I have friends in Paris.

I said, "Yes."

"Does anyone know you're in here?"

"I don't know."

A few hours later I sat playing rummy with Annika, when I heard the sound of something rolling along the rails of the balcony floor. Millie closed the book she was reading—something in French—and stood up again from the desk. "We have to stand at the door or else they won't give us our rations."

We lined up in front of the door, and I could hear what must have been the food cart roll and stop and then the rattle of keys, the groan of a door opening, and, after a minute or two, the door closing, and the cart rolling and stopping again before rolling onward. Finally it stopped just outside. There was the clattering of keys and our door swung open. Another girl prisoner pushed the cart and a matron stood over her. The prisoner handed us a chunk of bread, the same exact size for each of us. The door slammed closed again and I could hear the clink of the keys, and the cart went rolling off.

Annika sat back down on the bed and ate her bread, one small piece at a time. Millie set hers on the desk untouched. She said, "I don't have the stomach for it anymore. You won't have the stomach for it either after a while." I looked closer at the bread and it looked like there was something moving in it. I pinched it off and held it in my hand.

"What is that?" But I already knew because I'd seen what happened to dead birds and squirrels left too long in the woods, and I knew what sometimes happened to the hog meat that we dried and stored in winter.

"Maggots," Millie said.

I picked one out, pinching it between my fingers, and then picked out another and another until the bread was full of holes, just like cheese. The maggot bodies lay on the floor, squished and shriveled. I didn't even feel bad for killing them. I tore off a piece of bread and stuck it in my mouth, trying not to think too much, trying not to feel sick. I decided right then that I would eat everything they gave me because I needed to keep up my strength. I wasn't staying here one more minute than I had to.

That night, Millie and Annika gave me the cot, even though I told them I was fine on the floor. Millie said, "Don't be ridiculous." Then she dragged one of the other mattresses into the corner across from the door and lay down. She closed her eyes and stretched out, feet hanging off the end, but I could tell she wasn't asleep.

Annika handed me the one toothbrush they had between them, the one the guards had let Millie keep when she got there along with a bar of soap and a washcloth. Annika said something and made a motion like she was brushing her teeth. Then Millie, eyes still closed, said, "You're welcome to share the toothbrush. Just wash it clean when you're done."

Afterward, I lay down on the bed, facing the window. Our one light was out and there was no way to turn it on, so there was nothing to do now but sleep. Outside, it was sunset, and through the glass you could see the outline of the iron bars. The air was so close and stale, I could barely breathe. It smelled like a springhouse on a hot summer day when all the fruit lay rotting. I said, "Do they ever open the windows?"

"No."

Annika said something. I said, "What did she say?"

"We could open them if we only had a knife."

I thought: I can't sleep like this. I can't stand it another minute. It's bad enough to be in prison, but this isn't even the prison I was supposed to be in. I can't even breathe.

The prison matrons were called *les souris*—the mice—by the prisoners. Except for my hairpins, the wooden singing girl, the seashell, and Ty's compass, which was still hidden in the shoulder pad of my blazer, the mice had taken everything—my money, my lipstick, my identity cards, the chewing gum, even my rip cord. They had sealed up my bag in an envelope and made me sign a receipt for the money they took from me, which was over fifty francs.

If only I could breathe.

I reached up and pulled a bobby pin out of my hair. In the half dark, I slid the rubber tips off the end and felt the sharp points against my finger. I stood up and went to the window and let my eyes get used to the fading light. With my fingertips I found each screw that held the window shut and I reached up and started unscrewing them, one by one.

I heard shifting behind me and Millie said, "What are you doing, Clementine Roux?"

I said, "I'm getting us some air."

Millie said, "If they catch us they'll send us to the dungeon."

I didn't know what the dungeon was, but I could imagine. I said, "I'm only doing it for a minute and then I'll put it back."

Annika pushed herself up off her mattress and walked over, saying something to me in Russian and reaching up her hands to help. A moment later Millie was there. She hissed, "What did you smuggle in?"

I ignored her and kept working. I worked until I'd unscrewed all the bolts for one of the panes, and then I swung the window open. The bars on the outside were as thick as arms, and made of a cold black iron. I wondered if I could fit through the spaces between them, but they were too narrow.

On one side of me, Annika stood with her eyes closed, the breeze blowing her hair. On the other side, Millie was staring straight into the row of courtyards that ran past the building. The corners of her mouth were turned down and her head was thrown back in a proud way, but her eyes were watering. The air hit me in the face like spring, and I leaned my head out as far as I could and breathed.

By Friday, I had learned the routine at Fresnes Prison for myself. Six o'clock in the morning was when you found out who was going to be interrogated by Gestapo headquarters later that day. We lay awake listening for the clanking of the iron-wheeled coffee cart, which stopped in front of the cells of the prisoners they were taking. We listened to the opening and closing of doors, wondering if it would be our turn. Sometimes women didn't come back, and when they did come back we knew they had been tortured in ways they didn't want to—or couldn't—talk about.

After a breakfast of ersatz coffee, we washed our faces, taking turns with the soap and the washcloth, and made up our beds and tried to tidy the cell as much as we could. There was loose straw and dust everywhere, and we started a contest to see who could catch the most fleas. After that, we sat on our sofa of mattresses and played cards. Millie, who had been there longest, said that every two weeks you were allowed a hot shower, that once every eight or ten days the food cart stopped by with books, and that there was a Catholic mass once a month before dawn.

Air raid warnings sounded almost every day. We knew that Paris was abuzz, that the Allies were close, and that the Liberation would be any day now. When the sirens started wailing, we ran to the window to see if we could see anything—B-24s or B-17s or bombs falling toward the earth.

Once a day they opened the door into the main hall balcony and left it open for half an hour. Twice a week they gave us a "promenade," which meant we were allowed in the courtyard outside our cell for twenty minutes. On Saturday, August 12, Annika and Millie and I were let out of our cell and taken down the stairs to the ground floor, and the matron opened a door into one of the courtyards, which was just a little plot of grass surrounded by concrete.

The three of us walked round and round in a circle, looking up at the sky. If we stopped moving, one of the guards would shout at us, so when we got tired of walking we jumped and somersaulted and cartwheeled on the grass, which made me think of physical education, or PE, back in Sweetwater, Texas, when I was training to be a WASP. We weren't allowed to talk to anyone outside our own cell mates, but back in our cell Millie and Annika showed me how you could talk with your neighbors by tapping out Morse code against the walls or whispering through the faucets. You could also take the metal soup bowl and hold it against the wall and speak through it, pressing your ear against the bowl to hear the reply. And you could communicate with the prisoners on the floors below by using the hot air shaft, sending messages and food up and down by strips of cloth tied together.

Through the walk outside and the talking to other prisoners, I was learning some things about Fresnes. The walls of the prison were a heavy stone, about twenty inches thick. There was a matron named Agathe, who worked Tuesdays and Thursdays and every other Friday, who would look the other way sometimes if you gave her a bribe.

The hardest thing about prison—harder even than wondering what Émile and Barzo were doing, and if they knew where I was, and if I would ever get out—was feeling closed up like a bird in a cage again, like I'd felt living with Harley Bright back on Devil's Courthouse. I hadn't felt so closed up and closed in since then.

Nighttime was the worst. After the sun went down, we opened the window and stood breathing in the air for half an hour. Sometimes I pressed my face against the bars and stared out at the grass and the trees, pretending I was free. And then we would screw the bolts back into place and lie down on our straw mattresses.

After we went to bed, we talked about the meals we would have once we got out of there. We invited each other to made-up dinner parties, telling about where we'd be going and what we'd be eating. When it was Annika's turn, Millie would translate as best she could, and when it was my turn I described one of Granny's home-cooked meals. I would say, "You're invited to Fair Mountain for the weekend. It's a warm day in fall, but not too warm. The trees are just changing colors, and it's such a beautiful clear day that we will eat outside on the banks of Three Gum River. We'll have sweet tea and hot biscuits and country ham and fried apple pies, and after we're done with that, we'll have corn bread and fried ramps and honey sweet potatoes and three-week slaw and barbecue chicken and molasses sweet bread."

Sometimes I took them to Nashville, to the Lovelorn Café, famous for their fried chicken, and other times I took them to the Italian restaurant I'd eaten in with Ty, in Blythe, California, or the Balsam Mountain inn, where Harley and I spent our honeymoon, and where I ate lime pepper steak at every meal.

After we were finished describing the food, our voices faded off until I knew, even though I couldn't see Millie or Annika, that we were each lying there with the dark and the fear and the lonesomeness crowding in on us. This was when my heart was heaviest, and when I felt like it, I sang to them—"Yellow Truck Coming, Yellow Truck Going" or "Beyond the Keep" or one of Butch's songs that he used to play me, or the "Hymn to Avenger Field." Sometimes I would hear the women from other cells, the ones nearby, humming along.

After the talking and the singing, there was nothing to do but lie on our mattresses and wait for sleep. This was the part of my day I dreaded most. I worried about Eleanor, this woman I'd never met who was my responsibility, and I worried about Gossie and Cleo and Émile. Most of all I worried about myself.

I couldn't get Mama's voice out of my head. I kept seeing her face fading into her pillow, after she took to her bed, and kept hearing her voice telling me to go to the window, saying, "Live out there. That's where you belong, Velva Jean."

Live out there had become a kind of chant in my head. I heard it with the wheels of the cart rolling down the balcony in the morning, at noon, at night. I heard it when I was walking the courtyard. I heard it when I was brushing my teeth or cleaning the cell or playing cards. I heard it every time I looked out the window, the air cooling my face. I was as far away from out there as I could be. Mama never would have told me to live out there if she'd known what was going to happen, that I was going to end up here, locked up tighter than I'd ever been locked up anyplace.

For the first time in my life, I was angry with Mama for ever putting the idea into my head, and that was worse than maggots or fleas or not knowing if I would get out of Fresnes prison at all—if maybe Émile hadn't found someone else to do his mission for him—or falling asleep to the sound of my own stomach, growling with hunger, or wondering if there really was a heaven at the end of everything or if it would just be me in the dirt in the ground forever.

TWENTY-EIGHT

*A*t six o'clock on the morning of Monday, August 14, we heard the metal clanking of the coffee cart rattling across the brick floor. We heard the doors opening and closing, until the cart was right outside. The door to our cell swung open and one of the matrons stood looking in. It had been my turn to sleep on the cot, and I lay on it now, trying to disappear. Her eyes, far apart and small as peas, moved from me to Millie to Annika. She said, "Clementine Roux?"

I said, "Yes?"

"You're to be ready at seven." She held out a cup of coffee and as she did I knew it could be my last. I stood up and took it from her and then I sat back down, legs shaking. The matron slammed the door closed and I heard the cart clattering away across the balcony.

I wanted to say: You don't want me. I'm not Clementine Roux. I'm Velva Jean Hart. I'm not the woman you think I am.

Millie said to the door, "Always a pleasure." And then she was up and sitting on the edge of the cot, her knees knobbing out in front of her, pinning her hair back from her face, a hand coming to rest on my arm. "Just remember—tell them nothing, no matter what they do to you. The traitors are the ones who talk before they're even touched. But I assure you, there's nothing they can do to you that's worse than your own conscience." She pushed up her sleeves and turned her arms so that the bottom sides were facing up and I could see the long red burn marks from the elbow to the wrist. "Hot irons. One of their favorite devices." She smiled dryly.

I reached out to touch the scars. "They did this to you?"

She rolled her sleeves back down. "Jesus. Did no one warn you about them?" I thought: There wasn't time. Émile would have warned me, we would have gone over it, but I was picked up too soon. "Stand up to them, but don't be belligerent. Speak slowly because if you hesitate, they're less likely to notice. Be dignified, calm, but vague. Don't look too observant. It's better if you act confused or frightened or even stupid. They might try to torture you, but their biggest weapon is mental torture. They'll try to break you down that way first. They want you to be uncomfortable or afraid. They want to throw you off balance. Always stick to your cover story. Never tell an unnecessary lie."

Annika walked over and handed me something—a handkerchief, and inside were some crackers and sugar. Millie nodded at her. "Yes," she said. "You could be there awhile, and you need to keep up your strength."

"Thank you," I said, thinking it would take more than sugar and crackers, but it was all we had.

"Whatever you do, don't eat anything they offer you. Not because it's poisoned—it shouldn't be—but because it's something they do. They offer you a feast, your first decent meal in days, and you're so grateful you start talking." She shook her head. "At the most, take a bite or two, but no more, no matter how good it smells or looks."

I was learning to keep time without a watch. When the matron came back to get me at seven o'clock, I was ready. Annika said something as I got up to leave, and Millie listened and nodded. "She says you don't need Nazi food because it's her turn to have us to dinner tonight, and she's preparing an extra special meal for you after this day. So hurry up and get back here. And knock 'em dead, kid."

I wanted to hug both of them, these women I would never have been friends with in real life, in the outside world, but instead I nodded and did my best to smile, and then I followed the matron out of the cell and across the balcony and down the stairs. She led me into a dark hall and another and then, instead of going outside into the courtyard and to a waiting car, which would take me to Gestapo headquarters, she opened the door to a room and pushed me inside.

The lamp on the desk was lit and in the light I could see the square bread-dough face and glasses of a man. It was a face I'd seen before. He said in French, "This must be Mademoiselle Roux. Sorry. It is 'Madame' instead, is it not?"

I had already told myself I would think over every question before I answered, to make sure I didn't slip up. I would answer slowly, just as Millie had said.

"Oui."

The office was warm as an oven, and he had the windows closed, even though they would have let in the breeze. The desk was small and wooden and plain. The man sat half in light and half in shadow. In English he said, "Of course, I should be speaking in English. You are American, after all." He paused, waiting for me to thank him for being so reasonable. "The thing is, you aren't Clementine Roux, are you?"

I said, "My papers say I'm Clementine Roux. You must have them because they took them from me." Why was I here? Who was this man?

He got up, unfolding himself as if he had all the time in the world. He walked around the desk and stood in front of it, so that he was just two feet away. He offered me a cigarette from a sleek silver case.

"No thank you."

"I forgot—you don't smoke." He took a cigarette for himself, and then held out his hand. "I'm being rude. Sergeant Bleicher."

The spy hunter. The one who had captured Eleanor. I wanted to spit in his hand, but instead I made myself shake it. "Clementine Roux."

He smiled, and the smile made me like him less. "Of course. Madame Roux." He said my name as if he were underlining it. "I have some questions for you. About the Brunets." I thought: I have some questions for you too. He settled himself on the end of the desk, feet on the floor, arms at his sides, hands resting on the edge, unlit cigarette poking out from his fingers.

"I have nothing to say." Who is Eleanor and why is she so important? Why did you go out of your way to hunt her down?

Sergeant Bleicher's face folded in at this, as if I had just broken his heart or run over his dog, but it was a pretend sad. He was playing nice with me, showing me he was the good guy in all this. "The Gestapo will send for you." I knew it was a warning, but he said it like it was the last thing on earth he wanted. "I don't think they'll be nearly as understanding."

In my head I kept questioning him: What is it Eleanor knows that you're so afraid of? Is she a spy? Why didn't you shoot her on the spot instead of putting her in prison?

He leaned forward, as if he were getting ready to tell me a secret. "As far as I'm concerned, the Nazi war effort can go to hell. I myself am counterintelligence. I work for the Abwehr. Or what used to be the Abwehr." He said it in a bitter way. "I hate to think of your family, wondering where you are, missing you. Look at you. You are very young and very beautiful. You are here in Paris, the city of lights. You should be enjoying yourself. I am assuming it's your first time here."

I didn't say anything.

He said, "Would you like some new clothes? Jewelry? A lovely girl like you shouldn't look so ragged."

I looked at him as if I didn't understand a word he was saying, as if the thing I wanted to do most in this world was to sit there and have him ask me questions. I thought: How many other people have you captured? How do you even sleep at night?

He said, "Perhaps you would like to go to the theater? Or the opera?" Something must have passed over my face because he said, "Ah, the opera then. I am sure this could be arranged."

I said, "No thank you." I wouldn't take a thing from him, not even a chance to go home this minute.

He said, "Now, the Brunets." His voice turned brisk as an afternoon walk. "If you could tell me anything you might know, it would be very helpful for my investigation." He gave me a charming-type smile, but it didn't suit him.

I said, "I rented a room from them."

"Did you know them before you came to Paris?"

"They are friends of the family."

"Good friends then."

"I didn't know them before renting the room, but they are nice people."

"You know, of course, that they're involved in the Resistance."

I didn't answer and he said, "You will talk, madame. To me or to someone else." And then he walked by me, so close I could feel the whoosh of him passing and smell the cigarettes on his breath. He opened the door and called for the matron, and then he stood in the doorway as she led me out. "I will see you again soon."

As I walked out, he said, "We have a mutual friend, you know."

I turned to look at him. The matron had her hand on my arm, her fingers pinching into my skin like claws.

"I believe you know him as Fritz. He was of great help when I was tracking you." I tried to keep my face still so that I wouldn't react, but he could see he'd surprised me. He nodded at the matron. He lit the cigarette. To me he said, "We will try again tomorrow."

The following morning, August 15, the matron led me across the balcony and down the stairs into a dark hall and another and then, instead of going into the office from the day before, she led me deep into the belly of the prison, down stairs that grew narrower and hallways that grew darker, and through a maze of passages with low ceilings just a few inches higher than my head. The mildew smell of earth and damp made me dizzy, and I followed her down a hall that was more like a cave leading to a tomb, walking past closed doors on either side with no peek holes. One of the doors at the end of the hall sat open, and Sergeant Bleicher stood inside smoking a cigarette.

The room was as small and tight as Monsieur Brunet's office, and there was only one small window, up near the ceiling, with bars on it. A single bulb hung from the ceiling and it gave off a dim light.

Sergeant Bleicher said, "How nice to see you again."

Once again he offered me a cigarette and once again I said no. He offered me a seat on the concrete bed. I told him I would stand, and then he asked me stupid things like how had I slept and how was I finding it here at Fresnes. He asked me more questions about the Brunets and I still didn't answer. He said, "You are not who you say you are, but amazingly there is no record of you. Just where do you come from, madame?"

I said, "I have nothing to say."

"Where did you first land in France?"

I have nothing to say.

"When did you land?"

I have nothing to say.

"Who are you working for?"

"I'm not working for anyone."

"Who are you working with?"

"I am by myself."

"What contacts did you make in France?"

I didn't say anything to this.

He sighed. "You mustn't take me for a fool, Madame Roux. I am a very patient man, but I have my limits. I should have you shot, but I really don't want to."

He said this as if he were giving me some wonderful gift. I stared at him without blinking, keeping my gaze steady and calm. He said, "We executed a prisoner yesterday, a young woman who ran an escape line for Jewish people. She was a wife and the mother of two. Her body is still lying in the courtyard."

I said, "I'm sorry to hear that." I thought: Don't let the fear in. Push it away.

He inhaled deeply and dropped the cigarette onto the floor, where it lay burning, the end of it glowing red. He lit another cigarette. I thought: He is on edge too. He needs to calm his nerves. He probably didn't smoke nearly as much before the war started.

He said, "How do you like this cell?" His eyes moved around it and he waved his cigarette hand at the walls, the ceiling. "The very best in solitary confinement. Only our finest accommodations for our least accommodating prisoners."

The sink was concrete and there wasn't any toilet, just a hole in the floor. The floor itself looked like it was moving but it was only the spiders and cockroaches. A person could dig up the dirt floor if she had something to dig with. A person could even dig with a shoe or a toothbrush or her very own hands if she was determined enough.

I said, "It could use some pictures on the walls, but otherwise I like it fine."

That night, back in my own cell, I heard the tapping of a spoon against one of the pipes. It was a message in Morse code, which said the Allies were in Chartres. When I asked Millie how far this was from Paris, she said it was less than a hundred kilometers.

The next morning, August 16, the matron came and led me away and Sergeant Bleicher was waiting, this time in a dungeon so deep down in the prison, I thought we must be in the middle of the earth. This one was even smaller and darker than the one before because it didn't have windows. It looked like a place where you wouldn't put a rat, but there was another dirt floor that could be dug up if someone worked hard enough.

I was learning the layout of the prison from the girls who had been there longest. This floor was below the ground, but the cell from the day before was at ground level. If I wasn't able to break out of cell 401, I figured the trick was to do something bad enough to get thrown into the ground-level cell, but not bad enough that they would shoot you.

After two hours of asking me questions that I still wouldn't answer, Sergeant Bleicher stared at me and I stared at him, and then he said, "You can't keep this up much longer."

I thought, That's what you think.

He led me all the way back to my cell himself, and before the matron locked me in he said, "There is no point in my coming anymore. But know this—the Gestapo won't be so easy to talk to. If you would only talk to me, I can promise you your life." I looked at him and thought, Like the life you promised Eleanor? And then I thought: How can anyone promise anyone else their life? I'm the only one who can promise that to myself.

I said, "Thank you," and vanished as far into my cell as I could go, turning my back on him. I stood looking out the window, but what I was really doing was drawing a map in my mind. Every time I left my cell, I memorized the walks **they took** me on so that I had an idea now of which way the hallways **ran and** what was on each level of the prison. The Allies would be here soon, but just in case, I was planning my escape.

On the morning of August 17, the six o'clock hour came and went without anyone opening our door. That night I slept better than I had in days. Sergeant Bleicher was a spy hunter, I was sure of it, but maybe he wasn't going to come around anymore. Maybe he had given up.

I lay in bed and thought, I might die here. Émile didn't believe in heaven. He believed that you were alive and then you were dead and then there was nothing. All this time, I'd been counting on seeing Mama again, and everyone else I loved who had died and gone on ahead. That's what Aunt Zona called it, "going on ahead." I could just about get through anything if I knew there was something on the other side of all this.

I closed my eyes and thought about how this day was another day that I was still alive, and for now I would have to be happy with that. And then I went over the map of Fresnes in my mind three times so that I wouldn't forget it. Every time I went over it, I saw something new—a window without bars, a guard who didn't pay attention, a door that wasn't watched as carefully as others, a closet where someone could hide if they somehow got out and needed to give the slip to the people chasing them.

I lay still another minute, and then I watched as Annika sat down by the hot air shaft and pried off the grate. She pulled up the heavy string that hung there, tied just inside, and wrapped it tight around a book, which she then dropped into the vent and started lowering. She reached inside the shaft and tapped on the pipes, a kind of code, and waited. She was answered with a tap, and she kept on lowering. I watched as she waited and then there was another *tap-tap-tap*, and she pulled the string back up. Something was tied to the end of it—a bar of chocolate.

If the hot air shaft was wide enough to send books through it, it might also be wide enough for a person, especially one who hadn't eaten in a while. I crossed over to the vent and sat down and felt around the edges. I took a bobby pin out of my hair and started chipping at the stone. It crumbled away, and then I stopped chipping and put my head through—the opening was just wide enough—to see how far down the shaft went, if it was blocked anywhere. I knew the vent eventually emptied into the yard below. From there, a person would have to get past two or three guards, depending on what day it was, and break through the fence.

Millie said, "What do you have there, Clementine?"

I said, "I don't know." Maybe a way out.

TWENTY-NINE

On Friday, August 18, I woke before sunrise to the sound of keys outside our door. All three of us sat up and looked at each other. It had been over a week since either Millie or Annika had been taken in, and I knew they worried about being next. The keys stopped their clinking and it was quiet, and then suddenly the door swung open and there was the matron's unhappy face. "Roux," she said. "You are to be ready by seven o'clock."

Millie said, "You're so popular, Clementine." To the matron she said, "You're making the rest of us feel like the ugly ducklings at a dance." The matron gave her a look that could scare a haint and banged the door shut so hard that it echoed for a full five seconds.

This time the matron marched me down the stairs and through the hall and through the maze of other hallways till we walked outside into the early morning sunshine, where a police van was waiting. Inside the van were wire cages, and I was locked inside one of these. After what seemed like hours, the van came to a stop. The doors opened and the guard stood glaring at me.

They guided me into a building that was bright and white and elegant, all windows and cast iron. I could tell right away that something was brewing because the Germans seemed jumpy and they were everywhere, like swarms of bees. One of the guards locked me in a cell with other prisoners, all men, and went away without saying a word. The men were handcuffed and bleeding. One of them had a swollen face, his left eye closed and puffy. Another wore rags wrapped around both hands, like mittens, and blood was soaking through. They didn't say anything to me, and something told me to let them alone.

I'd been there maybe twenty minutes, sitting on the cold floor, my knees pulled up under me, when the cell door opened and a man was pushed inside. Blood streamed down his face from his head, and he slumped to the floor. He mumbled something to himself and it sounded like a prayer.

Without thinking, I got to my feet and went to him. I said in French, "I don't know if you can understand me, but I need to see if you're okay." I tipped his face up, and his mouth was swollen and so was his nose. His breath was ragged, and he opened his eyes and looked up at me and through me as if he couldn't see me at all.

In English he said, "I've been here three days and I haven't eaten." His words were faint. His accent was strange. Maybe Irish. Maybe Australian.

I pulled out my handkerchief and said, "Open your mouth." Then I scooped some sugar onto a cracker and fed him, just like you'd feed a baby or a bird with a broken wing. He ate this slowly, and for a minute I was afraid he wouldn't keep it down. But he swallowed and ate some more and swallowed, and I fixed him another cracker and another, till they were almost all gone. I thought he really did look like a bird, kind of narrow and beakish and small. I fixed crackers for the other men and handed them around till the handkerchief was empty.

I thought: Maybe you should have saved some for yourself. You don't know how long you're going to be here, and there you are, giving all your food away. I knew the guards had put me in here on purpose so that I could see the suffering firsthand, and so that I would be scared enough to tell them anything they wanted to know. I thought: We'll just see about that. If I tell the truth, they'll only arrest more men like this and do horrible things to them, and I won't let that happen, no matter what they do to me.

The young man I'd fed sat back, his head leaning against the wall. Color was creeping into his cheeks. He said, "The Germans are in an especially bad mood today. I heard them say the police and subway workers and mail carriers are all on strike. The radio has stopped broadcasting. Resistance groups are defending themselves in the streets." He took a long pause between each sentence, catching his breath. "The Paris Liberation Committee has called the people of the city to revolt."

"The Liberation?"

"Soon." He shut his eyes as if the eyelids were too heavy to lift. He said, "I hope I live to see it."

I wished I had Monsieur Brunet's chewing gum so that I could blast us out of there. "You will," I said, but after I said it I wished I could take back the words. He might not live to see it and these other men might not live to see it, just like Perry and Ray and Coleman hadn't lived to see it. Just like I might not live to see it myself.

Hours later I stood in a room with a desk and a table and a couple of straight-backed chairs. The office was hot and airless and the large windows were closed, shutting out the day. An open bottle of wine sat on the table beside a plate of hot food. I could see the steam rising off of it. For a minute, my eyes watered and my stomach growled, and the food smelled so good that I didn't even notice the man who sat behind the desk and the girl who sat behind a typewriter. The girl looked younger than me and bored silly. She kept yawning behind her hand, and I noticed the nails were painted red, just like Millie's, only the polish wasn't chipped.

The man was young too and smelled like cologne. He wore a suit and his hair was smoothed back from his face and parted in the middle. He wasn't bad-looking, but there was something twitchy about him that reminded me of a stick insect.

The man said, "Before we get started, perhaps you'd like to eat. He held the plate up. "Meat and gravy, enough for all of us." He set down the plate. "But it is for you."

The smell shot straight up my nose and into my head so that I felt the room slide out from under me. How long had it been since I'd eaten anything but coffee and soup and bread with maggots? Only a few days. I didn't need their food. I would rather die right there before eating it. But I thought maybe a bite or two would help me focus and keep my head clear.

I ate four bites of the meal, and even though it wasn't as good as Granny's, it was the best thing I'd had in weeks. He offered me wine, and I shook my head. After the fourth bite of meat, I made myself push the plate away and said, "Thank you. It was delicious." My head felt less spinny, my stomach less empty. In my hand, I was holding a potato, which I'd managed to slide off the plate when they weren't looking. I poked this into my pocket.

The door opened then and Sergeant Bleicher walked in. He nodded at the man and at the girl, and, without saying a word to me, he took a seat and lit a cigarette. The young man frowned at me and then frowned at the plate. He said, "What is your full name?"

"Clementine Roux."

He asked me to spell it.

I spelled it.

The girl sat at her typewriter and clacked away at the keys every time the man said something or I said something. Hugo Bleicher sat smoking like a chimney, his legs crossed, his wide dough face a blank. The other man asked me silly questions, boring questions—things like where are you from, how old are you, did you go to school— because this was the way they tricked you into relaxing, into feeling at home enough to tell them what they wanted to know.

The man said, "What is your home address in the United States?"

I didn't say anything to this and he asked me again. I was remembering something in my hazy, spinny brain—something I'd read about the Geneva convention, way back when, in Texas or at Harrington. Something about prisoners of war only having to answer certain questions but not others. Then I thought, I am a prisoner of war.

Somehow the thought made me sit a little taller. Just wait till I tell Johnny Clay, I thought. I thought it as if I knew where he was, as if I could tell him tomorrow. And then I remembered that he wasn't anywhere right now and I might never see him again.

I said, "I'm not required to answer that question," which was what the Geneva convention said you should say.

"But you will answer it."

"I won't."

"You will tell me who you are working with here."

"I have nothing to say."

"Do you know a woman named Cleopatra Breedlove?"

I didn't flinch, not even a little. "No." My throat had gone so dry I was afraid I wouldn't be able to say anything else. I stared at the man without blinking, praying he wouldn't look close enough to see the sweat that was starting to gather on my upper lip and forehead.

The questions came faster then, like rifle fire. "Are you working for the OSS?" "Are you working with the SOE?" "How long have you been involved with the Resistance?" "What is your real name?" He paced the room back and forth, sometimes sitting down, and then popping up again to pace some more.

I finally stopped saying, "I know nothing." "I have nothing to say." "I don't have to answer that." And I just sat there looking at him and not saying anything. Hugo Bleicher coughed into his hand.

The man said, "It will be easier on you if you answer me."

I blinked at him, and that was when he slapped me hard across the face. My head went light and my eyes stung with tears. I tried fast to think of everything I'd learned in the WASP about survival training. The girl stopped typing and yawned again, not even bothering to cover her mouth.

I reached my hand up to feel my lip, at the split in the middle, when he grabbed me by the shoulders, up out of the chair, and pushed me against the wall. He held me there and said, "Tell me your real name."

"My name is Clementine Roux." I thought: Go away, Velva Jean. Run as fast as you can. Let me take care of this. I am Clementine Roux. I am Clementine Roux.

He put his hand to my throat and lifted me up the wall till my feet were hanging just off the floor. The room started to blur. His hand crushed my neck so that I couldn't swallow or breathe.

The man said, "Tell me your name. All we want is your name. Tell us this, and we will let you go." Beyond him, Hugo Bleicher examined his nails and the girl picked threads off her dress.

I could hear my breath—shallow, rasping, fighting for air. I said, "My name is Clementine Roux." My voice was just a croak, faint and distant. *My husband was Pierre and when he died I stayed in France because the war was on and I couldn't leave. Besides, where else would I go? He was the only man I ever loved, and this was his home. It's the place that reminds me of him. He would have wanted me to stay and fight for the country he loved. Pierre was a pilot. He died in an accident. He flew into the side of a mountain. He was too young. We'd only been married a year. He wrote me a song before he died, but I never heard him sing it. . . .* In my mind, I could see the crash site, could smell the smoke, could feel my young married heart break when they told me what had happened, that he was dead, when the letter came for me after he was already buried, the last letter he'd written me, the one with the words to the song.

The man let go of my neck and when he did, I fell onto the floor, all the while remembering to hold on to the potato, to make sure it stayed in my pocket.

I heard something from outside and it was the sound of gunfire and shouting in German and in French, and I thought: That's why the windows are closed. You don't want to hear what's going on out there, and you don't want us to hear it either. I looked at Sergeant Bleicher and smiled.

The other man said, "Get up."

I said, "I can't. I've hurt my leg." This was a lie, but I thought it would give me more time. I wanted a minute, just a minute, to catch my breath.

He kicked me in the back, once, twice, and pain shot through me, changing colors—it was blue then red then a hot, bright yellow. My eyes started burning like I was going to cry, but I wouldn't cry because I was on the other side of crying, in a place where there was only pain and anger. His boot came down on my shoulder, pressing me against the floor so that I felt as if I might go through it, down into the dungeons below, down into the earth. He pressed harder and harder until I was sure I'd feel the bone snap, but instead of crying I stared up at him without blinking.

Suddenly he lifted his boot off me and walked to the table and poured himself a glass of wine from the bottle that sat there, opened and waiting. He took a drink and set the glass down. I wished I had the pills with me, the ones Émile had given me, and that I'd kept the L pill, the lethal one, so I could pour it into his wine when he wasn't looking.

He said to Sergeant Bleicher, "See that she doesn't sleep."

They kept me awake all night. The minute my eyes drooped, I was splashed with water or made to walk about the room or slapped across the face. They brought a bucket of water in at one point and they held my head under until all the breath was gone out of my lungs. I stopped fighting and my mind drifted off and I thought: It can't get worse. What else can they do to me? Death can't be any worse than this, even if there won't be a heaven to go to.

At the thought of never seeing Johnny Clay or Mama again, I wanted to cry, but I couldn't because my head was underwater, held there by a man I didn't know, and my mind had gone foggy. I wondered what any of it meant—driving or flying or Ty or the WASP or Butch Dawkins writing me songs. What did it matter how many songs he wrote me if this was all it added up to? What did it matter if Émile loved me or didn't love me or never kissed me again? If it all ended the same for everybody, whether you were Velva Jean Hart or Clementine Roux, then why bother fighting?

> *I had to know you somewhere,*
> *maybe long ago,*
> *on some forgotten highway. . . .*

I knew a boy somewhere, maybe long ago. A boy, half-Choctaw, half-Creole, with a steel guitar and a Bluesman tattoo. He called me something once . . . what was it? Something different, something lovely . . .

> *Or maybe on a pathway*
> *where I knew that I was lost. . . .*

Down-home girl. He said that's what I was because, whatever happened—no matter how many people I lost or how many things happened to me that were bad—I just kept on. He said I had no choice because that was the kind of person I was.

I'll love you forever
and on the day when we die . . .

They let me up just as I closed my eyes and gave in, drifting away with the song. I sat in a chair dripping water on myself and no one gave me a towel. Sergeant Bleicher walked in and stayed with me for three hours, and after that a round of guards came in and out, on shifts.

In the morning, the Gestapo from the day before came to interrogate me. He brought in his breakfast and ate it in front of me while I sat and watched him. I was still wet, still shivering, but I watched him just like I was warm and dry and well fed. I watched him like I didn't give two cents, like I didn't mind that he was eating in front of me when I was hungry and tired. But even though I watched him, I was really far away in my own mind. I was hosting a dinner party for all the people in this world who I loved. I thought about each dish, each place setting, right down to the napkins—cloth ones from Deal's General Store—and I was practically through dessert by the time the man finished.

And then I put all those people I loved away, as if I were shutting them into a room that I'd already left. They would be safe there.

Run away, Velva Jean. Lock yourself in that room and don't come out.

I turned my mind to Pierre, my dead husband, and the friends I still had in Paris, his friends, his family. I was too young to be a widow, and I didn't care what happened to me, which made it easier to fight. I had nowhere to go in this world, and so it was just me, Clementine Roux. There was no room for anyone else.

The German said, "I hope you're feeling more cooperative this morning." He wiped his mouth with a napkin and folded it beside the plate, so that I could still see and smell the eggs and potatoes and bacon that were left over.

My stomach turned. But my head was clear. Clementine Roux was a down-home girl too. I said, "Not really."

At noon, I was driven back to Fresnes. Inside my cell, Annika sat under the window on top of the mattresses, the blanket covering them, but Millie was gone. When she saw me, Annika ran to the door and I thought again how much she belonged outside in the sun. She held her hand out to my lip and said something I couldn't understand, and then she plucked the washcloth off the hook in the wall and wet it under the faucet. While she dabbed at my lip, careful not to hurt me, my eyes went past her to the desk chair. A woman sat there with thick glasses and gray-black hair and a face like a sheep. She watched us, and I said, "Millie?" I looked back and forth from Annika to this new woman.

Annika said, "Gone."

When Annika was done cleaning my lip, the new woman stood and held out her hand and said, "Inés." She was French.

I shook her hand. "Clementine."

She said, "She is Russian?" She waved at Annika.

"Yes."

I sat down on the mattress sofa and pulled the potato out of my sleeve. I held it up and Annika grinned and Inés took the potato from me and washed it under the faucet. I watched her hands, which were small but clever. She washed the potato as if it were made of gold, and I thought she might be a surgeon or a baker in real life, but I was too tired to ask her, too tired to get to know anyone else who would only go away soon.

I handed Inés a bobby pin and showed her how it became a knife, and then she set the potato on the desk and sliced it into pieces. While we ate, I told them what had happened, in English and in French so that Annika might understand some, and afterward I explained the daily routine of Fresnes prison to Inés, just as Millie had done for me.

We let Inés have the cot that night and as I lay on the floor I wondered when I would be taken away. I was too tired to chip at the vent, too tired to think of a way out. I wondered where I would go and who would be explaining me to the next person, and what they would say.

I am Clementine Roux.

There wasn't much they could say because they didn't know any-thing about me, and it would be just like I had never existed at all.

Sometime in the night I woke up to the air raid siren. I lay on my mattress listening to the hum of engines, which sounded as if they were almost overhead. I got up from the floor and went to the window, and Annika joined me. We pressed our faces against the glass and we could see the German guards, running for the underground shelter that was outside the prison walls.

Annika bumped my arm and pointed to the sky. A group of planes flew low over the prison—the B-17 Flying Fortress. I could almost feel the throttle in my hand, feel the rattle of the motor, see the lights of the controls spread out like stars. I wanted to say, "I flew one of those across the ocean," but I didn't say it because that was another girl from long ago and not Clementine Roux.

As I watched, one of the planes seemed to tug a bit to the left, throwing the formation off. It wobbled and turned, and I could see that it was struggling to right itself.

Suddenly the nose of the bomber pointed down and it went speed-ing toward the earth. I heard a second plane explode like a firecracker and a third, and we couldn't see chutes or men jumping or where the other B-17s had gone. All we could see from the window were pieces of plane dropping from the sky, and a distant glow of fire.

Annika rested her head on her hands, which were holding on to the windowsill. When she looked up again I could see she was crying, and I put my arm around her. We stood there, watching, waiting.

The moon hung low in the sky. I thought: I know you're out there, Émile. I know you're trying to find me. Maybe you're looking up at this same moon right now.

Annika started to hum "Hymn to Avenger Field." She said, "Sing, Clementine."

She started to sing it and I let her sing on her own for a while before I joined in. When we were finished a voice behind me said, "I know that song."

Inés was sitting up, rubbing her eyes. She reached for her glasses, which she tucked over one ear and then the other. She sang, " 'In the land of crimson sunsets, skies are wide and blue,' " in a warbly, off-key voice.

I tried to make out her face in the dark. I said, "How would you know that?"

"I worked on the Comet Line south of Nesles, and there was a girl pilot."

I said, "Comet Line?"

"The Freedom Line. This girl was American and she was always singing that song. Not well. She didn't have a voice like yours. But she was a nice girl. Smart. A lady."

"What happened to her?" I was afraid to ask it. Inés was here at Fresnes prison. She might have been caught and captured anytime, or Helen might have been with her.

"I sent her with a guide and two other pilots—both male—to Spain."

"Do you know if she got there?"

"I don't know. Three days later I was arrested."

I suddenly didn't want to talk anymore. I was thinking: Helen's alive. She's okay. She must have crashed too, but she's fine. I wanted to cry, but I couldn't cry.

Inés said, "You know her?"

"Yes," I said. "I used to." From a very long time ago, back when I was a pilot too, back when I was a girl from North Carolina named Velva Jean Hart.

THIRTY

The next day was Sunday, August 20. Behind the prison walls, we could hear the sounds of planes over the city. Every time a prisoner was taken to headquarters, they brought news from the outside. We knew the BBC was warning the French to stay off the highways because Allied planes were bombing and strafing every moving object they could target. There had been a second Allied landing on the coast of southern France, and now the Allies were nearly to Paris, where police, subway workers, and postal workers were all on strike, and the Resistance was leading citizens to attack the Germans.

Just after six o'clock the next morning, the coffee cart rattled down the halls, starting with the first floor, moving up to the second, then the third, until it reached our floor. One by one, I could hear the cell doors banging open. So many. Too many. It sounded like every single one of them was opening. The cart was making its way toward us. I heard a cell nearby open. Then another. Another.

The cart stopped outside our door. I held my breath. Everything was quiet. Annika and Inés and I looked at each other, waiting. Go on, I thought. Keep going.

The cell swung open and one of the matrons said, "Clementine Roux?"

"Yes?"

She said, "You are to leave here at noon today. Be ready."

"Where am I going?"

She said, "I do not know where they're sending you, but you should have your things together." Unlike the other matrons, she had a pleasant face, fresh and scrubbed as a whitewashed fence.

I sat up. "Something is happening out there. We can hear it."

She said, "The Allies have advanced within fifteen miles of Paris."

I said, "Then Liberation is almost here." I felt a hopeful rise in my heart.

She said, "Yes. For some," and she walked out, shutting the door with a bang.

The hours crawled by so that I lost all sense of time. At what must have been noon, the matron came back and waited while I said goodbye. I gave Inés a hug, even though I hardly knew her, and then I hugged Annika good and hard. I handed her one of my bobby pins and said, "We'll see each other again," and then in French, "See you soon. Take heart. Be strong."

Downstairs, I stood in line with a dozen other prisoners in that first room where we were searched the day we got to Fresnes. The prison guards gave me back my handbag, and I dropped the seashell, the wooden girl, and the hairpins into it, along with the green scarf I'd used as a turban. Ty's compass was still hidden in my shoulder pad.

There was a mirror hanging on the wall of the room, just by the door, and I looked up and caught my image there. At first, I thought it was someone else because the face was too pale, too thin, and the hair was too dark and short. The eyes looked blurry and the freckles had faded. The ones that were left stood out like chicken pox.

They loaded us into the prison car and locked us in our chicken cages. I couldn't tell where we were headed—if it was back into the city or somewhere farther out. Some of the women were crying, but I opened my bag and pulled out my lipstick, Révolution Rouge. *Revolution Red.* I painted my mouth a deep, blood red. I wasn't going to cry, no matter where they were taking me. I decided Clementine Roux had cried enough, that she didn't much like to cry to begin with, but with a dead husband she hadn't had much choice. She'd done a lot of crying, but she wasn't going to cry anymore.

*   *   *

I recognized Romainville from the map I'd eaten. It sat on top of a low hill, fat and swollen, a thick stone fortress that looked exactly like Death's Waiting Room should look. I stood in line in an office where there was a long counter, and behind this sat a half dozen German men in uniforms. I wondered if one of these men was Niklaus Reiner, Émile's contact.

When my name was called, I stepped up to the front, and a young officer sorted through my bag. He handed it back to me with everything still in it, but he held on to my identity paper.

"You are American." His English was clear and he didn't have much of an accent.

"Yes."

"I lived in the United States before the war, in New York City." I thought: He's trying to lull you in. He's making friends with you so that you'll tell him things.

I said, "Why did you leave?"

"The war. I had to return for mobilization, but as soon as the war is over I'm going back."

He handed me my driver's license. He said, "Perhaps I'll see you there." His voice was kind and warm. I wondered if he was the one Émile had talked about. If he was, did he know it was me, the one they were sending? And if it wasn't him, how was I supposed to know who I was looking for?

I said, "Perhaps." And then I held out my hand. "You know my name but I don't know yours." I thought, Please be Niklaus Reiner.

The other officers stared as he shook my hand. He said, "I am Josef."

The barracks building was surrounded by a barbed wire fence at least ten feet tall, maybe taller than that. Guards stood at either end with searchlights and machine guns. My cell was on the ground floor and was shared with six other prisoners. There was a sign on the door that said *"Alles Ist Verboten." Everything Is Forbidden.* The room was large, with a gravel floor, two-story wood bunks with rotting straw mattresses, and a wide window without bars. I could see right away that two of the girls were pregnant—one looked as if she were ready to have her baby any day now. An old woman, brittle as a dried leaf, stood beside a younger woman leaning on a crutch. Behind them, sitting on the floor, was a girl no older than sixteen and what looked to be her mama, because they had the same big nose and small chin and the same sad eyes like a cow. I didn't bother telling them my name and they didn't tell me theirs.

The old woman said that until a few days ago they'd been let out in the courtyard to take in the sun. She said it was better here than at Fresnes and worse too. She said every day at four p.m. there was a roll call, and that was when thirty or forty women were rounded up and sent to Germany to one of the camps. She said sometimes they were taken out of the cells and beaten, for no reason at all, and that they weren't allowed Red Cross packages, but had to get by on soup with maggots, bread, and rancid cheese.

She said in French, "You have to be careful who you talk to because the Germans have filled this place with informers. They're here to catch spies and Resistance fighters." She said this like she was accusing me of something. Her mouth broke into a sly, ugly smile. "It's not safe to talk to anyone, even to you. You might be working for them yourself."

I said in French, "I might. But I'm not."

She said, "You look like just the sort to work for them."

I said, "I'm sorry you think so." I wanted to slap her across the face, but instead I turned to the other women and asked if any of them had a piece of paper and a pencil.

The old woman said, "You aren't allowed to write letters home."

"I don't want to write a letter." I wanted to write a song.

"No paper," she said. "No pencil." She narrowed her eyes at me.

"I have paper," the girl with the sad cow eyes said in French. She carried a bag like mine over her shoulder and she stuck a hand inside and pulled out a few sheets of paper, torn in fourths, and a stubby pencil. I took one of the sheets from her and the pencil, promising to give it back. She said, "We write messages and hide them." She waved me over to a corner near the window and showed me where part of the stone wall was crumbling away. "Here."

The old woman frowned at the girl, at the wall, at me. She started clucking to herself under her breath. The girl said in English, "If one of us leaves, we take them to give outside." She meant to the outside world.

I said, *"Merci."* Then I said, "Do you know of a guard here named Niklaus Reiner?" The old woman was watching me. I wondered if she could be a spy or an informer for the Germans.

The girl said, "No. But they are always changing guards. He may have been here or may still be here, I do not know. Sometimes the guards become too sympathetic and they are removed."

"Or shot," the old woman said, and her eyes gleamed like a crow's.

I sat down on the floor, my back against the wall, and told myself to let them be. Better not to ask too many questions or call too much attention. I tried to think of a song. I held the pencil over the paper, waiting. I tried to think of everything that had happened to me and everything I might want to say.

> *Never confess.*
> *Good-bye forever to France.*
> *I am afraid.*
> *Don't talk.*
> *Life is beautiful.*
> *Live out there.*

The words went swimming through my head till they blurred together and started looping around and around. I looked down at the paper and it was still empty and blank, and the pencil still sat in my hand, my fingers wrapped around it, the dull point of it hanging just above the page.

That night, I lay in my bed, in the top story of one of the bunks, and went over the map of Romainville in my mind. I made myself remember every detail and as soon as I remembered it once, I remembered it again and then again. From what I could tell, I was in the eastern part of the building. In my mind, I counted exactly how many doors were between my cell and the main door, the one where they'd brought us in. I also counted how many doors were between the cell and the door at the end of the hall, which led out into the courtyard.

Bedbugs lived in the wood frame of the bed, and I lay itching and scratching and remembering the locusts at Avenger Field. I climbed down, trying not to wake anyone up, and lifted the straw mattress off the frame and set it on the floor in front of the window.

At curfew, a guard had come to count us and then double-locked the door, but we were allowed to keep the window open. I breathed in the night air. If I closed my eyes, I could almost trick myself into thinking I was in Nashville or Texas or even up on Fair Mountain. But then a great beam of light would sweep past—the spotlight they used to search the grounds—and then another, with exactly sixty seconds in between each sweep.

I couldn't count on Niklaus Reiner. I had to be ready to do this on my own. I could use my hairpins to open the window wide enough so that I could fit through. The yard was only a couple of feet below, and the drop would be easy, but before I tried to sneak out I needed to find Eleanor. Émile and Barzo might have already found a way to move her out of Romainville. I had asked the women in my cell if they knew of someone by that name. I had described her to them, but no one knew anything, or said they didn't. She could still be there in another cell, or she might be locked up by herself. I knew from the map where the *cachots* were, the underground cells where they kept their most dangerous prisoners.

I was still planning as I drifted off. From somewhere in the distance there was the thunder of a cannon, and then the answer of machine guns. I felt myself drifting into the clouds, which hung in the sky outside the window, up above the courtyard. I drifted high and free and then I heard my mama's voice singing.

The old woman had told me that once a week they'd been allowed a hot shower, a sunbath, and a chance to wash their clothes, but that now they wouldn't let us out for any of these things. I was sure it had something to do with the Allies and the fighting and the cannon sounds in the night. The girl with the cow eyes showed me a piece of paper, which she kept hidden inside the hole in the wall, the one that held the messages. On it, she was tracking the progress of the Allies as they drew closer to Paris.

The next morning, I painted my lips for no reason, other than that it made me feel better and stronger—like Carole Lombard or Constance Kurridge. Or like Clementine Roux, who had made a promise to herself after her husband died to only wear red lipstick. One of the pregnant girls taught me to play bridge and Belote, a French card game, and I tried again to write a song, but I spent most of the morning at the window trying to figure a way out.

The guards here had let me keep the package of chewing gum. I thought about all the ways I could use it. I could blast the window, but then I'd have to make my way through the courtyard and past the guards who watched it. I could blast the cell door, but then I'd have to get past the matrons and the guards on the other side. If I could get to Eleanor, I could blast her out, but first I had to find her.

I said to the old woman, "What does it take to get put in the *cachots*?" I wanted to ask what was just enough to get you in there but not so much that they would kill you instead.

She narrowed her eyes and for one horrible moment I thought she was going to put a curse on my head. "What do you want with the *cachots*?"

"Are they as terrible as they say?"

"I have never been." She spat on the floor and fixed her eyes on me. "You'd best not be up to something." And then she let loose with a stream of angry French.

One of the other girls said, "The prisoners there are spies and murderers. Thieves. Traitors."

"Do they lock them there when they first get here or are they sent there along the way?"

"Both."

The old woman was still glaring at me. She said, "You ask too many questions."

At four o'clock that afternoon, we lined up in front of our cells, and the guards marched up and down, their hobnail boots like hammers on the stone floor. While the guards read the list of names of those who would be deported, I searched the faces for the woman, Eleanor. I looked for the face in the photograph, but all I saw were cheeks that were too pale, and arms that were too thin, and eyes that were too hollow.

Four of the women from my cell were called—the old woman, the two pregnant girls, and the one with the crutch. The mother and daughter hung on to each other, and seeing them made me think of the little girl and boy, the sister and brother, at Fresnes. Where were they now?

Josef, the German from New York, stopped in front of me. "Looking for someone?"

I said, "There are just so many."

"Not as many as there once were." As the women were called, they shuffled forward and followed the guard past us, their chins high, their backs straight. Most of them stared at the head of the woman in front of them, but others waved to us and said, *"Au revoir!" "À bientôt!" "Vive la France!"*

Good-bye! See you soon! Long live France!

As I watched them pass, I thought: You are completely alone, Clementine. The only person who can save you is you. As if he knew what I was thinking, the German said, very low, so that only I could hear, "The Liberation is almost here, and I do not think you will be evacuated to Germany."

His words made my heart lift, but I didn't want it to lift if it wasn't the truth. With my mind, I pushed my heart down again, back to where it was anchored around my stomach. I said, "What are you saying?"

"I think we'll both be headed back to America before long." Even though I knew he only wanted it to be true too, I let my heart go just a little.

On my mattress that night, a warm breeze blowing in through the window, I looked at the mother and daughter, still clinging together, their mattresses pushed side by side on the floor. The rest of the beds lay empty. After we'd been returned to the cell, now that we were all that was left, they had asked me my name. "Clementine," I said. Before they could tell me theirs, I asked them, "If we go too, where would they take us?"

"Germany," the mother said.

"And how would we go?"

"By train." And then she'd drawn the route for me, as best she could.

Now I held the pencil in my hand, above the paper. Her map was on the back of it, and I studied this. I turned it over. Every time I started to write something, I stopped myself. I could only hear fragments of sentences, just a word here and there. Somewhere, far off, as far away as Rouen, maybe as far as Lisieux, I heard music, the faint, shadowy beginnings of a melody.

I think we'll both be headed back to America before long.

A hopeful feeling surged up in my heart. It felt like spring. I let it rise a little higher in my chest, and I thought: Maybe I won't have to get myself thrown into the *cachots* so I can find Eleanor. Maybe we'll all be set free before that.

I wrote: *Life is beautiful.* As I looked at the words, small on the page—just words, just letters, nothing more than that—I felt a cold, dead creeping, like something was sneaking up on me from behind.

Underneath them I wrote: *I am afraid.*

THIRTY-ONE

I was holding my Mexican guitar and standing at a microphone. I was playing but I wasn't singing, and I could feel the rough wood of the stage cool under my bare feet. I thought: Where are my shoes? Where did I put them? I tried to remember. I opened my eyes and stared down at my feet, and sure enough, they were naked. Then I looked up and out, and I was at the Grand Ole Opry, only all the seats were empty. I said, "Hello?" and my voice echoed back to me.

I almost walked off that stage, but then I thought: It took you an awfully long time to get here. Maybe if you start playing someone will show up.

I strummed the guitar again and opened my mouth to sing. I was trying to sing "Yellow Truck Coming, Yellow Truck Going," but the words came out in French. So I started to sing a new song, one I knew I hadn't written yet. These words were in French too. I thought: I wonder what that song is? I wonder if the words are any good?

No one was showing up, and I started to get mad. I lay my guitar down on the stage and said into the microphone, "What's the good of being up here playing like this if there's no one to listen?" I said, "I might as well just go on home as stand here." I said it like a threat, but there was not a soul there to hear it. "All right," I said. "Okay then. I mean it."

I picked up the guitar and suddenly there was a scream, only it didn't sound like a person. It was more like an animal or a monster. It sounded as if it were coming from outside the Opry, maybe as far away as the Lovelorn Café. I told myself: You're dreaming. It's only a dream. Wake up.

It was the worst scream I'd ever heard, and I lay the guitar back down and sat myself on the stage and decided I wasn't going anywhere as long as that monster was outside.

On second thought, I told myself, don't wake up. Don't you do it. If you wake up, it might be something bad. Stay in the dream.

I put my hands over my ears, but the sound came in anyway, and as I looked out into the black of the theater, I saw a white face shining there, watching me. At first I thought it was the monster, but then I could see that it was Judge Hay, the man who decided who sang at the Opry and who didn't. Even as I covered my ears, I thought: I hope he's not disappointed that no one came to hear me. I hope he doesn't think he made a mistake.

He said, "They are coming," but to be sure of it I took my hands off my ears and said, "Sir?"

"They are coming." His voice was high and girlish, and it didn't make sense with his face, with the cigar that stuck out of his mouth like a hand ready to be shaken. His lips weren't even moving, but he kept saying it. "They are coming. They are coming, Clementine."

I wanted to tell him that this wasn't my name, that I'd had another name, a long time ago, but I couldn't think what it was.

"Clementine!" Suddenly I opened my eyes and the girl, the one who'd given me paper and a pencil, was standing over me, her thin face, sallow as candle wax, staring into mine. The screaming was louder than in my dream, but it wasn't a monster at all—it was an air raid siren. I could see her mother brush behind her, dark clothes fluttering like bird's wings. The girl said, "They are coming for us."

Romainville was like a military fort, with cold stone walls and long, low brick buildings that sat in a square. The courtyard was in the middle of this, and we stood in the courtyard, some three hundred women, carrying our bags and purses and, in some cases, suitcases— whatever they'd let us keep—and waited. They divided us into groups by the letters of our last names and told us the buses were coming to pick us up, but they wouldn't say where the buses were taking us. Then they handed out parcels from the Red Cross and told us these had to last us for the journey, but they wouldn't say how long that journey would be.

We weren't allowed to talk to each other, so we waited in silence, under a blinding sun, and an hour went by and then another and another. I stood, my legs going to sleep, sweat running down my back, my hand at my side, my fist closed up around the paper messages, which I'd taken from the hiding place in the wall of our cell. I'd only had time to write two words on my piece of paper, so that besides *Life is beautiful, I am afraid,* it now said, *Leaving here.*

I made sure I was last in my line. I thought: Maybe the buses won't come and we'll go back to our cells and I can figure out how to find this Eleanor. I looked for her in the crowd, but all the faces were blurring together until they looked the same—thin, pale faces with eyes like tree hollows.

Maybe they won't come.

At three o'clock, there was the sound of something in the distance. At first it was a rumble, and then there came a grinding of gears like a tank was trying to make its way down the hill toward us. The guards started hollering, and the gates to the courtyard were thrown open so that we could see the buses. They were painted a dark, ugly green.

Men came down from the buses and started shouting at us. These were the SS, Hitler's personal bodyguards. They were the cruelest of all the German soldiers. They waved their guns and jabbed them into our backs and every single one of them, handsome or plain, had a horrible, sharp face, mean as a jackal's. A woman behind me said in French, "Thank God we are leaving. There will be a massacre in the prison."

Some of the women stumbled as they climbed into the first of the buses. The guards shouted and one of them raised the butt of his gun and hit a young woman on the side of her head. Up on the bus, it was like breathing into a hot, wet towel. The air lay still and heavy and for one terrible moment I thought I was going to faint. The door closed behind me, and I was standing by the driver because there wasn't anywhere to sit and there wasn't anywhere else to stand. He was a Frenchman.

The driver was to the left of me, and there was an SS guard on my right with his gun pointed at the door, waiting for someone to rush past him. He moved his eyes over us like one of those prison spotlights, sweeping up and then back, up and then back. The buses behind us were filling up with the other groups, and so we waited there, the engine idling, the air growing hotter and heavier till I was breathing with my mouth open, as if I were underwater.

I felt someone poke me from behind and then there was a piece of paper tucking into my hand, the one that was empty. I felt another piece of paper there and another. I wanted to say: No. Keep them. You'll get me in trouble. Someone rapped on the door to the bus and I almost jumped through my skin. The SS guard pushed the door open and leaned out to talk to the guard outside.

I said to the bus driver, "*J'ai des messages.*" *I have messages*. I held out my hands, trying to keep them low. When I opened them I saw the franc notes someone had passed me. "*Et l'argent.*" *And money*.

The driver slid his hand out and took them from me. Before I could say thank you, he said in English, "I have been driving prisoners all day and yesterday. From Fresnes, from Cherche-Midi, now here. I am sickened."

"Are all the prisoners being evacuated?"

"Yes."

"Where are the Allies?"

"They are here."

"Then the Liberation . . . ?"

"It is soon."

The SS guard clattered back into the bus and shouted an order at the driver. I pretended that I'd just been standing and not talking and not doing anything but waiting. We lurched backward, all of us falling and grabbing on to anything—the seats, windows, one another. The driver was trying to get that bus up the hill, but there were too many of us. He surged up and then back, up and then back, and finally they made us get out and follow the buses on foot.

At the top of the hill, they loaded us in again, and we rumbled off through the streets of Paris, passing shops and cafés and parks where people were gathered like it was any other day. As we rattled by, they stopped what they were doing to watch, their faces washed over by fear and pity, and gratitude that it wasn't them.

Most Paris rail stations had been destroyed by bombing, but Gare de Pantin sat in a neighborhood just outside the city, and it hadn't even been touched. Boxcars were lined up, as endless as the Scenic. In every window in every car faces crowded together. Eyes peered out of narrow openings and the cracks of half-closed doors.

Where are they going?

Other green buses arrived, and these carried male prisoners. The men looked as thin and pale as the women. For the first time, I wasn't sure I could do whatever the next thing was, and I froze. I told myself: Move, Clementine. Move now before they make you move. But my legs were rooted like a tree.

Behind me a voice said, *"Allons-y maintenant." We must go now.* She spoke in French, but she didn't sound French. There was a hand on my back, pressing me forward, then a hand in mine, guiding me. I closed my eyes and let myself be pulled. I should never have come. I should have gotten myself home on the Freedom Line. I wasn't a soldier or a spy. I was just a girl who could drive an old yellow truck and sing some songs and fly a plane.

All of a sudden I was bumped and shoved off the bus, herded up and moving toward a boxcar that said "30 horses—40 men" on the side. It didn't say anything about women. Before I could think to run or scream, I was inside the boxcar, swept in by the tide, and squeezing together with sixty other women. The woman still held my hand. She said, *"Ici." Here.* We sat down near the door. A thin layer of straw covered the floor, and we sat with our backs against the walls of the car or against the backs of one another, knees tucked up tight to make room for everyone else. Some of the women had a suitcase or box with them, and they stacked these along the walls.

The woman said, "Magda." She held out her hand to me. I thought:

Don't make me learn your name. You'll disappear, and I'll disappear, and I would rather not know it because you'll just be one more person I know who's gone.

I shook her hand and said, "Clementine."

One of the women said in French and then in English, "Breathe the air while you can. Remember the feeling of it." I closed my eyes and breathed it in, and it was the warm, sweet air of summer.

I opened my eyes and took in the wide blue sky, and I saw that Red Cross workers were moving up and down the line of cars. One of them came to us and she was young but looked old. She held out drinking water to everyone, and arms and hands reached for it, for her. She said, "You'll never get to Germany. You will be liberated before then." But all I heard was *Germany*.

When it was my turn, I reached my hand out for water, and I reached my head out too so that I could breathe the air in. Women were being shoved into the boxcar next to mine. They all looked the same—thin and ragged and frightened. They each had the look of a dog with mange, which was how I looked and how the rest of us looked too. One of the women turned just then. From the back I thought she was a girl, but she was actually older than me, though I couldn't tell how much. She had black hair and a heart-shaped face and arched eyebrows that gave her a fierce look.

Eleanor.

Before I could think what to do, the door to the boxcar slammed shut and there were only slivers of light, thin as reeds, falling across our legs and faces. The women at the back of the car, the ones in the corners, started grumbling, and I was suddenly glad about where I was sitting. I rested my face against the door and felt the air coming through the cracks, into my ear, onto my cheek. I tried to keep sight of Eleanor, still outside, but all I could see was earth and sky.

Minutes later, there was a tug that knocked me backward, and then another and another as the train began to move. I planted my feet into the sawdust and shifted my weight so I wouldn't topple over. The train built up speed till we were clacking along the tracks. I put one eye to the crack by the door, watching as a blur of colors rushed by.

I suddenly remembered my compass, the one in my shoulder pad. I pulled at my jacket, trying to get it off, which was almost impossible since I was smashed against women on my left and right, front and back. I was finally able to wrench it off, nearly ripping it in two, and set it in my lap. Some of the women were starting to cry and argue. I felt in the shoulder pads with my fingers until I found the compass and tore it free, and then I held it in the flat of my palm up to the light, trying to keep my hand steady.

Northeast. Just as the Red Cross worker had said. They were taking us to Germany.

Fifteen or twenty minutes later, there was the clear gonging of bells. Magda said, "Notre Dame. It's the largest of the bells, Emmanuel. The last time it rang was midnight on June 14, 1940, the day the Germans entered Paris."

The women in the car started singing "La Marseillaise," their voices rising above the bells and the clattering of the wheels against the tracks. I sang along in French and then I switched to English. Someone else nearby was singing in English also, and even in different languages, I thought we sounded better than any chorus on the Grand Ole Opry stage.

> *March on, march on!*
> *All hearts resolv'd*
> *On victory or death!*

The song spread to the other cars until everyone, women and men, was singing. The bell chimed on, even after our voices faded off, and I thought: Emmanuel is telling us good-bye.

We rattled onward into the night, pressed together in the heat without air or water. A woman next to me licked the sweat off her wrist. Some of the women stripped down to their underclothes. A tin bucket sat in the corner of the car, and this was the toilet.

I opened my Red Cross parcel, which was sugar and crackers and a tin of jam and a bar of chocolate. I opened the chocolate and a woman behind me said, "It might be poisoned." She sat with her parcel closed up on her lap. Some of the women were talking and I could hear the edge in their voices, which sounded too high in the dark boxcar, and too bright. A few of the women were still crying, and others sat silent, staring in front of them at nothing.

We slept in shifts because there wasn't enough room to lie down. Half of us stretched out as much as we could the first part of the night, and then the other half slept during the second part. I sat up the whole time, my head bumping against the door. I was too tired to lie down and too tired to take shifts.

Sometime the next morning, we passed into a tunnel, the yellow splinters of daylight disappearing all at once, leaving us in blackness. The train churned to a halt, still inside the tunnel. One of the women had a book of matches, and she lit them over and over while another woman, who had a watch, kept a record of how long we were there.

After one hour, we were still sitting on the tracks. The air was thick with black smoke, and we could hear the sound of the heavy German boots as they ran alongside the boxcars. The Germans shouted at each other. One of the women said, "They are trying to asphyxiate us."

Another said, "The tracks were blown. They are trying to figure out what to do."

Two hours later, we hadn't moved. The women on the left of me and the right of me took my hands and held them. *You are not alone,* they were saying. *I am here. We are all here together.* Down the line of cars, women and men were shouting: "Give us air!" "Give us water!" "Give us food!" The women in my car started shouting it too, banging on the walls, on the door. I thought: They are leaving us here to die. The Germans have gone off and left us and when the war is over they'll find us here, hundreds of us on this train. They'll write it up in the newspapers for the folks in England and back home, and the headline will call it "Death's Waiting Room."

The women started shouting at one another. One pushed past us and threw herself at the door, crying out in French. She clawed at a crack in the wall until her fingers started bleeding, and then another woman pushed her away and started to scream. Magda squeezed my hand like she was strangling the women. She said, "Idiots. They are causing a panic. They will use up all the air."

The women were pushing each other and crying out: "Give us air!" "Give us water!" Before I even had a song in my head, I started to sing, and it was a song I'd never sung before except in a dream. In the dream, I'd sung the words in French, but now I sang them in English. It was a song for Mama, like a prayer. It was a song about living out there and being lost and making a new start, which was also an old start. It was about finding your way.

Little by little, the women in our car started to settle, quieting down and sitting down and drawing themselves in until all you could hear was their breathing.

While I sang, the hairs raised up on my neck and my arms and my back, as if I'd seen a ghost. Those words and that tune came out of nowhere, out of the thin, close air of the boxcar. I thought: Maybe there isn't any heaven and maybe we stay in the ground when we die, just like weeds or roots or the red beads Daddy Hoyt offers to the earth after he takes something from it, but as long as there is music, I believe.

THIRTY-TWO

Sometime after sunup, they opened the doors to the boxcars and marched us to the top of a high, steep hill that dropped down like a waterfall into the trees and empty fields and a village no bigger than Alluvial that sat on the flat land at the bottom. Not counting the guards, there must have been three thousand of us, spread out across the hilltop like an entire city of sad, lost people. Some of the men had stripped off their shirts and stood half-naked in the sun. One of the SS guards perched below us, one leg bent up the hillside, and in French and then English shouted at us about not trying to escape. He said for every person who tried to run away, they would shoot ten prisoners and leave them on the hillside or in the woods for the animals to feed on.

For the most part, the guards seemed calmer and braver the closer we got to Germany. We could hear them in the night and in the morning, picking off people on the sides of the road with their guns, just like they were playing a game of Shoot the Can. They rounded up people into groups, from one boxcar to the next, and barked at us to pay attention, to not give them trouble.

I slipped to the back of my group and into the one from the next car. Without calling attention to myself, I stood still, scanning the crowd for Eleanor. When I didn't see her, I moved up a little and then up again. I bumped into one of the other women and she snapped at me in French.

Then, to the left of me, I spotted a woman with short black hair.

From the back she looked like a girl. I slid over to her, careful not to bump anyone, until I was standing next to her. In the bright of day, I got a look at her for the first time. She was shorter than I was by a good four or five inches and had black hair that waved into a widow's peak and eyebrows drawn in neat arches. Her eyes were blue and bright and she had a small, delicate face shaped like a heart. Those bright eyes passed over me and then moved off as if they were bored, as if there were nothing much to see, and settled on one of the guards. Without moving her head, she followed him, and I wondered if she was trying to judge how much time she had to escape.

At first sight, I didn't like her. I thought: That's it? That's her? There was nothing so special or different about her, nothing to make her stand out in a crowd, to make you think, That must be someone so important that the Germans would capture her and lock her away and England would want to rescue her and three men—Coleman, Perry, Ray—would die for her. To look at her, she didn't seem worth the fuss.

The SS moved through our ranks, lining us up two by two. They handcuffed us to the person next to us, then they started marching the first group down the hill. Our group fell somewhere in the middle, and I made sure I was handcuffed to Eleanor. Guards moved in front of us and guards moved in back and guards stalked along the sides of us too. We stumbled over the hill and through the fields, skirting the woods toward the village.

In French I said, "I was supposed to free you."

In French she said, "Sorry? I can't understand what you're saying to me." Her voice was chilly and British, neat as a pin.

"I was supposed to free you."

"Sorry. Your accent is impossible."

I said, as slow as could be, "I was supposed to free you."

She stared at me, and I knew she'd understood. "You were supposed to free me? *You?* Bloody hell."

"We were supposed to free you, I mean. My team." I looked ahead and she looked ahead, so that no one would see we were talking. "But I was captured early and they sent me to Fresnes instead."

She said, "I wondered where in the bloody hell you were."

I told myself: She's been through a lot. You don't even know what. She may have been tortured. She's important to the Allies. For some reason they need her. Do not kill her even if you want to.

I said, "I'm Clementine."

She said, "Eleanor." But I knew it was a name that had been given to her, and along with it was a whole story about an Eleanor March-and or an Eleanor Dupree, and not a word of it was true. I couldn't help myself—I wanted to know everything about her. What was her real name. What kind of work did she do. How did they catch her. Why did they catch her. What kinds of secrets did she know. She said, "Are you OSS?"

"No."

"Not SOE?"

"I'm a WASP." When it was clear she didn't know what this was, I said, "A pilot."

"They sent me a pilot? A woman pilot? Not even a woman, but a girl. How old are you?"

That did it. I said, "I'm sure you've been asked the exact same question. I'm sure there are plenty of people who aren't too thrilled by you doing what you do and being a woman."

She drew her mouth in and looked away.

Finally I said, "Why did they make us get off the train?"

"There was trouble on the line. Someone sabotaged the track. Probably the Allies are too close and they want to hide us away before we're intercepted."

Or maybe they're taking us into the woods to kill us, I thought. Maybe they're going to shoot us dead and then leave us there for the animals.

We slowed to a shuffle because there was a bridge up ahead, and we had to march across in lines of eight. I was suddenly so scared of being shot that I didn't talk to Eleanor again until we'd passed through the village and down a long dirt road with fields on either side. As soon as we were on the road and the guards were spread out farther, she said, "Does your team know where you are?"

"I don't know." I wondered if the bus driver had delivered my message by now or if he would. The messages could be lying in a trash heap or in the hands of the Germans. Or something could have happened to Émile. I pushed this last thought out of my head. I said, "We may have to do this on our own."

"That could be tricky."

"Maybe before they load us onto another bus or train. Maybe in all the confusion. There's always a way." I wasn't sure this was true, but it was usually true about most things.

She said, "Maybe."

We marched for two or three miles under the hot, white sun. The clouds had burned off and my hair was damp and sticking to my neck. My head had gone light and I was making myself concentrate as hard as I could so that I would keep going, even if they were making us walk all the way to Germany. When a woman, thin as a broom handle, wobbled and swayed and then crumpled onto the ground, one of the guards shot her in the dirt, right where she lay, and then he shot the woman handcuffed to her just so he wouldn't have to go to the trouble to bend over and unlock her. He stepped over them and shouted at the rest of us to stay on our feet or he'd do the same to us.

Eleanor said, "If you faint or fall, so help me, I'll kill you before he can."

I thought, Right back at you, sister. I almost wished I could shoot her right then. I wondered if she'd been hard before the war or if it had turned her this way. I hoped I wasn't turning hard too.

I tried not to look at the dead women, tried not to think about them. I kept my eyes on the road, on the sky, on the trees, on the person in front of me. I thought: Just one step. One step at a time. You don't have to do them all at once.

We came to a place in the road where the trees were blown down, like a storm had swept through. Some of the trees lay across the road, and we had to climb over or walk around. I kept thinking: Is now the time? If we ran away now, how far could we go?

Eleanor nodded at the trees. She said, "The Allies were here, trying to slow the Germans down."

We passed wrecked gliders, their cockpits and wings completely ripped apart. We passed bombed-out fields, dead cows, and houses burned to the ground, which I knew meant we were getting closer to the battle action. We came across a bridge that had been destroyed, still smoking from the fires.

I put my hand over my mouth and nose so I wouldn't breathe in the smoke. The bridge was on the edge of a village, and the village was nothing but rubble. People climbed about in the shells of buildings and houses and stood on hilltops of brick and stone, digging and sifting and searching. As we marched by, they stopped what they were doing and stared at us, and even though their homes had been knocked down and their town was gone, they looked at us sadly, like they were sorry, like they were grateful that, as bad as it was, at least they weren't us.

Some of the male prisoners called out, *"Bon courage. Vive la France!"* *Take good heart. Long live France!* And a young man slid down from a mound of ash and stone and ran alongside us. A woman two rows in front of me was dragging a heavy bag. Her arms were thin as bird wings and she was sagging from the heat and the strain. The young man took the bag from her and another bag from someone else, and he walked beside us carrying them. The guards ignored him and let him be.

A mile later we reached a flat field of land with train tracks running through it. A small building grew up alongside the tracks, looking as if it had somehow shot up out of the earth like a tree. A long freight train sat there, all its doors open so that we could see it was empty. As we got closer, I saw figures in white moving about on the platform.

I said, "The Red Cross is here." The sign of their clean white uniforms made me hopeful. At least we aren't forgotten, I thought. At least someone remembers we're here.

The guards said the train would leave in an hour, but instead of crowding us back into the boxcars, they let us sit down on the side of the tracks, on a little rise in the ground, and eat our potatoes and drink our milk. I said to Eleanor, "We could climb this hill and go down the other side." I wondered if there was a way to slip behind the station while everyone was boarding, to lose ourselves in the crowd and then pull away at the last minute. The station building was built up on bricks so that there was an open space, narrow and dark, running underneath. I wondered if we could roll under there and hide and wait till the train was gone.

She was studying the guards just like I was. She said, "They're watching us too closely. They're too on edge. Any sudden, strange movement, and I'm afraid they'll shoot everyone." I thought she was giving up too easily and I said so. She said, "Maybe. But it's been a long war. You Americans have been fighting in it the day before yesterday, but we've been in it for years. Maybe the fight's going out of me."

I said, "Because it's a long war, that's when you should fight the hardest."

I started telling her about my brother Beachard, who was over in the Pacific, and how no one ever thought he would live to grow up, and now he was something like a major in the Marines, when he'd only started as a medic who didn't carry a gun. It was a story meant to inspire her, but suddenly she started singing "Five Foot Two, Eyes of Blue." She sang it like she was bored silly, like she was telling me I was free to leave, that she was done here.

I said, "Do you know how many men have died to save you? Three of my team members were killed on this mission, eight if you count the original team that flew to France from England, five of them who died when we crash-landed, not to mention all the members of my crew, which makes a total of fifteen. I don't think it would hurt you to show some manners. And I'll tell you this: I'm not going to Germany if I can help it. And you're not going either if I can help it. But I am not doing this alone."

She had stopped singing. She sat a long time, staring off toward the train and the guards. Her expression didn't change, but she tilted her nose slightly, in such a way that I could tell I'd offended her. Good, I thought.

*   *   *

The sun was beginning to drop in the sky when they loaded us onto the train. We pulled out of the station, and once again I sat by the door. A guard was assigned to each car. They locked the doors and then they rode with the other guards, two or three cars away.

Eleanor and a few of the other women spoke German, but the guards didn't know they spoke German, which meant that they could tell us every little thing the guards said to one another. The car next to ours was a hospital car, filled with women who were ill or dying. Eleanor said the Germans planned to leave these women in a place called Bar-le-Duc and let them fend for themselves. She said the Germans considered these women dead already and didn't feel the need to carry any extra weight.

A lock hung on the outside of our door—we could see it through the crack—and I was going to try to reach through the opening and crack the lock open with one of my hairpins. If I could get my arm out and if I could reach the lock and if I could unlock it, we were going to jump. If I couldn't unlock it, I'd blast it open with the chewing gum explosive. We'd roll into the bushes or grass away from the train and then we'd hide there till it pushed on past. Eleanor said there were two more stops before Germany—Bar-le-Duc and Nancy.

I kept an eye to the crack and every now and then a sign blurred past. This was how I knew we were still in France, because all of the writing was in French. This filled me with hope because it would be easier for us if we could break free before we crossed into Germany. The air in the car was hot as an oven. The women who had the energy fanned themselves with their hands, and the others just closed their eyes, their faces wet and red from the heat.

Eleanor sat beside and behind me, so that she could block the view of the door. I pulled a bobby pin out of my hair and flicked off the rubber ends, and then I tugged on the side of the door and tried to slip my free hand, the one that wasn't cuffed to Eleanor's, out through the crack. I couldn't move the door an inch by tugging it, so I worked and wormed my hand out. The crack was only a couple of inches wide. My hand slipped out, holding the bobby pin, but I still couldn't reach the lock. I wriggled and wiggled my arm, which was thin from weeks of not eating much, but not thin enough. The skin scraped raw and began bleeding in spots, but I kept wriggling, kept wiggling, until finally I could just feel the warm metal of the lock in my fingers.

In French, one of the women said, "What are you doing? What is she doing?"

Eleanor said, "She wants some air. She needs to breathe."

The woman said, "We all want air. We all need to breathe."

Another woman said in English, "She will get us killed."

Eleanor said, "She won't get us killed, you fool." And the women began to bicker and buzz. Eleanor said to me, "For God's sake, hurry."

Careful as I could, I turned the bobby pin over in my fingers till it was pointed toward the lock. Signs and trees were rushing by, and I wondered if we could die from jumping at this speed. I couldn't see what I was doing, so I did my best to feel my way, tapping the hairpin across the top of the lock until I felt it click into the hole.

I thought: Eleanor's smaller than I am. Her arms are as thin as reeds. She probably knows how to pick locks like an expert, and I've never picked one in my life. It seems like she should be doing this instead, especially if she's as important as everyone says she is. I was beginning to think she didn't seem like much of a secret agent.

I slid the pin into the lock and then, because I wasn't exactly sure what to do, I began jiggling it around, trying to find the catch. All of a sudden, I pitched forward, banging my head against the door. The train had lurched and then lurched again, and then you could feel the wheels grinding into the metal of the rails. We were coming to a long, screeching stop.

I pulled the bobby pin out of the lock, and when I did it fell to the ground. I yanked my arm back in through the crack so hard that I fell back into Eleanor. "Here." She handed me a scarf and told me to wipe the blood off. I dabbed at the scrapes and cuts and then I stuffed the scarf into my own bag and rolled my sleeve back down so that it covered most of it.

My heart was skipping beats and my throat was dry. All I could think was: They knew what I was doing. Somehow someone saw me, and now they've stopped the train so they can take me into the woods and kill me.

Eleanor said, "Can you see what's going on?"

I looked out the crack and I could see some of the guards dragging four men away from the train. The men were prisoners, and I recognized one of them. He was one of the downed airmen from Gossie's.

The guards made the men stop in a field beside the tracks and stand facing the train. Then, one by one, they went down the line and shot each man in the back of the head. One by one, they fell to the ground.

Suddenly, the guard for our car was unlocking the door, the hairpin shining in the dirt underneath his boot. Don't look down, I thought. Please don't see it. He slid the door open and started counting us. Then he marked the number on the side of the door with chalk so that he would know how many of us there were the next time. He said, "We shall be counting and recounting you from now on, and if there are any other attempts at evasion, ten hostages will be shot from the car where it occurred."

Then he slammed the door closed again, turned the key in the lock, and marched off toward his own car, leaving the hairpin glinting silver in the dust.

The next morning, the train pulled into the village of Nancy, and the door was opened and we were counted again. This time the guard, who had a long, unpleasant face, was smiling. He made a show of counting us, and then he wrote the tally on the side of the car. His hand on the door, he said, "Congratulations. Paris has been liberated." The door slammed closed again—a heavy, grating sound of metal on metal that sent a chill through me. Through the crack, I could see his face, still smiling, as he lit a cigarette and inhaled and then held it out to us as if he was saluting, before walking away.

Eleanor said, "We are almost to Germany. If we're to be saved from deportation, it must happen now." I tried to remember how many days we'd been traveling so that I could know what day it was that Paris was liberated. I remembered Perry saying something about the Liberation, about how we would be there to see it.

I tried to picture what Paris must be like right now. I saw Gossie's face and Cleo's and the faces of the people in the street. I thought of all the downed airmen who wouldn't have to escape to Spain. They were probably kissing French girls on the sidewalks and singing. Everyone singing. Everyone laughing. Everyone drinking champagne. The bells of Notre Dame would ring, all of them this time. The flame would be lit again at the Tomb of the Unknown Soldier. Émile could go to his mother and get her out of the hospital. They wouldn't have to hide her anymore.

Émile. I touched my lips and shut my eyes, just for a moment, trying to crawl inside the memory of him.

Eleanor said, "We must do something."

I opened my eyes and suddenly I was back in the boxcar. I thought: You do something. I'm tired of thinking of what to do.

But instead I ran my fingers along the crack in the door, feeling the air, the warmth. The door was closed tighter this time. The space was smaller. I started fishing in my bag for the chewing gum. Before Eleanor could say anything again, I said, "I'm thinking."

THIRTY-THREE

*W*e crossed over into Germany an hour or so later. Except for the signs that we passed here and there, you couldn't tell we were in another country, but as soon as we went over the border, the mood in the car grew heavier and gloomier, like a storm was coming. Some of the women began to cry.

The train pulled to a stop and the guard counted us, and his long, unpleasant face was lit up like a Christmas tree. He told us we could get out and stretch our legs, and I thought: Of course we can get out now that you've gotten us away from France. You feel safer just being home.

Running beside the train tracks was a road, and just past this road, on the other side of it, was a row of small houses. As we wobbled down off the train, our legs bowing and buckling, the people came out of their homes—the German people—and stared at us. One of them shouted something at the guards, and a guard shouted back to him, and then the people were bringing us water to drink and bread to eat. Some of them filled up buckets with water and brought these so that we could wash our faces and arms and hands.

With the guards pacing back and forth, a few of us sat down on the grass that ran between the tracks and the road. I pushed up my sleeves and threw my head back and tried to soak up the sun. For that minute, I didn't try to think of a way to escape. I just wanted to live in the day.

One of the guards said, "You there." He stopped in front of me, leaning on his gun. "What happened to your arm?"

I looked down as if I'd never seen my own arm before, at what he must see—the scrapes and scratches and raw skin. I said, "I got into a fight."

He glanced at Eleanor and then he stared down at my arm as if it might tell him the real story. Finally, he smirked at me and said, "You'll need to get along better than that. We still have days to travel before we get to Ravensbrück."

At this, Eleanor said, "Damn," so low that only I could hear her. The guard was already striding away.

I said, "What's Ravensbrück?"

"A concentration camp for women."

Something in me sank as low as the grass. But at the same time I felt something rise in me too. We might have a better chance of escaping from a concentration camp than we would from the train. The chewing gum explosive might work, but I needed a match to light the fuse, or something to smash the gum with once it was wet and sticking on the door of the train. The woman with matches was in another car now, and no one else seemed to have any because the Germans had taken their cigarettes and matches for themselves.

I said, "Once we get there, we'll figure a way out."

She was quiet for a good long moment. Then she turned to me, the sun behind her, so that I couldn't see her nose, eyes, or mouth. She said, "No one ever leaves Ravensbrück." For the first time, her voice was kind, but it was also sad and distant, like she didn't need it anymore and was just this minute going away, leaving it behind.

~ ~ ~

Two days later, sometime after sunset, we passed a sign that read "Kaiserslautern—5 km." We went clattering past, and I was just turning to Eleanor to tell her where we were, when there was the great boom of a thunderclap, and all of us—every single woman—went flying across the boxcar into one another, slamming into the walls before we went flying back again. We landed in a pile, the car skidding into the car in front and the car in front of that. We rolled back and forth across the floor until the train started to slow, still shaking, like it was underwater or moving through mud. I lay there, trying to hold on, smoke scorching my lungs, my leg throbbing, my head pounding. I could feel something cold and wet on my arm, my knee. I waited to die, to be burned up like a plane engine.

When I didn't, I tried to pull myself up out of the bodies, some struggling, others lying still. One side of the boxcar was blown half off. We were still moving forward. Before I could think, I pulled Eleanor with me and we squeezed through the opening and jumped through the blackness of the night. We hit the ground and began to roll, coming to a stop in a ditch just beyond. Outside, the air was damp and misty, but hot from the fire. Clouds drifted across the sky, the moon, just a sliver, disappearing and then reappearing again.

Something exploded to the left of us, shaking the earth so hard I lost my footing. I looked up, expecting to see bombers flying overhead, but the sky was empty except for the smoke that was rising fast into thick black clouds and the blazing orange-red of the fire. The boxcars slid one into another, grinding, screeching, metal on metal. The cars piled up like matchsticks, upended until they were standing on their sides or turned over completely, wheels in the air. The prisoners scrambled out the doors and over the sides, stumbling their way into the surrounding woods and fields, still chained together. The first car, the one that belonged to the guards, lay separated from the others, as if the impact had come from the front of the train. Nothing much was left of it but wood and the bones and burned flesh of the guards trapped inside.

I started to cough from the smoke. Eleanor was saying something but I couldn't hear her. She finally reached her hand into my bag and pulled out my scarf and hers, which was still stained with my blood. She left me hers and then tied mine around her nose and mouth and waved at me to do the same.

The ground seemed to rise up under our feet, threatening to split open and suck us in. Ash and embers rained down from the sky like snow, and the fire grew around us. The earth swelled up and lurched downward by the front of the train, into a great crater. Steam rose up in a black, evil mist from another crater, just behind. The metal of the tracks was twisted but most of the cars sat on the track, as if nothing had happened at all. Whoever had done this had made sure to target the first boxcar, the one with the guards.

Men were shouting in German, in English, in French. People ran in all directions. In the night and the smoke and the wreckage, it was hard to tell who were the Germans and who were the prisoners.

I suddenly thought: This is hell. This is exactly what hell would be like. I knew in that moment that it existed, just like heaven, because hell was things like this—train explosions and fire and smoke so thick it filled your head, your nose, your lungs.

My heart was racing but my mind was faster. This was our chance and we had to take it, but where could we go? People were everywhere, debris was everywhere, fire and smoke were everywhere. Some of the cars were lying on their sides, people falling from the doors or the place where there used to be a ceiling, a floor. I heard the rattle of gunfire.

I grasped Eleanor's hand and we started to run. We ran through the ditch and down the line, and suddenly I stopped because the last two cars were sitting on the track, closed up tight. I could hear the people shouting for help. I dragged Eleanor over to the first car, pulling her behind me like a kite. I yanked a bobby pin from my hair and flicked off the rubber tips and started working at the lock.

Eleanor said, "Hurry, Clementine. For God's sake." Her eyes darted to the right of us, toward the front of the train, toward the fire and the smoke and the guards. Finally, she grabbed the hairpin from me and started working at the lock herself.

Seconds later, she pulled on the lock and it came off in her hand. Together, we pushed open the door and the women spilled out, dropping to the ground and running in every direction. Eleanor and I ran to the last car and she slid the bobby pin into the lock and twisted and turned and jiggled it, but the lock wouldn't give. Below the car the track was split, just like it had been blown.

I pulled a stick of gum from my bag. I said, "Here." Then I spit into my hand and wet the gum and stuck the gum on the lock. I shouted to the people in the car, first in English, then in French, "Stay back!"

In the ditch there were stones of all sizes, and pieces of boxcar, blown all the way from the front of the train. I picked up a stone and dragged Eleanor back, away from the car. Then I threw the rock as hard as I could so that it smashed against the chewing gum. At the same moment, Eleanor and I dropped to the ground and covered our heads as the lock blew right off. From inside, there was a kicking and a banging, and then the men began to push and pull until the door was half open.

I jumped at the sharp crack of a gunshot close by. Eleanor tugged at my arm with the chain. I said, "Unlock us." She worked for a minute. There was another crack of a gun. Then she threw the cuffs onto the ground and grabbed my hand.

We ran away from the wreck as fast as we could, leaping over the ditch and over the tracks and into the woods. Out of the corner of my eye, I saw two of the guards start after us, one of them shouting, the other aiming his gun. A shot sounded, and without thinking I turned in time to see one of the Germans fall to the ground. Standing over him, in the haze and the smoke, I saw a figure. It had the lean, proud face of a boxer, with a chin that sliced into the night and a shock of dark hair. "Barzo! Barzetti!" I shouted it over the noise. "Barzo!" The face turned in my direction. There was war paint on the cheeks. It wasn't the face of a boxer at all—it was the face of a warrior. He seemed to be saying something, waving me on, telling me to go, but a second later he was swallowed up by the crowd, disappearing into the smoke.

Eleanor tugged at my hand. The other guard kept after us and then I tripped over something and went sprawling, bringing Eleanor down with me. Before she could swear at me to get up, I saw what I'd tripped on—the man who had guarded our boxcar. His eyes were open and staring up toward the treetops, up toward the new moon. A single line of red seeped down the middle of his forehead. I watched as it ran toward his ear. He'd been shot clean through the head. I thought of Perry, lying in a field in France, blue eyes like still, dead pools.

Without saying "I'm sorry" this time, I took the gun out of the guard's hand and Eleanor took the knife off of his belt, and we kept on running. I heard another shot behind us. Instead of getting farther away, the gunfire was getting closer. In the distance I could see the lights of a town, and in the other direction there was nothing but blackness. A river, a mountain—it was hard to tell in the night. On the back of my leg, I felt something wet and warm, and I thought: I'm hit. Someone shot me.

Eleanor stopped suddenly and I ran right into her. We stood, both of us, not sure which way to go. Back toward the train or through the woods and the field ahead toward the town? Or into the blackness that might be anything at all? The only other way was the road, but we were in Germany now, which meant we had to stay hidden. I could hear the sound of someone running after us, and I didn't want to wait to see who it was.

I said, "The town isn't far."

Eleanor said, "We should stick to the woods." She was holding her arm, which was twisted at a strange angle.

I looked back where we'd come from, off toward the wreck. The fire and smoke filled the sky, reaching high above the trees. Through the trees I could see figures still running every which way. I said, "Let's go."

Just in case we were being followed, we loped off in a zigzag through the field and toward the black that lay beyond. As I ran, I freed up the safety on my gun. Eleanor said, "This way." I followed her through a break in the trees and then we doubled back to the right, to the left, to the right.

She said, "They're coming." Her voice was hoarse from the smoke. We pulled off our scarves and kept running. Suddenly, up ahead and to the side—it was hard to tell in the dark—I heard a cracking in the trees, and for a minute I thought it was the pop of a gun, aimed in my direction. The sliver of moon dipped behind the clouds again and at just that same moment, a figure broke out of the trees and it was big and dark and rushing for us.

The brush snapped as Eleanor and I ran forward, blind as bats, reaching our hands out in front of us, trying to find our way by touch. All of a sudden, the clouds shifted and the moon reappeared, and we could just make out the line of a creek to our left and, up ahead, a field, and beyond that, nothing, like everything ended there.

We ran toward the field, and the figure kept coming. I turned around and fired off a shot, and a voice said, in English, "Goddammit." Good, I thought. I hope you're hit. I hope I hit you smack between the eyes.

I ran a few more paces, not thinking, just running. The dark figure was almost on top of us. I turned to fire again, and it yelled in French, "Stop shooting at me! Who do you think blew up the goddamn train?" Suddenly the figure was caught in the pale, thin glow of the moonlight. The hair was gold, the skin was gold, the cheekbones high and wide. There was a scar over one eye now and a smear of blood on the face. "You nearly blew my head clean off." He spat on the ground and said in English, "Shit."

It can't be.

I tried to say something, but I couldn't because my throat was closed up tight, like someone was choking it.

From the shadows, Eleanor hissed, "Clementine."

The figure walked up closer and took my chin in his hand and turned my face this way and that. I couldn't breathe or talk, just stood there blinking back the tears. He whistled long and loud. He said, "Great Holy Moses, girl. I thought you was French. What the good God almighty did you do to yourself, Velva Jean?"

Everything faded away right then—the fire in the distance, the stench of smoke, so thick it felt like my nose was burning, the gunfire, Eleanor, the Germans, Germany, the war.

He said, "I'll be goddamned." And there was something in his voice that made him sound worlds older than the last time I'd seen him, when he was running off from Nashville to join the war. He started blinking fast, which he'd always done, his whole life, ever since I could remember, when he didn't want to be caught crying. "What in hell are you doing here?"

Finally, after what felt like two centuries, I could feel my throat loosening up and my mouth starting to work. I said, "Johnny Clay

Hart, don't you ever go off and leave me again." It came out as a kind of croak. And then I punched him right in the nose.

He swore and wiped his nose and there was blood on his hand, which made me feel good and mean and happy. And then I jumped on him and started squeezing him as tight as I could, and he picked me up and swung me around while I cried right into his neck.

When I opened my eyes I could see another man standing behind Johnny Clay. Even in the darkness, I could see the dark gypsy eyes and the heavy mouth that could be cruel and also sexy, and the smug set of his face. It was a good face, I thought.

His eyes moved to Johnny Clay and then to me, our arms still around each other. He said, "Clementine," and in that word I could hear a question, but I could also hear all the worry that he'd been carrying.

THIRTY-FOUR

*W*e ran toward the blackness ahead. I said, "Barzo was back there. I saw him in the crowd." He'd shot the German chasing us. He'd saved our lives. "We have to go back for him." As I said it, I craned my neck around to look at Johnny Clay, to make sure he was still there.

Émile said, "He's gone, Clementine."

"No, I saw him. He was there. He shot the German who was chasing us."

We were running but in the wrong direction. We should have been running back toward the train wreck and the rail lines. Barzo might be hiding in the woods or the field. He might be lying in a ditch, Germans surrounding him, waiting for us to come.

I turned myself around and said, "I'm going back there."

Suddenly Émile was in front of me, grabbing my arms. For one minute, I thought he was going to slap my face, but instead he said, "He's gone." He shook me like he was afraid I was hysterical. I knew what his words meant by the tone of his voice, but I'd just seen Barzo. He was alive. I wanted to ask what happened, if it was the German guards, but then I didn't want to know, not really.

I looked at Eleanor and she looked back at me, her face pale and drawn. I thought, Now that makes sixteen men who have died for you.

Émile took my hand and dragged me on and I let myself bump along behind him for a while before I started running again on my own.

We didn't know how many of the Gestapo were behind us or if anyone was chasing us at all, but Émile said it was only a matter of time before the Germans called reinforcements from the nearby villages, and we couldn't be caught in the area. The Gestapo knew someone had blown the rail line. There had been two other men besides Émile and Barzo and Johnny Clay, but they'd been shot by the Germans before they could get away. The Germans had seen their faces, all of them.

The great darkness ahead was a forest—I could see it now, long and unending across the horizon, trees and mountains rising up like something in a murder song. Émile and my brother and the other two agents, the ones on Johnny Clay's team, had blown up the rail line on the outskirts of Kaiserslautern, and now we were headed south, away from the city, toward the forest and France, which Émile said was about two hundred kilometers away, maybe less, over the hills and mountains. He said if we were lucky we could cover the distance in two weeks. We didn't have enough food to last us, so we would have to hunt when we could and take our water from the mountain streams and rivers. This was different than being on the run in Normandy because this time someone was chasing us and this time we were escaped prisoners and criminals, wanted by the Germans.

My head whirled from everything—freedom, Barzo, Émile, Johnny Clay. I turned and looked at my brother, who was running behind me, strangely silent. His silence made me nervous because it wasn't like him to be quiet unless he was in a temper. I hoped the war hadn't changed him.

Johnny Clay's alive. He's okay.

I had to keep looking back at him to make sure he was real.

Johnny Clay is an agent too.

It hit me then, like a knock in the head. The thing that smarted most was that he'd felt he couldn't tell me. He'd been sworn to secrecy by the OSS and ordered not to tell a soul, but rules like that had never bothered him, and they'd never applied to me. Our whole lives, we'd always told each other everything, and suddenly he'd gone behind my back and lived a whole other life.

I was suddenly so tired. I thought: Maybe they should go on. Maybe it's enough to know Johnny Clay's okay now. My leg and arm hurt from being thrown around inside the boxcar. My knee was bleeding and also my hand. I thought: I can just stop here under one of these trees and rest for a while.

As if he could read my thoughts, Johnny Clay ran up beside me, flashing me a challenging sort of grin. Even in the pale moonlight, his skin was like gold dust, and it was almost like we were back on Fair Mountain again, racing each other home. My feet and legs picked up speed like they always did when we raced. I wanted to stop and catch my breath and ask questions like where had Johnny Clay come from? Where had he been? How did he know Émile? Did he know him from before the drop in France? I wanted to tell Émile that Johnny Clay was my brother, the reason I'd come to France in the first place. But there wasn't time to stop because my legs were pushing forward, the pain forgotten, trying to outdistance my brother, trying to beat him for once and let him see how it felt to be left behind.

I heard him say, "Clementine? What's he mean, 'Clementine'?"

I said, "Don't call me Velva Jean. Do you understand me? Velva Jean doesn't exist out here." She doesn't exist anywhere.

"Suit yourself." And then he sprinted ahead so I had to catch him.

After crossing the field, we entered the woods and I felt at once as if I'd passed into another world. There was something ancient feeling and gloomy about those woods. The air suddenly changed and went darker, and the night grew blacker. You could tell just by stepping into it that it was a mighty forest, as large as a country, and filled with mystery and legend. The weather misted and fogged even more and the clouds rolled in overhead like a ceiling. I felt a raindrop on my cheek and then two more, four more, six more, until the rain was falling, splashing against the leaves above our heads, making a soft, clean tapping sound like a thousand far-off hammers. I could tell we were in some sort of valley and that the valley grew up into hills. We would have to cross over these to get to France.

As we began to climb, first Émile, then Eleanor, then Johnny Clay and me, I could see the red of the fire in the distance, see the smoke still hovering in the sky, and hear the sound of gunfire.

We couldn't risk building a shelter or a fire, and so we kept going. Émile said we were in the Palatinate Forest, the largest forest in Germany. He said it spanned some eleven hundred miles from Germany to France, and that it ended at the Vosges Mountains, which was where we were heading. He said that General Patton and his Third Army were heading there too, that they were preparing for a battle with the Germans who were fleeing France, that Gossie had told him so because she'd listened in on a telephone conversation between the President and Patton himself.

Gossie was okay. She and Cleo were fine, and now they would be celebrating the Liberation with the rest of Paris.

Émile said that above anything else, we had to get Eleanor back to England.

We were walking, not running, now, and as we walked I stared at the back of her head, small and wet, and tried not to resent her just because the military thought she was more important than my brother or Émile or me.

We took stock of our injuries—Eleanor had bruised her arm. At first she thought it was broken, but Johnny Clay said it was only a bad sprain. Émile had gotten another aid kit from somewhere, and he wrapped a bandage around my leg to stop the bleeding and one around my hand. Johnny Clay and Émile were both banged up and bloody with cuts and scrapes, but otherwise we were in good working order.

We crept through the undergrowth and through the trees and we climbed up and down the mountains, which were rolling and steep and green, like our mountains back home. At some point, the rain stopped, leaving behind a warm, wet fog. In some places we could hardly see two feet, and so we felt our way up through the forest. When it became too thick to see anything we stopped and Johnny Clay said, "Shit."

Émile said to me, "Do you have your compass?"

"Here." I pulled Ty's compass out of my bag and handed it to him. As I did, I felt the initials carved into the back: N-E-T.

Émile turned it over to look at the initials but didn't say anything. He held the compass flat in his hand and we all peered in to see. "This way," he said, and we began to walk again.

Half an hour later, the fog was as thick as gravy, and we took shelter in the ruins of what Émile said must have been a castle, built right into the side of a hill. He said the forest was littered with castles, or what was left of them. He said, "If we can't see in this fog, the Germans won't be able to see either. I think we can stop until it clears and keep going then."

We found a stone staircase going up, and we climbed it, feeling our way. At the top of the stairs was a room that was almost completely whole—stone floor, stone walls, and a great, high ceiling. Émile stood in the doorway, taking the first watch. I let Johnny Clay and Eleanor go inside ahead of me, and then I said, "I'll watch with you."

"No," he said. "I think I will find a higher place. There must be a tower that will let me see more. You must rest, Clementine." He wasn't looking at me, just staring away into the trees. I stood waiting for something, I wasn't sure what, before following the others into the room.

Inside, without any moonlight to see by, it was dark as a tomb. I felt around on the floor, and then I sat down in a small clean space and hugged my knees in. I heard the others settling around me.

Someone was just to my right, and I reached out my hand. Johnny Clay said, "You almost poked my eye out."

I said, "Why did you tell me you were in England? Why did you write me that letter when you weren't ever there?"

He was quiet a good long time, and finally I heard his voice: "I did go to England. That part wasn't a lie. I was supposed to go to Upottery. I had my bag all packed, but then I heard in a roundabout way of this opportunity, and it was one of those opportunities you can't pass up. Top secret. Dangerous. Only the toughest men. I said, Yessir, that's for me. Only thing was they didn't want me at first because I don't speak

French and I ain't all that educated, but I let my record speak for itself, and there wasn't another fella at training camp that was faster or tougher or smarter. I told them so myself, and I wouldn't let 'em be till they let me in." I thought about the way I'd written to Jacqueline Cochran, trying to persuade her to accept me into the WASP program. I thought, Look at us, my brother and me, about as far away as you can get from Fair Mountain.

He said, "They sent me into Normandy on D-day, only I dropped in with two other guys, not two hundred. It was just me and them and my weapon."

He told me about organizing Resistance groups and how he'd destroyed German tanks and bridges and how he'd gotten himself caught after blowing up a munitions factory outside Paris. He said he'd talked his way out of being executed, that the Germans were holding the gun to his head and pulling the trigger when he'd told them he was a paratrooper and that if they shot him there'd be hell to pay. He said Hitler had issued orders to execute all agents, but they weren't allowed to kill paratroopers just because they'd landed in France. He said Hitler could have found himself in a heap of trouble if he did that.

He told me how he'd bluffed a German regiment—more than eighteen thousand troops running from Paris, tails between their legs—trying to get back to Germany as fast as they could. He was by himself, walking down a country road (he didn't say where the other members of his team were and why he was by himself), when he came across their commander and convinced the man, just by some fast talking, that he and his men were outnumbered. He said the man surrendered to him right there, and then Johnny Clay turned them over to the French in Reims, which was at least a hundred miles away.

From Reims, he went to Germany, where he and the members of his team killed two men who were high up in the SS, and afterward they broke into a castle, a lot like the one we were in right now, only, according to him, ten times bigger. He said the castle belonged to one of Hitler's right-hand men, a man who was a chief in Hitler's armed forces, and that Johnny Clay broke in during the daytime, not even at night, and that he met the girlfriend of the man, who was also his secretary, and she gave him a present because he charmed her. He said it was a gold bookmark that had belonged to Hitler himself, that it was given to him by Eva Braun, who was Hitler's mistress.

I said, "Johnny Clay." Now I knew he was pulling my leg.

He said, "I'm serious." Then he told me about how he'd been taken prisoner as soon as he got back into France, but how he'd hid the bookmark so they couldn't find it, and then disguised himself as a worker, escaping in a coal bin on a train that went all the way to Belgium.

I said, "I'm not listening to any more of your tall tales."

He said, "I ain't done. Halfway there, I climbed out of that coal bin and walked right into the passenger car and sat beside an SS officer, and he didn't even check my papers. Offered me a cigarette and even lit it for me, and I just sat there, cool as could be, covered in coal dust from head to toe."

I said, "So why'd you drop in from England then? I thought Émile was waiting on a new team from there, and that was you."

He said, "Aw, they sent me back to debrief me. Made me a first lieutenant. Said I'd done enough already and completed my mission. Said I could sit the rest of this war out after all I'd done, but I said, There's still a war to be fought here and I aim to fight every last minute of it."

I still couldn't see him, but I could picture his face, jaw stuck out like he was daring someone to knock it flat.

"Little sister, would I lie to you?"

I said, "Yes."

He laughed, and his laughter, even though it was soft and low, rang through the empty castle walls, bouncing over our heads and out of our reach and right back to us. I thought then about the people who must have lived there before, all the kings and queens and knights in armor. I thought of the wars that must have been fought hundreds of years ago, back when the castle wasn't ruins but was whole and new.

Johnny Clay went on for a while, and I believed some of it but not all of it because I knew better than that. But I was proud of him just the same. When he was done, I said, "I didn't think I'd ever see you again."

He said, "Shit." I could hear him shuffling his feet against the floor. "I didn't ask what you was doing here."

I said, "They said you were missing and I came to find you."

There was a long silence, and I waited for Johnny Clay to swear or make a joke or change the subject, because he never knew what to do when you got too serious or sentimental. Finally, he said, "Thank you."

Then he told me that Linc had been made a captain because of being wounded in Anzio, Italy, and that, last he'd heard, our oldest brother had helped to liberate Rome on June 4. He said Coyle Deal, who was now Sweet Fern's husband, had been there too, but was sent back to England to recover after being shot through the arm and shoulder. He said as far as he knew, Coyle was still there, but maybe he'd be going home soon because it didn't sound like they were going to let him fight anymore, which was a rotten shame, if you asked him. He said Jessup Deal was with the 4th Infantry Division, but he didn't know anything about him past D-day, when he landed on Utah Beach. He said Butch Dawkins and his group of Comanche Indian code talkers had landed with them, and that they might be anywhere now or nowhere at all. He said those code talkers were traveling through France scalping the Germans. He said he hadn't heard from Beachard.

Music played in some far corner of my mind as I tried to conjure up Butch Dawkins—his gap-toothed smile and the broken bottle neck and his head bent over his guitar. For one sweet moment, I could see him.

Johnny Clay said, "So this Frenchman."

My hackles went up. I said, "Which one?"

"The old guy. Charles Boyer out there."

I said a little too quickly, "He's not old."

"Oh really?"

Dammit, I thought.

Johnny Clay said, "What's he to you, anyway? How'd you get mixed up with him?"

Before I could tell him about Harrington or the crash that killed everyone but Émile's team and me, Eleanor's voice, sharp and annoyed, came wavering up out of the dark. She said, "I'm trying to sleep."

I looked over at the direction of the voice, and I couldn't help it. I started singing "Five Foot Two, Eyes of Blue."

Johnny Clay laughed, and then, together, we sang the rest of the song straight through, just like old times, just like we were sitting up on Mama's porch or walking home from Deal's.

THIRTY-FIVE

By morning, the fog and the rain were gone and the sun blinked through the clouds. I was on watch, climbing an iron ladder that led up to the highest tower. At the top, I stood in the small, round space, no wider than a well, my gun in my hand. I could see now that the castle didn't just sit on top of the hill, it was built into the rock of it, and that the hill was high and covered in dark green pine trees in every direction. From where I stood, I could see down into the valley beyond the trees, across a winding river and red sandstone gorges and fat stone houses dotted here and there through fields and farms, but these things were probably miles away because the forest itself was so big. Beyond all of this were mountains.

I sat on the ledge, my legs straddling the wall, and I looked down. I thought: What if I fell? After all I've been through, what if I just fell right off the side? I looked out toward the river and the houses and wondered about the people there.

A voice said, "Are you all right?" Émile's head appeared above the ladder and he came climbing up. In the daylight, I could see the bruises and cuts on his arms and face, and the dried blood over one eye.

I knew what he meant: Was I all right after all that had happened—Fresnes, Romainville, the train, the explosion, and whatever else had happened to me that he didn't know about or couldn't imagine.

I swung my legs over so that they were on the same side of the ledge, so that they were resting on the stone floor of the small round space. "Yes."

He sat down beside me, his leg an inch from mine. I thought about moving my leg over just enough so that they touched. His hands rested on the ledge and there was blood and dirt underneath the nails and a long, jagged scar on the back of the right one. "If anything had happened to you, I would not have forgiven myself."

"But nothing did."

"I tried to reach you before they sent you anywhere, but by the time I found out where they were taking you, you were already at Fresnes." He sounded angry, and I knew it wasn't just at the Germans; it was at himself. "I'm sorry. I should never have asked you to do this."

I said, "I'm not sorry." I'd already decided I wasn't going to let myself think about all that had happened to me and to the others I'd met. I wasn't going to worry about the people I couldn't save. I wasn't going to think about them. I wasn't going to let any of them in because there was nothing I could do.

"This new agent." He nodded his head down toward the rooms below us where my brother slept. "He is very brash and very young." I wanted to laugh because here he was talking about Johnny Clay just as Johnny Clay had talked about him. "Who is this man to you, Clementine?"

I thought: He's going to kiss me again. I could almost feel his mouth on mine. Without thinking, I reached up to touch my bottom lip, where there was still a split down the middle from where the German guard had slapped me. Émile's eyes followed my hand and then he looked away.

I thought about teasing him, about letting him go on for a while thinking whatever he was thinking about Johnny Clay.

I said, "He's my brother."

He stared straight ahead, and his face didn't move an inch. "Your brother."

"Yes. He's the one I came here to find. I thought he was missing."

"He is your brother."

"Yes." He crossed his arms and frowned out at the trees.

I said, "I thought you would be happy."

I stared at him and he stared at the trees, and then he stood and I thought he was going to climb back down without a word, but instead he leaned in, his arms on either side of me, hands resting on the wall. His mouth was just inches from mine.

He said, "When I saw you again, I thought that you are like that star you told me about, the one in the song. The one that lights the way for a traveler in the dark." And then he kissed me.

When we broke apart, he smiled, from his mouth, from his eyes, and I thought how nice it was to see him peaceful, almost happy, even for a moment.

I said, "Why did you say that like it's a sad thing?"

"Because no good can come of us, Clementine." And, just like that, the smile was gone.

Without thinking, I said, "Don't you believe in magic?"

"Magic? Like Harry Houdini?"

"Like stars that light the way. Like destiny."

"Destiny?"

"Like my brother being here right now. All this time, I was looking for him, and then he found me, right here in Germany. Of all the men they could have sent, they sent you a team that my brother was on, and he thought he was just doing his duty blowing up that train, and it turned out I was on it. I was the person he was trying to free, even though he didn't know it. That's what I mean."

He straightened so that he was looking down at me. His hands reached for mine. I looked at our hands, twined together. There was dirt and blood under my fingernails too.

I said, "Maybe we were supposed to meet." My heart rushed a little as I said it.

"I am glad we met, Clementine. But I don't know that it was fate. I think maybe it is a happy moment, in the middle of a war, and that it was a lucky thing for me, but that is all." He smiled his cat-with-the-canary smile, dangerous and sincere at the same time, so different from the smile that had come just before.

I studied Émile as if I were studying a map—strong, stubborn profile, full lips, dark liquid eyes, wide, broad hands that carried so much. I told myself he'd been hurt too often by too many people. I wondered what I would be like if I'd been through all the things he'd been through. I wondered if I would see the world the way he saw it, without magic or destiny or anyplace to go after you died except right into the ground.

He lifted a hand and ran his finger over my lips, barely touching them, resting on the split. He said, "Do not love me, Clementine."

Before I could say anything, before I could push him away or tell him to go to hell, a voice said, "About time we headed off, ain't it?"

I looked up and there was Johnny Clay, arm thrown over the top rung of the ladder.

I stood, dropping Émile's hand. I said, "Hey, Johnny Clay." I was so happy to see him, my heart just filled right up. But he wasn't looking at me. He was staring right at Émile, like he was Hitler himself.

The land grew flatter and the trees thinner, and then they started filling in again and the earth rose into green hills that grew higher and higher. We'd been traveling for six days when we entered the Vosges Mountains, which would take us into France. We drank water from the creeks and rivers and we gathered berries and nuts and hunted fish and rabbits and, once or twice, squirrels. At night we made camp under the trees and cooked the food over a low fire, which we stamped out as soon as we were done. By morning, my stomach would be growling and carrying on as if it hadn't been fed at all.

As we entered the Vosges Mountains, Johnny Clay walked beside me. He'd been keeping his eye on Émile and me, studying us like a hawk, even though there was nothing to see. Émile had told me not to love him and I was keeping my distance good and far even though I lay awake each night wanting him, knowing he was just a few feet away.

Johnny Clay started telling me about his plans for after the war. He said he'd already decided he was heading to the Gold Coast, down in Africa, to mine gold. He was going to marry a Negro girl with skin as black as night and buy himself a mine and then buy up all the other ones too so he could own all the gold in Africa.

Just as he said it, I spotted a flash of gold on the ground. I thought:

That's funny. Maybe there's gold right here in this forest. I bent down to pick it up and it was an empty shell casing.

I brushed off the dust and the dirt, and Johnny Clay said, "What you got there?" I held it out so the others could see it. We all looked left and right and all around. The breeze blew my hair so that it tickled my cheek.

Johnny Clay studied the casing. He said, "German. Maybe someone broke away from his unit." He fingered his gun.

Émile took the casing from me and said, "It's Allied. From one of our fighter planes."

Johnny Clay said, "Why aren't there more of them then? You can track the path of a plane by the shell casings."

Émile said, "It does not mean there aren't more ahead."

He and Johnny Clay stared at each other. They made me think of two dogs about to get into a scrap fight. Eleanor said, "For God's sake. We've lost enough time because of the fog." She kept on walking.

The next day and the next we came across more shell casings, one after another. The casings littered the ground like bread crumbs. At first, I wondered if someone had dropped them there to mark their way home.

Émile frowned at Ty's compass and said, "I think we should travel the rest of the way down below, on the edge of the tree line."

Johnny Clay said, "We'd risk being seen. The Germans are fleeing France. The border towns will be thick with them, not to mention the borders themselves."

Émile slid the compass into his jacket pocket. I suddenly didn't want him touching it anymore. Before I could ask for it back he said, "We'll still be inside the trees, but we need to get off this path."

Johnny Clay said, "I say we're better off up high, even higher than this, where we can see around us, see what's coming."

Eleanor said, "Let's just keep going. The casings aren't fresh. Some of them have been covered by the dirt and leaves for a while."

Émile looked at me. Johnny Clay looked at me. They were waiting for me to decide it, and I knew by deciding it I would be choosing one of them over the other. I looked back and forth between them. I thought about how Émile had led me through France, and I trusted him, even though I didn't much like him, much less love him, right now. But I'd known my brother my whole life and I trusted him too. He was my very best friend. Émile thought things out but Johnny Clay usually jumped right in, headfirst, without thinking much at all.

I wanted to choose Johnny Clay over Émile, but I knew Émile was right about this. So I said, "I think we should leave the path and go to the tree line." I wouldn't look at Émile. I didn't want him to think I'd said it because I loved him.

Johnny Clay glared at me but I stared at him in a way that showed him I wasn't going to back down, and then I followed Émile and Eleanor off the path and down the hill, picking my way through the brush and the trees and the carpet of leaves that had fallen recently.

From behind me, I heard a sharp popping sound and I turned, looking up. It was the sound of a tree limb cracking and dropping from a great height, but the trees were still except for the breeze, which shook the leaves so that they danced.

As I was turning back around, my eyes dropped from the tree tops to the ground, and I watched, just like time slowed down, as Johnny Clay fell. It seemed to take him forever to fall, and at the same time it happened so fast I didn't have time to think.

The next thing that happened was that Émile shot the German dead so that he fell faster than Johnny Clay. And then Eleanor picked up Johnny Clay's gun and shot the German who came up behind him. All the while, I leaned over my brother, trying to find where the bullet had hit him. His eyes were closed and he lay so still I was afraid he was dead.

Don't be dead. Don't be dead. Please, please, please don't be dead. . . .

His eyes fluttered opened and he said, "They got me, didn't they?"

The bullet was in his leg, right above the knee. I still wore the same skirt and blouse I'd been wearing weeks ago when they picked me up and sent me to Fresnes. I had Eleanor's bloody scarf tied around my leg, and I tore this off and wrapped it tight around him. There wasn't time to treat it any more than that. I said, "Can you stand?"

"Of course I can stand." He pulled himself up to his feet and I helped him when he couldn't come up all the way. He swore a blue streak. He looked at Eleanor and said, "I'll take my gun back."

Émile said, "There are probably more of them. They've heard the shots and they will be coming."

As if they were listening and waiting, two more Germans appeared out of the trees. There was a hard, loud pop that seemed to go right through me, and I watched as one of the Germans fell, the red blooming out of his chest. Then another pop, and the German behind him fell too. My brother and Émile stood, guns pointed, like some sort of movie cowboys.

Johnny Clay said, "You think that's it?"

Émile's head was still but his eyes were scanning the woods. He said, "No."

It was hard to tell which way the Germans had come from, ahead of us or behind us or maybe somewhere from the left or right.

I said to Johnny Clay, "Can you run?"

"Faster than you, faster than anyone."

The four of us ran through the woods, along the side of the hill, up the hill, down the hill, heading all the time toward France. I wondered if somehow we were in France without knowing it, if maybe we'd already crossed the border, or if I would know it when we did.

Up ahead, built into the side of a hill, was another castle, or what used to be a castle. We pushed through sticker bushes, tree limbs snapping in our faces, not bothering to look where we were going, just going, going, heading for the castle walls. We were just rounding the side of it when I heard the Germans. I couldn't tell if they were in front of us or behind us or what side they were coming from. They might have been coming from all directions. Shots were fired off in the woods, then there was machine gun fire and the hard, wild shouting of male voices.

We hid behind the castle walls, which were crumbling and tilted like old tombstones. They seemed to be sinking into the earth. Then we waited. The breeze shook the leaves. I could hear my brother's breathing over my own. Johnny Clay pulled a grenade out of his bag and tossed it to Émile, then my brother pulled out another, his finger on the split pin. Émile handed Eleanor a small pistol—a .32, just like the one I'd taken from Barzo's bag. I held my gun, resting it on top of the wall, scanning the trees. The woods had gone quiet except for the sound of our breathing.

I thought: Maybe they're gone. Maybe that was it and we got them all. Suddenly, there was a rumble to the east of us that grew louder and louder until it was a roar. We turned our faces to the sky, and there was the green-gray belly of a plane almost directly overhead.

And then, through the trees, I saw the green-gray of uniforms and the dull green of helmets, and they were coming toward us. Johnny Clay and Émile looked at each other and then, at the same time, tossed the grenades. We covered our heads and waited for the explosion, and the earth and the trees shuddered. We started shooting as men rushed out of the smoke. Some fired back at us and some dropped on the spot, and I didn't have time to think that one of my bullets might have killed a man.

We went running on, away from the castle, higher up the hill, pushing through the trees, until suddenly there was a clearing, more like a field, and we came up short at the edge of it.

I said, "What do we do?" There we were out in the wide open, nothing to hide behind, moving targets.

Émile said, "Cross the field to the trees." On the other side of the clearing, the woods grew up again, thick and dark.

Johnny Clay said, "Stay low."

I said, "How many are there?"

No one answered me because there was no way of knowing.

I said, "Can we make it to France?" What I wanted to know was could we outrun whatever was left of the Germans? Was France close enough to run to?

Émile said, "It's on the other side of these mountains."

I looked at my comrades then—Eleanor's face was flushed and angry; I could see Émile thinking, planning, two steps ahead of me, of the Germans; Johnny Clay looked fierce as an Indian warrior. I wondered how I must look, standing there with the rifle in my hand, dressed in a skirt and blouse, bag slung over my chest. I caught Émile's eye and he smiled at me, but I knew he was really somewhere else, thinking ahead, getting us to France.

I said, "No prisoners."

"No prisoners," he said.

We ran down the hill and across the field in a line going across, heading into battle together. We ran low as we could and every now and then I looked behind me to see if the Germans were coming. The field was empty except for us. To the right of us was a road, and up in the distance, on the edge of the road, was what looked like a village. We kept running until I thought my legs were going to fall off and my lungs were going to give in. I looked at my brother, running alongside me, long legs flying, and you couldn't even tell that he'd been shot.

Johnny Clay fired his gun back toward the woods, the ones we were running from. We all turned and fired as a handful of Germans appeared. One of them carried a machine gun, and he started shooting. Johnny Clay grabbed me and yanked me down, and while I was down I reloaded my gun.

Johnny Clay said, "Run. I'll cover you."

I said, "No you will not. We stay together."

The Germans were shooting and we were shooting, and then more of them spilled out of the woods, guns raised. For the first time in my life, I wasn't sure I would get out of this, not even with Émile to lead us, not even with Johnny Clay. A bullet hit Émile in the shoulder and he swore. Another one hit him in the arm, the ribs, I couldn't tell which. A bullet whizzed by Eleanor's ear, so close she had to duck. She put her hand to her ear and came away with blood, and I thought: Where's the one that's going to hit me? Where's mine?

There was nowhere to hide out there, in the middle of the field. We crouched as low as we could and then Johnny Clay said, "Goddammit." And he stood straight up and pointed his gun and fired three rounds. Three Germans fell until there was just one more, coming straight for my brother, who was reloading his pistol. I raised my gun and shot the German square between the eyes.

THIRTY-SIX

We ran for the trees and lost ourselves in the woods again, the air cool on my face, the leaves swaying in the breeze. We took shelter in the shade of a wide tree, breathing hard, breathing fast. Émile said, "There may be more Germans ahead." His sleeve was red with blood, and he pushed it up to examine the wound. He said, "Just a scratch." But he took the aid kit from Johnny Clay's bag and pulled out a bandage since his own kit was out. There was only one, so he tore it in half.

Johnny Clay sat down and stretched his leg in front of him and pulled out a knife. His left hand was wrapped and bleeding. Before anyone could say anything, he stuck the knife in his mouth sideways, tore the scarf off where I'd tied it, and ripped a hole in his pants, just above the knee, so that you could see the wet purple-red of the wound. He grunted, his teeth clenched around the knife, "I want you to take the bullet out."

I didn't know who he was saying it to, but Émile took the knife from him. I said, "But your shoulder."

Émile said, "It is nothing."

"Let me see it." I reached for him and he caught my hand before I could touch him.

"I am fine." He held my hand, the warmth of it flowing into me. He twined his fingers through mine. There was something in his eyes—a question, impatience, anger.

Johnny Clay said, "Don't mind me."

Eleanor said, "The hole's too small for that." Her voice was flat and irritated and she glared at the knife. She was bleeding from one ear, where the bullet had grazed her. I pulled my hand away at the same moment Émile dropped it. I ripped the bandage in half again and held it out to her but she shook her head. "Here." She rolled up her sleeves and bent over Johnny Clay and reached into the wet purple-red wound with her fingers. Johnny Clay didn't even flinch, just sat back, resting on one hand, holding the other, the one that was bleeding, in his lap. He watched Eleanor work even when I couldn't.

She said, "There." She held up a bullet covered in blood. "A souvenir." She wiped it clean on her sleeve and handed it to Johnny Clay.

He said, "Thank you."

She tore off the hem of her skirt and started wrapping his leg. "You should let me look at your hand."

He shook his head. "What's done is done. I think I managed to stop the bleeding." Little beads of sweat dotted his forehead.

Eleanor tied up his leg with her scarf, and then she took the bandage, the one I'd offered her, and wrapped this around him too. She said, "This will have to do."

Émile went to scout out the Germans, to see how close they were and how many. He had been gone an hour. I counted the time by the slant of the sun. Johnny Clay and Eleanor and I took shelter in a cluster of trees, thick with brush.

I looked at my brother's leg and hand and then at his face, asking him without asking him if he was okay. I thought his face was a little pale, a little clammy-looking, but that otherwise he seemed like himself. He said, "What you looking at, little sister? Ain't you never seen a man shot before?" He stared down at his leg and he looked almost proud. He said, "Yessir. I reckon I'll get me a real good limp out of this. I can't wait to see the look on Daryl Gordon's face. He'll probably go out and shoot himself in his own leg just so he can have one too."

I said, "Daryl Gordon's dead, Johnny Clay. He was killed in a place called Bataan. Daddy Hoyt told me when I was home last."

Johnny Clay was still admiring his leg. I stared at his head, gold in the light, the hair growing back in from when the army had cut it. When he finally blinked up at me, all the cockiness was gone out of him. He said, "When?"

"November 1942."

He nodded at this finally like, "Okay." Like, "Well that's the way it is then." His eyes wandered away from me over the ground. Then they came back to me, and he looked me square in the eye. He said, "You listen here. We are going to get home again. Do you hear me?"

I said, "Yes."

"We are going to get out of here. No goddamn German is going to kill *me* before I'm ready to die." And then he pulled himself up with his one good leg and his one good hand without any help from me or Eleanor, and stood, brave and tall, the sun behind him, setting him aglow. He took his pistol out of his belt and checked the magazine. He said, "I'm going to get us some dinner."

An hour later, Émile was back, just as the sun dropped behind the trees. We made a small fire, leaving it lit long enough to roast the rabbit Johnny Clay had caught, and then we covered the flames with dirt and stamped out the embers and waited for the night to fill in and grow black. The sky was starting to change colors. *Nighttime already.* How did it get to be nighttime again?

Émile said, "There are Germans dug in fifteen miles to the southwest."

Johnny Clay said, "How many?"

"Hundreds."

"Are they on the move?"

"Yes."

"Which way?"

"Some south, some north. They are getting ready for a battle, but some are fleeing." We let his words settle in around us like the darkness. "We keep on through the night."

He kneeled down and, with a rock, drew a map in the dirt. He said that as far as he could figure, we were only ten or so miles from the border, but with Germans up ahead and with the state of the borders unknown, especially now that the Germans were on the run, he thought we should head east, deeper into Germany. Émile said they wouldn't want to let anyone in or out of the country who didn't have German identification papers.

Johnny Clay said, "We should head west and eventually we'll come to the French border, faster than if we go to the east."

"If we head west, we run into Schirmeck. There is a concentration camp there and, if the Germans can be believed, more Germans. They are everywhere from here to Belfort." Émile stood, brushing the dirt off his hands.

Johnny Clay grumbled, but he started walking eastward, Eleanor just behind. Before Émile could go anywhere, I reached for his jacket and pulled it aside, bracing myself for what I might see. But there was nothing. No blood. No tear in the shirt.

"What are you looking for, Clementine?" He smiled the cat-and-canary smile. It was weary around the corners. "Is there something I can do for you?"

I said, "But you were shot." Not that I care, I thought. Not that I care if you die right here in the woods.

Émile pulled something out of his jacket pocket. A round disc that was dented in the middle, as if someone had pushed it in with their thumb. He said, "I am sorry about your compass." He handed it to me.

I turned the compass over in my hand. I fit my thumb into the groove, the place where the bullet had hit, and I thought about all the things this could have been—fate, destiny, luck, chance. I thought, He has to believe now. I waited for him to say this was proof of something else other than just the things you could see and touch. Instead he tilted my chin with his hand, so that I was looking up at him, and kissed me.

We traveled all night and day and into the night again, picking our way east. No one talked and I knew the others, including me, were concentrating on finding their way and not being heard or seen by the Germans who were living in the woods.

Johnny Clay walked ahead of me and I watched the way he favored his leg, the one that had been shot, and the way he held his wrapped hand close to his ribs. The beads of sweat still dotted his forehead. His skin had gone so pale he looked as if he'd just come out of a long winter. We hiked around the peak of the mountain and across to the other side. From that high up we could see into the valley that lay below. The spires of a city—a good-sized one—rose up in the distance. We started down, and part of the way was so steep that I had to inch along so I wouldn't go tumbling to the bottom.

I didn't let myself think what we would run into once we were out of the woods. Instead I stared at the ground, at the way it sloped ahead, dropping off to nothing. I made myself take one step and then one more step and not think about another thing.

At dawn, I heard a rumbling in the distance. I looked up and there came the green-gray belly of a plane, just like two days before. I stood watching that plane pass on by and Johnny Clay said, "Come on, you." His voice was low, like he couldn't get his breath. He wasn't going to call me Velva Jean but he didn't want to call me Clementine either.

I said, "There's an airfield nearby."

I said it more to myself than to anyone else, but Émile said, "How do you know?"

I said, "Because that plane's fixing to land."

We went as fast as we could down the hill. We reached the edge of the woods, and past the tree line I could see a field and a squat stone farmhouse, and beyond that a road, and beyond that the dark shadow of the city.

Johnny Clay said, "Which way?"

I wasn't sure if he was asking me or Émile.

Émile said, "We stay off the roads." His eyes burned at me. I looked away. He said, "Where is the airfield?"

The air turned cooler against my cheeks. I felt a slight breeze from the west. My hair blew across my face and I brushed it away. I stood with my back to the woods. I thought, I don't know.

I studied the land. If I were building an airfield here, where would I build it? Flat land, far enough from the mountains to have a good takeoff and landing. Far enough from the city to have space, but close enough to be easy to get to.

From the woods, I heard something pushing through the trees, something snapping the twigs. We all turned, all at once. Were we followed? Were we being watched? An animal, I told myself. Just a deer or a squirrel.

From over the mountains, I heard the engine. And then the plane was over our heads, pointed toward the city.

We sat low in the high grass that surrounded the airfield, Eleanor to the right of me and Émile to my left, Johnny Clay on the other side of him. Émile touched my cheek with his finger, and it was enough to send a jolt of electricity through me. For him the touch was like an afterthought. By the time I looked up at him, he was staring off toward the airfield. I tried to imagine again what it would be like to be with him outside of this war, in a world of regular things like suppers and breakfasts and sitting by the fire. I wasn't sure he was a man made for every day.

The airfield was a control tower, a flattened grass runway, and six planes, nothing sleek or fast. Two guards walked back and forth with guns, yawning, smoking cigarettes.

I eyed the different planes that waited there. The Fw 190 was the fastest but also the smallest. I knew it was a single-seater and that there was barely room for one person, much less four, which meant it might be harder to get off the ground and it might be harder to fly it at a higher altitude. The Junkers Ju 87 Stuka had a wing blown off, and the two monoplanes looked like trainers. Even if they could seat four, they couldn't fly the distance from here to England.

The large, four-engine plane was almost the same size as the B-17, but I wasn't sure about something that big that I'd never flown before. If I flew that one, I'd need a copilot, and Johnny Clay could do that, even as weak as he was, so that was something to think about. They might have left the keys inside it, but if they hadn't I'd have to jimmy the engine, which could be harder to do on a plane that size. I also had to think about takeoff and how fast I could get a heavy plane up into the sky. We'd need to go as fast as possible to get past the Germans.

We watched as the last plane circled the airfield. It was small and sleek as a bullet. The landing gear unfolded out of the wings, which was something I'd never seen before. I could tell the plane was at least a two-seater, which meant we might be able to squeeze four inside. It was a single-engine and had a two-bladed propeller. The only thing was that it was smaller than the others and might not be able to fly as far as we needed it to go.

I said to Émile, to my brother, to Eleanor, to whoever could answer me, "What kind of plane is that?"

Eleanor said, "A Heinkel He 70. The Blitz. They use it as a mail plane. Not as powerful as the Fw 190 or the Stuka, but it's built for long distances and speed. It has its problems, though. It's made of a kind of metal that burns in the air when heated, so a single hit from a machine gun can set the entire plane ablaze."

I couldn't read German. I'd never flown a German airplane, but I figured a plane was a plane. I didn't think there was anything I couldn't fly, even if I was rusty.

THIRTY-SEVEN

Ten minutes later, the sky was beginning to lighten. The rain started to fall again and the air was so cold I could see my breath. I had to stop to think what month it was because suddenly it felt like winter. I'd lost track of the date, but I figured we must be into September by now. Back home the days would still be hot but the nights would be cool, but not cool like this. They would be just cool enough so that you could feel the breeze blowing in your open window and hear the end-of-summer crickets humming in the trees.

The Heinkel He 70 rolled to the end of the taxiway, pointed east. From what I could tell, it had a wingspan of around forty to fifty feet It stood about ten feet high and looked to be about forty feet long.

Johnny Clay would take care of the pilot. Émile would take care of the guards. Eleanor would be on the lookout for any crew that might appear. I would climb into the plane and get my bearings. We didn't know how far the plane had just flown or if it had taken any hits. In my mind, I ticked through the list of things that should be done to get the plane ready to fly again: an engine run-up; running the cowlings; checking the rudder cables, prop blades, elevator cables, vertical and horizontal stabilizers—or the rudder and the elevator—fuel system, fuel lines, static port; checking for damage; refueling. There wasn't time for any of it.

Émile said, "No shooting. No shots fired. Do not call attention."

Germans behind us. Germans in front of us. I didn't turn back to see if anyone was following us because I needed to look forward, to think about the plane. What if I couldn't fly it after all? We might get into the cockpit only to have me figure out that I didn't know what I was doing. The thing might not be able to take off or have only a gallon or two of gasoline. We weren't far from the French border—even if the plane needed refueling, we would be okay, or at least safer, as long as we could get out of Germany. The He 70 had come in strong, landing gear down, no sputtering or shaking. I decided there had to be enough gasoline in the tank for the trip to France.

The guards walked up and down, pacing, guns over their shoulders. We slunk through the grass, moving fast and silent. We stopped every few paces and waited, careful not to make a sound. When we were just feet away, we crouched low and watched as one of the guards called to the other and offered him a cigarette. They stood smoking, looking out toward the woods, talking in low voices. Every now and then one of them laughed.

When they were done smoking, they ground out their cigarettes and one of the guards strolled off. The other one stood looking out toward the forest as if he could see through the trees. I wondered if he knew about the Germans who were hiding there.

Finally, after what seemed like years, the guard turned around and looked the other way. He called out something to his friend, and then he started patting his pockets, like he was searching for more cigarettes.

I watched then as Émile crept through the grass, half-crawling, half-walking. The rest of us waited. The German still had his back to us and he was only two or three feet away. Émile rose up and all of a sudden he was just behind the guard, the knife pressed to the man's throat. I started crawling toward the plane. The guard let out a yell that was cut short before he fell to the ground. I was halfway between Émile and the second guard, when I saw the man turn in our direction. I saw the whistle around his neck, saw him fumble with it.

Before Émile could run for him, I reached into my bag and pulled out my lipstick and threw it as hard as I could. The lipstick hit the man smack in the nose and he dropped the whistle and covered his face with his hands. "You can turn anything into a deadly weapon," I said. Then I jumped for him, punching out my fist like a claw, and when he took his hands away I jabbed him right in the eyes.

Émile was there with his knife. His arm went around the guard and he dragged the body down into the grass. He grabbed my hand and his hand was wet. I tried not to think of the man's blood on him, on me, as we ran for the plane.

I could see Eleanor running ahead and Johnny Clay standing up on the wing, reaching into the cockpit, when I heard the shot. It rang through the morning like the bells of Notre Dame. I felt it instead of heard it, as if it were going through me, and for one minute I thought it *had* gone through me. I looked down at my arms, my legs, and then at my stomach, expecting to see blood. I pressed my hand to my stomach, right on my side, just below my ribs, but the only blood was from the guard.

As if in slow motion, Johnny Clay slumped over, onto the wing, one arm hanging off the side. I stared at the hand at the end of that arm, the way it was swaying back and forth, back and forth, till it came to rest, the fingers limp and pointing at the ground.

Before I could think or move, Émile was up on the wing. I heard a muffled shot, and the pilot's body dropped out of the plane. Then Émile was shouting at me and Eleanor was pushing me, and I was climbing onto the wing and into the plane, and there was a compartment with four seats, two on each side, facing each other. Half a dozen cylinders were stacked on top of one another like a woodpile, and even in my haze I knew these were bombs. The forward fuselage was shaped like a rectangle, with the machine gunner's station at one end, under the cockpit cover, and the crew compartment sitting under a framed canopy off to the port side. There were cartons in there of mail or something else, which made the compartment look like a storage room.

Émile rushed into that compartment, carrying Johnny Clay, blood soaking through my brother's shirt, right at his ribs and waist, blood soaking Émile and the floor of the plane. I watched as Émile laid him down, turned his own bag inside out and then Johnny Clay's, grabbing his aid kit, opening it, throwing it aside, and sprinkling white powder over Johnny Clay and all that blood. Émile threw off his jacket and then his shirt, ripping it in half, and he wrapped this around my brother like a bandage.

I felt a poking and a pushing and there was Eleanor, and I found myself in the cockpit, which had two seats, one in front of the other— the pilot's seat on the left side of the plane; the other seat, the one behind it, on the right side—and I was strapping myself in, running my hands over the controls and levers.

The engine was off. It had just been running. The pilot must have shut it down before Johnny Clay got to him. Maybe he'd shut it down because he'd seen Johnny Clay and he knew he wanted the plane.

I said, "The engine's dead." *Johnny Clay's dead or he might be dead. Velva Jean Hart is dead. Everything is dead.*

Eleanor sat behind me in the navigator's seat. She said, "He's still breathing. He's alive." I turned my head and Émile was bent over Johnny Clay, his black hair catching the daylight, which shone in through the hatch. Had he shut the hatch? Had I? I couldn't remember, but somehow we were locked in. I could see the gold of my brother's hair, the gold of his skin growing paler. Émile was working over him just as he'd worked over Captain Baskin all those weeks ago, when I was first flying to France.

> *You are lost and gone forever,*
> *Dreadful sorry, Clementine.*

"Can you fly it?"

The voice was coming from a long way away.

"Clementine. Can you fly this plane?" I turned and Eleanor was staring at me, her face wet, blood on her cheek, on her hands. She rubbed at the blood, trying to get it off. Not her blood, I thought. The guard's blood. My brother's blood.

I said, "Yes." I didn't know if this was true or not. I might not be able to get it started. The plane might not have enough gas. There might not be enough room to climb before they shot us down.

Émile said, "Sing, Clementine." It was a command, an order, but there was a gentleness behind the voice, and something else that seemed to wrap around me and let me know I was safe.

I thought, Sing, Clementine. But I suddenly couldn't remember any words. I thought: Sing, Velva Jean. Why is everyone always telling me to sing? I couldn't remember the tunes. I sat there feeling like two people sewn up the middle, like one person cut into halves. I was Clementine Roux. I was Velva Jean Hart. I wasn't Clementine Roux. I wasn't Velva Jean Hart. I wasn't anyone anymore. I was just some girl who'd lost herself. I was some girl whose mama had told her to live out there, and now I didn't know who I was or where I fit in or if I'd ever fit in anywhere again.

Émile began to sing, his voice rough but warm. It was an honest voice. It was a good voice. I didn't recognize the song or the language. It sounded like the kind of song you would sing around a campfire or in a dark saloon that smelled of whiskey and cigarettes. A gypsy song.

Eleanor leaned forward and laid a hand on my arm. "He will be fine," she said. For a moment I thought she meant Émile—that Émile would be fine—and then I realized she meant Johnny Clay. It was the first moment I liked her.

I stared hard at the controls and suddenly they came into focus. On the right side was a smooth panel and underneath this was a compartment. Inside there were a dozen or more switches and these looked like circuit breakers. I figured the Germans probably turned off all their breakers when they finished flying, so I reversed them all, thinking this would turn them on. The gauges lit up and we had power.

"I need the starter," I could hear myself saying. I said it over and over. Eleanor leaned forward and ran her eyes over the control panel, reading the words of each dial and lever. She pointed at a metal T-handle on the right side of the cockpit that had a word on it, written in German. *Anlasser.* I pulled it. Nothing happened.

I could hear the voice of my first flying instructor, Duke Norris, the man who'd taught me to fly: *If pulling the starter doesn't work, push it.*

I pushed and I felt something catch, like something was winding up. I pulled the handle and the engine started up, low and throaty at first—kind of sputtering and muttering—and then it seemed to kick in and began to hum. I tried to find the gas gauge to see how much fuel we had, but I couldn't figure out which one it was. There were five buttons behind the throttle, two in front and three in back. I pushed one of the front buttons and then another, but nothing happened.

The sun was rising, turning the sky a sleepy gold and pink, and I could see figures inside the control tower. They would be wondering why their pilot was starting the plane up again after he'd just landed, never thinking for a minute that it wasn't their man at all but a girl.

To the east, I could see the glow of the sun as it climbed up above the horizon, dulled behind heavy gray clouds. To the west there was nothing but the heavy, sprawling green of the forest. Because of the mountains, we would have to fly south and then west and then northwest.

I taxied south, the woods on my right, the control tower on my left. I gave it more gas and pushed the throttle, and there was that moment, the one that happens just before a plane takes off when everything seems to drop into the feet—heart, stomach, knees. It's the moment when anything can happen, when you feel as if you can do anything and everything and live forever. It's the moment when I can suddenly hear all the songs there are to write in this world and see all the places there are to go. It is ceiling and visibility unlimited. It is beyond the keep.

The moment only lasted seconds, and then we shot up into the air. I flew too high too soon and the plane started to shake and tug back toward the ground. I wrestled the throttle and the wheel until it evened out. I pushed the throttle full forward and cleared the meadow that surrounded the airfield and a fence that sat at the edge of it. I was fence-hopping again, like I'd done with Ty in Texas, back when I was training to be a WASP. Down on the ground, men ran out of the control tower.

I pushed one of the three buttons and the flaps started coming down. I pushed the next button and they went back up again. Okay, I thought. I know what these do. But then I ran my eyes over the other controls—so many buttons and levers and knobs—and I thought about how much I didn't know, which was almost everything.

Over the engine, I shouted to Eleanor, "Tell me what you know about this plane."

She shouted back, "That's all. It's not used much anymore, just as a trainer and for mail delivery. They replaced it with the He 111."

"Miles per hour?"

"I don't know."

"Maximum range?"

"I don't know."

I thought, What *do* you know?

"Well," I shouted, "there's only one way to find out."

I felt a tap on my arm, and there was a headset hanging in midair. I took it from Eleanor and fitted it as best I could around my head and over my mouth. "Can you hear me?"

"I hear you." In my headset, her voice was scratchy and too loud. "I'm studying the maps and trying to get you a distance."

I tried not to think of my brother lying in the belly of the plane bleeding to death. Instead I told myself I was Constance Kurridge. I was Flyin' Jenny. I was Pancho Barnes, the fastest woman on earth. I kept thinking: I just stole an airplane. A plane I don't know anything about. I don't know how fast it can go or how far. We have to cross hundreds of miles of enemy territory in an enemy plane. Pilots like me are going to see this plane and try to shoot it down because it's German, and there's no way to tell them we're on their side.

Eleanor's voice said, "Five hundred fifteen nautical miles. That's how far we have to go. We head northwest over Germany, then Luxembourg, then Brussels, and then over the Channel to home."

Your home, I thought. But not my home. My home was so far away it would take three planes to get there.

We didn't know anything about the airspace over Germany, Luxembourg, and Brussels or what air battles might be going on. I said, "Is there a manual back there?" I knew by the size of the plane that it couldn't have more than six hundred miles of range.

"No. But I'm still looking."

I said, "Get Émile and tell him to drop some of the weight. The cartons in the crew compartment and the bombs, but make sure they're not armed. Tell him to wait till we're over the forest and the mountains. Tell him to get rid of them."

We needed to lighten our load if we were going to have enough gas to make it to England. We'd get there faster that way and be able to fly higher, which would keep us safe from ground patrols.

I pointed the plane to the northwest. As we flew over the mountains, they looked so much like my mountains that my heart caught, but then I could see they weren't as high or as far-reaching. The air above the mountains bounced the plane and I climbed higher to get past it. We flew like this for a good hour and I started to relax into the flight and into the plane. The throttle buzzed in my hand. The control panel was lit up like the Fourth of July. I looked around, out the window, and thought how beautiful it was up there, above the earth where men were shooting each other with guns and cannons and leaving each other for dead, above the clouds where you could actually see the sun and feel it on your face.

That little plane soared along like a racehorse. I opened her up and my speed climbed to 241, 289, 321, 354 kilometers per hour. Maybe it was going to be okay. Maybe no one was going to come after us or try to shoot us down, and maybe we were going to get back to England without a hitch. I thought that whatever happened to me or Johnny Clay or Émile or Eleanor or this Heinkel He 70, it was good to be flying again.

THIRTY-EIGHT

Ten minutes later, I heard Émile's voice on the headset. He said, "We are not alone."

At first I wasn't sure what he meant. I said, "Where are you?"

"The machine gunner's station. There's an MG 15 machine gun here."

"Are they Allied?"

"German. Three in all. Focke-Wulf 190's. Maybe just scouting right now, trying to get a read on us." There was a blast of static and then nothing.

From behind me, Eleanor said, "That's not right. There should be four of them, unless one got shot down. The German formation is four. They call it the swarm."

"Émile . . . Émile!" It sounded like I was talking into a box, like my words were bouncing back to me.

Eleanor said, "The intercom's dead." She shouted it. I pushed my headset off so it fell around my neck and hung there like a necklace. Without Émile, I couldn't know what was happening around us. I couldn't see the bandits, and the thought that kept going round in my mind was that we were a flying time bomb. If the Germans didn't get us, the Allies would, as soon as they spotted us. And if they didn't go after us over Germany or Belgium they'd go after us as we were crossing the Channel.

I thought through everything I could be doing that I wasn't doing. Maybe if we lightened the load even more. The He 70 was fast, but it wasn't as fast as the Fw 190. Maybe if we tried the radio, but then the Germans would only intercept us and that might bring more after us, and we had too many after us now.

I shouted to Eleanor, "Can you see them?"

"No!"

The sky was empty and this made me more jittery than if I could see what was going on. They must have been coming at us from the rear.

Think, Velva Jean. Think, Clementine. Think, both of you.

I thought we must be at least over Luxembourg by now. If only I knew where the Allies were and what the airspace was like over these places. I might be flying us right into the middle of a battle zone.

I tried to take stock of where we were, watching the ground for landmarks, for forests or rivers that might tell us how far we'd gone, how far we still had to go. From up there, everything looked the same—forest, field, farm, cows, trees, houses, what was left of a village here or there.

Eleanor shouted, "We've got company. Under the wing."

I turned my head in her direction, and I could see she had the map spread across her lap. I turned my head to the left and there, under the wing, was an Fw 190. *The fourth one.* He was cruising along beside us, matching our speed. He was so close that I could almost read the instruments in his cockpit. We couldn't touch him under our wing like that, and he knew it, because the only gun we had was in the middle under the canopy.

I thought, Please don't let him look over here. I reached up to touch my bare head. I wasn't wearing a helmet, which meant he would see I was a girl, and he would know I wasn't supposed to be flying this plane. I stared ahead, as if this would keep him from doing anything but staring ahead. I thought of taking the plane up or down or veering away from him, but he made me nervous being so close, right under the wing.

Suddenly I couldn't help it—even though I knew I shouldn't look, I did. The first thing I saw was his oxygen mask, then the goggles sitting on top of the black helmet, and then his eyes, staring out at me. I heard Eleanor say, "Damn."

Without thinking, I reached for the autopilot aileron control, or where it would have been on a B-17 or an AT-6 or an Aeronca. At the same time, I lowered the left wing toward the Fw 190, bracing myself for the jolt of metal on metal. The 190 shot away, like out of a cannon, and I felt a shudder go through the He 70, which meant Émile had started firing.

The plane dropped out of my sight, and then it was back again, the engine smoking, the canopy torn off. The cockpit was empty and the plane started spiraling, and I saw a blur of color, and there was the pilot, dropping fast, his chute opening above him like a mushroom. Beyond him, I could see two more planes, both smoking, both heading for the ground.

I sped away from them, scanning the sky for the other plane, for new planes, but there was nothing but clouds and sun and a faint trail of smoke. I decided from then on to fly low so we'd make a more difficult target.

Twenty minutes later, I could see the choppy blue-black of water, wide as an ocean. *The English Channel.* As soon as I saw it, I thought: We're almost home. We're almost there. Hang on, Johnny Clay. Hang on, little plane.

We only had to cross the Channel and fly to Harrington, about 230 nautical miles. I turned to Eleanor. I said, "My brother . . ."

Before I could finish, she unlatched her safety belt and felt her way to the belly of the plane. I concentrated on flying and on counting each second. I wouldn't let myself think about anything more than that. One minute ticked by, and then two minutes, three minutes, four minutes, five. I wanted to leave the wheel and climb back there to see what was going on, but instead I made myself stare straight ahead and keep counting.

Two minutes later, Eleanor returned. In my ear she said, "He's holding on," and then she took her seat, strapping herself in again.

"Thank you," I said. *Thank you. Thank you. Thank you.*

And then I saw them—three airplanes flying in formation, heading right for us. They weren't just planes; they were B-17 bombers.

That's my plane, I thought. That's the one I flew across the Atlantic. They were probably on their way home when they saw us. They've come to bring us in. They're making sure we get back safely.

The bombers split off and surrounded us. Suddenly the controls went slack and I knew we'd been hit, and that's when it struck me: They think we're the enemy and they're going to shoot us down.

I waited for the fire or some sort of explosion, but instead we kept right on flying, although the engine began to chug like it was trying to get its breath. The oxygen pressure dropped by nearly half, and I increased the rpm and boost. I shouted at Eleanor to find Johnny Clay and put an oxygen mask on him, and then I grabbed for my own mask and pulled it on. "And tell Émile to hold his fire! Tell him not to shoot! I'm not going to kill our own men if I can help it."

I turned to make sure she'd heard me, and I saw her scrambling away toward the belly of the plane again. I turned back and thought about how I'd been in worse situations—like having to crash-land a B-29, the largest bomber in the war, over my very own mountains. I told myself if I was able to survive that, I'd be able to survive this.

The sky was filled with the flak that comes from ground fire. As I dodged the plane left and right, up and down, I thought the flak looked like large gray snowflakes. I didn't want to do too much dodging because what if I flew into the bullets instead of around them?

One of the planes rolled toward us head on, firing away. The B-17 was only a little faster than the He 70, but it had a service ceiling of thirty-five thousand feet and a rate of climb of nine hundred feet per minute. There would be more of them somewhere. Even if they were flying in Tail-end Charlie formation, which was three squadrons of three flying lead, high, and low, there should be at least nine or ten other bombers with them.

I remembered what Second Lieutenant Glenn had said about our flight from Harrington to France: *The trick is to fly in a dogleg pattern, which means you never fly a direct course for longer than thirty miles.* I went back in my mind, not to Camp Davis or Avenger Field, but to a little farm in Nashville where a man named Duke Norris taught my brother and me to fly. I remembered the spins and dives and stalls that

Johnny Clay had done and that I'd done too. I remembered the ones I'd learned from Puck when I was training to be a WASP.

Okay, little plane, I thought. Let's see what you've got.

I went into a break first, which meant I tipped the plane sideways and applied the rudder to make a fast turn. The B-17s were faster but heavier, and they kept on going straight away from me. I pushed the plane on, and minutes later the bombers were heading back toward me. This time I did a barrel roll, breaking to the right and rolling away while the Allies rolled to the left. I did a high barrel roll and then a low barrel roll, rollaways and scissors and yo-yos. I pushed the oxygen mask off my face so I could see, and then I sent the plane into a dive and hoped the Allies would think I'd been hit and was going down. Maybe they would leave us alone. We went down, down, down like a meteor, and when we were eye to eye with the treetops, I righted the nose and brought us level.

From below I could see the Allied fighters, high above our heads, limping along in a straggly, ragtag formation. Two of the B-17s were smoking, the wings on fire where they'd knocked into each other. I saw the parachutes dropping, one plane spinning toward the earth, but not on purpose like us. I saw the balloon of fire and smoke as it hit, and then I pushed the He 70 up and up so we would get lost in the clouds, out of sight of the two fighters that were still there.

The plane climbed to ten thousand feet, then twelve thousand, then fifteen thousand, then sixteen thousand, until the world went white around us. In that field of clouds, it felt as if we were floating. It was like being in a cave—no flak, no fire, no sound at all. Everything slowed down. I felt light, like I didn't weigh a pound. If I let go of the throttle I thought I might slip away through the cabin and out the window and into the fog. I would float there like an angel, like Mama, and I would be free as the clouds. I would live in the clouds and live in the sky, nothing pulling me down or keeping me planted or rooting me in place like a tree. I am living out there, I thought. Are you happy, Mama? This is living out there, just like you told me to do.

I wanted to go higher. I wanted to go as high as the sun or the moon. I wanted to open the window and step outside and feel the air lifting me, holding me. My head felt sweet and blurry and it was the first peaceful moment since I'd left America behind. My eyes were heavy and I wanted to sleep. Just for a minute. Just a quick rest. I hadn't rested in a long time. When was the last time? I couldn't remember. It must have been months, maybe more. Back in Nashville. Back at the Lovelorn Café. With Gossie in the next room and Johnny Clay keeping us up late talking. And we were learning to fly.

Johnny Clay. There was something about Johnny Clay. . . . My eyes were closing and my head was blurring. Johnny Clay . . .

Suddenly I felt a sharp sting on my cheek. I tried to hide my face by turning in to my shoulder, but there was a sting on my other cheek. I was weak and I was weary, and I didn't have much breath left in me, and then there was something being tied around my head, around my mouth. I tried to push it off, but the more I pushed, the harder it pressed against my face.

A voice that sounded just like mine said, "You're dreaming, Velva Jean. Wake up. Come out of the fog."

I opened my eyes and Émile was bent over my seat, wedging himself into the small space, his hands gripping the throttle and the wheel. He said, "Are you mad, Clementine? You pulled off your oxygen mask."

I felt the mask, and then I looked around. We were out of the smoke and there was nothing but clear sky. No enemy planes. No bursts of flak. I wanted to go back and lose myself. I wanted to pull off the mask and shut my eyes.

I shouted, "Did you slap me?"

"Yes! Take the wheel and get us out of here."

"Johnny Clay . . ."

"He has a fighting chance as long as you don't fall asleep again. Go."

I said, "We're hit."

The engine was running rough. From what I could tell, we didn't have rudder controls or hydraulic pressure, and the oxygen was low. Émile shouted, "There's a leak in the bomb bay cross-feed. I opened the bomb bay doors to try to stop an explosion."

A red light on the instrument panel started blinking on and off. In all the planes I'd flown before, this meant the plane was close to running out of fuel. I chopped the throttle and flew the tightest pattern I could, and then I gave it all the gas I could.

I took the plane low because of the oxygen supply. I let down three hundred feet per minute, which let me increase our speed, and then I throttled back to save fuel. I throttled it back even more and reduced the rpm. We were losing gas and I didn't know what this meant for us, if we could make it to Harrington or even another ten miles. Down below us, the land gave way to the blue-black water, and suddenly we were over the English Channel.

Émile was shouting something about Manston, England. Not Harrington. Manston. It was an RAF emergency landing field. It was closer. It sat right on the coast. It had a three-thousand-foot runway, which was perfect for a no-flaps, no-brakes landing. They could handle emergency landings there. They had all the equipment. Take us in there, Clementine. Take us in there, Velva Jean. Take us in there.

I brought us down through the clouds, lower and lower, and suddenly, rising out of the water, there were these giant white cliffs, topped with a bright green, running from east to west as far as I could see. Just beyond them was a long gray-black road that wasn't a road at all but a runway.

I started cranking the main gear down, and then I leaned in over the instrument panel—the red light flashing—searching for the green light that would tell me the gear was locked, but I didn't know what I was looking at. We came in fast over the water and passed over the cliffs, and the whole time, I was trying to shake the gear into a locked position. Heavy bombers were scattered across the airfield, and this made me grip the throttle tighter, so tight my knuckles went white.

I pulled up hard to set up for landing. I pitched up and eased the throttle back and punched the buttons that would put the flaps down. I could feel the flaps coming down, but the landing gear didn't move, and then the flaps seemed to stop, just like that. I punched the buttons again, but they stayed where they were, half-down, half-up. I closed my eyes, just for a minute, and thought about flying blind. This was flying as blind as they came, and without looking I punched the buttons and pulled the levers, right where I would have found them on a plane I knew.

Nothing happened.

I looked toward the ground, and that's when I saw the ground crew. The air defense men had ripped the tarps off the quad .50 machine guns that sat around the field in a circle. I turned around to look for Émile, but he was gone again. Eleanor was gone. It was just me.

I couldn't worry about the machine guns pointed at us because I had to worry about landing the plane. The engine was choking, and the gauges were spinning. I used something called a sideslip to slow the plane, which meant I cross-controlled the aileron and rudder to slip the He 70 down, putting the side of the aircraft into the wind to increase drag and decrease speed. I lined up with the runway and all the guns followed me. I stared so hard at the runway that I made the guns blur away. All I could see was that gray-black road stretched out in front of me.

I would have to land the plane on its belly, and I didn't have any way of telling Émile or Eleanor what I was doing. I flashed my downward recognition lights—or tried to—which would let the men on the ground know I was in trouble and, hopefully, that I was friendly, and then I brought the He 70 lower, lower. I brought her even lower, and there was a jolt as we hit the ground, the metal of the plane's stomach grinding across the hard pavement.

The cabin filled with smoke and I was in the clouds again. But instead of floating away, I flipped the safety release on the escape hatch. It didn't open and I thought of Sally trapped in the cockpit of her plane. I flipped it again. Men with guns were climbing on the wings and they grabbed for me. I tried to undo my seat belt, but my hands wouldn't work. The men were pulling me, and one of them yanked me out of the plane so hard the seat belt snapped in half against my legs. He threw me down onto the runway.

The plane was smoking like a chimney, and the men dragged me away from it, just as they were dragging away Émile and Eleanor and Johnny Clay. My brother's head was limp against his chest, his arms thrown out to his sides. I started kicking the men and slapping them. I said, "He's hurt! Be careful with him!"

The men dropped me onto the ground. "You let him go right now, you hear me?" A fire truck came roaring up, and I shouted at the firemen, "That man is dying and you'd better make sure he doesn't. I don't care what you do to me, but you'd better take him to a hospital right now."

There was an ambulance now and they were loading Johnny Clay into the back of it. I tried to get up and run for him, but one of the men blocked my way and another came up next to me and said, "We've got a Frenchman, an Englishwoman, and this one. The Englishwoman may be a German." His voice was cold and British.

I said, "Please let me go with my brother." The ambulance door shut with a click. The driver climbed into the cab.

The man blocking my way said, "I'm sorry. Not until we can verify your identity."

I watched as the ambulance rolled away with my brother inside.

I thought: Good luck. Maybe once you figure out my identity, you can tell me just exactly who I am.

THIRTY-NINE

W e were held in a cell in the decontamination center, where we were interrogated, one after the other. When it was Eleanor's turn, Émile and I sat side by side on a bench and waited.

"How long will they keep us here?" I said.

"I do not know." He took my hand. "He has lost some blood, but he is strong. He is a fighter like you."

I didn't bother moving my hand away. I was so tired. I leaned my head back against the cold stone wall and closed my eyes. After all that time trying to find Johnny Clay and worrying about him, he had been fit as a horse. And then I'd found him and now he was dying and once again I couldn't even see him. It was good to be on land, especially safe land, where there was no one to run from or to shoot at you, but I could feel the dark clouds gathering around me. All I wanted to do was sleep.

Émile talked to me about the Heinkel He 70 and Manston, and he told me about Westgate on Sea, how it was built right on the cliffs, which were the famous White Cliffs of Dover. He said they were made of chalk—or calcium carbonate—which was why they looked white, and that on a clear day you could see them from France.

I opened my eyes. I said, "Like the song."

"The song?"

"'(There'll be Bluebirds Over) The White Cliffs of Dover.'" I started to sing about laughter and love and the peace that would come once the world was free again. "I've heard that song a hundred times, but I never stopped to think about the words."

He said, "They will be sending us to London. I need to go with Eleanor, to deliver her into the proper hands."

"I'm not leaving here without my brother."

"I know."

"What will you do?" I meant in the rest of the war but I also meant in life.

"I will volunteer for another mission."

"In France?"

"France is all but free now. Somewhere in Europe though, or perhaps French Indochina in the Pacific."

I didn't want to think of Émile going back to it. I didn't want to picture him organizing the Resistance in the Pacific or blowing up rail lines or freeing spies.

"Eleanor is a double agent," I said.

"Yes."

That's good, I thought. That's important. I wasn't sure it was worth the lives of Perry O'Connell or Ray or Coleman or Barzetti, but it was something.

"So is this good-bye?" It wasn't really a question because I knew it was good-bye. I wanted to say, Will I ever see you again?

"I will try to come back before they ship me out, to check on you and your brother." I wondered if he would try and if I would watch for him or if we both knew that this was the end. He turned his whole body to face me. He took both my hands in his. He said, "I don't want you to wonder why we met. I want you only to remember the rough and surly Frenchman you knew and how you were like a star that lights the way. I want you to remember that good did come of this, no matter what an idiot Frenchman once said."

I sat not moving, not talking. I thought, You will not cry.

He said, "Maybe you will come to France someday, just for pleasure. You will see it the way it is meant to be seen. We will climb the Eiffel Tower and drink champagne and toast our fallen comrades."

I thought: No. I won't ever go to France again, and if I do, it will be years from now and you will be married to a good French girl with a gap between her teeth, one who understands what you say and where you come from.

I said, trying to sound light and bright, "And then maybe you'll come to America, and I'll show you Fair Mountain and my family and Nashville. Maybe even the Grand Ole Opry, where I'll be singing with a Hawaiian steel guitar and a suit made of rhinestones." I sounded as breezy as a spring day, but inside my chest my heart tightened like someone was squeezing it.

He said, "I look forward to it."

And then he leaned in and kissed me. He held my face in his hands and when we finally pulled apart I said, "Do not love me, Émile Gravois."

He laughed, with sadness. "I am afraid it may be too late for that." He put his arm around me and we sat, side by side, not talking.

Afterward, they let us shower and gave us new clothes, and I brushed my hair for the first time in weeks. Right down the middle of my head was a thin gold-brown line, like a road, where my own color was coming back. I thought, It's good to see you again.

The clothes had been donated by the Ursuline Convent, which was a few miles away in Westgate on Sea. When I asked about my brother, the officer who'd brought us the clothes said he had been taken to the RAF hospital.

"Can I see him?"

"We will take you there later."

They released us then, and I wondered if the SOE and the OSS and Jacqueline Cochran herself had confirmed who we were. Outside, the station commander was cross and unsmiling. He said someone was waiting to transport Émile and Eleanor to London right now, and me to Harrington, and he began walking us to an RAF transport plane, which sat, engine running, on the taxiway.

I said, "I won't go without my brother."

He said, "Your brother is immovable at this time, Miss Hart."

"Then I'll stay here until he's able to go himself." I stopped walking.

"But you will need to be debriefed, and your commanding officer will do that at Harrington."

"I don't have a commanding officer, sir, unless you're talking about Jacqueline Cochran. I don't work for the OSS or the SOE or any branch of the military. I'm a WASP, and we're civilians."

The station commander said, "I am sorry, but it's procedure."

"That's exactly what I'm trying to tell you. It may be procedure, but I'm not. I've got nothing to do with procedure in this war."

Émile said to the man, "If I may." The man looked at him, and I suddenly saw Émile through his eyes—dangerous and commanding. "I would like to save you a good bit of time and a great deal of energy by suggesting you do not argue with her. You will be much better off letting her do what she's put her mind to do." Émile looked at me and smiled.

The man walked away, shaking his head as Eleanor came toward us. She held out her hand to me. She looked pretty and fresh now, like a regular girl and not some important spy in a war. I thought about hugging her, but instead I put my hand in hers and shook it. Her grip was softer than I'd expected.

Over the engine, she said, "Thank you, Clementine Roux. Because of you—because of your team—I can see my daughter again."

I was surprised at this because I didn't know she had a daughter. But then, I didn't know anything about her. I said, "You're welcome."

As she headed for the plane, stopping just feet away, waiting for Émile, I tried not to feel lost or alone. After everything we'd been through—Eleanor and me, but mostly Émile and me—now it was over, and I was glad and relieved and thankful, but I was empty too.

Émile stood in front of me, smiling down with his dark gypsy eyes. I pulled off Clementine Roux's wedding ring and handed it to him. I said, "Thank you." My hand felt free and empty. I wiggled my fingers just a little, letting them breathe. I didn't think I'd ever wear a ring again.

He said, "Keep it. As a memory." He placed it back into my palm. "Good-bye, Velva Jean Hart."

I said, "I don't even know your real name."

He said, "You know more than that." And he took my hand and pressed his lips to it, holding them there so I could feel them burning into my skin.

———

September 12, 1944

Dear family,

I'm writing to tell you that I found Johnny Clay. We'll give you the whole story when we see you, but we met up in Germany, and now you'll be glad to know we're back in England.

Even while I'm writing this I'm not sure what to say, but there's something I've got to tell you and it's a hard thing to hear. Johnny Clay was hit by a German bullet and he's in the hospital on base. I haven't seen him yet but I'll see him soon. They don't want any germs near him right now, so they're keeping him to himself.

But they did tell me this—he was hit in the abdomen, just below his ribs. The doctor said it's amazing that his stomach didn't rupture and that he didn't die before he got here because usually that's what happens—the acid in a person's stomach can get into their bloodstream and kill them. They're worried right now about his spleen and his liver. He's lost a lot of blood and he might be bleeding inside where they can't see it. They've been giving him transfusions, which means I've been giving them as much of my own blood as they'll take. The doctor's going to operate, to make sure the bullet didn't hit a major organ, and we won't know much more until they do. I don't think Johnny Clay's in pain because he's sleeping right now. He's been asleep ever since it happened. The doctor's worried he might not wake up.

Let me tell you something about where we are because this might make you feel better about him being here. Manston is a fighter airfield for the 11 Group Airforce, squadrons 600 and 604. It sits on the White Cliffs of Dover, just like the song, and it's also a graveyard for heavy bombers because it's so close to the front line, and airplanes are always limping in, like we did, after being hit by ground fire or air attacks. Because they've had so many emergency landings, the RAF built a hospital so they could treat the wounded on the spot instead of shipping them off somewhere else. This hospital has sixty beds, and the staff is made up of Red Cross doctors and nurses and the Princess Mary's RAF Nursing Service, and also the Royal Navy.

So you see it's a very good hospital with very good care and Johnny Clay's getting the best of it. I'm going to write you every day to let you know the news and also when we'll be home again. He won't be able to travel for a long time, but the doctors seem to think he'll come out of this, just like we all will.

I surely do miss you.

Love,

Velva Jean

P.S. The little plane we stole limped in here with 188 shrapnel holes in the waist and tail, a 20-mm dud in the gas tank, severed rudder cables, shattered elevator cables, shrapnel in both main tires, and the number two prop blade blown in half. The head mechanic at Manston said it was a miracle we were able to fly as far as we did.

TELEGRAM

TO: Velva Jean Hart
FROM: Hoyt Justice

October 3, 1944

Aunt Junie working for Johnny Clay from here. She says remember how you said the verse over Harley when she healed him. She says to say this verse now—Ezekiel 16:6. Take care of that boy and you.

Love,

Daddy Hoyt

FORTY

On October 4, they let me see Johnny Clay. The first thing I saw when I looked at him lying in his hospital bed was Mama's face. He lay on his back, eyes closed, his face fading into the pillow, just like hers had after she took sick, right before she died. I stood in the doorway of the room and couldn't move.

The doctor was a white-haired, sad-faced Scottish man named McTeer. He said, "Go on. It's all right." And I wanted to say: It's not all right. It's all wrong. That's my brother, and he looks too much like Mama, and I can't see him like this. Johnny Clay belonged to the gold mines and the rivers and the trees and the mountains and the sun. He didn't belong to a white bed and white walls and tubes and bags hooked up to him. I wanted to yell at him and shake him and tell him to get up right now and wake up already, to stop acting, stop pretending. I wanted to holler, "Dammit, Johnny Clay," till I couldn't holler anymore.

Instead I took the chair the doctor held out for me and I sat down with my hands folded in my lap and I stared at my brother as if he were someone to be suspicious about.

The doctor said something about the operation, about cutting something out of Johnny Clay and patching the ends of something else together. He talked about a coma, and about more blood transfusions, and would I be willing to give more blood.

I said, "Of course, of course," but I was looking at the black of my brother's lashes against his skin. I was looking at the Cherokee cheekbones, so much like Mama's, and the broad mouth, and the gold hair that was coming back in. A beard was growing in too, a darker gold than the hair on his head, and I thought how much he would love looking scruffy like that, like an outlaw. He was thin, just a shadow of himself.

The doctor said, "We weren't able to save his finger."

I blinked at the doctor because I didn't know what that meant and then I remembered: Oh yes. His hand. I looked at my brother again, at his left hand, which lay at his side on the bed. The middle finger was bandaged.

The doctor said, "He might be able to hear you. Talk to him. Tell him you're here."

I wanted the doctor to go away and leave me alone. I said, "Thank you," but my voice was someone else's. I said, "I'm here, Johnny Clay. It's me. Velva Jean. I'm sitting right here and you're safe and so am I." The doctor nodded at me as if I'd done something good and smart, and then a nurse walked in and she stopped when she saw me and kind of tiptoed the rest of the way in. She began to adjust all those tubes and bags.

I said, "We got all the way here from Germany, and we're almost home and I need you to hang on because I will be mad as Sweet Fern if you leave me. Do you know what I went through to find you and get you here?" I started telling him about crash-landing in France and the prisons and Hugo Bleicher.

The doctor and the nurse both stared at me, but I didn't care. I said, "I want to tell you something else. I will never speak to you again if you don't wake up. Do you hear me? Not even if you're in heaven and you decide to haunt me. I'll pretend I never knew you. I'll act like I don't even know your name."

The doctor cleared his throat, but I just talked louder. I said, "I want you to know that I'm going to be here every day. I'm going to sit in this chair and I'm going to tell you every last thing you ever did to make me mad, starting with when I was ten and you were twelve and you would leave me after school so you could go off with Hink Lowe and the Gordon boys. Then, after I'm done, I'm going to dare you to get out of that bed and tell me off. If you don't, I'm going to tell everyone between here and America that you're a yellow chicken."

I glared at the doctor and glared at the nurse, and they were both staring at Johnny Clay with eyes like saucers and mouths that hung open, as if they were waiting for him to sit up in his bed right then.

I thought: I am just getting started. I was so mad, I was shaking. I said, "You listen here. We are going to get home again. Do you hear me? You mark my words."

Then I took his hand, the one that was bandaged, and before I could say anything else, the coldness of it went through me. I could tell from the touch of it that he was barely there, that he was still here but that he was probably someplace else too.

I said, "Dammit, Johnny Clay."

My voice broke in the middle. And then, while I could still talk, I started repeating the verse of Aunt Junie's. She was the witch healer that had once lived in our mountains and had cured Harley when he almost died after burning up in the Terrible Creek wreck. She had talked the fire right out of him.

I said, "'And when I passed by you, and saw you weltering in your blood, I said to you in your blood, Live and grow like a plant in the field.'" I said this three times, holding his hand, my eyes closed, and then I sat with him until it was night and the doctor told me visiting hours were over for the day.

Johnny Clay had a second operation on October 6. Dr. McTeer said, "It was successful. We think the bleeding has stopped. Now we need him to wake up."

I said, "I'll discuss it with him, sir."

I went in and sat with Johnny Clay and held his hand and told him how much we all needed him to wake up. I said to him, "There's no reason not to because you had your surgery and the pain won't be nearly as bad now. So open your eyes. Please."

When his eyes stayed closed, I repeated Aunt Junie's verse. And then I fussed at him about the time he'd stolen my best marbles, and the time he told Daddy I took his pyramid-head steel rivets, the ones he used in his blacksmithing, when in actuality Johnny Clay had used them as bullets for a pop gun he made so he could shoot blue jays.

In the afternoons, after visiting hours were over at the hospital, I took long walks on the Cliffs of Dover, looking out at the sea and thinking about all that had happened over there, in France. I wondered if Eleanor was home by now with her daughter and how old her daughter was and if Eleanor was a good mama in addition to being a spy. I wondered what secrets she knew that might help us win the war, and if she would go back to spying or if maybe she was going to stay home now and be a mother.

I had decided not to think about Émile. Not yet. Instead I tried to remember who I'd been before the war and who I was now.

At night, I ate my meals alone, still eating with my left hand because it was just as natural as brushing my hair or putting on my lipstick, and then I went back to my barracks to a room all my own, and I wrote letters home. I wrote every day, even when there wasn't anything new to tell. I wrote pages and pages about nothing—the Cliffs of Dover or the breakfast I'd eaten or whether it was rainy or sunny and if the moon was full. I wrote as much as I could so I wouldn't have to think, because as soon as I finished at the hospital and finished with dinner and finished with my letters, I had to get into my bed and face a long night of lying awake, staring at the ceiling, and worrying about Johnny Clay.

The thing that kept running through my mind was, What will happen to me if he dies? I wasn't anyone's daughter and I wasn't anyone's wife. I wasn't anyone's mother. I was just a weapon of war, but now my war was over and the only person I belonged to in this world was my brother, and he belonged to me. He was my best friend, and if he died, I would be alone and I might as well be dead too.

On October 13, Special Force Headquarters ordered all the American and British agents who were still in France back to England. The British agents were reassigned to India and Ceylon. The French went to French Indochina. The Americans—all but my brother—were sent to China.

Sometimes I sat beside Johnny Clay's bed and sang him songs. I tried to remember the song I'd made up on the train about living out there, but I could only hear it in bits and pieces. I decided to write it over again, so I asked the nurse for a piece of paper and a pencil, and she brought me a stack of paper and two pencils. I looked at them and thought about the days when I could have filled up that paper and used every bit of that lead, but now I wasn't sure I could fill even half of one sheet.

I picked up the pencil and I wrote two lines:

> *You are lost and gone forever.*
> *I am afraid.*

I pulled my knees up close to me so that I was hunched over in the chair. I tapped the pencil against my chin and said to Johnny Clay, "I haven't written a song in a very long time. But I'm writing one now. I'm writing one for you and for Mama. And for me too. It's for all of us." My eyes started stinging and I blinked, even though there was no one to see me cry. It was the thought of the three of us together in one place, even if that place was just a song written on a piece of paper.

> *A star that lights the way.*
> *No prisoners.*

I wrote line after line, in no real order. Just wrote them down as they came to me.

> *I was lost for a while.*
> *The Freedom Line.*
> *The war is over for you.*
> *Life is beautiful.*

Every morning at mess, one of the officers would announce the weather forecast for the day. Almost every day, it was the same: "Dull and showery." "Misty and cold." "Cold and windy." "Cold, dull, bleak."

The weather made my mood worse. I wasn't sleeping. I could barely eat. Even when it rained, though, I went walking because I needed to do something when I wasn't at the hospital. An OSS officer had flown to Manston from Harrington to debrief me, and each morning I had to go over everything that had happened, again and again.

The thing that made it worse was the newspapers. Even all the way over in England, they were talking about the WASP. A London paper reprinted an American story with the headline "Not Created by Congress," which quoted people who claimed the program would be ending soon and all the WASP would be sent home. One of the men they interviewed said, "We'll wake up one of these mornings to discover there are no more WASP to sting the taxpayers and keep thoroughly experienced men out of flying jobs."

I asked the officer in charge if I could have the paper and he said yes. I marched outside into the damp and the cold and walked down to the sea ledge. There, I tore the newspaper into a thousand little pieces and watched them sail away across the water.

~ ~ ~

The weather forecast for Thursday, November 2, was "Clear and sunny. Visibility—very good." I spent the morning walking in the wind along the Cliffs of Dover. The sun was so bright I had to squint. But it was also cold. It wasn't time for visiting hours yet, but I knew I could sit inside the hospital and drink hot tea and get warm.

Instead I kept walking. I wanted to feel the bite of the cold on my face. I wanted to push myself to walk a little farther today. On the way to Dover there was a fishing and mining town called Deal, and this made me think of Mr. Deal and the Deal boys—Jessup, the baby, and his older brother, Coyle, who was married to Sweet Fern, and Danny, who'd been married to her first, before he died.

There was a castle in Deal that had belonged to King Henry VIII, and one day I asked someone to tell me the history of it. I closed my eyes while he told me and I pretended it was Émile telling me instead. Then I walked along the Goodwin Sands, which was a sand bank that ran for ten miles beside the cliffs. More than two thousand ships had wrecked on the beaches there, and I thought, When Johnny Clay gets better, we can come down here and go searching for buried treasure.

If he gets better.

My birthday was in three days. I was going to be twenty-two years old, but I felt three times that. As I walked, I looked out at the blue of the Channel and I could see the crooked coastline of France curving along in the distance, just twenty-five miles away. The cliffs of France were also white, and I wondered if they were the cliffs that circled Omaha Beach and Utah Beach and Juno Beach. I heard the words to the song I was writing, the lines that I had so far. And all at once I couldn't help it—I thought about Émile.

I pictured his dark gypsy eyes and the proud set of his mouth. I heard his voice and the funny songs he would sing. I saw his hands, large and strong, and in my mind they weren't covered in dirt or blood, and one of them was wrapped around one of mine.

I sat down on the sand and I watched the waves lap in and out, in and out. It was a sleepy rhythm that was like a kind of lullaby. I could almost hear my mama singing me a song. I lay back on the sand and rested my hand on my breast, where Émile's had once been, and made myself think of him.

I didn't know how to feel about Émile. I didn't even know his real name, so maybe I didn't have the right to feel anything. But I thought I loved him. Maybe you couldn't help but love someone, even for a little while, when you went through a war together. Maybe it was okay to love someone for a moment. No one else, not even Johnny Clay or Butch Dawkins, would ever understand what Émile and I had been through—crashing in the French countryside, running from the Germans, working with the Resistance, losing Coleman and Ray and Barzo, burying Perry, escaping from the Nazis in a stolen plane.

And now he was back in France or somewhere in Europe or maybe Indochina with a real name I didn't know and would never know—he wasn't Émile at all, but maybe a Lucien or a Gerard or a François— and I was here on the Goodwin Sands in England but soon I'd be home again, and even if I had loved him, it would be like I'd never known him at all.

That afternoon, when I got to the hospital, one of the nurses said, "Dr. McTeer's been looking for you." My heart nearly stopped, and before I could think or breathe the nurse said, "No, Miss Hart. Your brother's fine. He's awake, don't you see? He woke up an hour ago."

When I walked through the door of Johnny Clay's room, he was lying in the bed, propped up on two pillows. His eyes were shut and he looked just like he always looked except that he was sitting up a little higher. I thought the nurse must have been wrong. Maybe she was thinking of someone else's brother. The hospital was filled with wounded and dying men.

I stood watching, though, in case she wasn't wrong, and the only sound was the tick of the clock that hung on the wall beside the window. A minute ticked by. Another minute ticked by. I felt the cold, dull, and bleak settling in around me.

And then Johnny Clay's eyes opened and he looked out toward the end of the bed and up at the ceiling and finally his eyes wandered over to me.

He said, "Well hey there, little sister. I was wondering where you were," just like I was the one who'd been gone awhile. His voice was weak, and now that he was looking right at me I could see how thin he was and how tired. Everything he'd been through was there on his face.

I stood watching him, and suddenly I couldn't move. I blinked my eyes over and over to make sure what I was seeing was real and not a dream. Before I could run to him and throw my arms around him, he said, "For your information, I didn't steal those pyramid-head steel rivets from Daddy. I won 'em off Beachard, who stole 'em from Daddy. And it wasn't me that stole your best marbles. Don't you remember? Hunter Firth ate the three little ones and when he almost died Sweet Fern threw the rest away. Said someone was likely to kill himself on them."

I burst into tears. I stood there crying my eyes out. I cried so hard that I gave myself the hiccups. I put my hands over my face and cried and cried and hiccupped till I couldn't breathe.

Johnny Clay said, "Come on now, Velva Jean. Or are you still Clementine?"

"No," I hiccupped. "Not anymore."

"You knew I was going to be okay." I dropped my hands and looked at him. He shifted and twitched around in the bed, his face thin, his eyes wet. "I'm too stubborn and mean to die. I told you that a long time ago. Why don't you ever listen to me?" He was crying now too, the tears rolling down his cheeks. He rubbed the tears away with the back of his good hand and then he sat looking at me, letting the tears go. He said, "Come on now. We've got to be men about this."

I ran right to him and threw my arms around him and hugged him, all the while trying not to hurt him or hug him too hard. I felt his arms go around me and he didn't feel so big and mighty anymore, but he was my brother and he was alive.

I said, "Don't you ever do that again, Johnny Clay Hart."

November 21, 1944

Dear Clementine,

I am writing for three reasons. First, to say I am happy to hear your brother will pull through. Second, to say I am sorry I wasn't able to see you before I left England. Third, to send you the words to the song so that you can take them home with you.

Un Petit Cochon (A Little Pig)

A little pig
Hanging from the ceiling
(Pull its nose
it'll give some milk)
Pull its tail
It will lay some eggs
(Pull it harder
It will lay some gold)
How many of them do you want?

(I am sending the English words so that you can see how the song is not so pretty.)

Remember that, in the end, it is only a song about a pig. Perhaps when you sing it, you will think of me, just as I am thinking of you.

Love,

Émile

FORTY-ONE

By December, the Soviet Union had invaded Germany. United States troops had landed in the Philippines. German field marshal Erwin Rommel, who they said was in on the plot to kill Hitler, had committed suicide. And the French had captured Strasbourg, the city near the Vosges Mountains, where we stole the Heinkel He 70.

On December 5, the BBC news reported that all German women over the age of eighteen were being asked to volunteer for the army and the air force as test pilots. They were needed by the Luftwaffe for jobs like ferrying planes so that they could free men for service at the front.

On Friday, December 15, Captain Glenn Miller flew out of RAF Twinwood Farm in Clapham, Bedfordshire, 150 miles northwest of Manston, in a single-engine UC-64 Norseman. Captain Miller was traveling to Paris to start a tour of Europe with his Glenn Miller Army Air Force Band. He was going ahead of the band to make arrangements, but somewhere over the English Channel, the Norseman disappeared and everyone on board went missing.

The weather report for that day was "Hard frost with local fog in the morning." We didn't see the sun again that whole week. Every day was damp and overcast, with a bitter, cold rain and a thick mist that rolled in off the water. I was beginning to hate England. I hated the dull and the damp and the dreariness. I hated the boiled potatoes at breakfast, lunch, and supper. I hated sitting there while the war was still going on. I wasn't in it and I wasn't home. I was somewhere in between, and all I wanted to do was *something*. But the main thing I wanted was to get Johnny Clay out of the hospital and back to himself again.

Dr. McTeer said my brother wouldn't be able to travel for a month or two, maybe more, and as much as he wanted to, he wouldn't be allowed to rejoin the fight.

For you, the war is over.

He would recover, but it was going slower than he wanted. One week after he woke up, an official-looking man flew in from Harrington and said he was with the OSS. For three days, he locked himself away with my brother and debriefed him. When he was finished, the man told me they had to do this with all the special agents. They had to deactivate them like time bombs because they found that most of these men, especially the American ones, were like a law unto themselves when they came home.

When I saw Johnny Clay after his deactivation, he seemed both tired and angry. He'd exchanged all the French francs he had and they added up to five hundred dollars. He sealed most of this into an envelope and made me mail it home to Daddy Hoyt. Then he took the rest of the money, nearly ten dollars, and spent it on scotch. I never found out who smuggled it in to him—one of the officers, one of the nurses who was sweet on him—but he drank for four whole days and then stopped. When I asked him about it, he said, "I figured I drank enough, Velva Jean. Now I got to get myself better so I can get out of here."

He could walk now and eat, but he got worn out quicker than Aunt Bird, who was at least eighty years old. He had to stop and rest his hand on my shoulder, the whole while pretending he was just trying to decide which way to walk or that he was studying a painting on the wall, when I knew he was only trying to catch his breath.

There was a lot he was mad about these days. He was mad because he wasn't well yet. He was mad because he was missing half his middle finger, right down to the second knuckle, and he said how was he ever supposed to play guitar or pan for gold again. He was mad because "everyone is fighting this war but me." He was mad that he didn't remember stealing the plane and flying out of Germany. He said he would have shot those Germans down if only he'd been conscious. Missing finger or not, he would have shot every last one.

I tried to take his mind off things by telling him about Gossie and Paris and Hugo Bleicher and prison and Helen and the song we'd used as a signal so we would each know the other was okay. I told him about the song I was writing now, the first one since I'd left America. I was almost finished with it.

He said, "Is it good?"

"It's taking the most out of me. I've never had so much trouble writing a song before. The way I wrote it is Mama singing to me and me singing to Mama, a kind of back and forth."

"But is it good?"

"I think so."

"Don't you know?"

"I guess."

"You used to know."

That's true, I thought. I used to know a lot of things.

I said, "I met a woman in the war who talked about how important it is at times like this for art to survive. She said if stories and beauty can make it through the war, that means life can be created from them again."

He seemed to think this over. He said, "Maybe that's one reason it's so hard for you to write. Because you got a lot to get through. There's a lot riding on this song. But that makes it even more important to write it, doesn't it?"

"I guess so."

"We got to be men about it, Velva Jean." His voice caught and he said he was tired then and would I mind letting him rest. Before I left I told him, "Just think of the limp you're going to have, Johnny Clay. And just think of the stories you'll tell."

The next day, when we walked down the hall outside his room, he made sure not to lean on me at all. Whenever a nurse walked by, he played up that limp like he was Hopalong Cassidy.

~ ~ ~

On Friday, December 22, after breakfast, I trudged through the winter chill and mist to the hospital. Twenty planes had made emergency landings since I'd landed there, and the hospital beds were always full of the wounded. Now that he was out of danger, Johnny Clay shared a room with nineteen other men, ten beds in a line on either side.

Sometimes I would find him playing cards with one of the other soldiers, and sometimes he would be lying flat on his back, staring into space. I dreaded those days because there was no cheering him. He didn't want to hear any war news or talk about anything much other than the weather or what I'd had to eat at the mess hall. His mind would drift off somewhere and I worried that not all of him had come back from wherever it was he'd been when he was asleep. I wondered if he was in two places, because sometimes that was how it seemed.

When I walked into Johnny Clay's room the morning of the twenty-second, there was a girl sitting in the chair beside his bed, her legs crossed. She was dark and slim, and I thought, What is Eleanor doing here?

Johnny Clay looked past her and said, "Well hey there, Velva Jean. You should see your face." He grinned at me, and the first thing I thought was, Thank goodness it's going to be a good day.

The girl turned and it wasn't Eleanor at all. She was wearing a WASP uniform—the Santiago Blues—and for the first time in a long time I thought about how I didn't have a uniform anymore and how Perry had promised to get me a new one.

She said, "Hartsie." And then she flew to me and wrapped her arms around me and hugged me for a good minute.

"Helen and I've been talking," Johnny Clay said. His eyes were shining and I thought, Oh no. But I was happy because he was happy and looking like his old self.

Helen said, "He's been talking, mostly." She didn't sound very impressed, and I thought, Now that's a first. Usually girls went mad for Johnny Clay.

I pulled a chair up next to Helen's and we sat side by side, close to

Johnny Clay's bed. She picked up a bag—my bag from Harrington, the one I'd left behind with all the things I owned in the world—and said, "I thought you might want this."

Then she crossed her legs again and took my hand and held it tight and told us about where she'd been—how she'd crashed in France near Falaise and how members of the Resistance had helped her get to Paris and the Freedom Line. She traveled for days on trains and bicycles and also on foot with one French guide after another and two male pilots, until she crossed the Pyrenees Mountains into Spain. From there, she flew back to England, back to Harrington, and ever since she'd been ferrying planes from base to base for the RAF, just like she was back at Camp Davis.

Johnny Clay said she was one of the bravest girls he'd ever met, and to be so beautiful too. Helen stared at him as if she didn't understand a single thing he was saying to her. I wondered what on earth she made of my brother.

I said, "I guess we'll be back at Camp Davis before too long." The thought of it made my stomach sink, but there was something comforting about it too.

She squeezed my hand. "No, Hartsie. When I found out you were here, I wanted to come myself to let you know."

"Let me know what?"

"The WASP were disbanded. It's official. Jackie Cochran sent a telegram."

She unfolded something from her pocket and held it out to me. I took it from her, but I didn't read it.

Helen said, "No honors, no ceremony. We're just supposed to pack up our flight suits and our parachutes and go home."

I looked down at the paper and the words were blurred. I thought: Well. You are really and truly on your own now. I wasn't a part of the military even though I'd flown their planes. I wasn't really a spy, even if I had worked with the Resistance and helped rescue a double agent for the SOE, because I wasn't an actual member of the OSS. And now I wasn't a WASP anymore. I wasn't Clementine Roux and I was barely Velva Jean Hart, that girl who dreamed of the Opry and a suit made of rhinestones, who used to save every penny she earned just so she could sing there one day.

Helen said, "What will you do, Hartsie?"

I said, "I don't know." For the first time in my life, I didn't know. I didn't have a single thing planned. "What about you?"

"I don't know either."

I said, "What about you, Johnny Clay?"

He said, "I don't know, Velva Jean." The brightness had gone out of his voice. He scowled down at himself lying on the hospital bed. You never knew when his mood was going to change these days.

We sat staring out at the room of wounded men, some who would survive to plan a future, some who wouldn't. Johnny Clay would make it home, but I worried that, like his left hand, maybe only part of him was making it home after all. No one said anything for a while.

From his bed, Johnny Clay started to sing: "In the land of crimson sunsets, skies are wide and blue. . . ."

Helen and I looked at him.

He said, "Isn't that the song you were going to use to find each other if you got lost?"

I thought: Yes, it was. Only I'm more lost now.

He said, "Look. Once a WASP, always a WASP. I don't care what the government says or what the military says. They can come to me if they got a problem with it. I say you girls earned your stripes as much as any man I know, maybe more so. Just as much as any of these men here. But the thing you got to remember is this—when plans change on you, you figure out something else, something better."

Crow Lovelorn had told me the same thing back in Nashville, when I asked him if he missed making records and singing at the Grand Ole Opry. *Sometimes dreams change, either because they have to or because life has something else in mind for you.*

Johnny Clay looked down at his hand, at his leg, and then he glared up at us and said, "So go on then. Sing it to me. Those are the only two lines I know. I want you to sing me that song."

I was crying by then, and Helen was too—tears pouring down like the rain outside the windows.

*   *   *

Helen said she would stay through Christmas Eve, and then she was due back at Harrington. When she asked me to come with her, I said no. I was done with the war for now. Besides, I needed to stay with Johnny Clay.

That night, after she went to sleep, I sat on my bunk and opened the bag she'd brought me. I laid everything out on the bed and thought: There is your life, Velva Jean. That's who you are. It was like looking at clues to a mystery, pieces of a puzzle. A Mexican guitar. A mandolin. A navy dress with a skirt that twirled. A green emerald that shone when you rubbed it. Clover jewelry. A secret decoder ring. Bakelite hair clips. Mama's wedding ring and Bible, where she'd noted important dates and events. Two letters from my daddy, written when Mama was sick and he was trying to get her help. A wood carving of a girl, her mouth open like she was singing. Songs and letters written to me by a boy named Ned Tyler and a boy named Butch Dawkins. A record produced by a man named Darlon C. Reynolds with two songs, one on each side. A *Life* magazine with me on the cover. A framed picture of the Grand Ole Opry stage. A Comet Red lipstick.

I added in the wooden flying girl, the rip cord, the seashell, and the compass, dented by a German bullet. I added in the letter from Émile. I almost added Clementine Roux's wedding ring, but instead I slid it onto my finger. And then, in my mind, I added in the things I didn't have anymore—a perfume bottle that sprayed poison gas, a lipstick gun, a scarf that was really a map, and a telegram from Jacqueline Cochran, congratulating me on being the second woman in history to fly a bomber across the ocean.

Together they didn't add up to much, but then again, they added up to just about everything I had.

~   ~   ~

Christmas Day was clear and bright. Frost covered the ground and the planes that lined the airfield, but the sun shone strong, a giant yellow-orange that rose up over the water.

All of the sharp lines and angles that had sprung out on Johnny Clay were beginning to fill in, and to celebrate his progress and the sunshine, he and I ate our Christmas breakfast on the cliffs. The water was a deep blue, and the waves smacked against the beach down below. France rose up in the distance, the cliffs there as white and high as the ones we were sitting on.

I said, "When you look over there, it's hard to imagine all the things that happened."

He said, "Or that we were ever there at all."

Then I thought: Just over those white cliffs is Rouen, where Joan of Arc was burned at the stake. And to the southwest of that lives a girl with a gap between her teeth who delivers messages on a bicycle. And to the southeast of that is Paris, where Gossie and Cleo and Rose Valland and others like them, and maybe a rough and surly Frenchman going by the name of Émile Gravois, are working to win this war, not just for France but for everyone. And to the right of us, over the land, and over the ocean, is America.

With his right hand, Johnny Clay fished something out of his pocket. Two bullets, gold and shiny. He pinched them between his fingers and raised them to the sky. He said, "I'm going to take these back home and give them to Granny along with that bookmark from Hitler. She can show them to everyone on Fair Mountain. She can keep them on her mantel."

I said, "You don't really have a bookmark from Hitler." I was daring him to show it to me, and he knew this.

He sat blinking into the sun, and then he turned to me and winked and said, "Like hell I don't." I waited for him to take it out, to prove me wrong, but instead he said, "You asked me a question the other day that I was too tired to answer."

"What question?"

"What am I going to do. Well, I was thinking about it, and there are lots of things—once we get back to America, I'd like to hang around New York City awhile and see what that's about. Maybe see those Rockettes, the ones that kick their legs out all in a line. Maybe go to Grant's Tomb. I wouldn't mind riding the rails again and visiting the places across America that I still haven't seen. I'd like to see Mexico. I got a wild hair to go back to Hollywood. I reckon I could be a movie star by Friday."

When he was done, I said, "We aren't even home yet, Johnny Clay, and already you're wanting to leave." Even as I said it, I felt the old itch in me that I knew was just like my daddy's. It was the one that told me I'd be wanting to go before too long myself because, like it or not, that was the way I was made.

Johnny Clay said, "There's a great big world out there, Velva Jean. What we got up on Fair Mountain is only a little part of it. It's a good part, but it's just a little part." For a moment his face went cloudy. He reached down, like he wasn't even thinking about it, and rested his left hand, the one missing part of a finger, on his bad leg. He said, "Yessir. It's a good part, but it's just a little part." His voice drifted away over the water.

I reached my hand out to let him know I was there, that it was going to be okay, that we were going to be okay, but he shifted just out of reach. My ring caught the sun and held it.

"It's the best part," I said.

Johnny Clay raised his mug of tea. He was in an easy mood, but his eyes had gone serious. He said, "To home."

I raised my own mug and we clinked them together, the sound of it carrying away on the wind. "To home."

"Live Out There"
(words and music by Velva Jean Hart)

"Live out there," my mama said,
but somehow I lost track—
lost myself, then found myself
and now at last I'm back
And making a new start.

She'll be with me all the way—
I'm not scared 'cause I've got her heart—
And I'm growing closer to her day by day—
I'll hold on to her memory and prayer—
I'll live out there.

"Mama, don't make me go," I said.
"I want to stay right here."
"You have to go," she told me,
"Don't be afraid to live out there."

Lost and gone forever like last night's moon—
the unknown soldiers in makeshift tombs—
They lived out there.

Joan of Arc on the funeral pyre—
Courage born in fear and fire—
She lived out there.

Beyond the crimson sunsets in a deep blue sky—
Beyond the bright clouds where women pilots fly—
Live out there.

The power of an airplane resting in my hand—
the mystery of the air that helps me soar and land—
Live out there.

Floating over mountains far, far away—
Flying close to heaven day by day—
Live out there.

Learning to use my compass to find my own way
To freedom, liberation, and a glad new day—
Live out there.

Fighting loud and brave to be a weapon of the war,
Never forgetting I'm just a down-home girl
Out there.

Walking for miles on that Freedom Line,
Life is beautiful, life is fine—
If you live out there.

Traveling in the dark with a star to light the way,
Brightening the path to a brand-new day
Out there.

I'll sing myself awake from a deep dark sleep—
I'll fill myself with hope from beyond the keep—
And when the war is over and peace has come
I'll sing myself a pathway all the way home—
Living out there.

I'll keep a seashell for luck,
And my compass in my hand,
And faith in my progress
Toward the promised land.
Like a pig spinning gold,
Like the magic of the heart,
Miles don't matter 'cause
We're never far apart—
Out there.

"Just remember," Mama said,
"That's where you belong—
Up above the clouds,
Lost inside a song—
Live out there.

"I am always with you
In the blood and the bone
Precious child of mine,
Person all your own—
Live out there."

Now I'm making a new start,
And you'll be with me all the way.
I'm not scared
'Cause I've got your heart—
And I'm growing closer to you day by day.
I'll hold on to your memory
I'll hold you in a prayer,
I will live out there.

I was lost for a while,
but now I'm back.

The Story Behind the Story

The best stories are rooted in truth. When I was thinking up Velva Jean's next adventure, I looked—just as I did when writing *Velva Jean Learns to Drive*—at my own family history for inspiration. My father, Jack F. McJunkin Jr., was an Army Intelligence officer on Okinawa and in Vietnam, and received the Joint Service Commendation Medal and the Bronze Star. The first three years of my life were spent in Okinawa, and I remember vague, hazy explanations of where my father was and what he was doing during his long absences from my mother and me. His work in intelligence always fascinated me, even as a little girl, and I was convinced my dad was off somewhere being a superhero. Going further back, women spies run rampant in my family, although none of them, to my knowledge, spied in World War II. They spied in the Revolutionary War and the Civil War. One of these women, Jane Black Thomas, was a Revolutionary War hero and South Carolina's first feminist. She not only spied for the Patriots; she single-handedly fought off—with a sword—a battalion of Tories to protect a crucial supply of ammunition and the family home.

Those women have always fascinated me, as has World War II. Jack F. McJunkin Sr., my beloved grandfather—the one who helped inspire Johnny Clay—fought in the war. Unfortunately, I never knew much about his wartime experience, only what I was able to piece together here and there. He enlisted as a private on April 6, 1943, at Camp Croft, South Carolina. He was twenty-eight. He was married to my grandmother Cleo by then and their only child, my father, was eight months old.

When Granddaddy went to war, Grandmama went to work—the only time she ever worked outside the home—to support herself, her mother, my dad, and his cousin Paula, just a baby, whose own mama had died at seventeen. Granddaddy never talked about his experiences in the war, and after both he and Grandmama were gone, I inherited her jewelry box, where she kept a handful of newspaper clippings detailing the battle of Anzio, Italy, and the movement of the Fifth Army: "Anzio No Beachhead, Assert Men There, Dodging Shells"; "Anzio Vet Describes 84 Days Under Fire. . . ." One of these clippings showed a map of the country and the campaign area. In Grandmama's handwriting, there is just one word—*Jack*—with an arrow pointing to Anzio. And there is a letter she wrote to her sister-in-law on July 11, 1944:

> *Jack's outfit was one of the first to go into Rome. He was awarded a combat badge for exemplary conduct in action against the enemy. All I do is write Jack and pray for his return to us soon. War is such a horrible experience even for the brave. I firmly believe this war will make a difference in everyone.*
>
> *Jack and I have great plans for our future. If only God sees fit for him to return to us. I work all the time and try and save. Jack is the most important thing in my life—without him, I'd be lost. We are terribly in love—people say as you are married longer you grow out of it, but we seem to grow more in love with each passing day even though separated.*

The rest of the story is lost. All I know is that after fighting at Anzio, Granddaddy, with the Fifth Army, went on to liberate Rome, and later to free the most prominent and highly guarded prisoners from Dachau concentration camp after they were transferred to Tyrol, Austria, where the SS planned to either keep them away from the Allies or kill them. By the time I knew him, Granddaddy was missing part of the middle finger on his left hand, from the middle knuckle up. The story of that finger changed each time I asked him about it, but some family members say it was hacked off by farm equipment when he was just a kid working in the fields, and others say it was shot off in battle. However he lost it, I remember it always itched and he often rubbed the end of it. For years, he kept a crude silver ring that was given to him by a prisoner from Dachau, one the prisoner had forged himself.

Of course, Velva Jean's story doesn't come only from family history. None of my ancestors were WASP or members of the OSS and SOE's operational groups, but these two divisions of military history have always intrigued me most. Women pilots! Women spies! I knew from the beginning—when I was first conceiving the Velva Jean series—that I wanted to pay homage to the daring girls who appeared in their own adventure stories of the 1920s and 1930s, inspiring girls like Constance Kurridge and Flyin' Jenny, who were comic book heroes, and who spied and flew and acted and sang and fought crime and did exactly what they wanted to do and were well ahead of their time.

The Women Airforce Service Pilots, or WASP, formed in 1942, training women to fly military aircraft so that male pilots could be released for combat duty overseas. Over twenty-five thousand women applied, but only 1,074 were accepted. As WASP, they flew almost every type of military aircraft—fighter planes and bombers, including the B-17 and the B-29. Before they were disbanded in 1944, thirty-eight WASP lost their lives flying for their country, some in accidents caused by the male pilots they worked with, who refused to accept them as equals.

The head of the WASP was Jacqueline Cochran, then the most famous and well-respected female flier in the world. In 1941, she was the first woman to pilot a bomber across the Atlantic Ocean. In this book, Velva Jean becomes the second woman to do so, but in reality no WASP flew overseas during the war. Because this is fiction, however, I did take the liberty of letting Velva Jean enjoy that particular adventure. After all, it seemed to me like something she would have done, had she been there, especially with her brother missing in Europe.

When she crash-lands in France, Velva Jean is thrown together with an operational group from the OSS, or Office of Strategic Services, the predecessor to the CIA, which was known as a real cloak-and-dagger army. General William Donovan envisioned soldiers organized in small groups and trained with guerrilla capabilities, who could be parachuted behind enemy lines to conduct sabotage, covert operations, and guerrilla warfare, all of which would support the Allied advance. These groups operated in France, Italy, Greece, Norway, Yugoslavia, and China. Another OSS faction, the Jedburghs, dropped in groups of three and worked mainly to support, supply, and direct Resistance groups, while the operational groups were involved in commando-type action. The United States military thought of them as shadow warriors, but to the enemy they were terrorists. They were the forerunners of today's U.S. Army Special Forces.

The operational groups took many forms—saboteurs, guerrillas, commandos, and agents. These soldiers were from all walks of life: dentists, chemists, psychiatrists, police detectives, bankers, safecrackers, journalists, doctors, international playboys—and women. Many of these women were wives and mothers. Odette Sansom, Violette Szabo, Virginia Hall, Nancy Wake, Princess Noor Inayat Khan, and Julia Child were just six of these, but some two hundred women worked in England or dropped into France or Africa or the Pacific. Many were captured and executed by the enemy.

Agents were not the only women to fight in World War II. I had to be careful, when researching, not to get too distracted by women like Suzanne Spaak, a mother of two who worked to save the lives of Jewish children being deported from Paris to the German death camps (and who was eventually executed at Fresnes prison), or Rose Valland, overseer of Paris's Jeu De Paume museum, who kept track of the artwork stolen by the Germans. There were women like Lee Miller, who reported the war, often from the front lines, and the Russian female snipers, some two thousand in all, who fought alongside the men.

When the war in Europe ended in May 1945, there were 460,000 women in the military and over 6.5 million in civilian war work. In Nazi Germany, Hitler forbade women to work in German weapons factories because he felt that a woman's place was at home. There is no doubt that without the contribution of women, the Allied war effort would not have been nearly as strong or as successful.

Sixty-seven years after the war's end and the liberation of the prisoners in Tyrol, the ring given to my grandfather has been lost. But, thankfully, the stories of the men and women who fought in the war live on.

Resources

Two particular women did much to inspire and inform Velva Jean's story—Hélène Deschamps, a member of the French Resistance who was later recruited by the OSS, and Virginia D'Albert-Lake, an American in Paris who worked for the Resistance while also helping to free Allied airmen on the Freedom Line. I was also fortunate to get to know Dr. Margaret Emanuelson—clinical forensic psychologist, author, and former agent of the OSS—who was generous in sharing her vast knowledge and the memories of her experiences.

Although this is a novel, I have examined numerous resources and conducted extensive research in an effort to make the events, the setting, and the period as authentic as possible. Perhaps the greatest resources were the members of the OSS Society and its president, Charles Pinck, and Roy Tebbutt and the Carpetbagger Aviation Museum (a.k.a. the Harrington Aviation Museum), in Harrington, England. Espionage expert Linda McCarthy, founding curator of the CIA Museum, was a terrific resource as well. I also owe much to the comprehensive (and recently declassified) National Archives and Records Administration OSS Collection, and the Churchill Archives Centre.

In addition, the following books were most helpful: *Is Paris Burning*, by Larry Collins and Dominique Lapierre; *An American Heroine in the French Resistance: The Diary and Memoir of Virginia D'Albert-Lake*, edited by Judy Barrett Litoff; *Americans in Paris: Life & Death Under Nazi Occupation*, by Charles Glass; *Operation Jedburgh: D-Day and America's First Shadow War*, by Colin Beavan; *The Jedburghs: The Secret History of the Allied Special Forces, France 1944*, by Will Irwin; *Sisterhood of Spies: The Women of the OSS*, by Elizabeth P. McIntosh; *Spyglass: An Autobiography*, by Hélène Deschamps; *Cast No Shadow: The Life of the American Spy Who Changed the Course of World War II*, by Mary S. Lovell; *The Wolves at the Door: The True Story of America's Greatest Female Spy*, by Judith L. Pearson; *The Women Who Lived for Danger: The Agents of the Special Operations Executive*, by Marcus Binney; *Women at War: The Women of World War II—At Home, at Work, on the Front Line*, by Brenda Ralph Lewis; *Undercover Tales of World War II*, by William B. Breuer; *France: The Dark Years 1940–1944*, by Julian Jackson; *And the Show Went On: Cultural Life in Nazi-Occupied Paris*, by Alan Riding; *Operatives, Spies, and Saboteurs: The Unknown Story of the Men and Women of WWII's OSS*, by Patrick K. O'Donnell; *The Women Who Wrote the War*, by Nancy Caldwell Sorel; *World War II Day by Day*, by Sharon Lucas, Michael Armitage, Lord Lewin, and John Stanier; *The Routledge Atlas of the Second World War*, by Martin Gilbert; *Agent Zigzag: A True Story of Nazi Espionage, Love, and Betrayal*, by Ben Macintyre; *Secret Agent's Handbook: The Top Secret Manual of Wartime Weapons, Gadgets, Disguises and Devices*, by Roderick Bailey; *OSS Special Weapons & Equipment: Spy Devices of WWII*, by H. Keith Melton; *Jane's Fighting Aircraft of World War II*, by Leonard Bridgman; *Ghosts of the Skies: Aviation in the Second World War*, by Philip Makanna; *Normandy*, by Clare Hargreaves (Cadogan Guides); *Heinkel He 70/170: Blitz*, by Refael A. Permuy López, Juan Arráez Cerdá, and Lucas Molina Franco; Berlitz *French Phrase Book & Dictionary*; World War II *German Phrase Book*; *Letters Home: 1944–1945 Women Airforce Service Pilots*, by Bernice "Bee" Falk Haydu; *Warriors: Navajo Code Talkers*, by Kenji Kawano, Carl Gorman, and Benis M. Frank, USMC; and *As You Were: A Portable Library of American Prose and Poetry Assembled for Members of the Armed Forces and the Merchant Marine*, edited by Alexander Woollcott.

I visited and revisited several films, videos, and radio programs as well. Among the best: *Carve Her Name with Pride*; *O.S.S.*; *Wish Me Luck*; *War in Color: France is Free*; *War Zone: Air Wars*; *Secrets of War*;

OSS and SOE training films (courtesy of Real Military Videos); *The Lady Was a Spy*; *School for Danger*; *The Train*; *Band of Brothers*; *The War*; *Fly Girls*; *The Rape of Europa*; *B-17: The Flying Fortress*; *The Great Escape*; *Honey West*; and one I could watch again and again, *The Dirty Dozen*.

Also available from bestselling author Jennifer Niven

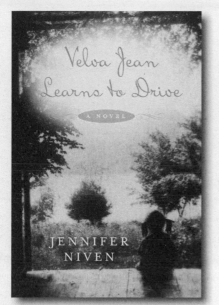

ISBN: 978-0-452-29740-1

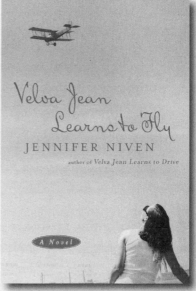

ISBN: 978-0-452-29740-1

Available wherever books are sold.
www.jenniferniven.com

Plume
A member of Penguin Group (USA) Inc.
www.penguin.com